Douglas Jackson turned [...]
Rome and the Romans i[...]
turing Rufus the slave. H[...]
the Scottish borders, and now lives in Bridge of Allan.
His first book, *Caligula*, is also published by Corgi
Books.

Also by Douglas Jackson

CALIGULA

and published by Corgi Books

CLAUDIUS

Douglas Jackson

CORGI BOOKS

TRANSWORLD PUBLISHERS
61–63 Uxbridge Road, London W5 5SA
A Random House Group Company
www.rbooks.co.uk

CLAUDIUS
A CORGI BOOK: 9780552156950

First published in Great Britain
in 2009 by Bantam Press
an imprint of Transworld Publishers
Corgi edition published 2010

Addresses for Random House Group Ltd companies outside the UK
can be found at: www.randomhouse.co.uk
The Random House Group Ltd Reg. No. 954009

The Random House Group Limited supports The Forest Stewardship
Council (FSC), the leading international forest certification organisation.
All our titles that are printed on Greenpeace approved FSC certified paper
carry the FSC logo. Our paper procurement policy can be found at
www.rbooks.co.uk/environment

Typeset in 11.5/14.5 pt Sabon by Falcon Oast Graphic Art Ltd.
Printed in the UK by CPI Cox & Wyman, Reading, RG1 8EX.

2 4 6 8 10 9 7 5 3 1

Mixed Sources
Product group from well-managed
forests and other controlled sources
www.fsc.org Cert no. TT-COC-2139
© 1996 Forest Stewardship Council
FSC

For Gregor

Roman Britain at the time of Claudius

1 AD 43. The legions of Rome land at Rutupiae under General Aulus Plautius and consolidate before marching westwards.

2 Togodumnus, brother of the British war leader Caratacus, bids to hold the advancing Romans at the River Medway but is defeated.

3 The decisive battle on the River Thames. Caratacus attempts to draw Plautius into a trap.

4 Claudius takes command and rides into battle on Bersheba, the Emperor's elephant.

5 Claudius marches eastwards to take Camulodunum (modern Colchester) and the surrender of the rulers of southern Britain.

North Sea

Irish Sea

CARVETII

BRIGANTES

PARISI

DECEANGLI

ORDOVICES

CORNOVII

CORIELTAUVI

ICENI

DEMETAE

SILURES

DOBUNNI

CATUVELLAUNI

5. TRINO-VANTES

4

ATREBATES

3

2

DUMNONII

DUROTRIGES

BELGAE

REGNI

CANTIACI

1

English Channel

0   MILES   100

Prologue

Britain AD *43*

The scarlet of their tunics spread across the land like a bloodstain.

From his position on the crest of the hilltop he could see the tight, disciplined column moving steadily through the trees. He tried to gauge their numbers. Thousands certainly, perhaps as many as ten thousand. And these were only the advance guard.

His spies had given warning of their coming but he had travelled days beyond his own frontiers to see for himself. The legions of Rome. They had been here once before, when his father was still a boy and Julius Caesar led them across the sea, but they had soon left, laden with gold and hostages. Some primal instinct told him that this time they were here to stay. The warriors of Britain had long forgotten the legions' power and their fearsome potential, but he had remembered the old tales – and learned. Any refugee from Gaul knew he would receive a welcome among the Catuvellauni, and it was the way of the Catuvellauni chief to question such refugees, gently, about the threat that had driven them from their lands. Now he could see that threat with his own eyes and he felt an unfamiliar stirring low in his belly. So this was fear?

'Lord? It is time.'

He looked over his shoulder to where his escort waited, hidden below the skyline. Ballan was right. If they stayed longer they could be trapped by the auxiliary cavalry which undoubtedly accompanied this force. But his eyes were drawn back to the marching column and the occasional glint of sun on burnished armour. In the serene quiet of the morning he could hear the faint notes of horns. Even at this distance it sounded alien. Aggressive.

'Lord? Caratacus?' Ballan's voice was louder and more urgent. He was pointing to a saddle between two hills about a mile away, where a dozen small specks had just come into view. Horsemen. Another few minutes and they would be cut off.

'Go,' he shouted, running down the slope and vaulting on to his pony. Caratacus, king of the Catuvellauni, rode north to prepare his people for war.

I

Rufus felt soft lips caress his cheek, barely disturbing the three-day stubble. He had been asleep for only a few hours, except that the chill from the damp earth seeping into his bones meant it hadn't been real sleep, more a dozing just beneath the surface of waking. Not sleep, but at least rest, and he needed rest after a long day on the march. For a moment he resented the attention, but he had dreamed so long of a woman's touch, a woman's tenderness; of hair the colour of spun gold and the texture of silk ... He opened his eyes and looked lovingly into two hairy nostrils.

'Bersheba,' he groaned, pushing away the long, sinuous trunk that nuzzled his face. 'It can't be time to feed you already.' He turned over and pulled his cloak closer around him, but his tormentor returned, plucking insistently at the heavy cloth. He sighed and sat up. He might as well give in now.

She was standing over him, and he could just discern the faint outline of her massive bulk against the first hint of dawn that painted the sky a cadaverous, purple-bruised grey, the faint light reflecting liquid brown eyes filled with timeless wisdom. Bersheba had been his charge for almost seven years now, first under the psychotic Caligula – four terrible years he wished he could erase from his memory – and latterly in the more benevolent service of his successor, Tiberius Claudius Drusus Nero Germanicus. The Emperor's elephant. And why, he asked himself for the hundredth time, are the Emperor's elephant and her faithful slave stranded in this strange and dangerous land when the Emperor himself is a thousand long miles away in Rome?

He struggled to his feet and walked to the bullock cart to collect Bersheba's feed and the little red apples she loved. Gaius and Britte were still asleep among the hay. He smiled down at his son and listened to the soft, regular breathing with a pleasure only a father could know. Gaius was tucked in close to the big slave girl who had been his wet nurse since his mother's death at the hands of the man the world believed was also Caligula's killer. Rufus was one of only two people left alive who knew the true story and that was the way he intended it to stay. In a few minutes Britte would rise and prepare the oats for their only proper meal between now and nightfall.

Within the hour, they would harness the bullock cart and march another twelve miles.

It had been like this for a week. A relentless trudge across a rolling landscape of forest and downland as the soldiers of four legions sought to bring the tribes of Britain to battle. The whole army, forty thousand men from the furthest corners of the Empire, could sense their general's frustration. Aulus Plautius Silvanus had promised his Emperor a swift victory, but all he had to show for his efforts were a few burned-out huts and the heads of a dozen British warriors taken in the endless, futile skirmishes that hampered his progress. Rufus gave thanks he was positioned with the baggage train of the Second Augusta, in the centre of the miles-long Roman column, and unlikely to be involved in any fighting. He had warned Narcissus that Bersheba wasn't meant for war. Why had he trusted that scheming Greek?

The unexpected call to arms had come two months earlier, in the sheltered little park by Bersheba's barn on the Palatine Hill. It was the day he'd met Claudius's freedman when Narcissus had returned from the coast of Gaul, where Plautius had gathered his forces for the invasion of Britain. The balmy days of April had given way to the hard-edged heat of May, and the Mediterranean sun bounced off bone-hard ground and radiated from the gleaming white marble of the great Corinthian-columned palaces. Both men's lives had changed markedly since

11

Caligula's death. Rufus was still a slave, but one who held an honoured position in the imperial household. Narcissus was the Emperor Claudius's trusted adviser and wielded the kind of power only granted to potentates. But Rufus knew he tired of the constant demands on him as Claudius's eyes and ears. Tall and bald as a pullet's egg, the ageless Greek looked thinner and more careworn, but his eyes were the same deep azure blue and had lost none of their hypnotic intelligence.

'I must be too many people now, Rufus, far too many. Negotiator, diplomat, counsellor and enforcer. All things to all men,' he had complained soon after the Emperor inherited the throne following his predecessor's untimely, but well-merited, death. 'Life was easier with Caligula. At least then all I had to worry about was staying alive.'

Claudius had honoured Plautius, the irascible governor of Pannonia, with command of the invasion because he was one of the few military commanders he trusted. Aulus Plautius was related by marriage to the Emperor and owed his position to that bond. He was renowned as a disciplinarian and legendary for the savagery with which he had put down the insurrections of the mountain tribes under his rule. The soldiers he led were the finest the Empire could provide. His shock troops were the élite Twentieth legion, five thousand battle-hardened legionaries who had learned their trade on the upper Rhine penning the German hordes east of the river. The Second

Augusta and Fourteenth Gemina had joined them on the march from their bases further upriver. Ninth Hispana travelled furthest, from the upper reaches of the Danube, where they had been headquartered for almost thirty years. The four legions were reinforced by auxiliary units hand-picked for their fighting qualities: cavalrymen from Germany, Thrace and Gaul, tough little Syrian bowmen gifted by their king, and Batavian light infantry who could swim like otters. It was a mighty force. But there was one problem.

'The whole army was on the verge of mutiny. The men of the Ninth were at the heart of it; they said they refused to leave the known world. The known world!' Narcissus spluttered. 'We have traded with the tribes of Britain for a hundred years. The sailors of the invasion fleet know the waters of the south coast better than they know their own. The Ninth have been headquartered in Pannonia for so long they have put down roots. A legion should be moved every ten years if it is not to become part of what it has conquered. They did not want to leave their cosy barracks and their pretty mistresses. They thought if they could hold out for long enough Plautius would give in and send them home and call for another legion. Emperor Claudius feared they would make him a laughing stock and he blamed me.

'But now they will sail and, yes, the credit is mine, although it cost more than I like to remember, including my dignity.' Narcissus shook his head ruefully. 'The Ninth are good soldiers, but they are led by a weakling. Once they began making demands the cancer spread to disaffected elements of the other legions, the way it does if you don't put the hot iron to it. Plautius was behind me, of course, and I exempt the Second from my tale of woe. Their commander, Flavius Vespasian, is a different animal: intelligent, a true disciplinarian and as hard as granite. He will do well, Rufus, mark my words. The usual bribes didn't work. The rot had eaten too deep for the tribunes to remind the legions of their loyalty. In the end, I had to give them what they wanted. Land.'

He had promised Plautius's legions that, when the conquest of Britain was complete, each veteran would receive a grant of prime land to go with his pension and scroll of thanks on his retirement.

'They kept me waiting for two days,' the Greek continued. 'At the end of it, when I demanded an answer, they laughed at me, said they would be happy to take orders from a former slave, and cried, "Io Saturnalia."' Rufus smiled. Saturnalia was the winter festival when slaves were served by their masters, and he could imagine Narcissus's reaction to the jibe. But the Greek was unperturbed. 'It was I who had the last laugh. Now all they need is a favourable wind and they could be in Britain within a week.'

Rufus congratulated him, but he could read Narcissus well enough by now to know that there was more to come.

'I promised them something else,' he admitted. 'They were pleased with the gift of land, but it needed

14

just a little extra to tip the scales. I assured them their Emperor was with them in spirit and as a token of his regard he would send with them his most treasured possession.' Rufus listened with growing unease. Narcissus was looking beyond him now and the familiar 'harrumph' from over his left shoulder told the young slave what was coming next. 'His elephant.'

It was madness! Rufus had argued and pleaded. He even threatened. But Narcissus only stared at him with the puzzled expression of a father confronting a recalcitrant child. 'Did not your Emperor create you a member of the Praetorian Guard?' he demanded.

'Yes, but . . .' Rufus distinctly remembered the words temporary and unpaid. He had worn the dark tunic and silver breastplate on the day Bersheba pulled the golden statue of Caligula's sister, the goddess Drusilla, to its place on the Capitoline.

'And was that order ever revoked?'

'No, but . . .' How could it be revoked when the man who had given it was long dead?

'Then you are subject to military authority, as Bersheba is subject to the Emperor's authority. Deny that authority at your peril.'

'I cannot go,' Rufus insisted.

'Will you disobey your Emperor?' Narcissus demanded in astonishment.

'What about Gaius? Who will look after him while I am at war?'

'Ah,' the Greek said in that perplexed way of one who had just remembered something terribly

15

important he should never have forgotten in the first place. 'Arrangements will be made. Your son shall accompany the invasion.'

Now Rufus's hand stole to the lion's tooth charm he wore at his throat as he looked down at the sleeping three-year-old. Gaius had weathered the sea voyage better than his father, along with Bersheba, who, standing four-square on her bridge pile legs in the cramped hold, had proved the most natural sailor of them all. The little boy's face was set in a tight-eyed frown, but it was still possible to discern the fine-boned features that had made his mother such a beauty. Rufus felt the pain of guilt like a half-healed knife wound when he thought of his wife. Livia had been the lead acrobat in a troupe of dwarf entertainers and Caligula had conducted the wedding ceremony as an entertainment to amuse his guests. Their relationship had been short and tempestuous and ended on the day Gaius was born. Had he truly loved her? He couldn't hide from the answer. Not enough.

Reluctantly, Rufus shook his son awake and Gaius moaned peevishly until Britte spooned cold porridge into his gaping mouth as if she was feeding an orphaned jackdaw. Around them was a buzz of what at first appeared chaotic activity as thousands of men were nudged and kicked awake by their officers, accompanied by the familiar dawn chorus of coughs, farts and muttered complaints.

The legionaries were bivouacked in eight-man

sections. As they gathered in their ranks, ten of those sections combined to make a century, which then formed on those already in position, six centuries creating the 480-man cohort which was the basic fighting unit of the Roman army. Each legion consisted of ten cohorts plus a cavalry troop 120 strong. Decurions pushed and bullied the individual soldiers into position, while the centurions, identifiable by their distinctive cross-plumed helmets, struck out with their gnarled vine sticks and shouted themselves hoarse until the disorganized mass became a tight-knit formation in marching order and ready to do battle. Watching the Second Augusta assemble, Rufus was struck by the difference between these men and the polished Praetorian Guards he had known in the palace. Their arms and armour were well used and equally well cared for, but the real difference was in the men of the Second themselves. They had a hawk-like confidence that set them apart. Where the Praetorians were well fed and softened by years of barrack life, these were creatures of the wild. To a man they were lean and wiry, unburdened by an ounce of spare flesh, and their faces were burned nut brown and the texture of old leather from constant exposure to the elements. They toted the crippling load of their personal equipment on five-foot poles over their left shoulders. In their right hands they carried the *pila*, the two throwing spears they would use to slow a charging enemy. They called themselves Marius's Mule, after the old general Gaius Marius, father of the modern legion and the man responsible for the sixty-pound burden they carried. But it was said with pride. They were hard and uncompromising. Invincible.

Rufus picked up his son and Gaius squealed as he was swung into the cart to take his place among the hay and the mealy bags from where, each day, he seemed to see the world with new eyes and greeted each experience with a fresh wonder. His cries made Britte laugh – a soft chuckle that seemed too gentle for her broad, pink-cheeked face – and her dark eyes twinkled with innocent pleasure. Like Rufus she had been taken as a slave while still a child, in a punitive raid on one of the tribes of central Gaul. She was as tall as most men and almost as broad in the chest as Bersheba. Rounded was the best word Rufus could think of to describe her. Round breasts, a round belly and a round backside that quivered when she laughed. While Britte took her place at the bullock's side, Rufus climbed on to Bersheba's shoulders and a few minutes later they were on the move. From his perch high on the elephant's back, he had an elevated view of the surrounding countryside as the column snaked its way across the grasslands and trackways of southern Britain. The land, bathed by a summer sun much gentler than the one which turned Rome into an oven at this season, was a carpet of greens so vivid and varied that he could never have described them all. Dark green water meadows shot with the white of wild flowers, emerald-green stands of young beech trees, shadowy green clearings, bright greens and dusty greens, greens that shone like silver and greens that were almost brown. He was no farmer, but such lushness told its own story. This was a rich land. A land that would support anyone prepared to turn the earth, work hard and defend what they grew. Italia, with all its abundance, was a desert by comparison.

He had heard they were in the country of a tribe called the Cantiaci, but there was little sign of their presence. The column passed farmsteads where not even a dog barked. Pasture that should have supported a dozen animals was empty, and fields were left unworked. It was the same in the small communities they came across. Occasionally, a half-wild cat would cross their path, but there was not a sign of a human being.

'Look!' He turned at a shout from one of the baggage slaves and stared towards a distant ridge where a group of tiny figures was just visible. As he watched, a horn sounded a series of harsh notes and a squadron of auxiliary cavalry galloped eastwards to see off the threat. The enemy.

II

The boy started screaming the instant he recognized the pointed stake. He had been taken captive in a raid on the Ordovici two years earlier and had heard the whispered tales of what happened behind the screen of oaks in the sacred grove. Now he would experience the dreadful reality. Caratacus frowned. The gods must have their sacrifice, but he wondered if it was necessary for the victims to suffer so much. On another occasion the boy might have been drugged, but Nuada, High Priest of the Catuvellauni, had ordained the threat so great that the victim must undergo the ordeal in the full knowledge of what was happening to him. Only then would the Druids be certain of the reply the gods gave to the gift of a soul.

There was no need for torches. A full moon flooded the grove with pale light, occasionally part shadowed by a wisp of cloud. A thin, misty rain drizzled down through the oak canopy and Caratacus could taste its sweetness on his lips. The new-life tang of damp summer grass filled his nostrils.

The screaming changed to a shocked whimper as the two guardians of the grove picked the boy up by the arms and carried him, struggling, towards the stake. It was set on a low mound at the centre of the clearing. The mound was surrounded by a circle of cloaked and hooded figures. Only Druids and kings could witness this ceremony. Caratacus stood outside the circle of priests beside another powerful figure in front of a carved wooden throne at the edge of the trees.

'Squeamish, brother?' the second man asked with a cold smile.

'I have seen blood before, Togodumnus. I only take enjoyment from spilling it in battle.'

Why must his brother continually antagonize him? It hadn't always been like this. Their father, Cunobelin, had raised them to rule together. The Druids had taught them the art of kingship and between them they had combined the strength and intelligence to make the Catuvellauni the most powerful tribe in southern Britain. They were so different, yet so alike: Togodumnus, a year older and stocky, with the heavy shoulders of a full-grown ox; Caratacus, tall and slight, but with a strength that always surprised his opponents; both of them hungry for a power that would not be shared. He couldn't point to a single incident that made them rivals. It had happened over time: a slight here, a disagreement there, and finally the moment when his brother challenged him to single combat. The king had forbidden it, of course, but Togodumnus never forgot the imagined insult.

The screaming began again when the boy felt the point of the stake at the opening of his anus, and grew to an agonized, throat-tearing shriek as it penetrated his bowels. He had been carefully chosen for his size and weight. The stake must penetrate his heart at the very moment the sun rose between the two most ancient oaks at the eastern side of the clearing if the ritual were to have its full effect. It was two hours till daylight.

The victim's arms were unbound. Their flailing would add to the Druids' understanding of the gods' message. The priests studied his torment with an intensity that was almost hypnotic, recording each change of expression, each shudder of agony and, when the screaming finally stopped as he lapsed into blessed unconsciousness, each dying gasp.

'Will your Dobunni fight?'

Togodumnus shrugged. 'That is for the council to decide. I am here to listen. Once I have listened I will take what I have learned back to my tribe and we will decide in the old way.'

Caratacus knew it would serve no purpose, but he couldn't resist goading his brother. 'A king is not a king if he cannot command his people.'

Togodumnus flinched and his hand went to his sword belt, but it grasped empty air. 'We will see who is the better king. It is fortunate for you we have left our weapons outside the shrine. A king's blood would have been more welcome to the gods than any slave's.'

The timing was perfect. The boy gave a final, convulsive shudder just as the first rays of the sun speared between the trunks of the twin oaks. The Druid circle drew closer and an intense discussion took place among them. Eventually, one of the priests broke away and walked towards the two brothers.

'What news, Nuada? What omens from the sacrifice?' Togodumnus asked respectfully. Before he had taken the tests, Nuada had been a prince of the Catuvellauni. He was an adept of the sacred rituals and in his youth he had travelled to Gaul to study among the learned men of the Veneti among the great Stones. It was said he was welcomed even in the highest councils of the society at the enormous sanctuary on Mona in the Western Sea. He was old now, older than any man in the tribe, but he still stood tall. His grey hair was cut short and his scalp shaven in a half-moon from his forehead. The cloak he wore was of the finest woven goats' hair and seemed to shimmer in the dawn light. At his throat was an amulet of Silurian gold in the shape of a bear, and where his right hand should rightfully have been a bear's razor-clawed pad was fixed by a leather socket that covered his lower arm. But it was his eyes that made men fear him. They were the colour of old amber and had the intensity of a stooping falcon's.

The Druid ignored Togodumnus and took his place solemnly on the throne in front of the two men. His breast heaved, and as they watched the amber eyes rolled back into his head, so the sockets were filled with the unnerving milky white of a blind man. From deep in his chest came a low growl, and the unearthly voice that emerged from his throat sent a shiver through Caratacus.

'The gods accept our sacrifice, but are puzzled why the invaders have been allowed to sully this land with their presence for so long without being swept back into the sea whence they came. The sacred places are defiled and their servants insulted and killed, yet the men of Britain stand aside and allow these Romans to advance ever further. Are the gods to believe that their warriors fear the invaders?'

Caratacus felt Togodumnus stiffen, but he ignored the implied criticism. Nuada had been one of the strongest advocates in council for an immediate counter-attack on the Roman army, and it was surprising how often the musings of the gods echoed his own viewpoint. This was merely the prelude to the true message of the prophecy.

'Yet the gods are both forgiving and generous. They understand the reluctance to attack an enemy of such power; understand, even, that mere men might hesitate.' The sound of Togodumnus's teeth grinding almost made Caratacus smile, but he maintained his solemn expression as Nuada continued. 'Nevertheless, victory is assured. When the time is right, Taranis will shower thunderbolts from the heavens and Andraste will call on the rains and raise the rivers to cleanse our land of the Roman filth. Epona will seduce their horses and drive them wild and Belenus will send a plague to strike their soldiers down. All this the gods pledge.'

Togodumnus relaxed at his side, but Caratacus sensed they still had more to hear. The support of the gods was welcome, but they were fickle masters. He had noticed that often everything would be in place for their intervention, only for some stronger or more deserving god to take precedence and cancel out what was to be. Nuada had not mentioned the Roman gods, so perhaps the fear he spoke of was not only felt by 'mere men'. Certainly, they would have power in their own lands, but would that power extend to the island of Britain? Caratacus knew only one thing with certainty: when it came to the fight it would be man against man, sword against sword, and shield against shield, and only the god within each would affect the outcome.

Nuada's voice grew in intensity. 'Only this do the gods ask of the men of Britain. That they stand firm in the face of the threat, even if the enemy appears to have the ascendancy. For the gods to prevail, men must have faith, and it is by your courage that your faith will be proved. That for each victory, large or small, the gods should be rewarded appropriately from among the enemy champions, for it is from the souls of the strong that they themselves gain strength. Finally, they require that that which is broken must be mended, and that that which is divided must be joined, and that the festering wound which is weakening the men of Britain must be healed.'

The Druid slumped forward in his throne. After a few seconds he raised his head, and the eyes which looked up at them were the eyes of Nuada and not the prophet. When he spoke, his voice was the voice of an old man, gentle and slow.

'Go now. The gods have spoken.'

Togodumnus hesitated as if he were about to speak, but thought better of it. Caratacus could feel his brother's confusion, and understood why. The message from the gods, though couched in the archaic, coded language the Druids favoured, was a straightforward one: if the warrior tribes of Britain would fight, the gods would aid them. But the final part was different. It was more the kind of riddle with which Nuada had taxed them during the long winter nights when he had tutored them for the kingship. It contained a hidden message which Caratacus had already untangled, but which his brother's furrowed brow demonstrated was still not clear to Togodumnus. This was one of the reasons Togodumnus was now king of the Dobunni, a numerous but not influential tribe who acted as a buffer between the civilized peoples of the east and the wild savages who populated the untamed lands of Siluria and Demetia in the west. Caratacus acknowledged his brother was a prodigious warrior who had bested many enemies, but their father understood he did not have the temperament to maintain peace and discipline among the British tribes at a time of ever-growing pressure from the Romans. That took intelligence and cunning. The kind of intelligence and cunning that allowed Caratacus to stay silent during the long minutes until his brother worked out the answer.

They were approaching the settlement when the final piece clicked into place and Togodumnus whirled round to face him. 'This was your doing,' he snarled. 'Somehow you put Nuada up to this.'

Caratacus gasped, feigning shock at his brother's sacrilege. 'You would accuse me of interfering with the gods?' he demanded. 'You impugn not only my honour but that of the holiest man in the tribe, a priest who has communicated with the gods since before we were born and whose prophecies guided our father before us and his father before him? Are you mad, brother? Even to make such a charge is to invite the three trials before Esus. Only my love for you holds me from returning to the sacred grove and demanding immediate justice.'

Togodumnus hesitated. He had witnessed the three trials of Esus, and he knew a man's chances of surviving them were slim. 'You must excuse me, brother. My mind is confused and I spoke hastily. It is just that the message . . . You understood the message from the gods, surely?'

Caratacus pretended to accept his sibling's apology with as much grace as he could muster, but there was still an edge of false exasperation to his voice when he replied grudgingly, 'The message is not clear to me. I was turning it over in my mind when you attacked my integrity. Perhaps you would enlighten me?'

'Not your integrity, brother; never your integrity. But I admit I questioned your judgement, and now that judgement has been confirmed by the gods. I was suspicious, but I see I was wrong.'

'And what is it you gleaned from Nuada that I have not? It was always obvious we must face the Romans, but it will be at a time and a place of our choosing. I will not sacrifice warriors on the whim of anyone, not even Taranis. I do not have enough of them.'

'But do you not see, brother?' Togodumnus was excited now. 'That is the message the gods sent: "That which is broken must be mended, and that which is divided must be joined, and the festering wound which is weakening the men of Britain must be healed." Surely what is broken is our friendship, and what is divided are the two tribes we rule—'

The light of understanding gleamed bright in Caratacus's eyes. 'And the festering wound is the enmity we have allowed to grow between us! You are right, Togodumnus. I see it now. The gods wish us to put aside our rivalry and combine our strengths to meet this greater threat.' He grasped his brother by the shoulders and looked him in the eye. 'I for one bow to the will of the gods. What of you, brother? Will you join me and smite the Romans such a blow that the ravens and the foxes will feast on their flesh and the frost will crack their bones when winter comes?'

Togodumnus hesitated for only a second. A tiny twinge of doubt told him something was out of place here, but his brother's confidence and all that he had witnessed this night overcame any scepticism that remained. 'The Dobunni will fight with the Catuvellauni and the Trinovantes,' he said firmly. 'And with the aid of the gods we will sweep the raiders into the sea.'

'Not just the Catuvellauni and the Trinovantes, brother, but the Cantiaci and the Atrebates, and the Durotriges, the Iceni and the Cornovii, the Corieltauvi and the Brigantes, the Parisii and the Dumnonii.' Caratacus listed the roll call of the southern tribes. 'I will even make accord with the Silures and the Ordovici if it means we can turn back the armies of Rome. The messengers have set out. The chiefs will be here in three days. Will you stay for the council?'

Togodumnus nodded, stunned by the scale of his brother's ambitions. They parted, Togodumnus for the roundhouse whose family had been evicted to provide suitable accommodation for the honoured guest, Caratacus for the modest home he shared with his wife and family in a wing of the royal palace.

Nuada was waiting for him. 'Well?' The Druid raised an eyebrow.

Caratacus gave him a weary smile. 'We have one pigeon in the net. It is yet to be seen whether we can ensnare the rest.'

Nuada shrugged. 'That is the will of the gods.'

III

Rufus swung his mattock savagely at the dry turf and forced another foot of sod from a meadow that was so reluctant to give up its bounty he had to assume it had been bewitched to resist the invaders. When the grassy square was free he carried it over the ditch and placed it firmly against the sloping bank of the temporary marching camp. All along the top of the bank men of the Second were carefully positioning sharpened four-foot wooden stakes to create a defensive palisade. He laid the mattock on the ground to rest. His arms ached and he was struggling for breath. Each evening every fit man in the legionary column helped dig an eight-foot ditch with an earthen rampart round a perimeter of more than two thousand yards. Only then were they able to pitch their leather tents and sit back to watch the squealing

31

antics of squadrons of playful scythe-winged swifts against the perfect blue of the skies as they prepared their evening meal.

'What's wrong, elephant man? All those nights with the big Gaulish bitch tiring you out?'

Rufus looked up to find a grizzled legionary with close-set, spite-filled eyes, and a mouth that seemed to contain a single blackened tooth, sneering down at him. He picked up the mattock and stared up at the man. He was tempted to take up the challenge, but he knew it was what the soldier wanted. Rufus was a slave, the soldier was a Roman citizen; a citizen from the gutter, but still a citizen. The merest breath of an insult and he would be dragged before the legionary's centurion and whipped until he bled.

'Leave him be, Paullus,' the man working next to the soldier said. 'He's doing all right for a slave. Look at his hands.' Rufus noticed for the first time that his palms were coated in blood from burst blisters. 'He's one of them pampered ones. Not used to this, he ain't. Not like you and me. Come on, old mule; nearly finished now. We'll soon be tucking into some hot grub and I'll be skinning you of every sesterce you've got, same as usual.' Rufus relaxed as the first soldier gave him a hard look and turned to follow his comrade.

'I see you still make friends everywhere you go, Rufus.'

He turned at the sound of the familiar voice. He hadn't seen Narcissus since they set foot on the beach as part of the third wave of Plautius's invasion force. Now he barely recognized him. It was obvious the tall Greek hadn't washed for a week. He'd swapped his immaculate palace clothes for a coarse woollen tunic of the type the Celts favoured, and a muddy pair of breeches of similar material. An untidy shale-dark beard disguised the lower part of his face and his pale scalp was hidden beneath a crumpled leather cap. He sat astride a small native pony that was dwarfed by the horses of his escort, a section of auxiliary cavalry who formed a half-circle behind him.

Rufus smiled. For all his complaints, he had come to enjoy Narcissus's company during the long round-about journey from Rome. Not that he deluded himself he had got to know Claudius's aide well; quite the opposite. He seemed to end every conversation attempting to unravel a labyrinth of contradictions and enigmatic hints which, after prolonged consideration, revealed nothing about the giver, but somehow induced him to divulge more than he wanted about his own thoughts and fears.

His hopes, too.

Narcissus read his face. 'The Emperor will free you, Rufus, I have his word on it. But at a time and in a place that benefits you most. And whatever happens to you, your sons will grow up free men.'

Rufus laughed. 'It doesn't matter. I am as free as any man in this army. We all march and we all dig. We eat, then we march again.'

'The marching I can do nothing about,' Narcissus

admitted. 'But no more digging. The keeper of the Emperor's elephant is an honoured member of the legate's staff. I will talk to Vespasian and ensure you are excused fatigues.'

Rufus knew such preferential treatment was certain to increase his troubles with the likes of one-toothed Paullus, but he accepted in any case. It didn't surprise him that Narcissus would approach the Augusta's commanding general over such a trivial matter. The Greek had an influence in this army far beyond his diplomatic status and he enjoyed using it. Rufus changed the subject. 'You have been busy, I see. Is there any news of the enemy? The soldiers say bringing the Britons to battle is as difficult as pinning down smoke with a tent peg.'

Narcissus smiled wearily. 'After a week in the saddle I feel part horse and I'm raw in places that may never heal. There have been times when I thought I would never see another dawn, never mind a soft bed, but my efforts are close to bearing fruit. Your friends will see more smoke than they bargained for soon enough. Is that not so, Verica?'

A straw-haired young horseman at Narcissus's right shoulder grunted a reply. Rufus thought there was something familiar about the trooper. The Greek noticed his interest. 'I brought Verica to see your elephant in Rome. Surely you remember? He fell over the moment the beast came out of the barn. Thought Bersheba was going to eat him. He's one of the reasons you are here.' He gritted his teeth as he swung his

34

right leg over the pony's back and slid gingerly from the saddle. 'See to the horses, Verica. I will rest here awhile with my young friend.' He threw the reins to the Briton and the group rode off.

'Come, show me Bersheba. Does she thrive in this country? I was wrong about it. Not about the people: they are crude and uncultured. But it is good land, and beautiful. If it were not for the natives I might be tempted to stay here. It's more dangerous than it looks, though.' He waved a thin arm at the gentle contours of the horizon. 'You can't see them, but their scouts are behind every tree, in every fold in the ground. I have come to respect them. Some of them, the Cantiaci and the Atrebates, are actually part civilized. Their warriors don't know fear, but I think their leaders can be made to see sense. Most of them. Not the Druids. The Druids would have them fighting till the end of time, but if you could separate them . . .' His words tailed off aimlessly as his train of thought faded. He shook himself like a wet hound and resumed his monologue. 'Verica speaks Latin like a dog barking, but I've grown quite fond of him. He is of the Atrebates who hold land towards the south coast around their capital Calleva. His grandfather, Commius, was an ally and friend to Divine Julius in the days before Gaul was a province. Verica, too, has been a friend to Rome. But the Catuvellauni are the real power in Britain. When the old king, Cunobelin, died, his sons, Togodumnus and Caratacus, did what princes always do: they marched on their weaker

35

neighbours and threw Verica out. Now he wants us to give him his kingdom back. Poor Verica; he'll probably be killed. He knows Plautius won't hand him a crown unless he earns it, and he can only do that by proving himself in battle. I've been sitting by the campfire with him every evening and he's taught me his language, after a fashion. Of even greater interest is the information he has provided. The Britons are more divided than in the days of Julius. When they are not at each other's throats, they glare at each other across their boundaries, spoiling for a fight. The Cantiaci, in the south, despise their neighbours the Regni; the Atrebates live in fear of the Trinovantes; and they, the Iceni and the Catuvellauni are in constant dispute.'

He was still talking when they reached the section where Bersheba was hobbled. Britte sat on top of the cart, stitching part of the elephant's harness. When she heard their approach she lifted her head and gave Narcissus a look that would have soured new-drawn milk and muttered a Gallic curse under her breath. But her features softened a little when the Greek drew a cloth bag from beneath his tunic and threw it towards her.

'Here. Fresh-baked bread, and cheese. The Britons make good cheese. You are well, I hope, lady,' he said with an overstated courtesy that made the wet nurse's eyes narrow with suspicion. 'And little Gaius too, I see. The air here must agree with him. He seems to have sprouted another inch or more since last we

36

met.' He ruffled a hand through the little boy's untidy curls, and walked on a few yards with Rufus to where the elephant stood shovelling great trunkfuls of straw into her mouth.

'I see our secret is still safe in Britte's charge. Did I not tell you she was worth a full cohort of legionaries?' Rufus didn't react. The matter Narcissus referred to kept him awake at nights and made the inside of his head buzz like a wasps' nest. He tried not to think about it.

The Greek changed the subject. 'Do you not miss Drusus?' Drusus was a year younger than Gaius and the son of Aemilia, who had been Rufus's co-conspirator, along with her brother, the gladiator Cupido, in the intrigues that led to Caligula's death. She had become his lover in the months that followed and Rufus was her son's acknowledged father. They were the only people who knew the true identity of the child's sire, and that was the way it would stay. Rufus conjured up a scowling, petulant face below a sparse clump of dark, tufted hair. No matter how he tried, he could never quite find the affection for Drusus that stirred him when he was with Gaius. 'He is his mother's son, more than mine. Better that he should stay with her in Rome,' he said. He and Aemilia had drifted apart. It had been inevitable, he thought. She may have been a slave, but she had been born a princess.

Narcissus put a hand on his shoulder. 'Aemilia still believes we had a hand in her brother's death,

37

although we both know the blame, if blame there be, lies closer to home.'

Suddenly, the air lost its warmth. Rufus glanced up and noticed that the sun had slipped behind a silver-grey mountain of cloud. At first it was still bright beyond the fragile curtain, but he watched its power dim as it neared the centre of the huge mass. It reminded him of the light fading in Cupido's eyes as he died in Aemilia's arms.

Bersheba sensed the change in his mood and reached out to run the tip of her trunk over his face. The familiar touch of warm, wet flesh restored his humour and he absently patted her wrinkled cheek. 'Why are we here?'

Narcissus didn't answer directly. 'Did you know it is less than a week until the Festival of Fortuna? In Rome, the gardeners will be preparing the flowers for the ceremonies, and the year's new vintage will be almost ready to drink.'

Rufus shook his head. On the march one day merged into the next, one step into the next. But the question carried his mind back to his home, among the palaces and temples on the Palatine. The festival to the goddess of Fortune was the only one, apart, of course, from Saturnalia, he'd ever taken part in. His head had ached for three days afterwards.

'Verica has been very useful to me,' Narcissus continued, obliquely returning to the subject. 'He has introduced me to his cousins, and his cousins' cousins, his friends and their friends. Important men

38

and utter nobodies. Clever men and fools. From them all, high or low, I have learned something of value; each, willing or otherwise, wishes to contribute to our cause. Do not mistake me: they hate Romans. But they hate their own countrymen more. In our presence they see opportunity; the chance for the restoration of the fortunes Caratacus and his Catuvellauni lords took from them when Verica was deposed. They will support us. But first they want to see if we can fight.'

Rufus stared at him. 'The soldiers say the barbarians are great warriors who believe they cannot be killed.'

'There is only one certainty, Rufus – war is coming and it will be hard and it will be bloody, for that is the nature of war. But I will tell you something you must divulge to no other. When we meet the enemy you will have an important task to fulfil. You and Bersheba will stand in the front rank of the army facing the countless host of our enemy and it is *you* who will know no fear. That is what I came here to tell you. There is a great service you can do for your Emperor. Can he trust you?'

IV

Early the next evening the column camped on the edge of a forest, with the flank of the earthen fort protected by the sweeping bend of a wide, slow-moving river. When the ditch was dug and the guards were set, Rufus unshackled Bersheba and led her to an area of shallows a hundred yards downstream from the legion's watering point. His body was chafed where his clothing had rubbed against skin caked in the salt sweat of an interminable, stifling hot day. When Bersheba waddled out into the stream with a trumpet of pleasure, he pulled his tunic off and followed her, settling languorously into the clear water until it reached his haunches.

He watched as Bersheba filled her trunk and curled the delicate tip to her mouth, gulping down gallons of water at a time. When she had drunk her fill she bent at the knees and flopped down, creating a wave that almost swept Rufus away, then rolled, scrubbing her back on the big pebbles of the river bottom. Her obvious delight made him laugh, and when she rose to her feet with all the grace of a queen finishing her morning bath, he called out to her. 'Thank you, great Bersheba, monarch of all elephants, for as you frolic you save me work. You were so heavy with dust I feared I would have to wash you down with a bucket.'

Bersheba replied with a playful jet of water from her trunk that took him full in the chest with so much force that he lost his balance and ended submerged. He came up spluttering and it was a few moments before he noticed a vague figure through the damp curtain of his hair.

'Narcissus assured me there would be fifty elephants. War elephants.'

Rufus swept the hair from his eyes and splashed to the bank where Verica stood. Bersheba remained in midstream spraying her wide back with river water over each shoulder in turn. Sometimes, when the fine droplets caught in the sun, she gave the illusion of blowing smoke from her trunk.

'Narcissus often exaggerates,' he said, as he carefully dried himself with his tunic. 'Rome doesn't fight with elephants, it fights with men; well-trained, well-armed and well-disciplined men. Legions.' He and Narcissus had once discussed Bersheba's potential as a weapon, a role which, fortunately, she had never

41

been called on to carry out, and now he quoted the Greek's words. 'Elephants have never been part of the Roman order of battle. They are too ill-disciplined. They can be as dangerous to their friends as to their enemies.'

Verica eyed Bersheba doubtfully. Rufus guessed that he and the Briton were around the same age, in their early twenties, but where he was athletically slim, the Atrebate prince had a stocky warrior's physique, and the ends of his long blond moustache flopped below the level of his chin.

'I have heard stories of great victories. There was a general, Scipio, who fought with elephants?'

'Borrowed elephants.'

Verica blinked. 'Borrowed elephants?'

'Yes. He borrowed them from a prince of the Indus, where they thrive, who loaned him little brown men to drive them and archers trained to fire from their backs.' He didn't know if it was true, but it sounded plausible. He had discovered that if he spoke confidently on the subject of elephants, however unlikely the claim, he was accepted as an expert. He had a vague memory of Narcissus spinning him a similar tale.

Verica looked at Bershcba wistfully. 'I wish we had more elephants. It will take more than men to defeat Caratacus.'

'You haven't seen the legions fight,' Rufus assured him, with more confidence than he felt. 'Anyway, where is Narcissus? Shouldn't you be with him?'

'He is with the general,' Verica said. 'They are discussing the timetable for the return of my kingdom.'

Rufus thought this was unlikely, but decided it wasn't worth arguing about. 'I saw you once, in Rome. The first time you set eyes on Bersheba, you fell over.'

Verica gave him a look of irritation. 'I wouldn't have noticed you, a mere slave. I was a guest of the Emperor.'

The words 'mere slave' were meant to wound, but Rufus ignored the insult. It was true. He had been sold into slavery when he was six years old, by his father, a Spanish colonist who couldn't feed a family of five from a few square yards of parched Mauritanian earth that produced more rocks than grain. He had been brought to Italy in the belly of a packed galley and counted himself fortunate that he had been bought by the family of Cerialis, a baker, and more fortunate still when he had passed into the ownership of the animal trainer Cornelius Aurius Fronto. The old man had sensed a talent in him he wasn't aware he had: a talent to train animals for the arena. It had given him fame, of a kind, and it had led him inexorably into the clutches of Caligula. So, yes, he was a 'mere slave', but that didn't make him any less of a man.

Verica mistook Rufus's silence for disbelief. 'It is true. I was in exile in Gaul when Narcissus heard of my plight. He summoned me to Rome to put my case to the Emperor. When I convinced them of the justice of my cause, Emperor Claudius vowed to create a mighty army to help me regain what was mine.' The Briton's voice held a faint hint of doubt, as if he didn't quite believe the outcome himself, and Rufus decided this new, charitable Narcissus must be some kind of benign twin to the ruthless schemer he knew so well.

'You are fortunate, then. But I am curious. How did you come to be in Gaul?'

'When my father died I was proclaimed chief of my tribe, the Atrebates. We hold lands between here and the coast. Soon after I took the throne, the Catuvellauni, our neighbours to the north, demanded a cut in the taxes levied on their goods passing through my country. They are a warlike people and their king, Caratacus, is very powerful, so I agreed to a modest reduction. A week later I received a similar demand from the Dobunni, who are ruled by Caratacus's brother Togodumnus. When I refused, they turned my cousin Etor against me. Of course, I had to kill him, but the Catuvellauni and the Dobunni joined together and invaded my land. If I had not fled when I did, they would have taken my head.' Verica spoke matter-of-factly, as if losing a kingdom was an everyday occurrence. 'Soon I will have my throne restored, and with Rome's support, and Caratacus and Togodumnus gone, I will rule the south. Already my enemies fear my coming.'

Rufus remembered Narcissus's reference to 'poor Verica'. He suspected this guileless young man would have to bathe in British blood before Plautius handed him the kingdom he assumed was his by right. The Celtic noble's hopes, based as they were on courage, honesty and trust, had as much chance of being fulfilled as Bersheba had of joining the long skeins of snowy-white swans which occasionally flew over the column in the early morning.

V

The fire burned bright in the centre of the meeting house as Nuada carried out the ceremonies of cleansing and called on Esus to ensure the success of their enterprise. Caratacus, in the place of honour directly opposite the doorway, allowed his glance to wander round the circle of seated men. There were twenty in total, kings and princes all, but only a dozen of them mattered. It was more than he expected, but fewer than he had hoped. They represented the tribes of southern Britain; the dam which must hold back the legions of Rome. But if any part of that dam should fail . . .

They had gathered at a temporary camp on the southern border of Caratacus's lands, from where his warriors could cover all the likely river crossings the Romans might use. He knew each man in the hut by sight or by reputation, had drunk with some of them and taken land and cattle from others, sometimes both on the same night. A few of them liked him, some of them hated him, but they all respected him.

He had placed Togodumnus at his right hand so all should know the rift between them was healed. Antedios, king of the Iceni, sat to his left, his chest torn by an occasional cawing cough. He was an old man now, but in his youth he had been the most fearsome of Iceni champions and his people would still follow him. Closer to the doorway Bodvoc, the Regni chief, was a warrior king in the prime of his life, massively muscled and with a fortune in gold at his neck and on his upper arms. He grinned fiercely and raised his cup in salute when he noticed Caratacus looking at him. Bodvoc could be trusted to fight. Epedos, whose claim to the Atrebate throne Caratacus had supported when the feckless Verica had proved incapable of holding what he had, would not meet his eyes. Why? It was something he must find out later. Adminius, king of the Cantiaci, was studying him with frank distaste, but that was to be expected; born of the same father, but to different mothers, they had clashed in the past and would clash again. There were others, the Parisii, the Coritani, the Cornovii, whose support he must have, but who could be counted on to follow where the strong led. She was not here. Why had she not come at his summons?

'I see no Silure or Ordovice representatives,

brother. I was certain they were part of your grand design.'

Togodumnus, as always, had found a way to irritate him, the buzzing insect never far from his ear. 'They do not feel the threat as we do,' he replied, keeping his voice emotionless. 'But they know it exists. The time will come when we have common cause, but it is not yet.'

'What is to stop them from raiding the border villages when my warriors are off fighting your Romans? Is that not the Silure way, to stab you in the back when you least expect it? We should combine now,' Togodumnus raised his voice so the others could hear, 'combine now and destroy the power of the Silures so that when we advance on the invaders there is no threat to our rear.'

Bodvoc growled his assent, which did not surprise Caratacus. Bodvoc would fight anyone. The others looked to him, awaiting his reply, but it was Adminius who intervened.

'Why should we fight at all?' he asked.

His words had the same effect on the gathering as red-hot coals dropped into a pail of water. The tensions which had been held in check just below the surface erupted in an explosion of spluttered fury and demands to speak. Caratacus cursed beneath his breath. He had lost them. No. He had never had them. Like a fool, he had allowed Togodumnus to sow the seeds of disruption. He had to do something. But before he could get to his feet there was a sharp crack as Nuada rapped his staff against the centre post of the meeting hut.

'We should fight for the gods,' the Druid growled, pinning Adminius with a glare that dared him to speak, and gave Caratacus a moment to step into the void. The Catuvellauni king knew he had only one opportunity, and when he spoke it was with all the power of a lifetime preparing for just such a day. His voice was strong, but devoid of any harshness, and it seemed to fill the roundhouse with its resonance. Its message was that he bore none here ill-will, not even those who opposed him. That he spoke because it was his right. That they should listen because he had won their respect a hundred times over.

'We should fight because we are warriors, the protectors of our people. We should fight because if we do not fight we will be enslaved. We have all lived through the plagues that ravaged this land. All felt the sorrow of a loved one lost. Unless we fight we will feel that sorrow a hundred times over – no, a thousand – and we will condemn our children and our children's children to suffer it also. Do not mistake me: this is a plague more deadly than any we have faced. A human plague that will strip the land of Britain clean and condemn its people to death or slavery. These Romans have not come here for a season, but for a lifetime – perhaps many lifetimes. Nuada is right. We should fight for the gods, for only by fighting for the gods will we deserve the help of the gods. But the gods have their own battle to win, the battle against the gods who watch over the Romans. So it will be men, men with iron in their souls and blades of iron in their hands, who will defeat the red scourge.

'You are all here because you know that if each of us stands alone we will be crushed into the dust the way a dung beetle is crushed beneath a wayward foot. We all have courage.' He waved a hand to acknowledge them as warriors who, each in his own way, had proved their worth many times. 'But courage alone will not be enough. Nuada, whom you know by reputation, has sent a messenger to the gods and the message he received in return is that only united will we prevail. My brother, who sits at my right hand, witnessed it, and he and I have put aside our grievances to meet this greater threat. Come, brother.' He took a startled Togodumnus by the arm and raised him to his feet. 'Give me the embrace of friendship.'

Togodumnus's face was frozen somewhere between a dead man's grin and a wolf's snarl, but he allowed himself to be taken into his brother's arms. 'You take unity too far, brother, and push my patience further still,' he said through gritted teeth into Caratacus's ear.

'It is a small price to pay, brother.' Caratacus turned back to the circle of kings, and when he spoke the power in his voice grew with every word. 'I do not ask you to do as my brother and I have done, but I do ask you to forget your grievances; to set aside the blood feuds and the border disputes that have long sapped our strength, and combine with me in one great battle against the enemy. Together we will destroy them, and the vanquished will take the tales of our valour back to their villages and their towns and their cities, and their stories will ring down the generations and ensure no Roman returns to these shores for a thousand years.'

Bodvoc started it. Each man in the circle had his war shield with its personal crest laid out on a frame in front of him. The Regni leader thumped a giant fist against the leather-covered ash in a rhythmic, measured drumming that was taken up by each king in turn. Caratacus saw Epedos hesitate before joining in the rhythm and taking up the chant that now rattled the wooden rafters of the hut. 'War! War! War! War! War!'

Caratacus waited until they were hypnotized by the steady beat of flesh upon wood, their blood was racing through their veins and the savagery of their shouts was mirrored in their eyes before he raised a hand for silence. He opened his mouth to give orders for the muster. In his mind he had already chosen the sites for the stores of food that would sustain a great army until the harvest. Knew even where he would bring the Romans to battle if the gods favoured him.

'Am I to be denied my say?' Adminius demanded.

'We do not need the words of a coward and a Roman-lover.' Togodumnus was on his feet, his face flushed with the honeyed ale he had consumed and

51

the battle-rage Bodvoc had inspired. 'If you want to lick this Claudius's boots, take your little tribe and go. Leave the fighting to real warriors.'

Adminius rose and would have walked out, but Epedos laid a hand on his arm. 'Adminius is a king, as we are kings. He is my neighbour, and we have had our differences, but I say he should speak.'

The last thing Caratacus wanted was to allow Adminius to speak, but Epedos was central to his plans. He put a hand on Togodumnus's shoulder and forced him down. 'This is a gathering of friends. You are of my blood, Adminius, but even if it were not so you would have your say, though I fear it will not be what we want to hear.' He gave way to his half-brother with a bow.

Adminius acknowledged the courtesy with a curt nod and rose to his feet. He was smaller in stature than Caratacus and Togodumnus, but with a girth and a pair of greedy eyes that told their own story. Yet his fine clothing and the gold torc at his throat marked him as his brothers' equal, and when he spoke it was with a ponderous sense of his own dignity. He looked slowly round the room.

'So we are all friends?' He paused and took in the puzzled stares which answered him. 'That will be why Bodvoc here encourages his warriors to steal my grain and take my young maidens for concubines.' Bodvoc's face split in a grin of acknowledgement. The Regni chief's passion for auburn-haired Cantiaci girls was a byword in both tribes. 'And why the king of the Atrebates allows my *friend*' – Adminius's voice was slick with sarcasm – 'Togodumnus to cross his land to raid my northern estates for plunder to repay some disputed debt that we have both long forgotten. And why you, my brother, do not have the will to stop the Trinovante nobles, over whom you claim kingship, from causing havoc with the river trade on the Tamesa that is the lifeblood of my people.'

Caratacus didn't answer. He didn't have to. Everyone in the room knew it was all true.

Adminius continued: 'King Caratacus is correct. One thing we can learn from the Romans is unity.' He paused again to allow his words to sink in to drink-addled skulls. 'But it is not the only thing.'

Togodumnus gave a growl and would have risen to his feet again if Caratacus hadn't held him down.

'It was the Cantiaci and our Atrebate allies,' he bowed to Epedos, 'who bore the brunt of the fighting when the Romans came before—'

'And who've forgotten how to fight now.' Bodvoc belched. 'Or you'd still have a few more of your pretty wenches.'

Adminius ignored the laughter and continued as if he hadn't been interrupted. 'It is we, the Cantiaci, who control trade with Gaul, who provide you with your wine, and the pretty pots and precious oils your wives covet. Therefore it is we who are best placed to understand the Romans, who have had lordship over Gaul for a hundred years and who have brought that land prosperity—'

He was interrupted for a second time by Bodvoc's growl. 'If you call prosperity a boot across your throat and six inches of iron in your gullet, then, yes, they have brought prosperity. But I for one can do without that kind of prosperity. Give me a warm hut and a warmer woman any day.'

'The kings of Gaul no longer live in huts,' Adminius countered. 'I have travelled there and I have seen their great palaces, the fine houses of their nobles, and their temples.'

'Temples for Roman gods.'

'No, lord king. Not Roman gods. Celtic gods. The Romans are pleased to allow the Gauls to worship their own gods if they wish. Of course, some see benefit in worshipping Mars alongside our own Teutates, Venus alongside Epona, goddess of the horses, but that is their choice. There is no coercion.'

Old Antedios coughed. 'Yet we hear of Druids abused and imprisoned, even executed.'

Adminius smiled indulgently. 'Not all Druids are of the calibre of Nuada. Perhaps the Druids as a society have placed themselves above the kings they profess to advise? Even above the gods they profess to serve. Does any of us here not know of priests who have overstepped their position?'

There was a low murmur of assent from Epedos, and even Bodvoc nodded. Caratacus sent an almost imperceptible signal to Nuada, who had listened to the insult to his sect with a face that could have been carved from granite. When the priest spoke, his words dripped with a contempt that stung Adminius more than any blow. He pointed his bear claw at the Cantiaci chieftain and the men on either side of Adminius shifted instinctively away.

'Before you were born, Adminius, the Druids of Britain were all that stood between this island and a maelstrom of blood and madness. Every petty king and chief of a dozen men or two dozen sheep fought the others for land, or for water, or for gold. No man could till his field without a weapon to hand; no woman was safe, even in her own hut. It was the Druids who wrought order from this chaos, who found the strong men capable of ruling, and who taught them how to rule. Men like your grandfather Tasciovanus, and your father Cunobelin, whose legacy you appear to hold so cheap. It is Druids who preserve the history of our tribes in song and story, Druids who bind the gods to the people, Druids who decipher the skies, without which the crops would fail. Who provide healing in time of plague and counsel in time of strife. Without the civilizing influence of the Druids, Adminius, you would still be living like a cockroach in the cave your ancestors inhabited.'

He paused and looked slowly round the men in the hut until his gaze fell again on the king of the Cantiaci. 'When I look upon Adminius I see a man driven by the desire not for peace, but for advancement. A man who twists the words and deeds of other men to suit his own purposes, and sees only that which he wants to see. Yes, the kings of Gaul have palaces of stone, but it is the stone we chain to a slave's neck to prevent him from escaping. Yes, they drink Roman wine, but that wine poisons their minds and influences their decisions in favour of their Roman overlords. The Roman gold that flows into their treasure chests only serves to divide them from their people. Is that the Britain you wish to inhabit, Adminius? A Britain where no man is his own lord and where the only freedom lies in death?'

Adminius shrugged, as if the question were beneath him. 'I merely point out that Rome is an opportunity as well as the threat you all perceive. It is a poor king who pushes his people towards a war he cannot win, when a few words would lose him nothing but his overbearing pride and gain him an ally with the power to extend his rule over all Britain.'

No one in the room had any doubt that the words were directed at Caratacus, who smiled for the first time. 'Is this the titbit you have come to offer me, Adminius?' he said softly. 'Is this the song your Roman friends have taught you to sing?'

'Do you deny it is your ambition?'

'I do not deny that Britain has never needed a strong leader more than at this moment.' He looked to each of the seated figures in turn. 'Who will unite our tribes and lead them to victory? You, Epedos? You, Antedios? Bodvoc?'

The big man grinned and shook his head. 'Not me. I have enough enemies already.'

Caratacus continued relentlessly. 'You? You?

You?' As he challenged each man in turn he felt Togodumnus fidgeting in the seat at his side and willed him to stay where he was. At last, he came to Adminius. 'And you, Adminius. Will you lead the warriors of Britain in this time of their greatest trial?'

Adminius stared at his half-brother. Was this a trap? Caratacus was offering him what he had always coveted. He had dreamed of uniting the tribes and leading them forward into a new prosperity, longed for the admiration and respect his people would give the king who brought the bright light of civilization into their lives. Then he looked at those who shared the room with him, savage men who ruled by the strength of their swords and the ruthlessness that rid them of rival and enemy. Saw the wolfish, mocking faces waiting for him to speak. And knew his dream was just that. A dream. He shook his head, and everyone in the hut recognized his defeat.

Caratacus accepted his triumph for what it was. He had forced the wild dog back into its lair. Now it was time to throw him a bone. 'You are correct, Adminius: the Cantiaci understand the Roman way better than anyone else in this room. The Cantiaci will be my eyes and ears in the south. Do you accept this task?'

Adminius nodded his assent, not trusting himself to speak.

'Then this is the way it will be. Togodumnus, you will . . .'

*

It took two hours of hard bargaining before he had his way, but that was to be expected. He was dealing with proud men not in the habit of accepting orders, even from other kings. Epedos had been easier to persuade than he expected, willing to accept his tribe's role in slowing the Roman advance and avoiding casualties. Caratacus knew the Atrebate leader would have difficulty restraining his men. The British approach to war was victory or death. To order a warrior to attack his enemy then vanish into the trees was like asking a bear to pin down its prey but not tear out its throat. It went against every instinct.

After everyone had gone, he sat with Nuada close to the fire, discussing what was said, and, perhaps more important, what was not said.

'There are not enough of them, not nearly enough. To stop the Romans we need every warrior south of the Tyne. The Silures and the Ordovici I can understand refusing my invitation, they have no reason to love us, but the Durotriges? Does Scarach believe he can sit behind the walls of that giant fortress of his until they go away? And the Corieltauvi? Do they think the Romans will ignore them because a wall of Catuvellauni dead lies between?'

'And the Brigantes,' Nuada said quietly. The Brigantes were the most numerous of the British tribes and held the mountainous north. With the Brigantes at his side Caratacus would have swooped on the Roman columns with the confidence of a hunting eagle.

'Yes,' he acknowledged, 'the Brigantes. Why did she not heed my summons?'

Nuada ignored the question, although he knew the answer well enough. 'Will Adminius fight?'

'No,' Caratacus said decisively. 'But even though I would give my right hand for the warriors he leads, it suits my purpose. Better to have him watching us bleed from the nearest hill than in the middle of my battle line less than a spear's throw from my back. However, Adminius is not the only one with doubts. I had a sense of men hiding behind their smiles.'

'Our scouts tell of groups of warriors riding hard by night,' Nuada said. 'Of meetings held where they would not be held by honest men. Wherever these men go the clay that binds us weakens and crumbles a little more.'

'Then tell our scouts to bring me the heads of these spies, or better still bring me one alive so we can discuss the nature of their meetings and who attended them.'

'The goddess Epona has been kind to them. The horses they mount are speedier and hardier than our British ponies. They allow our scouts to come close, then harness the wind to sweep them beyond our reach.'

'Then we must ambush them,' Caratacus said patiently, as if to an elderly relative. 'Find some hidden place and set a trap.'

Nuada raised one eyebrow, but otherwise showed no offence. 'It appears they know the tracks and the forest ways as well as any of our people,' he replied, with equal patience. 'Almost as if they *were* our people.'

A shadow fell over Caratacus's face. It was not unexpected, but when he thought of his countrymen collaborating with the invaders he could feel the hot coals of a fire smouldering in his belly.

'Adminius?' Nuada said.

'I don't think so. Not yet. He cannot openly oppose us until he has convinced his tribe we cannot win. He can question what we do, but he dare not act. It is not our enemies I fear, but our friends.'

Nuada opened his mouth to reply, but before he could speak a travel-stained figure burst into the meeting room.

'Lord, forgive me,' the man gasped, going down on one knee. Caratacus recognized Ballan, his chief scout, but he had never seen the man so agitated.

'What is it, Ballan?' he demanded, struggling to keep his voice calm. 'What brings you to me in such haste that you feel the need to break every convention of the meeting house? Are the Romans upon us?'

'No, lord.' Ballan looked up self-consciously. 'They are still thirty miles beyond the river.'

'Then we may lie safe in our beds?'

'But, lord . . .'

'Yes?'

'They have bent a monster to their will.'

Caratacus made the sign and despite himself he felt the hairs rise on the back of his neck. He asked the question, but he did not want to hear the answer. 'What kind of monster have the Romans bent to their will?'

'A dragon, lord – a mighty dragon that breathes smoke and fire.'

VI

The Senate was well attended when Lucius Arruntius Scribonianus was condemned. Claudius counted no fewer than nine former consuls from his elevated position above the throng, not to mention the cream of those of senatorial rank, though a few were missing who would normally have been there to witness the spectacle.

He looked down at the shrunken figure who had been dragged before him. What changes six months in prison could impose upon a man, even a proud man like Scribonianus. Claudius had seen men broken in body by torture, but he had never seen anyone quite so broken *within*. He remembered Scribonianus as a solid, almost portly figure, swelled by his own vision of his importance. Now his features were sunken, the ravages he had suffered written plain on the stark bones of his face. The governor of Illyricum; he had come so close, so dangerously close. With three legions he could have swept down from that place where Strabo said, curiously, that the natives lived in caves beneath their dung heaps, and taken Rome in a day. Only the Praetorian Guard would have stood between Scribonianus and the purple, and Claudius doubted they would have stood for long against twenty thousand veterans.

He realized he'd slumped lower in his seat as his thoughts wandered, and he straightened, attempting, no doubt in vain, to make his features look more imperial. It should not be so difficult; he did, after all, have the blood of Augustus running through his veins. Concentrate. By now Seneca had abandoned wit for bile, and was excoriating Scribonianus as a traitor and a coward. You could always depend on Seneca to frolic at the feet of power like some faithful puppy, ready to beg or roll over at the first sign of a sweetmeat, or cringe if he was shown the whip. He had become a little too familiar of late. Perhaps Valeria Messalina was right and it was time to send him back to Corsica?

He wished they would get on with it. Scribonianus looked as if he was going to die of his own accord. Three legions had joined him in the revolt, their officers seduced by promises of loot and advancement. But he had waited too long. Dilly-dallied nervously in his Dalmatian fastness until they sensed his lack of resolve. Still, they might have followed him, but for

63

Narcissus. Claudius smiled to himself. He was always amazed by the brilliant and ruthless intellect hidden behind that benign, almost childlike face. The Greek's spies had brought word of the revolt almost before it had begun.

Clever Narcissus, who always knew which to bribe and which to threaten. Within a week of his clandestine arrival in Illyricum, the legate of each legion was persuaded his interests lay in supporting the Emperor. Scribonianus was hunted down in a shepherd's hut as he attempted to flee to the mountains. Since then he had spent each day being peeled of information, one painful layer at a time; friends, relatives, casual acquaintances, fellow conspirators, he had eventually implicated them all. The soldiers, naturally, were safe from punishment. No point in throwing rocks at a hornets' nest. Those without influence – including, of course, the innocent but expendable – would die forgotten in the mines. But Scribonianus had not acted without allies in Rome, and that accounted for the gaps on the senatorial benches. Claudius was surprised how much the rebellion had unnerved him, yet now his enemies were unmasked he felt more confident; he would be able to face them one by one. They awaited his pleasure. Did that make him strong, he wondered. His grandfather Augustus had been a strong ruler. Tiberius too, in his own way. Gaius Caligula, that poor, insecure boy, had mistaken brutality for strength, fear for loyalty, and had paid the price.

The lictors were gathering now, a dozen for an Emperor, each carrying the *fasces*, the bundle of wooden rods that marked their master's *imperium* and his right to dispense justice. Behind them came his curtained litter, borne by six sturdy African slaves. It was not far to the execution ground, but he never walked when he could be carried. He had been born with one leg slightly shorter than the other. It was something he had learned to live with, but it gave him a clumsy, rolling gait which had always attracted ridicule and was, he thought, unbecoming in an Emperor.

The mob were out in force behind the ropes that cordoned off the stake; the arena might provide more in the way of excitement, but it was not every day they had the opportunity to watch a citizen of consular rank burn. No clean strike with an axe for Scribonianus. A traitor's death for a traitor.

The poor deluded fool must have convinced himself he would be sent into exile and somehow escape death. When the magistrate read out the sentence he had begun mewing in a disturbing, childlike way that reminded Claudius of a dog whimpering in its sleep. Did the man have no dignity? He began pleading as soon as he saw the raw baulk of timber with its chains and the pile of pitch-soaked brushwood at its base. 'Caesar.' The high-pitched cry echoed across the execution ground. 'Not this, I beg you. I throw myself upon your mercy. Remember my long service to the Empire. It must have some value. Caesar, please.'

The prisoner's shouts were greeted with laughter and from the crowd a dozen voices mimicked the condemned man, but Claudius kept his face cold. He closed his ears to Scribonianus's increasingly urgent cries and watched. Watched as the former governor was chained to the post and the brushwood piled high around his feet. Watched as the torch was put to the wood and the pitch-fuelled flames exploded in an instant. Watched as the fiery breath first consumed Scribonianus's clothing, then his flesh. Watched as his adversary's face melted from his skull like candlewax.

So die the enemies of Rome.

Tiberius had said ruling Rome was like taking a wolf by the ears, and it was true. Loosen your grip just a fraction and the wolf would turn on you. Scribonianus had not been the first, nor would he be the last, Claudius reflected, trying not to breathe in the stink of roasting flesh as he was carried past the smouldering, blackened ruin that had once been a man. He had never wanted this. Truly he had not. He had fought long and hard for a return to the Republic. Had risked his life for it. But it was for the best. If chance had not given him the imperial purple, the plotters would have served him in the same way as Caligula's wife and daughter, butchered on a silken carpet.

His mind went back to the moment the heavy curtain had been drawn aside, exposing his pathetic refuge on the palace balcony. He had stared death in the face. Seen it in the wild eyes of the Praetorian who believed he had discovered another of Caligula's assassins. Then had come that unforgettable moment of release when the man had recognized him; when the sword raised to strike him down was instead raised in salute. 'Senator Claudius?' A long, terrifying pause. 'Hail, Caesar!'

Sometimes he had difficulty believing he'd heard the words.

Narcissus, who else, had charmed, bribed and badgered the German faction of the Praetorian Guard to put the succession in place for just such an eventuality as this. It had cost 15,000 sesterces for each Praetorian, more for the officers. Expensive, but not excessive, for an Empire. From the palace, Claudius had been taken in a litter to the Castra Praetoria, the great red-brick Praetorian barracks to the north of the city. He learned later that he appeared so downcast as he was borne through the streets by burly, heavily armed legionaries that sympathetic Romans mourned an innocent man being taken to his execution. Even when the Guard proclaimed him, survival was not certain. There were those in the Senate who would sooner have seen him dead.

The crisis had hung in the balance as senators bickered over the merits of Republic or Empire. In the meantime, Narcissus had carefully salted the mob with supporters, and when a senator who had been well paid for just this moment finally stood up and mentioned the name of Claudius, the cry was taken up by a dozen more of the crowd, then twenty, then fifty, until eventually thousands chanted his name. Within the hour he had marched on the Senate with four thousand trained soldiers at his back, to take his unwanted and undeserved place in history.

Yet, three years on, he still had the wolf by the ears. When he looked out over the Senate, what did he see? Enemies? Yes; they were all there in plain sight, the ones who hated or envied him. But what of the friend with the dagger beneath his toga? What of the assassin who came in the night? When they stared at him, he knew they were searching for some sign of weakness. Weakness! How he despised the word. It had followed him since the day he was born. He was a weak baby, his mother said. A weak child. A cripple who couldn't take part in boys' games; who became the helpless target of his peers' cruelty.

If they ever discovered the true extent of his weakness they would be on him like a pack of rabid dogs. He slumped back in his litter and closed his eyes. He needed the support of the army. He needed a triumph, a triumph such as no Emperor had been offered before. Only one man could deliver it. He must trust Narcissus.

VII

Bersheba was nervous.

Rufus could feel the tension in her shoulders and from time to time she would raise her trunk and cautiously sniff the air. Her normally certain steps were uncharacteristically hesitant. Occasionally she would stop altogether – a massive grey dam – causing the long column to concertina behind them and the overseers to scream abuse.

He studied his surroundings to see if he could identify the source of her concern. Sometimes the scent of wolf or some other predator would affect her, but he could see no sign of any danger. A pair of young buzzards circled high above, their shrill 'ky-iiik' cries sharp in the clear air. He was tired and not a little nervous himself. He had been woken in the night by the shuffling of feet and the muffled clink of armour shortly after drifting into unconsciousness. It was pitch dark, so he could see nothing, but there must have been some movement of men from the front to the rear of the column. It was unusual, but not unknown. Nevertheless, he had cursed them for his hours of lost sleep.

The baggage train snaked through the centre of a steep-sided, wooded valley with a small stream wandering along it. On each side of the stream for a hundred paces the terrain was flat water meadow: sweet, knee-high grass scattered liberally with tiny flowers of blue and yellow. The meadow looked inviting, but the slippery sward made difficult going for the heavy-laden wagons and progress was slow. The cart containing Bersheba's feed had already become bogged down twice and they'd had to enlist a dozen slaves to push it clear. He prayed no one was wondering why such a light load should cause such a problem, and scattered the straw a little thicker across the cart's floor. A wide gap was developing between the drab-clothed baggage minders and the glittering plate armour of the close-ranked legionary formation ahead of them. As Rufus watched, a mounted officer galloped back to confront the quartermaster responsible for the Second's transport.

'If you don't get this column moving and catch up with the main force, General Vespasian will have your testicles for a paperweight and your cock for a fly whisk,' the horseman roared.

The quartermaster stared back at him contemptuously. He was a veteran of campaigns from the dusty African plains to the snowy wastes of Germania. He had been shouted at before and was not going to be cowed by any young staff peacock. 'If the legate thinks he can move this shambles any faster than it's going he can have any part of me he likes, and I'll throw in my poor old piles as a bonus. The fact is,' he said with exaggerated patience, 'whoever led us into this mud patch didn't take any account of my wagons. The only way we're going to catch up in the next hour is if you stop, and we both know Vespasian isn't going to do that. So you go back there and tell him we're doing the best we can, and that we'll make better time once we're out of this swamp.'

Rufus heard the younger man suggest that the gap in the column threatened the security of the legion. The quartermaster took a long look at the receding backs of the legionaries and spat on the grass beside the officer's horse.

'The more time we spend standing here arguing the worse it's going to get. Send back a squadron of cavalry if you like, but by the time you've got them organized I'll probably be sitting in my tent drinking wine and dreaming of women, which is what I generally do of an evening.' He pointed to the thin line of auxiliary infantrymen escorting the baggage train. 'We've barely seen a sign of the enemy for a week, and these lads are more than a match for a few spearmen.'

'The responsibility is yours, then.'

'The responsibility was always mine, sonny. That's what they pay me for, and nothing you pretty boys who wipe the legate's backside say will make it different.'

The young officer muttered an obscenity and galloped off after the main column, his horse's flying hooves spattering the quartermaster with muddy sod. For a moment the man stood grinning, pleased with his small victory, then he turned on the soldiers who had stopped to listen to the argument. 'What do you layabouts think you're looking at? Get back there and get these tortoises on the move. Use the whip if you have to. I want this shambles back with the main force before they make camp. Move, you lazy bastards.'

'The beating heart of the Empire.' The mild voice came from just below Rufus's left foot and he looked down to see Narcissus walking by Bersheba's side, four of his Celtic bodyguards at his back. The Greek still wore native clothes, but he was clean-shaven and his bald head glowed pink in the early-afternoon sun. He noticed Rufus's puzzled look. 'Men like these,' he explained, nodding to where the quartermaster stood shouting out his commands, 'are the beating heart of the Empire, for without them there would be no Empire.'

'Did a philosopher write that?' When Rufus had been an animal trainer for the arena, his master had paid for the young slave to be taught to read and write and given him access to an extensive library.

But Fronto had been accused by one of Caligula's aides of cheating the young Emperor and Rufus's chances of freedom had died with the trader.

Narcissus laughed. 'Yes, it sounds like something Cicero would have put in one of his speeches, but I'm afraid it's all mine. I quite like it. I must write it down and expand upon it. *Narcissus's History Of, and Peroration Upon, the Empire and its Officials*. It should sell well, don't you think?'

Rufus smiled politely. 'I didn't expect to see you again so soon,' he said, casting a wary eye towards the cart, where Britte sat beside a boisterous Gaius watching them suspiciously. Narcissus followed his gaze and shook his head ruefully.

'Women. They are such fickle creatures. I have been wooing a certain haughty lady who is important to our cause, but I fear she will be an expensive mistress.' Rufus was surprised. This was hardly an appropriate time for romance, and Narcissus seemed the least romantic of men. 'Do you notice anything different?' The Greek changed the subject abruptly.

Rufus shrugged. 'You seem to have lost your horses and you shaved this morning. I haven't shaved for a week.'

'Your personal hygiene is of no interest to me. And you know very well no sensible horse will come anywhere near this lumbering monster.' He patted Bersheba on the shoulder to show no offence was meant. 'No, do you notice anything about your surroundings?'

73

Rufus looked around him. Nothing seemed to have changed in the last hour. The valley was perhaps a little wider, the legionary formation ahead of them a little further in the distance. But there was something. The column itself. It seemed . . . thicker? The crowd of baggage slaves about him was packed closer and many of them were wearing their cloaks despite the afternoon heat. He gave Narcissus an enquiring look, but the Greek's only reply was an infuriatingly enigmatic smile as he kept pace by Bersheba's side.

It was one of those peculiarly beautiful British days when sharp, clean air and a cloudless sky seemed to combine to create an effervescence in the blood: a heady elixir that heightened the senses but, conversely, lowered the guard. Rufus felt the moment it changed, and he saw Narcissus's expression turn serious as he felt it too. Two heartbeats. A tiny oasis of calm in the midst of a thunderstorm. An unnatural stillness, as if for an instant the entire universe, god, animal and man, paused to take breath.

A pair of fat wood pigeons exploded from the trees at the edge of Rufus's vision. The earth sprouted men.

Rufus's eyes didn't believe what they were seeing. There must have been five hundred warriors hidden among the trees, but such was the level of concealment it seemed their gods had made them part of the landscape. One moment the valley was a tranquil forest scene, the next it was filled by an avenging army with a single objective.

Bersheba.

For the first heart-stopping instant of the charge the Celtic warriors ran in silence, but when they had covered half a dozen paces the air was split as five hundred throats united in a single scream that chilled Rufus's blood and made Bersheba shift uneasily between his knees. They could have attacked anywhere along the column, but their chieftain had bided his time until the Emperor's elephant was directly opposite his ambush. Every eye in that sweating, racing mass of men was focused on her. Every sword and every spear thirsted for her blood. None of the warriors wore armour, because this was a lightning attack designed to break the thin screen of auxiliary troops. Its power was in the speed and momentum of the attackers, which would take them through and beyond the defensive line and into the mass of unarmed baggage slaves. To slaughter. To Bersheba.

'So that is their intent?' Narcissus said calmly. 'Take your elephant and your family to the far side of the column. You will be safe there.'

Safe?

Only now did Rufus notice the figures around them shrugging off their thick cloaks, revealing the pot helmets with their neck-protectors and cheek-pieces, the faded red tunics, and the gleaming plate armour – the *lorica segmentata* – of the legionary heavy infantry that clinked rhythmically as they marched. They were already in their sections and they moved purposefully through the auxiliaries to form a double line, perhaps two hundred paces in length, precisely where the

British attack would strike. The first Britons were still fifty yards away when, at a shouted order, the legionaries hefted their brightly painted rectangular shields shoulder high and locked them in an impenetrable defensive wall. A second order and the razor-edged short swords they carried on their right hips sang free from their scabbards in a single practised movement.

Another enemy might have hesitated; might have seen their defeat in that wall of painted shields. But not this enemy. From his position on Bersheba's shoulders Rufus saw them, not now as an amorphous mass, but as individuals, mouths gaping and eyes bulging with pent-up hate. They fought naked from the waist upwards, though it was difficult to tell because their bodies were so densely covered in intricate blue-veined tattoos they appeared clothed. Each man was magnificently muscled and carried a seven-foot throwing spear or a heavy, straight sword. Many had limed their long hair into jagged spikes that made them appear even taller than they were. Their feet were bare, the better to find purchase on the slippery grass. Every one was a warrior, bred for battle.

The attack had no tactical formation, but it seethed with bloodthirsty intent. The fastest and strongest gradually emerged from the pack to take the lead. They were the champions, the battering rams who would smash great gaps in the enemy line and allow the long swords the space to carve left and right, cutting bone and sinew and enlarging the break still further. But the men facing them behind the big shields were warriors too. Each soldier of the Second Augusta was a battle-hardened veteran of the German frontier wars. He had eaten and passed wind, served and suffered, laughed and cried with the comrades to his left and right for longer than he cared to remember. They were his family and he trusted them, quite literally, with his life. For if their sword arms should fail them after an hour of hard fighting, or the curve-edged shields that protected them give way before a charging enemy, they were all dead. So he trusted them. And they trusted him. They had confidence, because they were the best-equipped army in the world and they knew it.

'The Second won't use their throwing spears,' Narcissus predicted. 'They want them in tight, buckle to buckle, where they will become entangled.' For the first time Rufus noticed that the front rank of legionaries had embedded the heavy metal-pointed spears they carried into the dry ground at the rear of the line, while the second rank held the heavy spears shoulder high in two hands ready to stab at any exposed throat or chest which showed itself.

Closer now, so Rufus could actually hear the muted thunder of a thousand charging feet slamming into the turf above the panicked gabble of voices around him. With twenty paces between the opposing forces one man broke clear of the other attackers, not a giant, but with long legs that flew across the grass.

'Hold. Hold. Hold.' The shout of a centurion was repeated along the line by the double-pay men.

The warrior with the long legs screamed a mindless, high-pitched message filled with venom and launched himself from ten paces, feet first, at the painted insignia of a legionary shield. It was a suicidal one-man bid to crack open the Roman line that appeared as if it must succeed. But the Romans were ready.

'Now . . . *brace*!' The centurion roared his command. Three hundred forearms tensed in the leather shield-straps, three hundred fists tightened on the hand grip behind the heavy bronze boss and three hundred shoulders pushed forward against the bare wood of the shield's rear surface. The attacker struck the centre of the line with the force of a charging bullock, but the shock of his flying leap was absorbed not only by the man whose shield he had targeted, but by those on his right and left who had, at the last instant, edged their own shields behind his. The Briton was smashed backwards to sprawl dazed in front of the shield wall and in the same second fifty of his fellow tribesmen hit the legionary line in an avalanche of bodies with all the power of hate behind it. When they met, the very air shook with the impact. The Roman shield wall buckled and contorted, but, incredibly, it held, and the frustrated warriors leapt to their feet and began pounding the hated insignia with their swords. But a long sword needs room to be swung and before they could make more than two or three swingeing cuts the main British force was crushing them forward against the Roman line. Trapped between the two pressures, they could only jab ineffectually at the helmeted heads showing behind the shields. Now it was time for the scorpion sting of the *gladius*. The legionaries' short swords with their needle-sharp triangular points had been designed for just this close work. Rufus heard the shrieks of surprise and pain as the first Britons died, their exposed bellies pierced as the defenders stabbed between their big shields at the nearest foe and wrenched the blades free in the classic gutting stroke. From between each pair of legionaries, the spears of the second rank darted and jabbed at neck, face and shoulder, ripping at eyes and throats. The first blood of the afternoon stained the crushed blooms of the blue and yellow flowers and ran down to nourish the fertile earth of the meadow.

The noise of the battle was an assault on Rufus's ears. A cacophony of grunts and screams; howls of mortal agony and roars of frustration; the mighty, reverberating clang of the British warriors' long iron swords against the hardened wood of Roman shields: the damp, butcher's-block thud of a sword edge hacking into muscle and bone.

He attempted to move Bersheba away from the fighting through the ranks of panicking baggage slaves with their mules and oxen, but even the elephant's enormous bulk could only make slow progress. As they went, he felt her twitch beneath him and he struggled to hold her as she danced and shuffled, threatening to crush the terrified men around her. Now another sound registered itself on Rufus's senses, a whizzing, quicksilver buzz like the high-speed passage of some giant insect. Suddenly he understood why she was so animated. He looked beyond the mêlée of warriors struggling to overcome the Roman line in what had become a great shoving match. A dozen men stood clear of the ruck and he saw one of them swing his arm four or five times in a circular motion before unleashing some missile towards them. This time he heard the smack as a round stone an inch across hit Bersheba on the rump, making her dance sideways. Slingers; of course the British would have slingers. They were at the limit of their range and the stones were as little threat to Bersheba as fleabites, but annoying just the same. Another missile whirred as it passed close above his head and Rufus realized with a thrill of fear that, although the elephant was safe from the attack, her rider was not. If any one of the stones which were bouncing so harmlessly from Bersheba's leathery skin hit his head it would smash his skull like an eggshell.

He was manoeuvring his way down her flank to a less exposed position when he noticed the spearman. The bright-blue boar tattooed upon his chest made him stand out even in that jostling crowd of warriors. He was tall, with the broad shoulders of a wrestler, and the arm that was thrown back was as thick as one of Rufus's thighs. His massive fist was wrapped round the shaft of a seven-foot ash spear. As Rufus watched, the arm whipped forward. It was an incredible cast, and he could barely believe the speed with which the spear crossed the hundred paces that separated them. Surely it must fall short? Please be short. But he realized with horror that its arc was bringing it directly towards him. To Bersheba. Its aim would bring it plunging into her ribs close to the top of her right foreleg. If it had enough force behind it, it could penetrate her lungs.

By now he was on the ground beside her. He saw the spear come as if time had slowed to a crawl. Watched it spiral on its own axis, the polished metal of the lethal leaf-shaped point glinting in the sun as it rolled. He screamed in impotent anguish as it dropped, increasing speed, towards her. No! With all the strength he could muster he launched himself into the air so he was almost half his own height from the ground. Still the spear came and for a split second he feared that he had mistimed his jump and that it would be his body that felt the murderous bite of that terrible blade. But the fingers that reached out to snatch the spear from the air a bare four feet from Bersheba's exposed flank were sure. He landed in a crouch with the long ash shaft clutched convulsively in his right fist, heavy and dangerous, the wood still blood-warm from its thrower's hand and damp with the owner's sweat. When he looked up every eye was on him, slaves and auxiliary soldiers staring with that not quite canny look he had seen aimed at Cupido after the gladiator had performed another seemingly impossible feat in the amphitheatre. For a moment he was no longer Rufus, the slave; he was Rufus the entertainer, who had once won over the mob in the crumbling magnificence of the Taurus arena. Very deliberately, he rose to his full height and brandished the spear above his head so all could see it. The acclamation began as a murmur but quickly grew to a roar that almost drowned the death cries from beyond the undulating wall of legionaries. When it reached its peak Rufus threw back his arm and hurled the spear in a great whirling curve over the heads of the Roman line and into the packed mass of British warriors.

Bersheba caught his mood. She turned her huge head in the direction of the fight, flared her galley-sail ears and raised her trunk to let out a trumpeting roar of defiance that echoed along the valley. It was an ear-bursting blast that made even Rufus, who had heard it a hundred times before, quail before its power. The violence and the terror of it cleared a half-moon among the awed baggage slaves in front of her and for a fleeting moment it seemed that even the battle paused. To the Britons she was the terrible beast they had come to kill: the Roman monster whose annihil-ation would shatter Roman hopes and weaken Roman hearts. Now they saw her in all her might and for a second the sheer visceral force of it unmanned them, but only for a second. For the battle was con-tinuing. Men were dying, Romans as well as Britons, because Rufus could hear the screamed curses as they were dragged, bleeding, from the front rank, and see that the shield line was noticeably shorter than before. If the Britons managed to outflank the legionary shields, only a few lightly armed auxiliaries would stand between them and the helpless baggage train. He looked round for some avenue of escape, but Narcissus touched his shoulder. 'Wait.'

A rasping signal sounded from the curved horn of one of the *cornicens* – an insignificant echo of Bersheba's trumpeted battle cry. Then, above the screams and the insane clamour of the battlefield, Rufus heard a rumble that reminded him of a distant waterfall, growing louder with each passing second.

They came simultaneously from both ends of the valley, as if they were practising a parade-ground manoeuvre. Two squadrons of cavalry, big men on big horses, recruited from the flat plains of northern Gaul, armed with iron-tipped lances and heavy swords. If the British war chief had seen them, he would surely have given the order to flee, but he was caught in the crush in front of the Roman line, cursing and screaming at his men to break through, to kill the beast. By the time the warriors at the rear realized what was about to happen, it was too late.

The squadrons came in three extended lines and at the full gallop. The first lines hit both flanks of the enemy attack in the same instant, the charging horses smashing men flat with bone-shattering force, ripping at faces with their yellowed teeth and crushing skulls with flying hooves. The elemental power of the charge gave the lances a killing capability that was almost beyond imagination, the long spears punching through a first body as if it were made of silk, then spearing another, then another, before the weight of dying men forced the cavalry trooper to drop the weapon and reach for his sword.

The first lines were followed ten seconds later by the second, with similar devastating effect, but the third rank of each squadron wheeled away to form an unbroken barrier between the attackers and the sanctuary of the tree-lined valley wall.

The Britons were trapped.

A growl of rage went up from the surrounded men. They understood they were defeated, but they were warriors, they knew how to fight and they knew how to die. If they were to go to their gods they would take as many Romans as they could kill with them. The intensity of the fighting in front of the shield wall, already savage, grew to a kind of wild-eyed mindlessness as men tore at each other to reach the hated enemy. Behind them, the heavy cavalry swords rose and fell, hacking at arms and shoulders and heads, until a spray of blood and brains fell like summer raindrops on killer and victim alike. A man screamed from what was once a mouth as he realized he would never see again because his face had been sheared off by a sword blade, the way a slave would peel the skin from a ripe pear. Another sobbed as he watched, stupefied, while his lifeblood drained from the stumps of his forearms. A few had helmets, but that did not save them. The force of the falling swords was enough to crush metal and bone alike.

'They're beaten,' Rufus said, his voice shaking in wonder at the scale of the carnage. 'Why don't they give up?'

'They are barbarians. They don't surrender, they die.' The voice was flat, emotionless. Not Narcissus, but a heavy-set man in elaborate, polished armour and a legate's scarlet cloak. He was accompanied by a staff of a dozen young officers and a twenty-strong bodyguard of cavalry who reined in their nervous horses well upwind of Bersheba.

'So you were right, Master Narcissus. They came for the elephant.'

'And you were right, General, to salt the baggage train with a half-cohort of infantry disguised as slaves. The gap in the column was fortuitous, but I ___ ___ ould have attacked unless they ___ k.'

___ commander of the Second ___ Vespasian had a way of hold- ___sted he had been carved from ___is mid-thirties, he had used his ___ rise steadily through the ranks ___ntil the only thing standing ___nsulship was a successful military campaign. He was tough, ambitious and intelligent, but if its owner was undoubtedly noble, the face was that of a provincial butcher, broad and puffy-fleshed, and only saved from being ugly by a rather handsome nose.

Vespasian frowned, as if Narcissus's attempt at flattery offended him. 'Nothing is certain in war. If the cavalry had been less timely it would have been hot work for a while.' He nodded in dismissal and forced his white stallion forward through the crush of the baggage train, to where his legionaries were still sweating to contain the snarling remnants of the British attack in front of their shields.

'Steady, comrades. You almost have them. A ration of the best wine for the third cohort tonight.' The encouragement was greeted by a ragged, dry-throated cheer. Then in a quieter voice to the stern-faced officer who commanded the cohort he said, 'Give them another minute and form wedge. That'll finish the bastards.'

The surviving warriors were trapped in a blood-slick square perhaps two hundred paces across, hemmed in by cavalry on three sides and the fourth an impenetrable wall of shields. Five hundred men had launched themselves from the forest, confident they would slice through the thin defensive line and destroy the enemy's talisman. Thirty minutes into the battle less than half of them were left standing, and more fell to join their dead and dying comrades with every swing of the sword.

'Wedge formation.' The centurion's command was obeyed in three well-practised movements which turned the infantry line into four arrowheads. The legionaries used their shields to batter their way deep into the heart of the enemy ranks, destroying any remaining cohesion or illusion of command. Rufus saw the panic spread through the British force like a ripple on the surface of a wind-blown pool. There was no visible evidence of surrender, only a palpable recognition of defeat. It was accompanied by a sound like a snarling dog as the warriors realized they could no longer fight, but only die. Some of them would have given in to despair, but the trap was sealed so tight they did not even have the choice of falling on their swords. Only one among them retained his composure, on the far edge of the slaughter where the cavalry screen was lightest and the trees closest. Somehow he was able to organize a concerted assault against the weak point of the Roman line. Fifty warriors broke through the gap and sprinted for the wooded hillside and safety.

'Let them go.' The legate's roar halted the cavalry pursuit. He turned to the tribune who was his closest aide. 'You must always leave a few to tell the tale, Geta. They'll think twice before they try to tickle us again.'

VIII

The taste of victory was the taste of blood.

Tiny droplets must have carried from the battle-ground on the breeze and settled on his thirst-dried lips, because when he licked them he could distinguish that unmistakable metallic tang.

Rufus hadn't realized that the aftermath of a battle could be as terrible in its own way as the battle itself. But Narcissus insisted he see the enemy at close range to understand the primeval force which opposed them. Now they were walking among the dead and the dying, the severed heads and the gobbets of name-less flesh, and the sword-chopped hands that seemed to beckon their former owners. At first he had tried to avoid stepping in the blood, but he quickly realized how pointless it was. There was blood everywhere. Not an inch of the killing ground was unpolluted. It stank, too. There were two distinct varieties of dead, he noticed. Those in the rear had all suffered terrible wounds to the head and upper body as the long, heavy cavalry swords had chopped down on flesh unprotected by armour. In contrast, those who were closest to the shield line had mainly died of stomach wounds, where the three-foot *gladius* had punched into belly and groin. Some had been almost entirely eviscerated and it was their exposed entrails, lying in obscene heaps and twisted strings, which gave the battlefield the odour of a well-used open latrine. It was quieter now; the groans and whimpers of the wounded had faded as the legionaries moved among them, slitting throats as casually as if they were sacrificing chickens and surreptitiously pocketing the golden bracelets they found decorating the arms and necks of the richest corpses.

'Magnificent, are they not?'

Magnificent? Rufus looked at Narcissus with puzzlement. An hour ago these had been vigorous, powerful young men full of the confidence that came with that stage of life when maturity of body and mind reached its pinnacle. The past was full of growing pains, the future an unavoidable fading. The present? It was for laughing and loving, and, yes, for fighting. But this? He had seen death before; in the arena and in the palace of Caligula how could one not? He had even killed a man, a man who might have been his friend. He remembered the feeling of having lost something for ever: an empty space deep at the heart of his being. This was different. The enormity of it, the scale of the suffering, numbed the mind and froze the body. It overwhelmed that part of him that cared, so he could stand here, in this obscene garden of the dead, and not go mad.

'Why did they do it?'

'They wanted Bersheba. They have never seen her like. She is a mystery to them. They fear her, so they must destroy her.'

'But Bersheba is . . .'

'Yes.' Narcissus smiled. 'We know that but they do not. We stumbled on their tracks about two days ago, when we were coming in from the north. They were shadowing the column, but keeping their distance; then a messenger came, and reinforcements. That was when they closed in and when I informed the legate. At first we weren't sure where they would strike, but Bersheba drew them like wasps to rotting fruit.'

'Will they come again?'

Narcissus cast a bleak eye across the sea of dead flesh surrounding them. His gaze settled on the big spearman with the blue boar tattoo who had almost killed Bersheba. The man's head was cleaved in two from the dome of his skull to the bridge of his nose, with the soft pink of his brains spread under him like a pillow. The unseeing eyes were crossed in a way that was slightly comical.

'Would you?'

*

Two marches took the legions through country where the land was gentler and progress more speedy, and Narcissus believed the Britons could not avoid battle for many days longer. 'Their king, this Caratacus, is gathering his forces. He has the support of many of the tribes – not as many as he would like, but enough to provide him with forty thousand warriors. Once he has them together, he must use them quickly. They are a fractious people, the British, not really one people at all: a hotch-potch of mongrel breeds, each claiming a more noble ancestry than the other. If he does not bring them to fight Plautius, they will begin to fight each other. Then his chance is gone.'

'What is he like?' Rufus asked, curious about this nemesis whose name was already legend among the invading army. 'Have you seen him on your travels?'

'Not seen him, no. I fear my first glimpse would have been my last. But I have heard much of him. If the tales are to be believed he is an eight-foot giant who eats Roman babies and slaughters Roman maidens for sport. He is said to have killed fifty men in single combat and used their heads to decorate the palisade of his capital at Camulodunum.' Narcissus shook his head. 'Just stories, but there are certain facts of which I can be sure. He has the support of the Druids, for without it he could not have brought the tribes together. He is a fighter, because no man who is not a warrior can rule in this land where a strong right arm and a well-whetted blade can win

91

a kingdom. And he is clever. A fool would have thrown his forces at us in small packages and we would have crushed them one at a time.'

'But that is exactly what happened in the valley.'

'True, and I find it puzzling. There was no plan behind it that I could discern, just a simple launching of troops at the column. Bersheba was the target, but there are more certain ways to kill her. I believe one of the chiefs acted alone, thinking to please him, but he will have been far from pleased by the result.'

'And now?'

Narcissus stared at the distant hills to the north. 'Now this defeat will eat at his confidence and at his authority. Only one thing can wipe away the memory of it. Caratacus needs a victory, and he needs it soon.'

IX

'So this is the great beast all the army has been boasting of. It is more fearsome even than I had imagined.'

Rufus turned, and discovered that the heavily accented Latin belonged to a tall man in the uniform of the *Ala Gallorum Indiana*, the Gaulish cavalry unit that had annihilated the barbarian attack a few days earlier. The cavalryman's face was hidden behind the god-mask of an ornate parade helmet with horsehair plumes, which he must have donned for a ceremony earlier that day. Rufus knew that such helmets, cast from brass and iron, were only awarded to the squadron's champions. He watched the soldier carefully remove the helmet's visor, with its enigmatic all-seeing expression, to reveal handsome, weather-worn features. The visitor was clean-shaven, with penetrating brown eyes that radiated intelligence and a strong nose that had been badly broken at some point. The column had halted before a line of steep, tree-clad hills while the engineers of the leading legion, the Twentieth, cut a road that zig-zagged up the face of the slope. Normally, the army would have stopped for the day and set up camp, but the ground was rocky and gully-strewn, and provided a poor defensive position. Plautius planned to push beyond the obstacle and force the pace on the enemy.

Britte had wandered off with Gaius to a small stream within the defensive perimeter, where the little boy sat throwing stones into the burbling water while she stood and watched. Bersheba was hobbled among the supply carts, munching contentedly at a pile of hay. They were twenty paces from her, but Rufus could tell that, even at this distance, the Gaul was impressed by the elephant's bulk.

'It must be very fearsome in battle,' the soldier continued. 'I have heard of these things, heard that the . . . that we had tamed monsters and made them do our bidding, but I had never believed it till now. It must weigh more than twenty horses, and those tusks . . . I have faced charging boars the size of a small bullock, but I doubt that I would stand before this.' He frowned. 'Does the monster truly breathe fire?'

Rufus laughed. 'There are times when her breath could knock you over at ten paces. But no, she does not breathe fire.'

'I have heard that it requires a hundred prisoners each day to satisfy its hunger?'

Rufus saw the glint of humour in the cavalryman's eyes, and grinned back. 'She would eat from dawn until dusk, but a cartload of hay and a basket of red apples is her daily ration. We keep the prisoners for Britte, who is truly a man-eater.'

'Britte? You have two of the monsters?'

Rufus laughed again. 'No. Britte is nursemaid to my son.' He pointed towards the stream, where the big slave girl and Gaius both now stood in the water. Britte held her skirts high to reveal calves almost as enormous as Bersheba's. 'She is one of your people, I think. You must stay and meet her. She has little opportunity to speak her own language.'

The Gaul smiled uncertainly. His expression changed as his eye was drawn to Gaius, whose high-pitched cries of pleasure rang clear to them. 'I too have a son of similar age, though I see little enough of him these days. I envy you your good fortune . . .'

'Rufus.' He extended his hand and the Gaul took it, his grip strong and his palm calloused and horny. A warrior's hand, hardened by constant practice with sword and spear. Rufus expected the man to reply with his own name, but instead he deftly turned the conversation back to Bersheba.

'So, Rufus, keeper of the monster, your beast does not breathe fire and does not eat prisoners, yet it must be terrible in battle?'

95

Rufus thought for a moment. When Bersheba was in a temper she was a truly frightening sight, but battle? Gentle Bersheba whom he had seen pick up an egg and place it back in its nest with her trunk? Bersheba, whose mighty strength was equalled not only by her intelligence, but by her compassion? 'She could be,' he admitted. 'But I doubt it is her natural state. I have heard of elephants bred to war, and truly they are terrible to behold. But they have been known to be driven mad by the noise and sound of battle, or by the pain of wounds, and they can be as dangerous to their allies as to their enemies.'

The Gaul gave a deep laugh. 'I have known men like that.'

'You did well the other day,' Rufus said.

'Well?' The cavalryman sounded puzzled.

'Against the barb— against the Britons. You and your comrades did terrible slaughter. I watched from the column. You probably saved Bersheba's life.'

The trooper's face turned serious and the humour died from his eyes. Rufus remembered his own feelings as he walked among the dead, and understood. When the battle-madness died and the glory faded, sometimes the reality was difficult to live with.

'They were fools, to attack as they did.'

'That is what Narcissus says.'

'Nar-ciss-us?' The name was obviously difficult for him, came out as a stumbling, fractured thing.

'He is . . . my friend. He is an important man. He says if this Caratacus, the enemy war chief, is half the

96

leader they say, he would never have ordered such a thing.'

'I am sure he is right,' the Gaul said with certainty, then returned to the subject of Bersheba. 'You say she is not warlike, so why is she here, eating enough rations for a cavalry squadron?'

Rufus looked proudly towards Bersheba. 'Because she is magnificent, because she gives our soldiers confidence, and because she is the Emperor's elephant.'

'The Emperor!' The cavalryman gaped in surprise. 'You have met the Emperor?'

'Yes—' Rufus was interrupted by a commotion behind him as Britte returned from the stream with Gaius. He turned at the sound of their voices. 'Britte, this is one of your countrymen.'

The wet nurse's broad face creased with puzzlement and he looked over his shoulder to find that the cavalryman had disappeared into the crowded ranks of the baggage slaves.

It took them two hours to climb the hill by the road the engineers had cut through the trees. By the time they broke for camp there were still four hours until dark but Rufus was exhausted. He felt slightly guilty that others would have to dig the defensive ditch and build the parapet, but all he wanted to do was wrap himself in his blanket and sleep until dawn.

'You, elephant man!'

He looked up and his heart sank. One-toothed Paullus. Now he'd have to explain to the legionary

97

about Narcissus's intervention with the legate and his exemption from digging. But Paullus already knew.

'Think you can sit back and get screwed while the rest of us work? Well, think again. Old Paullus has been ordered to put together a foraging detail, and guess what?' The sneer on his tormentor's face told Rufus everything he needed to know. Reluctantly, he rose to his feet.

'I'm on it?'

Paullus grinned. 'That's right, fancy boy, and I'll make sure that if there's anything heavy to carry, you'll be the one with the aching back. Want to do anything about it?'

Rufus thought for a moment. He could argue that the exemption from digging freed him from all fatigues, but that would only make Paullus more of an enemy than he already was. There was no point in arguing. He shook his head. The soldier grunted and marched him off to join a party of about twenty baggage slaves and a dozen bullock carts outside the main entrance of the camp. Paullus was in command of an escort composed of twenty-four soldiers from the Augusta's sixth cohort, which was largely made up of fresh-faced young men recruited just before the invasion. He lined them up within sight of the grinning guards leaning on the parapet beside the gateway and stood with his legs slightly apart and his hands on his hips.

'Right, I'm only going to say this once, so pin your ears back and listen. Our scouts have identified a village less than two miles from here where they reckon the Celts have a hidden store of food and grain. There are reports of a lot of coming and going between the huts and a wood a few hundred yards away. Whatever's in that wood we take and bring back to the column.

'Now, there shouldn't be any trouble, because there are only a few old men, women and children in the village, this whole area is crawling with our cavalry and there's been no sign of enemy activity, but . . .' he gave the final word an emphasis that had the escort leaning forward to listen to his next words, 'but if anything does happen, you know what to do. You, fat boy in the rear rank,' he barked at a sturdy youngster in a helmet that was too large for him, 'what is it you do if there's trouble?'

The soldier blinked and swallowed nervously. 'W-we converge on you in defensive formation, sir, and wait until help arrives.'

'And why will help arrive? Help will arrive because there's a squadron of cavalry within trumpet distance, which is why we have Julius, the cornicen, along for the ride. Or if the cavalry are as cloth-eared as you lot, we will always be within view of that.' He pointed to a signal tower the engineers of the Second had constructed on a hill overlooking the marching camp. 'And don't call me sir, son. I'm just a lowly single-pay man who must have offended Mithras because he's been dumped with the job of wet-nursing you. Right, let's march, and no straggling.

Keep a tight formation beside the wagons and your eyes open. We don't expect trouble, but we're ready for it. That's why we're the best.'

Rufus listened from his place on one of the bullock carts. Despite himself, he was impressed. Paullus might be a bully, but he knew his business. The unsprung wagons creaked in protest and their wooden wheels squealed as they lumbered into motion and moved across the rough ground away from the camp. At first, the soldiers seemed cheerful enough, but once they were out of sight of the palisade Rufus noticed the mood change. He felt it too, and understood it for what it was. They had all been part of the invasion column for so long that there was something unnatural about being detached from it. The landscape around, for as far as he could see, was gently rolling heathland – rough grass with a few clumps of trees dotted here and there – yet it was strangely threatening. It was all very well to invade Britain at the centre of an army of forty thousand soldiers, but to be part of this isolated little convoy made each man acutely aware of his own vulnerability, as if he were walking naked down a busy street. Even Paullus had gone quiet.

They marched beneath the smoke-black underbelly of a carpet of cloud that extended from one horizon to the other. The atmosphere was warm, almost liquid, and thick with the buzz of tiny insects. Soon everyone in the column was brushing sweat from their eyes or dashing at invisible tormentors. A dozen soldiers marched on each side of the carts, with Paullus leading the way, uncomfortable in the saddle of a chestnut mare whose temperament appeared to match his own. The horse twisted and stuttered beneath the Roman, and from his place in the second cart Rufus could hear the patrol commander muttering under his breath. He decided this wasn't the day to fall foul of the man and vowed to keep his mouth shut.

They were an hour into the march when Paullus noticed the first faint trace of white woodsmoke against the leaden clouds and halted the column at the base of a gentle rise. He called his section leaders to him and together they crawled to the top of the hill.

When they returned a few minutes later Paullus squatted over a patch of raw earth dug up by a fox or a badger, and used the tip of his sword to draw a rough map in the dirt. 'The village is here, overlooking the stream.' He sketched a tight circle beside a line which snaked from one side of the patch to the other. 'And this,' another larger circle on the far side of the snaking line, 'is the wood where the cavalry reports they've stored their food. First section will come in from the east, second section from the west.' He drew what looked like a bull's horns converging beyond the village circle from right and left. 'We'll give you to the count of one hundred to get into position before we move in. They'll try to run when they see us coming. Your job is to make sure no one escapes. Understood? Nobody escapes.'

101

When the two sections had moved off at the trot, Paullus formed up the wagons just below the brow of the hill. Rufus saw him frowning with concentration as he counted off the numbers in his head. Eventually he nodded to himself and clumsily remounted the mare.

'March,' he shouted, and the column moved off to bring Rome's bounty to a village that had lived happily without it for a thousand years.

X

In truth, it wasn't much of a village. When Rufus's wagon crested the hill behind Paullus he counted a dozen large huts and assorted outbuildings scattered haphazardly over a piece of raised ground perhaps two hundred paces across, which was half encircled by a loop of the stream. To his right was a network of cultivated fields and hedged trackways. To his left, beyond the river, a forest of mixed ash, birch and scrub oak stretched far into the distance. As the carts trundled down the shallow slope towards the village there was a flurry of movement on the river side of the compound, followed by a shrill cry that might have come from a woman.

Paullus grunted: 'At least someone's doing their job.' He urged his mount forward and the cornicen and the eight remaining legionaries jogged after him.

By the time Rufus and the other wagon drivers reached the huts the legionaries were methodically searching each house and stacking anything of value in front of Paullus. It was the first time Rufus had seen British buildings at close quarters. He was surprised at how sturdily constructed the roundhouses were. Long poles a foot in diameter formed the framework for the conical roof, which was covered by a thick thatch. The walls were of wattle, woven through upright wooden stakes, and the gaps filled with dried mud which made the houses weather- and windproof. They were each capable of housing an extended family of a dozen or more people and it was clear from their state of repair that this was a thriving community. Paullus looked at the pathetic booty of well-used copper pans, cracked wooden spoons and small heaps of powdery flour and shook his head.

'This isn't what we came for. You.' He pointed at the driver of the first bullock cart. 'You're the one who can understand their gibberish?' The man nodded nervously. 'Come with me.'

The prisoners had been placed under guard outside the largest hut. There were nine of them, not counting the plump woman, who reminded Rufus a little of Britte, lying crumpled in a pool of blood with a look of mild irritation on her face and a large wound between her breasts. The others were three elderly men, probably not fit to carry a sword, four terrified children of indeterminate sex, and two younger

104

women who stood weeping quietly and looked as if they expected to be raped at any moment.

'Ask them where the rest of the villagers are.'

The wagon driver approached the tallest of the three men and put the question in a sing-song accent. The elder, who had lank, shoulder-length grey hair and wore a ragged tunic and long striped trews, kept his head bowed and refused to meet his interrogator's eyes.

Paullus gave a thin smile. 'Ask him where the food's hidden.'

The wagon driver spoke again. Still the man would not meet his gaze, but this time he did answer, in the same lilting dialect. 'He says there is no food. What we see here is all they have.' He pointed to the little heap of plunder.

'Ask him again. Tell him we'll pay for it.'

The interpreter looked doubtful, but put the question to the old man, who looked up sharply and replied in a staccato burst. The interpreter shrugged. 'He says they've been starving for days. They have no food.'

Paullus's expression didn't change. Wearing the same thin smile he marched up to the nearest woman and grabbed her by the left breast, making her gasp. 'This one isn't starving. Plenty of meat on her, and the other one, and the brats.' He picked up the smallest child, a dirty-faced urchin with wide innocent eyes, and pinched his cheeks. 'See, if it was starving, it would be skin and bone.' Rufus didn't notice him draw the dagger – no one did until its razor edge sliced across the little boy's throat, flooding his tunic with blood. The child's eyes opened wider still and his mouth gaped, but he was dead before he could even scream. Without a word, Paullus dropped the still twitching body to the ground.

For a moment the world stopped – Rufus would swear his heart did not beat – then pandemonium erupted as the two young women shrieked, the one Paullus had abused dropping to kneel by the dead child. The surviving children keened a single despairing wail and the tall elder launched himself at the Roman patrol leader, who kicked him contemptuously in the groin, and stood over his writhing body.

'Now ask him where the food is hidden.'

The interpreter stared at him.

'Ask him where the food is hidden,' Paullus snarled.

The man complied, his voice shaking, but the only answer from the sprawled Briton was a glare of pure hatred.

Paullus shook his head as if the prisoner were a particularly clumsy recruit. 'Never mind. We've got plenty of time. Get a nice fire going and we'll see if Grandpa here is more talkative once he's been warmed up a little.' At his orders, two of the soldiers dragged the man into the hut and the other guards herded the surviving prisoners inside against one wall. 'String him up from there.' Paullus pointed to a beam about nine feet above the dirt floor. The prisoner struggled as he was stripped naked and had his hands and feet bound. He was thrown to the ground and when he looked up his eyes locked on Rufus's. They were the eyes of a helpless, terrified old man and they were filled with a mute plea to save him from this undeserved torment. Rufus turned away, sick inside at his lack of courage, telling himself over and over that this was not his fight. One of the soldiers tied a longer rope round the man's ankles and slung it across the beam, then he and his companion hauled on the rope until the Briton was suspended with his head three feet from the earth floor. Paullus nodded. 'That will do.'

Meanwhile, two of the guards had gathered brushwood and set a large fire slightly to one side of where the old man hung. He was sobbing now, some prayer in his own language, and his teeth were clenched tight with the agony of the strain on his ankle joints. Rufus watched from the open doorway, his mind struggling to deal with what he was witnessing. The murder of the child had been so sudden it still seemed to him some kind of dream, but what was happening in front of him was undoubtedly real. The old man's flesh was an unhealthy yellow-white and pinpoints of red covered his back where lice had recently fed. Fear had shrivelled his manhood and retracted it into his body.

Paullus drew his sword, then thought better of it and demanded one from the closest recruit. When the Roman plunged the blade into the heart of the fire, the soldier opened his mouth to protest, but the look in Paullus's eyes silenced him. Paullus bent and gripped the suspended Briton by the hair so he was looking directly into his captive's face. 'Now, Grandpa, let's continue our little chat.' The old man gasped something unintelligible and spat in his face, but the Roman only laughed. 'Give him a taste,' he ordered.

One of the young legionaries pushed the dangling prisoner so that the momentum swung him directly over the fire. The old man writhed and twisted, desperately trying to keep his body away from the heat. But the flames sought him out, and the hut filled with the acrid stench of singeing hair as his head was surrounded by a halo of flame that flared and died in an instant, accompanied by a grating scream of agony.

Paullus reached for the sword resting in the fire, but drew his hand back sharply when he felt the heat radiating from the hilt. He noticed Rufus watching from the doorway and grinned. 'You'd have liked that, elephant man. Old Paullus getting a bit of his own medicine.' He used his still bloody dagger to cut a square of cloth from a blanket and wetted it in a stone trough set to one side of the room. Steam hissed from the cloth when he picked up the sword, its iron blade shimmering red. He turned to the hanging figure, whose blackened tufts of remaining hair still wafted smoke towards a hole in the centre of the roof. 'Now let's hear the old man sing.'

The suspended victim shook his head wildly and

gibbered a high-pitched rush of words. Paullus looked towards the interpreter. 'Is he going to talk?'

The man shook his head. 'He says Esus will rot the eyeballs in your head and make you piss maggots.'

Paullus laughed and stepped forward with the glowing blade and brought the point slowly towards the powerless Briton's left eye. A commotion behind him stayed his hand a fraction before the red-hot metal kissed the old man's cringing flesh and the woman he had abused earlier burst between the guards and threw herself at his feet. He frowned. 'What's she saying?'

The interpreter listened to the sobbing woman for a few seconds. 'Her name is Veleda. This man is her father. She begs you not to harm him. She says she'll lead us to the grain and the fodder. It's hidden in a clearing in the forest, enough to fill all our carts and more.'

Paullus looked thoughtful. He turned to the leader of the legionary guards, a pink-cheeked young man with a square jaw and a squint in one eye.

'Agrippa, take the woman and the two old men, but bind them tight and keep a sword at their back. The others stay here. Tell her I'll gut her father and the brats at the first sign of a trick.' He waited until the interpreter had translated his words, then placed the sword a hair's breadth from the old man's wrinkled belly and looked hard at the woman. 'Understand? I'll gut him.' She nodded sharply. 'Take them away. Elephant man, you're in charge of the slaves. I want every grain of wheat and wisp of hay, or you'll answer to me.'

The legionary guards marched the woman and the two elders from the hut and Rufus turned to follow, calling to the other baggage slaves to bring the wagons across the river. As he walked from the doorway, he heard Paullus say conversationally: 'Now, ask him about the gold.'

The screaming started before they reached the forest.

It wasn't possible to take the carts into the trees. The villagers had been careful not to leave any marked tracks leading to the clearing where they had cached their precious supplies. Instead, they had created a dozen well-disguised paths that were scarcely wider than those trampled by foraging deer. It was along one of these that Veleda led them, with the point of Agrippa's sword at her back. Trees and thorn bushes grew tight to the track, plucking at the tunics of soldier and slave alike. Above them, the leaf canopy created a barrier that trapped the steamy heat beneath it, making the atmosphere in the forest depths oppressive and almost unbreathable. If anything, the day had grown even more humid and Rufus thought he heard the rumble of thunder in the distance. Eventually, Veleda stopped and pointed to an impenetrable wall of foliage. Agrippa studied what she was indicating with a look of suspicion, his squint growing more pronounced with each passing second. 'If this is some kind of trick . . .'

The British woman didn't understand the words, but she shook her head and approached the spot she had indicated. As they drew closer, Rufus saw it was a wall of still growing trees and plants, closely woven and carefully chosen to exactly match the habitat around it. Beyond this slim natural curtain was a clearing that contained a dozen small, raised wooden huts, which, on closer inspection, turned out to be storehouses filled with sheaves of hay and sacks of wheat and barley.

'They build them on stilts to keep out the damp from the earth and stop animals getting at the food. I've seen storage places just like it in Germania. There's enough here to feed a cohort for a week,' Agrippa said cheerfully.

Low earth mounds on the clearing floor covered pits containing different types of cereals and pulses, and Rufus ordered his fellow slaves to begin digging up the buried food stores. On the far side was a fenced stockade where a dozen small sheep with matted brown wool grazed in silence. Agrippa frowned when he saw them.

'I don't think we can take them with us. If we release them they'll just scatter into the forest and the wolves will get them. We should leave them here and send back some cavalry and a stockman to drive them in.'

'Paullus won't be happy,' Rufus pointed out.

Agrippa grinned. 'Paullus is never happy. I thought you'd noticed that. We'll need half a dozen trips to

111

get all this to the wagons.' He shouted to one of the other guards. 'Cestus, the old men and the woman can still carry something with their hands tied. Get the buggers to work.'

The slaves were already heavily laden. Agrippa ordered them into line with one guard in the van, with Veleda, and another bringing up the rear. 'We'll leave a couple of people to keep digging up what's in the pits. It shouldn't take us long to get back to the village.' Rufus nodded and picked up as many sacks as he could carry before following the Roman back into the trees. He felt a spot of cold liquid splash on to the bare flesh of his forearm, quickly followed by another, then a dozen more. In a moment, big droplets studded the earth of the clearing, lancing diagonally from the heavens and creating little brown pools in any indent or hollow. The noise of the rain hitting the leaves was so loud that Agrippa had to shout to make himself heard.

'This cursed country. Quickly, now. We need to get this into the carts and covered or we'll lose half of it.' He sheathed his sword and picked up a sack under each arm before trotting off after the column of slaves and captives, leaving Rufus to make his own pace.

By now the deluge was so fierce the young slave had difficulty following the track. He concentrated on Agrippa's retreating back and tried to keep his feet moving through the increasingly heavy tangle of wet grass. In the twilight world of the storm-darkened undergrowth, the trees and bushes seemed closer than before, the thorns longer and more persistent. The grasping stem of a dog rose obstructed him and he looked up to discover that Agrippa had disappeared. For a moment he feared he'd be trapped for ever in this frightening green jungle that threatened to bury him alive. Then, as suddenly as it began, the rain stopped, and it was as if a veil had been lifted from his eyes. He was no longer in a threatening, claustrophobic tunnel, just a pleasant green pathway. The thorn bushes were scattered with delicate pink flowers which the raindrops filled like tiny diamonds. He could hear a bird singing a sweet trilling melody, and the rhythmic tap-tap of individual drops falling from the canopy on to larger leaves below. And the sound of clashing metal. Metal? With a lurch his world turned upside down. Now the grass he'd been walking on was in front of his eyes, each individual blade etched sharp on his brain. For a second he was surprised. He must have tripped? Then the grass blurred, and faded, and his vision turned black as night, but not before his mind registered the leather-clad foot which planted itself an inch from his nose.

XI

There are different kinds of waking.

There is the restful waking in a soft bed, or even a hard one, when the brain is refreshed and instantly at the ready for whatever the day brings. There is the sluggish, glue-mouthed waking that is the aftermath of a half-remembered night of revelry that involved one cup of rough wine too many. Then there is the joyful waking, as one's hand unthinkingly finds firm, rounded flesh, and the mind strays to the wonders of the night before and the body anticipates the pleasures yet to come.

Rufus's waking was none of these.

He knew something was horribly wrong even before he opened his eyes. What was this unyielding, gnarled vegetable thing cutting into his face from eyebrow to chin? And another, trapping his arm beneath him and eating deep into his flesh. He was half upside down, with his neck forced at an angle by something crushing him from above. The thing was moving, enormously heavy, and at once hard and soft. He could barely breathe because of the weight bearing down on him. Warm, viscous liquid ran over his bare flesh – he was naked? – and into his hair and his eyes and his mouth. He tasted it, bitter and sharp and yeasty, as at the same time he recognized its smell. He choked and spat and his eyes snapped open with the shock. Human piss!

Still his brain took time to acknowledge the enormity of what was happening to him.

One eye was angled so it could see nothing but the pile of wood and logs at the base of whatever it was he was now part of. Because he was part of it, as much so as if he were jointed or nailed to it. The thing eating into his face was a twisted wicker strand, perhaps an inch across. His mouth was partially covered by the wicker and forced half open by the pressure crushing him. His other eye looked directly at a ring of grim, moustached faces. Two men were set apart by their bearing and the fact that they were clean-shaven. The one in the long cloak, with the shaven head; and a warrior . . .

There was an awful moment when realization took over from calculation and concussed bemusement was replaced by sheer horror. His body began to tremble, at least what little of it was capable of movement. He heard a high, whining sound come unbidden from his throat; a helpless, terror-stricken wail he now knew was being echoed by the nameless, faceless mound of living human bodies piled above him in this wicker trap. He closed his eyes again, hoping against hope that he was in some terrible dream; that he would wake once more and it would be gone. But there was no escape. Instead, his mind painted a picture of what was, and what was to be. He could see the giant structure, grotesque, yet vaguely human in shape. A great basket made up of wicker and tree branches, and filling its belly and breasts the human fodder that would soon fuel its fiery appetite. Sacrifices. *He was to be a human sacrifice.* He shook with helpless terror and felt urine shoot from him in short involuntary bursts. Now he understood. And there was worse occurring above him as his fellow captives began to realize the true horror of their fate. The stink of voided bowels filled the air. He could hear someone pleading from within the human tangle close by and thought he recognized the voice of Paullus, though it was difficult to tell since it sounded like the high-pitched bleating of a small boy. He felt the tree-man shudder as prisoners fought in vain to be free; to throw themselves on the merciful swords of their captors.

He had heard the tales of the Wicker Man, of captives put to death in the belly of Taranis, the thunder god, and trembled at the thought of it. He had never expected to see it. Now he was enduring its terrible reality. Why was he not going mad? Surely it would be better to be lost in babbling insanity than to lie here coldly considering his fate?

Soon they would begin to push the straw and branches into the basket between the living fuel. And then the songs would begin. Julius Caesar had written of the songs, or was it Strabo? What did it matter? He was going to die. When the Wicker Man was filled with enough flammable material, the Druid would come forward with his flaming torch, and then . . . 'No! Gaius! Bersheba! Please!' His wail rang across the glade where the British war chiefs had gathered to see Taranis receive the gift they prayed would turn the campaign in their favour. With one eye, he saw the warrior without the moustache frown. Was there something familiar about him?

The man had the place of honour beside the Druid. He was dressed in the finespun cloth of a Celtic lord, with a torc of twisted gold at his neck and a thick cloak about his shoulders, clasped by a bright, bejewelled brooch. On his left hip hung a long sword in an ornate bronze scabbard, its hilt decorated with rubies and glittering studs of precious metal. His left hand rested on a big oval shield with a swirling pattern etched into the copper and the figure of a charging boar at its centre. Some faint memory blew back the curtain of panic that surrounded Rufus. A charging boar. What was it?

The flicker of a torch in the Druid's hand drew a collective howl from the trapped men. In a high, clear voice Nuada began the gift song of Taranis, quickly joined by the deeper tones of a dozen warrior kings, including Caratacus, who stood tall and straight at his side. The Catuvellauni leader watched the men trapped inside the thirty-foot construction squirming in terror, and steeled himself against pity. What must be, must be. These Romans had invaded his land. Now they would pay the price. His whole upper body vibrating, he let the song boom from his chest, felt the mesmerizing power of it in his mind. The loss of a fine moustache was a small price to pay for the information he had gleaned about the 'monster'. He had resented it when his father insisted he should learn the language of the enemy, but now he acknowledged Cunobelin's wisdom. The old man had known the Romans would return, and that his sons were destined to oppose them. He was determined they should have every possible weapon at their disposal. Caratacus remembered his father's words as the trio sat by the fire in that fierce winter a dozen years before.

'To face the enemy without fully understanding them is like facing them without a sword or a shield. It gives them a precious advantage. Hate the Romans if you must, but do not allow hate to cloud your judgement.'

Caratacus had listened. Togodumnus had sneered that he wanted nothing to do with the Romans but killing them. That was the night, Caratacus knew, when his father had decided he should be king.

118

He brought his thoughts back to the present. The Druids were pushing straw and thin branches that would feed the fire into gaps in the structure, and the tinder-dry gorse bushes that burned so fiercely when they were in yellow flower. The shrieks of fear were an assault on his ears and he vowed to close them when the flame was lit. A pity he had been unable to spend longer with the young man in charge of the elephant. It had been a very revealing conversation. Now he was sure the beast was no physical threat he could concentrate on combating the power of its symbolism. Togodumnus, the fool, was still determined it should be destroyed. Would he never learn?

The attack on the column his brother had ordered without his knowledge had infuriated the British war leader. How many men had they lost? How many irreplaceable warriors cut down for nothing but one man's vanity? Three hundred, perhaps four. And worse, every man who escaped the carnage was now convinced of the Romans' invincibility and spread whispers about the power of the 'monster'. The damage was incalculable.

At last, Nuada was ready.

Rufus watched the Druid come forward with the flaming torch in his left hand. His mind threatened to freeze with terror, but he knew he couldn't allow it. He must find the strength. Think! The boar. There was something about the boar. Then the words came to him as clearly as if he was hearing them spoken inside his head: 'I have faced charging boars the size of a small bullock, but I doubt that I would stand before this.'

He forced himself to concentrate. The nose. Yes, the broken nose. That noble, who must be Caratacus, was the *Gaul*, the Gaul who had questioned him about Bersheba! He had only one chance. He opened his mouth wide to shout for the British king's attention. But he had drunk nothing for more than a dozen hours and it was as if his throat was filled with pebbles. All that emerged was a pale imitation of an elderly crow that was drowned by the moans and screams of those trapped with him.

Nuada was mere feet away, his hand reaching forward to push the torch into the straw, where it would flicker, then burn, then consume. Rufus swallowed desperately, working his mouth in an attempt to find something, anything, that would lubricate his throat. He tried again. If he failed, he was dead. 'Lord,' he croaked. 'Lord Caratacus. Bersheba. The elephant.'

Nuada's winged brows knitted in puzzlement at the words, but he shook his head and forced the flaming torch into the straw beside Rufus's head. The young Roman screamed in terror as he felt the first heat of the flames on his flesh.

'Hold.' The voice was firm and commanding and it was accompanied by strong hands beating out the fire.

'What is this?' Nuada's voice was thick with righteous outrage. 'It is sacrilege to deny Taranis his gift.'

Caratacus stooped to wipe his blackened hands on the grass at his feet and looked up at the Druid. 'Do not oppose me in this, Nuada,' he said quietly. 'It is the will of the gods.'

He straightened and turned to the kings and war chiefs, who were staring at him in astonishment. 'This man is a gift from Taranis to me, Caratacus, and I accept his gift. Does any man deny my right to it?' He stared at each warrior in turn, daring them to challenge his authority. None would meet his eye.

'I say burn them all.'

Togodumnus, of course. So be it.

He turned to his brother with his hand on the jewelled hilt of his sword. Togodumnus glared at him for a few long seconds, but recognized a deadly intent in Caratacus's eyes. He calculated his chances. 'Keep him then, but the rest burn.'

Axes chopped at the slim branches holding Rufus within the wicker figure and willing hands bent them aside, creating just enough space for him to fall clear, but not enough to allow another captive to follow. Barely understanding what was happening, he was dragged naked before Caratacus with the pitiful pleas of the men he left behind torturing his ears. He didn't dare look back for fear that what he would see would unman him.

'You are Rufus, keeper of the monster?'

Rufus realized his face was covered in dried blood from the wound he received when he was struck

121

down in the forest, and that his hair was wild and matted. He must be barely recognizable to this man he had met only once. 'Yes, lord,' he replied, his voice shaking with emotion. He knew a single wrong word could put him back in the wicker cage. 'I am the keeper of Bersheba, the Emperor's elephant.'

'And you have met this Claudius, whom we owe nothing, but who would have us pay homage to him?'

'Yes, lord.'

'Then truly, Rufus, you are among the fortunate.' Caratacus unpinned his heavy green cloak and shrugged it from his shoulders, then draped it over Rufus's nakedness. In the same movement he turned the young slave towards the sacrifice. 'See how fortunate you are.'

For the first time Rufus looked upon the full horror of the Wicker Man. Taller than five men standing upon each other's shoulders, it dominated everything on the bare hilltop where they stood. It was constructed from a framework of branches and its shape was that of a broad-chested male, his gender instantly apparent from the crude sexual organ protruding from between his legs, each of which was filled to overflowing with tinder-dry straw and branches. The head was a featureless ball, but the blank, pitiless face only made it all the more terrifying. Thrown haphazardly together within the chest cavity was a writhing mass of naked human figures. He could see Paullus, who had shown so little mercy to the village elder, now pleading for it with the last of his strength. Agrippa would be there in that pale jumble of limbs, Agrippa who had seemed too gentle to be a soldier, but who had participated so willingly in Paullus's atrocity. The interpreter. Slaves he had called his friends. He glimpsed Veleda, the British woman who had led them to the cache of stores, and the two elders captured with her. Presumably they had been tainted by their contact with the Romans. Some of them screamed, some of them, like Paullus, pleaded, others appeared to be shocked into silence. The more fortunate were unconscious or dead, smothered by the weight of flesh above them.

Nuada looked to Caratacus and the Briton nodded. Taranis received his sacrifice.

Rufus's eyes recorded every detail. As the flames licked the lower layers of bodies he saw mouths opening wider than any human mouth should be capable of, the bulging, disbelieving eyes, and the arms stretching out for assistance from the Roman gods who had forsaken them. Strangely, now, he heard not a sound. Perhaps his mind was protecting him from something that would ultimately destroy him. He felt twin streams of tears on his cheeks as the flames did their work. The gold and green gorse bushes burned quickly, the wood less fiercely. Quite soon the only movement within the giant wicker frame was of blackened corpses contorting and shrivelling in the intense heat at the golden heart of the inferno. The terrified faces of individuals were replaced by a wall of grinning skulls, white teeth stark against charred flesh, which demanded to know why he deserved life when they did not. He had no answer.

'Enough.' Rufus felt Caratacus's hand pulling at his shoulder, but he found he could not move. Somehow he knew that if his eyes broke contact with the flames he would be sucked into that whirling vortex of fire from which he should never have been allowed to escape. Only when the Wicker Man crumpled in on himself, taking with him his banquet of roasted flesh and scorched bone, was the spell broken. 'Come,' the Catuvellauni leader ordered. Rufus allowed himself to be guided between the lines of cold, staring faces towards the thatched huts hidden in the woods below. After a few steps an involuntary shudder racked his body and he vomited a fountain of bile on to the grass, staining the fine cloak in the process.

'I do not think you are made of the stuff of war,' Caratacus said gently. He led the way to the largest of the huts, which was set some way back from the others. It was clear this rough camp was only a temporary home to the British war leaders, but Caratacus's hut was nevertheless sumptuously furnished in the British fashion. The walls were hung with the thick fur of a bear and numerous beaver, fox and wolf pelts. The floor was covered with fresh rushes mixed with herbs which filled the interior of the hut with their sweet fragrance when they were crushed underfoot. At the far end, opposite the doorway, a frame had been set up on which hung the shields and standards of the British tribes. Caratacus's charging boar, the bull's head of the Regni, the galloping horse of the Iceni, and the crossed spears of the Dobunni were all there, though Rufus recognized them only as brightly coloured symbols of power. To one side, a child played on a rug of washed sheepskin, watched by a smiling, olive-skinned woman with the first silver of age dusting her hair. The boy reminded Rufus of Gaius and he struggled to stifle a sob. The woman looked up in surprise at the sound and her eyes widened when she saw the bloodstained, dishevelled figure wearing her husband's cloak.

Caratacus smiled an apology to his wife. 'Take Tasciovanus to see the ponies, Medb, and send Idres with a basin of water.'

The Briton took his place on a wooden chair in front of the banners and invited Rufus to sit at a nearby bench. They waited in silence until a girl of about thirteen arrived with the basin and without a word began to bathe the dried blood from Rufus's hair. He winced as she touched the raw flesh of a wound just behind his right ear. He reached up and gingerly felt a large bump. 'It is not mortal,' Caratacus assured him. 'We will have it dressed later. Nuada has much skill in these matters. He has stitched me up many a time.'

'Nuada?'

'You have met him. The Druid.' Rufus paled. 'Do

not judge him on what you saw today. He has his place in our society, as your priests do in yours, and carries his burdens as we all do.' He waved the girl from the hut. 'Now tell me about the Emperor Claudius.'

XII

'You seem distracted, husband. You should not let affairs of state burden you so.'

Claudius looked up from the plan he had been attempting to study and smiled benevolently at his wife. I am an actor, he thought, a player who shelters behind a dozen stage masks, or perhaps a coward hiding behind a dozen curtains. He seemed to have been hiding all his life. Hiding from small bullies who ridiculed his limp and his stutter and thought they would be doing Augustus a favour by drowning him in the latrine at the villa in Lugdunum. Hiding from Asinius, that disgusting brute, who had thought it a worthwhile experiment to determine whether a sound beating each day would cure a boy of the disorders that made his mother – his own mother – brand him a 'monster'. Guardian, he called himself, and tutor. The man was a *muleteer*. Eventually he had hidden in taverns and places of the most ill repute, trying desperately to rid himself of the knowledge that he was worthless; hardly a human being at all.

Only much later did he discover that a man's worth did not have to be measured by his prowess at the games or in the bedchamber, nor by the soundness of his limbs or the prettiness of his looks. It was the soundness of his *mind* that mattered. By then his nephew Gaius, called Caligula, had appointed him consul and given him the power that had been his right, but had been withheld from him all his life. For that alone he had Rome's most reviled citizen to thank. Yet the elevation had placed him in deadly peril. In the palace of Caligula every man's hand had been against him. He remembered Protogenes, he of the basilisk eyes and the coldest of hearts, and the way he had measured him an inch at a time, as if he was preparing a corpse for the tomb. So he had hidden again, this time behind a façade of drunkenness and senility, and endured the humiliations and contempt. And waited.

'I am a l-l-little t-tired, my sweet. You have b-been k-keeping your C-C-Claudius up t-too late and his people suffer for it.'

She was too good for him, he knew that. But he could not let her go. He would not let her go. He smiled at her again, and this time the smile was not a lie, but the plain truth. He loved her.

She returned the smile with one of her own, her

128

dark eyes glittering in the light of the perfumed oil lamps, and his heart fluttered and his stomach contracted as if he were some beardless boy in the thrall of his first real woman. Woman? She was a goddess. Valeria Messalina. The most wonderful thing that had happened to him in a life measured by the tidemarks of fear and pain and suppressed rage.

'It is l-late. You should retire, my l-love. Your b-b-beauty shines at its b-b-brightest after a p-proper night's rest.'

She rose from her place near the window in one graceful movement, stretched her arms and yawned. Then she came to him and stood by the couch where he was working.

'Darling Claudius,' she said, running her slim fingers through his thinning hair and caressing the nape of his neck. 'You care for me so much.' She bent close to kiss him on the cheek and the scent of her perfume made his head spin. He watched her walk from the room, the half-moons of her perfectly shaped buttocks shivering rhythmically beneath the azure silk of her gown. She half turned and smiled a farewell. She knew he was watching. Knew he liked to watch. Liked him watching.

When she had left the room he stared at the doorway for a long moment before giving a long, drawn-out sigh. *I wonder who will share her bed tonight.*

He shook his head to clear it of that melancholy thought and stared blankly at the plan again. It was the first inklings of his scheme to turn the swamp around the little harbour at Ostia into a port that would be a wonder of the world and the engine of Rome's future prosperity. But he could not concentrate. What was it she had said? Distracted? Of course he was distracted. He should have heard something by now. What was Plautius thinking? The invasion of Britain. Narcissus had made it seem such a fine enterprise, assured him of the swift defeat of a rabble of disorganized natives and at the same time the fame of outmatching the deeds of his ancestors. The answer to all their problems. Why did it now feel like a leaden weight round his neck or the heavy blade of a headsman's axe? He was by nature a cautious man. Yes, he needed a triumph, needed it the way a dying man needs his next breath, but now he could see that defeat, or even the wrong kind of victory, would be the end of him. Verica, that arrogant Celtic oaf, had given them the pretext for the invasion. Did he really believe the Emperor of Rome would gather an army from the four corners of the Empire so that he could wear a crown of tin and call himself the king of some barbarian hamlet? Yet Narcissus had seen his potential; had found the right lawyers who would declare his claim legitimate and his usurpers the enemy of Rome. Verica had promised them a mighty treasure in return: the mineral riches of the Durotriges and the Silures, pearls from the western shores, furs from the north, and slaves, thousands of slaves, from among the Catuvellauni he hated and feared. But why did Rome need to fight for such baubles when it had ready access to them, and more, through trade? No, plunder was not the objective. Not plunder. Glory.

He had provided Plautius with a great army, more men than the general would ever need to subdue the semi-civilized portion of the island they required for Narcissus's subterfuge. Four legions – the unstoppable champions of an Empire. Surely Plautius must have defeated the British tribes by now? He was ready. Had been ready for weeks. It only required that single performance in the Senate, perhaps the most important performance of his life. He must stand up before his enemies and persuade them, against their better judgement, of the righteousness of his cause. Was the actor up to the challenge? Would the mask hold in place? He expected to feel the knife-twist of fear, but all he experienced was the warm glow of expectation.

'Tell me again about Rome. Is it true a man would take an entire day to walk from one wall to the other? And that the buildings are like our mountains?'

Rufus tried to keep his eyes open. It had been like this for hour after relentless hour. Caratacus was insatiable in his quest for knowledge. The answer to one question would give birth to a dozen more, and they a dozen more in their turn. He felt as if his head had been squeezed until every crumb of information lay on the small table they had taken their meal upon

131

what seemed like hours earlier. He nodded, although he suspected the Briton knew a great deal more about the imperial capital than he gave away. 'It is true.'

'And the hill where the Emperor has his palace? The Palatine?' He ran the word Palatine around his mouth as if he were testing it for poison.

Rufus nodded again.

'If he has all this, accepts tribute from so many great cities – Carthage, you said; I have heard of this Carthage – and is the overlord of so many peoples, what does he want with us poor Britons? Everything he would wish from us we would be happy to give him, for a reasonable price. Why does he send four of his mighty legions to lay Caratacus low?' The warrior stared at Rufus from under low brows, and the young Roman realized he wouldn't escape with a one-word answer.

'He believes Prince Verica has been wronged and has guaranteed him the return of his kingdom,' he said, repeating what Verica had told him. 'If you would only agree to this, I am sure the legions would withdraw. I think the legates wish nothing more than a speedy return to Rome, and Aulus Plautius knows it.' He tried to inject as much sincerity into his expression as he could manage, given that he didn't believe a word of what he was saying.

'Pah,' Caratacus spat. 'Verica! I would not make Verica the king of a dog kennel, and neither would your Claudius. I know this now. The man you have described to me is not a fool, and only a fool would believe Verica worthy of a throne. Your Emperor may be crippled in body, but he knows how to wield power, and to survive. There is more to this than Verica. Why did Claudius send this Aulus Plautius to do his fighting for him?'

Rufus frowned, trying to remember whether they had gone down this path before, but there had been so many different paths he couldn't tell. He shook his head. 'Emperor Claudius is a great man, but he is no warrior. I could not imagine him on campaign.'

'Then why has the Emperor sent his elephant, his most treasured possession, on this perilous mission?' the British king demanded triumphantly.

Rufus opened his mouth to reply. He'd been asking himself the same question for the last month and he was no nearer an answer now than when he started. Caratacus noticed the slight hesitation and gave him a calculating look. 'Enough for now. I will think on it and we will discuss it further in the morning. I wish to know more about these invincible legions of yours. I have had a hut prepared for you and a sleeping mat. You will be guarded there, but it is for your own safety. Rome has no friends in this place.' He called out and two burly warriors armed with long spears appeared in the doorway.

Rufus went to them, but before they left the hut, he turned to Caratacus. 'Why did you burn those prisoners? You do not seem a cruel man.'

The king looked at him for several long seconds. 'Do your people not send messengers to the gods?'

'No, I do not believe so.'

'My people do, and we have never needed the wisdom of the gods more than we do now.'

'Am I to burn, then?'

Caratacus's eyes were in shadow, so Rufus could not see the message in them. The long hesitation again. 'We shall see.'

Rufus struggled to find sleep. Whenever he closed his eyes his mind filled with flames, and in the flames writhing, twisting shapes that might have been human. Instead he lay awake and used the time to go over his discussion with the king, attempting to divine some overall purpose or pattern to the remorseless probing. Initially, Caratacus had confined his questioning to Bersheba, her role in the campaign, and Rufus's part in preparing her for it. On the first point, Rufus had been able to supply limited information, for beyond parading her for the morale of the troops there seemed no good reason for her being here. On the second, he cheerfully expounded on the intricacies of looking after his enormous charge, her habits and her moods, the gentle, almost motherly compassion that was her most dominant characteristic, and the deep intelligence that confounded any who witnessed it. Staring into the dark, he wondered how she was faring without him. Was Britte managing in his absence?

Later, the Catuvellauni had moved to the subject

of the legions. What were their strengths; did they have any weaknesses? How had they defeated Togodumnus's ambush force with such savage ease? Their tactics?

Rufus supplied what information he could, suppressing an unease that sometimes made him squirm in his seat. He knew he was guilty of betraying his comrades, but the alternative was too terrible to contemplate. He was a slave. No one was paying him to suffer and die for Rome. There would be no land or pension for Rufus, the elephant keeper, at the end of his service. He wanted only to get back to his family, and the only way to ensure that was to give Caratacus what he wanted.

When he was satisfied he knew as much as Rufus about the column's forces, the Briton turned to the subject of Claudius. What kind of man was he? How long had he been in power? Did his people fear him? Love him? Respect him? Then he threw Rufus off balance by switching back to the legions. Did their short swords not make them vulnerable? After all, look at his own sword. He drew the blade of polished iron from its richly decorated bronze scabbard with a threatening metallic swish. This, he explained, was merely a decorative toy he wore on ceremonial occasions to impress uncultured brutes like Bodvoc. It had been made by a Gaulish craftsman who had visited Camulodunum five years before and was counted the finest in all Britain. But look, it easily outreached the little – what did he call them? *Gladius*? – the little *gladius*, it was heavier and had a fine edge; surely in open battle it must prevail?

Rufus wasn't certain, but from what he had heard among the legionaries, the secret was in the amount of space allowed a man in a fight. He told Caratacus how the shield wall had held the attack on Bersheba and of the dreadful carnage the 'little swords' had wrought on the tribesmen.

Caratacus frowned. 'Yes, I see it,' he said after a moment's thought. 'My people are warriors. They fight as individuals, for that is where their power lies. Each man is confident in his own strength and in the war skills he has learned from childhood. He goes into battle knowing that with the gods' aid he will overcome any enemy. But your Romans, they are soldiers. They fight as a unit, each man supporting the other. They have a discipline that I could never impose on my people. We are not like you.'

Always, though, he would come back to Claudius, and increasingly to his relationship with the invasion commander Aulus Plautius. What was the army's prime objective? After all, if it was only to restore Verica to his undeserved throne, they could have camped around the Atrebates' capital at Calleva, declared Verica king and dared any man to challenge him. Was there dispute between Plautius and the legates of the four legions? Who was the strongest of them? What of his character? Was Plautius operating independently or did he wait for instructions from Rome?

Eventually, Rufus fell into a dreamless sleep. But what seemed like only minutes later a rough hand shook his shoulder and a beer-soaked moustache was in his face. He raised his head, and winced. The wound behind his ear hurt more today than it had yesterday. The man pushed a bundle of clothing into his hands and Rufus discovered it was a remarkably clean pair of the patterned trews every Celt wore, and a rough woollen shirt, which he pulled over his head. He stood up to struggle into the trousers, which barely fitted him. Then he walked from the hut into a bright sunlight that sent pain flashing across the back of his eyes. When his vision cleared, he found himself at the centre of a circle of threatening barbarian faces. They were mostly old men, women and filthy, dishevelled children, but there were a few young warriors, and it was these who worried him most. They studied him with expressions of naked hatred.

The guard motioned him to where Caratacus and a small group of older tribesmen sat eating from wooden bowls at a crude bench. The British king rose to greet him, and offered a seat at his side. He was wearing a different cloak today, earth brown and of rough-woven cloth. The brooch that pinned it at his shoulder was the same, however, and Rufus could see now it was of remarkably fine workmanship; spun gold in the shape of a boar's head, with a ruby, its inner light burning like fire, for the beast's eye. His thoughts were interrupted when a bowl like the others was pushed in front of him and a large wooden spoon dropped into it with a splash that spattered his new clothing with thin gruel. Not daring to look at his tablemates, he picked up the spoon and stared at what was in the bowl. It made his stomach churn.

'Not hungry?' Caratacus asked politely. 'Do not worry. We don't poison our sacrifices.'

Given the choice between trusting his host or starving to death, Rufus decided he was hungry after all and spooned the unappetizing mess into his mouth. It was surprisingly good: boiled oats, sweetened with honey, but with a slightly tart taste that lingered on his tongue.

Caratacus said: 'I have decided not to continue our conversation.'

The spoon froze halfway to Rufus's mouth. He suddenly realized the smell he had thought was pork cooking for breakfast came from the smouldering heap of blackened nameless obscenity where the Wicker Man had previously stood.

'It is time to return you to your son, and to your larger charge.' Caratacus looked thoughtful for a second and then smiled. 'You are right. I am not a cruel man. I wish you to take a message to your commander. Tell him Caratacus of the Catuvellauni sends his greetings. That he fears neither his elephant nor his army, but wishes peace between our two peoples. Tell him he can return to Rome with every man he brought to these shores, or with none. I will give him two days to comply. If he does not, I will harry him until he bleeds from a thousand wounds, and at the time and place of my choosing I will destroy him. Do you understand?'

Rufus nodded. But Caratacus ordered him to repeat the message until he was satisfied. 'Good. Now, come. It is time.'

He led the way towards a group of four men who stood holding five of the small, hairy British ponies. Before they reached them, a young warrior stepped from the watching crowd and blocked their way. He stared coldly at Rufus, his whole posture radiating challenge, before drawing his sword very deliberately from its scabbard. Rufus instinctively reached for his knife but of course it had been taken from him. He laughed at his own stupidity and the warrior frowned at the unexpected sound. They stared at each other for a few seconds, and Rufus realized that the longer the stand-off continued the more likely it was to end badly for him. He turned to Caratacus. 'If he is going to kill me, tell him to get on with it. Better a clean death than the belly of the god. But I would have thought there is little honour in killing an unarmed man, even among your people?'

Caratacus laughed at the insult and translated Rufus's words to the warrior, who stepped forward so his face was close enough for Rufus to smell his sour breath. The young man launched into a spittle-laced tirade which must have found favour among the watching tribesfolk because they roared their acclamation at regular intervals.

The king translated. 'He says he is Dafyd, son of Cefn who fell in the battle of the valley when the great beast cast its spell over our warriors. Now he carries his father's sword. He says you will not always have the king's protection and that though you are a coward and a weakling he will hunt you down wherever you run, even if it is beyond the Great Sea. He will cut out your heart and sacrifice it to Taranis, your fingers will provide a necklace for his wife, and he will use your skull as a drinking bowl – once it has been properly cleansed of your filth. He makes this pledge before all the gods and asks them for aid in accomplishing it.'

Rufus took a step back and studied his opponent. Dafyd was a well-muscled young man of about his own age with a mesh tattoo covering one shoulder, but he sensed the Briton was less of a champion than he appeared. He had been in the arena often enough to know the signs. There was a tension in the way Dafyd stood that betrayed his anxiety, and his knuckles were a little too white where he gripped the sword hilt. Cupido, the gladiator, had taught Rufus enough moves with the sword to have confidence against most men. In any case, as he had already calculated, Caratacus had saved him from the belly of Taranis, and it was unlikely he would allow him to be butchered. He turned to the British king. 'Give me one of the little Roman swords and I will be happy to provide him with his opportunity to accomplish it now.'

Caratacus smiled and shook his head slowly. 'There will be a time, Rufus the elephant man, but it is not now.' He pushed the glaring young warrior aside with what sounded like a warning, and led the way towards the waiting horsemen.

'This is Ballan. He will escort you back to your people. Remember the message. I hunger for Roman blood, but I give your general one opportunity to make an honourable withdrawal. Farewell. I pray we will not meet again.'

XIII

They rode south and east, along valley sides lightly wooded with larch and thorn, and Rufus noted that Ballan took care never to be drawn to the valley floor when there was another possible route, even if the alternative was more difficult for his ponies. Neither did he expose himself on the skyline above the crest of a hill. The ponies were a uniform nondescript brown and Rufus realized that from a distance they would merge perfectly with the landscape they travelled across. One rider always scouted ahead, studying the hills and reconnoitring what waited over the next crest, while two wove their way along the flanks.

Rufus studied his companion, trying not to betray his interest. Ballan was short for a British warrior, but he had the kind of physique that made him appear as broad as he was tall. His legs were enormously muscled and he sat astride his horse as if he were part of it. Most Celts clothed themselves in homespun cloth shirts, but Ballan favoured a scuffed leather tunic worn over what looked like an auxiliary's mail shirt. He had a head that was almost square and he wore his hair short whereas his compatriots allowed theirs to grow to their shoulders in shaggy, lice-infested manes. His weapon of choice was an iron-tipped throwing spear he carried always in his right hand, but a sword and a curved dagger hung from his belt and Rufus had no doubt he knew how to use them.

The Briton spoke without turning his head. 'You ride a horse as if you were a sack of corn. My two-year-old son sits a pony better.'

Rufus ignored him, thinking it was a wonder anyone could stay on board these fractious, knobble-backed beasts that seemed to treat every bump as if it were an obstacle to be leapt over. His thighs felt as if they were on fire from the constant strain of keeping his seat on the sweat-slippery animal's back. Who did this barbarian think . . .

'Where did you learn Latin?' he asked in surprise. The Briton had spoken in a fractured accent that sounded to Rufus's ear as if it might be closer to Spanish, but it was Latin sure enough.

They travelled another hundred or so horse-lengths along the narrow path before Ballan deigned to reply. 'My lord insisted I learn the tongue of my enemy, for only then could I understand my enemy and be of true use to him. The only thing I would make you understand, Roman, is what it feels like to die. You were given to the gods. You should have burned. Are you some sorcerer that bent my lord's mind to your will?'

Rufus spat to ward off bad luck. To speak of sorcerers was to invite trouble. 'Your lord vowed I was the gift of the gods to him. Would you deny him? Would you gainsay Caratacus, king of the Britons?'

Ballan laughed, a great bellow that came from deep in his chest. 'Caratacus is no king of the Britons. The Catuvellauni may call him king, but not the Dobunni or the Regni, or even, though he may tell you different, the Trinovantes over whom he claims lordship.'

'But he leads a great army, the warriors of a dozen different tribes?'

'Leads them, yes, rules them, no. He holds them together by the power of his will.' Ballan held out his hand and clenched his fist tight. 'Let him but loosen his grip for an instant and they will fly like blackbirds from a nest.'

'You talk loosely for a spy and disloyally for a warrior bound to his lord by oath.'

The spear point came up as if it had a life of its own and stopped less than an inch from Rufus's right eye. One wrong move from the pony skittering nervously between his legs and it would skewer his skull.

'I have given Caratacus no oath. A man can only be held by a single oath. I did not give it and he did not ask it.'

'But the Catuvellauni—'

'Are beasts to be herded and milked by my people, the Iceni.'

Rufus recognized the name. Narcissus had described them as the easternmost of the major tribes. 'Yet you follow Caratacus, king of these . . . cattle.'

The spear point dropped and Ballan grinned, an expression that gave his face a curiously impish, almost childlike quality. Rufus realized with surprise he could grow to like this bear of a Celt who was so eager to kill him.

'Caratacus is different. He is the finest warrior I have ever seen. He uses tricks in combat that would make your eyes water, Roman, and your head spin. When he fights, he wins. I follow him because I trust him, and because he promised me enough loot to buy a hundred horses.'

'A hundred horses will be of little use to you if you are dead, which is what you will be when your lord finally decides to fight the legions,' Rufus pointed out mischievously.

The scout shrugged. 'What is death to a warrior? I would rather die with a sword in my hand and my feet in the mud of a bloody battleground than in a warm bed being spooned milk by one of my numberless grandchildren.' He kicked his pony sharply in the ribs and it spurted ahead. 'Come, get that nag moving or I won't be able to deliver you in daylight. I wouldn't give a cracked egg for your chances if you approach the column by night. Those legionary cavalry are twitchy in the dark, but they're good.'

They rode on until Rufus's breakfast was a long-forgotten memory. The only halt Ballan would allow was when they came to a broad, shallow river and he could water the horses, but the Celt's vigilance never waned. The horsemen approached the stream individually, with the others keeping watch. Rufus marvelled at the Briton's stamina and fortitude. When he complained he was tired and hungry Ballan threw him a leather bag that contained a few crusts of stale, iron-hard bread that would have broken his teeth if he'd tried to bite them. The only way to make the food edible was to keep it in his mouth until his saliva softened it, then chew it gingerly until he could swallow.

Late in the afternoon they halted at the entrance to a rock-strewn valley cut by a stream through the line of hills parallel to their route. Ballan reined in his pony and took Rufus's halter.

'This is where we part, Roman. You can walk from here.' He pointed into the gully. 'Follow the river until the valley begins to rise. You'll know the place when you see it, because there's a big old oak tree growing almost horizontally out of the left bank. When you reach the tree, climb up that side of the hill. Once you get to the top you should be able to see your army. We've been watching them for days and they never turn from their line of march; very predictable and very careless. I've told Caratacus we should ambush the buggers, but he doesn't want to lose any more of his precious warriors.'

Rufus slipped from his pony and almost collapsed. Walk? He could hardly move, his legs were shaking so much from the strain of a day on horseback.

Ballan laughed. 'A bit stiff? You'll feel better in an hour or two.' He reached inside his leather tunic and threw something that glinted in the sunlight. Rufus caught it in his right hand. It was the lion's tooth set in bright metal he had been given by the master of the slave ship that had carried him from Carthage to Rome. It had been stripped from him with the rest of his possessions before he was placed in the Wicker Man. He had thought it was gone for ever, and felt the lesser for its loss. His fingers instinctively rubbed the smooth surface, and he nodded his thanks.

'Caratacus believed it was precious to you. What is it? I have never seen a fang like that one.'

'It came from a cat as big as your pony. It's a charm that was given to me as a child.'

The Briton snorted in disbelief. 'No cat was ever that size. A charm, though, I can understand. The brooch Caratacus wears is such a thing, they say. A thing of power, though I have never seen it used.' He shook his head as if such superstitions were of no interest to a warrior, hauled on his mount's halter and, leading Rufus's pony, began to move off.

'Farewell, Ballan. I do not grudge you your reward,' Rufus shouted. 'But I fear the only hundred horses you see will be in your dreams.' The squat

Briton didn't look back, but Rufus heard him chuckle.

'A hundred horses, a fat Gaulish concubine and an elephant, that's what I'd like. But what would I do with the elephant?'

Rufus stood for a while after the Briton was gone, feeling unaccountably lonely. With an effort he roused himself. Don't be a fool, he thought. Soon you'll be back with the column and with Gaius and Bersheba. The knowledge gave him strength and he started off at a brisk pace, keeping the stream to his right and following the valley floor. It was an intimidating place, narrow and claustrophobic, where damp moss covered the gully walls and the sun penetrated only when it was directly above. He had been walking for an hour when the reaction to his ordeal finally overcame him. It was less than two days since he had awoken in the horror of the Wicker Man's belly; but for the merest chance he would be a grinning, burned-out skeleton, like Paullus, his flesh charred and his bones blackened; empty eyes staring from a flame-scorched skull. He stumbled and almost fell, his vision blurred and his world spinning. He decided to rest, choosing a hollow in the valley wall where the roots of a fallen tree had torn a hole just large enough for him to wedge himself inside. The earth was dry and soft, and somehow he found its closeness comforting. Should he not feel guilt for having survived? What had he done to deserve life when every other member of the forage party had died screaming in that fiery cage? The truth was that he didn't feel guilty at all. Only relieved. He was lying here in this cool chamber that might have been his tomb, but his heart was beating, he could smell the fresh earth in his nostrils and the air he breathed was clean and heady. Nothing else mattered. Not Paullus or Agrippa, or the British woman Veleda. Not the dead child. He was alive. Alive! His last thought before he was overcome with exhaustion was of Aemilia, far away in Rome. How he missed her; she smiled at him, and she was beautiful, but then her hair was on fire and it wasn't Aemilia, it was Veleda, and the flesh fell from her face to leave a grinning skull.

The sound of hooves clattering on rock woke him. It was close to dusk but there was still just enough light to see, even in the shadowed depths of the gully. Romans, he thought, with a surge of hope. It must be a Roman patrol. They would be searching for the missing forage party. Surely they would have discovered the abandoned wagons at the village by now? But what if it was Celtic scouts? Perhaps Ballan had changed his mind and decided to take him closer to the legionary column? There was only one way to find out. He slipped out of his impromptu burrow like a mole from the earth. Judging by the noise of the hooves there couldn't be more than two horses, which seemed to rule out a Roman patrol. Ballan then, but be careful. If it was the Briton he would be on the alert for the enemy. A friend's spear thrown in error wasn't any less sharp.

Left or right? Upstream or down? It was difficult to tell. He chose upstream, but now he remembered Ballan's wariness, the way he had avoided the valley floor. Taking care not to disturb any loose rocks he clambered halfway up the gully wall until he was among a tangle of low bushes. The going was much harder here, but he was part hidden from anyone following the stream below.

It quickly grew clear the horses were not finding the terrain easy as they picked their way through the boulders that littered the riverbank. He could hear their riders urging them forward, but this was no place for a pony, not even the sure-footed steeds the British scouts rode, and he could tell he was making ground on the horsemen. Barely daring to breathe, he pushed aside a small bush and gave himself a clear view of a length of valley ahead. About thirty paces in front of him two Celtic warriors were arguing loudly. He couldn't understand what they were saying, but it was abundantly clear they held different opinions about their next move. When he looked beyond them the reason was obvious. A rock fall had brought down a small landslide and partially blocked the gully, making it impassable for the ponies. One of the men seemed to want to leave their mounts and carry on on foot. The other didn't have the same enthusiasm for whatever mission they were embarked upon, and was arguing for a return the way they had come. The first warrior had his back to Rufus, but the way he held himself triggered some memory that made the young Roman uneasy. The dispute grew more heated, and it was clear the first man, despite arguing the louder, was the junior partner. The second warrior, who was broader in the shoulder, turned his pony and began to make his way back downstream towards Rufus. The first, every movement betraying his reluctance, turned to follow and Rufus took an instinctive step backwards.

Dafyd! The Briton must have delayed until Ballan set out and then followed his tracks. But would he have brought only a single companion? A shout from further downstream proved not. There were more of them. Rufus froze, fighting an impulse to move backwards up the slope away from his enemy. The two horsemen were directly below him now and any movement would alert them. They were still debating and Rufus wished he had some way of knowing what they were saying. Would they return to Caratacus? Or was Dafyd's hatred and the honour of the blood feud strong enough reason for them to continue the chase? He waited until the voices were far downstream before he moved, making his way stealthily in the opposite direction and edging further uphill with every step. It was a few minutes before he noticed something that made him stifle a cry of frustration: the bushes and thin saplings he was negotiating formed only a slim fringe clinging to the flank of the hill. Below it, the rocky ground fell away too steeply for anything except moss and the occasional sapling to grow. Above was open moorland, with barely enough vegetation to provide cover for a mountain hare. It had been his plan to get as far above them as he could, possibly even slip over the hill, but that vast expanse of open hillside made his spirit quail. He had no choice. He would have to keep to the wood until he reached the oak tree Ballan had described and then take his chances.

At first it was simple enough. The bushes and trees slowed his progress a little, but every step he took increased his confidence. He moved silently, avoiding the broken branches which littered the ground. His caution saved his life. He heard Dafyd come before he saw him, a thundering crash as the British warrior burst from the undergrowth a dozen paces behind. Dafyd screamed in triumph as he took up the chase with his father's sword in one hand and a long spear in the other. They were killing weapons and if he had the opportunity to use either Rufus knew he was dead. But they also slowed the Briton down in the constricted space among the trees and that gave Rufus his chance. He sprinted uphill and into the open, hoping his speed would give him an advantage.

Not daring to look back, he took a diagonal course across the hillside. He understood he was leaving his back exposed to Dafyd's spear point, and his spine anticipated its agonizing punch with every step. But he prayed to Jupiter that the Briton would not gamble on a single cast; that he would want to slay his father's enemy with his father's sword. He could hear the young warrior grunting not far behind him as he tried to keep pace. Now Rufus gave thanks for all the long hours he had spent in training with Cupido. He could outrun Dafyd if he could only stay on his feet in this rough ground.

But there were some things he couldn't outpace. The stone whistled by his ear so close he felt the wind of its passing. He dared a glance to his right and almost gave in to despair. Beside a crumbling earth-work two horsemen – no, three – were visible on the brow of the hill, riding parallel to his course. He tried to visualize his position. Dafyd behind him with another man, possibly two. The horsemen on the hill-top would keep pace, cutting off his escape route. All they had to do was continue the chase until they wore him down. Then he was dead. Not up, then. Down? He darted to his right and took the slope at a head-long gallop, plunging through the trees and into the rocky gully below, knowing that the slightest stumble could leave him at the mercy of his hunters. The sudden move caught Dafyd by surprise and he felt a thrill of hope as he heard the warrior's roar of frus-tration. Instantly, he turned back downstream, praying the abrupt change of course would gain him another few vital seconds. He had no idea what he would do next. No plan. Only understood that every second he stayed alive increased the chances of keep-ing him that way. It must be close to nightfall and the darkness that would cloak him from his enemies for at least a few hours.

The sides of the gully were a blur; his feet danced over the stones and the boulders, occasionally dipping into the chill waters of the little stream. When the stocky warrior who had accompanied Dafyd stepped into his path it was too late to stop or even turn aside. The man grinned in anticipation as he waited with his sword held high, ready to chop Rufus down in his headlong rush. Flailing desperately, the young Roman tried to stop himself, but his left foot skidded on a weed-covered stone and he flipped upside down, soaring through the air until he landed on his back in the middle of the stream. As he lay winded, with the cool waters flowing around him, he knew death was coming, but he had lost the will to evade it. He opened his eyes. The sword point was poised less than an inch from his face. An impossibly long way above it the owner held the pommel two-handed, ready to plunge the blade into his brain. For a second, his mind filled with visions of Gaius and Bersheba and the freedom that would never be his, but a barked command brought him out of his death reverie. Dafyd! Of course Dafyd wouldn't let him die by another man's hand. Rough hands hauled him to his feet and turned him to face his executioner.

The Celt stood over him like a young god, his chest heaving and his body bronzed by the sun. Beside him, Rufus felt bedraggled and somehow unworthy as he swayed, dripping into the stream. He remembered the death he had been promised, and hoped it would be quick. Perhaps he should kneel, and Dafyd might consider taking his head off with one merciful blow, rather than the gutting stroke he appeared to be preparing for. Rufus had seen men die from stomach wounds and it wasn't an experience he was eager to share. His whole body began to shake in anticipation of the terrible violation about to be done it.

Dafyd smiled and spat in his face before launching into a rambling monologue which must have been some paean he had composed to his father. Rufus closed his eyes. Get on with it! Please. Just get on with it. The words ran through his head, over and over again. Was this how Fronto had felt when he watched Caligula's executioners folding the chains with which they were about to beat him to death? He tried not to cry. Not to plead. But the tension was becoming too much. Was the last thought he would take to the Otherworld that the Celts would never use one word where ten would do just as well?

There was a sharp 'thunk' close by: the wet sound of a butcher chopping a piece of beef. At first he thought Dafyd must have struck and that his body was declining to pass on the message. Then something splashed into the river beside him. He looked down to see the staring eyes and gasping mouth of the warrior who had been at his back. The man was struggling and wriggling like a beached fish in the reddening water and his hands flapped helplessly at the emerald-flighted arrow buried in his throat.

Rufus glanced up into Dafyd's face. The astonishment in the Briton's eyes mirrored his own. As the young warrior hesitated, something flashed over his shoulder and fell into the water at Rufus's feet. It was one of the long swords the Celts used, a twin to the one in Dafyd's right hand. Slowly, never taking his eyes from his enemy, Rufus bent to pick it up.

'Now we'll see if you can fight as well as you can talk, Roman.' Verica was sitting casually on a large rock a few feet behind Dafyd to his right. The British warrior half turned in surprise at the sound of the voice. He stared at the Atrebate prince and then his eyes flickered to the man with the arrow in his throat, who now lay deathly still, before finally returning to Rufus. Without warning he swung his sword in a mighty, sweeping slash that was designed to cut his opponent clean in half. Rufus was momentarily distracted by Verica's unlikely appearance, and the contest should have been over in a single blow. But the British blades were heavy and the cut was laboured, and he was given a fraction of a second that allowed him to step back as the edge missed him by the width of a piece of parchment. The power Dafyd had invested in the blow made him stumble and that gave Rufus time to take the measure of his opponent. They were of a similar height and reach, but the Briton was undoubtedly the stronger, and Rufus realized that strength could be a deciding factor in this contest. He was outmatched, and he knew it, but strangely he felt no fear. Somewhere, he knew, Cupido was watching over him, and that was enough.

He caught Dafyd's next cut on the blade of his own sword with a ringing clash that echoed from the valley walls, and the power of it almost broke his wrist, confirming his earlier judgement. In this kind of fight the stronger man would simply bludgeon his weaker opponent until his guard was overwhelmed. It was the British way. But Rufus didn't fight the British way; he fought Cupido's way.

For the next few attacks he allowed Dafyd to force him backwards. It was a dangerous strategy and it was all he could do to stay alive, parrying thrusts and roundhouse cuts with deft movements of his sword that deflected the Briton's blade without allowing it to bring its whole power against his own. With each step he tested the ground beneath his feet. He understood he couldn't win on these treacherous, slippery rocks that could have a man on his back and at the mercy of his enemy before he knew it. He needed firm ground and he thought he knew where to find it.

Just below the point where his path had been blocked he remembered a flat area of dry sand beside a deeper pool. Every step he retreated took him closer to it. But every step he took also increased Dafyd's confidence, and the more confident the Briton grew, the more dangerous he became. Rufus heard Verica hoot as one thrust ripped a hole in his tunic and came close to disembowelling him. Bastard! He'd teach him a lesson – if he survived. Still the same weed-slick rocks. Make it soon. Make it . . . Sand. Lovely, firm, packed sand. He almost smiled, but Cupido never smiled. Cupido only killed. Three more steps and he was ready. The British way was raw power. Cupido's way was speed. Now Rufus could move, dancing away and around his opponent, knowing no slippery pebble was going to betray him. Dafyd snarled his frustration and turned to follow him. When the Briton's sword swung it found only air, and each fumbling stroke opened his defences to Rufus's counter-attack. But it was still too soon. Rufus made no attempt to take the fight to his opponent. His own sword was as heavy as Dafyd's and he knew the weight would sap his strength as it was already sapping the Briton's. He was content to twist and turn, keeping his distance and watching the anger and the confusion grow in Dafyd's eyes. One chance. He only needed one chance.

But so did the young Catuvellauni, and over-confidence was Rufus's enemy just as it was Dafyd's. In the next instant, the Briton twisted left when he should have turned right and luck brought him within range of Rufus with a low cut that would have hamstrung the Roman if he hadn't jumped two-footed into the air. Enough.

That was the moment Dafyd came for him with all the speed of a charging leopard. The Briton's arms were numbed by the constant labour and his legs were beginning to tire. He knew he had to strike soon. This time Rufus let him come, and when Dafyd raised his sword to strike the Roman made a disguised thrust towards the British warrior's exposed throat. Now it was Dafyd's turn to step back, slightly off balance. As he did, Rufus deftly switched his sword from his right hand to his left. Cupido had been expert with a sword in either hand and it was the first skill he had taught Rufus in their endless sessions in the Palatine gardens. He had never become as adept as the gladiator with either right or left, but he had learned enough. He saw the confusion on Dafyd's face turn to panic as the Briton saw danger from an unexpected angle and was forced to make the awkward parry Rufus had been waiting for. The young Roman screamed in triumph. Now.

It was a terrible blow. A fearful blow delivered with all the strength of fear and anger and frustration. He didn't want to be here. He didn't want to be in danger and he didn't want to kill. But if he must he would. He swung the blade from low to his left beneath the pathetic defence of Dafyd's flailing sword, using the power of his wrist to sweep upwards, turning and twisting the blade as it went. The razor edge took the young Briton in the V where his legs met and sliced up through soft flesh and hard bone, through muscle and sinew, and up again through offal and lung until with a sudden wrench Rufus ripped it through his enemy's already dying heart. It was as if Dafyd had exploded. Blood and torn guts erupted from the obscene cavity the long sword had created. The Briton's life fled from him in a moment of horror that transformed him from a bronzed young god into a grey-faced, drooling old man; the way his father must have been when the legionaries took away his life in the battle of the valley. The thing that had been Dafyd collapsed backwards into the pool, where the current slowly turned him, dead face to the skies, arms spreadeagled, until he floated gently away, to be caught between two boulders in the shallows a little downstream.

Rufus stood for a moment, unmoving. He felt something growing in him, something untameable, primeval. He turned. To kill Verica.

'That was an interesting move – you must teach it to me. I—' The Atrebate was walking towards Rufus across the sand, but when he saw the look in the Roman's hooded eyes he stopped in mid-stride and mid-sentence. It was followed by a long awkward moment when Verica knew with certainty that this gore-stained young slave held his life in his hands.

The spell was broken by a rattle of hooves that heralded the arrival of a dark-skinned young man with a wispy beard. He was wearing the distinctive pot helmet and green tunic of the Syrian auxiliary cavalry unit attached to the Second Augusta. Across his back was slung a short curved bow and he rode one horse while leading two others. From his saddle hung two heads that bore all the signs of having been recently harvested.

Rufus felt everything in his body slip down into his legs and it was suddenly difficult enough to stand, never mind kill Verica. The Atrebate saw the light of murder die in Rufus's eyes and felt the liquid feeling in his stomach fade away. He let out a long sigh, and realized he'd been holding his breath for a full minute.

He laughed, but it came out high-pitched and nervous. 'This is Hanno,' he said, indicating the man on the horse. 'He can put an arrow through your eye at two hundred paces. He spotted the men tracking you. He saved your life, but you can thank him later.'

Rufus swayed. His head was spinning, but he knew there was something important he had to say. He searched his mind for the word. 'Caratacus . . .' he croaked finally, and Verica's eyes widened in interest.

'You have seen Caratacus? I think that will be important to Narcissus, and to the general. We should return immediately, then.'

'Caratacus wanted me dead.'

Verica frowned and splashed his way through the stream towards Dafyd's body. He reached down and held the head up by the blood-sodden hair. 'Not Caratacus. I recognize this cur. Knew his father. See the tattoo, the way the pattern forms the outline of a hare? His clan is of the Catuvellauni, but their loyalties have long been in the keeping of Togodumnus.' He spat. 'Caratacus's older brother. If these men tried to kill you it was at his behest, not Caratacus's. Move, elephant man.' Hanno dismounted to give Rufus a helping hand on to the big Roman cavalry mount. 'Unless I miss my guess you've just become someone worth keeping alive.'

161

XIV

Verica led them back to the mouth of the gully, where they were met by a dozen other Syrians. 'We had given you up for dead when we found the forage wagons,' the Briton explained. 'It was obvious that the detachment had been ambushed, but the attackers nailed one of the legionaries upside down to a tree just in case we didn't get the message.'

'What did he look like?' Rufus interrupted. For some reason it seemed important.

Verica shrugged. 'Dead. Blond-haired. Young. One eye looking at you and the other one somewhere else.'

Agrippa. So he at least had been spared the fire.

It was full dark by the time they reached the day's encampment and Verica approached cautiously, shouting the password as he rode. They swung past the earth barrier in front of the main gateway and for the first time in forty-eight hours Rufus felt safe. The only thing he wanted now was to get back to his son. Instead, Verica insisted they go directly to Narcissus's tent in the headquarters section.

Claudius's freedman sat hunched over a tiny folding table, scratching with a metal *stylus* on a wax writing tablet by the light of the smoking oil lamp. When he saw Rufus, his tired eyes lit up with pleasure. 'So, you survived. I told them you would. Verica here wanted to give up the search, but I insisted, didn't I, Verica? What was it you said? "They will leave none alive, especially not a miserable worm of a slave whose only purpose is to shovel elephant dung." He has such an elegant turn of phrase, don't you think? Verica was of the opinion that they would sacrifice every Roman prisoner, yet plainly they did not?' Narcissus was smiling, but there was a question in his voice and the smile didn't quite reach his eyes. 'Why was that, do you think?'

Rufus shook his head to clear it. 'They said they wanted a messenger.'

'Clearly not a messenger to the gods, so your message must be for the general. And whom, pray, is the message from?'

'Caratacus.'

Five minutes later he stood before Aulus Plautius, commander of the British invasion. Rufus knew that Vespasian, legate of the Second, had a reputation for

163

sharing his soldiers' hardship. Plautius was an entirely different animal.

An elderly slave carefully washed Rufus's feet at the doorway of the huge cloth pavilion which was erected for the general at the end of each day's march. Soft slippers were placed on his feet and with Narcissus at his side he was escorted across woven carpets to Plautius's inner sanctum. The general sat in a padded chair at a large wooden desk, behind which hung a wide drawing of what Rufus realized must be the outline of southern Britain. Much of the map was blank, but he knew that each day of the campaign more and more of it would be filled in as the scouts and reconnaissance patrols brought in their reports of a valley here, a village or a hill fort there; of forests that might or might not be impenetrable. Of wide rivers. It was the rivers that interested Plautius.

The general raised his head as they entered, spearing the intruders with granite-chip eyes in the face of a startled eagle. He wore his grey hair cropped tight and Rufus could see the pink indent his helmet had created on his forehead during the day's march. It was rumoured the general wore the richly decorated helm even in his sleep, and the young slave was mildly surprised to see him without it. An aide waved them forward, while another entered behind them and scuttled past to update the map with another report. Rufus could see a red line snaking across it from what must be the coast at Rutupiae. He thought it would be longer. As he watched, the second aide carefully drew a ribbon of blue directly across the column's line of march.

'You said you had urgent news for me, Master Narcissus. This,' Plautius waved a dismissive hand towards Rufus, 'does not appear to be worthy of that title.'

Rufus became acutely aware of his dishevelled appearance. The ragged British clothing stained by Dafyd's lifeblood; the fact that he had not washed for three days, and that the physical manifestation of his earlier terror seemed to be that he stank like a pole-cat. But Narcissus was well versed in the etiquette of the Emperor's court. He smiled his acceptance of the Roman commander's judgement.

'That is very true, General, but appearances can be deceptive. This young man is the keeper of the Emperor's elephant, which you know has an honoured position in the mighty force you have brought to this land. He has also recently been a guest of one you wish to know better.'

Plautius raised his head; a predator sniffing the scent of his day's meal.

'Caratacus.'

The general's face broke into a smile that was even more frightening than his normal expression. 'Tell me everything you know about this man.'

In a way it was a mirror image of his interrogation at the hands of the British king; shorter, but equally disconcerting. Rufus would describe an element of his meeting with the enemy leader. Plautius would stare at him with the utmost concentration before firing out a series of staccato questions. 'Did his people look thin, undernourished? Were their weapons well cared for? How many warriors did you see? What were their tribes?'

The Roman commander was so fixated on the character and the mettle of his opponent that it was some time before he realized he had neglected to discover one important point. He frowned. 'And how did this meeting come about?'

Rufus related his tale of the ambush and of regaining consciousness inside the Wicker Man. And what followed. As he finished he heard a retching sound as one of the young aides was sick outside the pavilion doorway. Plautius stared in disgust. 'Have that man replaced. I have no room for weaklings in my command.' He studied Rufus with new respect. 'It seems the gods protect you, or fortune favours you. I can make use of that kind of fortune. You march with Vespasian?'

'Yes, sir.'

'I may call on you and your elephant. Be ready.' Rufus bowed, and he and Narcissus turned towards the doorway. 'There is one more thing.' Rufus froze. He knew what was coming. Plautius's tone was mild, but his innocuous words carried the threat of a death sentence. 'You were with this Caratacus for almost twenty-four hours?'

'Yes, sir.'

'Yet in all that time he never questioned you upon our dispositions or our intentions?'

Rufus felt Narcissus tense at his side. 'He questioned me, sir, but I did not know the answers to his questions. I am only a slave. I care for the Emperor's elephant and I do my duty. I know nothing of strategy or the intentions of great men.'

Plautius stared at him for a long moment, the gimlet eyes attempting to see into his soul. Then, not quite satisfied, he nodded his dismissal. They had walked twenty paces from the pavilion, along a lantern-lined pathway and past the outer ring of the commander's personal bodyguard, before Rufus dared breathe. Narcissus laid a hand on his shoulder. 'You have missed your vocation, young Rufus. You should have been on the stage. Now come with me to my tent.'

Rufus protested that he needed to return to his son, if for no better reason than to show the boy he was alive.

'Nonsense,' Narcissus insisted. 'I have already sent word of your unlikely survival and that the general seeks your counsel. We will share a flask of good wine, for I think you need it, and you will reveal to me what truly passed between you and this Caratacus. Hold nothing back, for it could be vital to our endeavours. You may trust me.'

The words sent a shiver through Rufus. Every time he trusted Narcissus someone died.

*

Two hours later he was not quite drunk, but not quite sober either. Waves of exhaustion threatened to overwhelm him, but every time he tried to leave Narcissus found some new morsel about Caratacus to chew over. 'So, King Caratacus is aware that our Emperor hounds his servant, Aulus Plautius, and demands an early victory.'

It was only a rumour, Rufus tried to say – but by now coherent speech was beyond his powers – I betrayed no one.

Narcissus stared at him, and his eyes, normally so expressionless, were filled with fire. 'You have done your Emperor a true service by staying alive. What you have told me may have great bearing on the success of this enterprise. If I read it right you have dealt our enemy a blow at least as great as was dealt to them on the day of the ambush. Go now to your family. You may tell your companions of your experiences and of your interview with Plautius, but say nothing of our talk.'

Rufus didn't go directly to Gaius; he had another duty to perform first. Bersheba scented him when he was many yards away, raised her trunk and welcomed him with a series of gentle grunts. He stood with her for a while talking quietly and feeding her from the supply of sweet little apples, until the turmoil in his mind calmed and he felt ready for sleep. Gaius lay in Britte's arms on a blanket in the bullock cart. He kissed his son's head, marvelling as always at the silky softness of his russet hair, then lay down at his side, exhausted beyond life itself. He feared he would dream of pain and death, but he dreamed only of a great and glorious victory. Which was the same thing.

XV

Caratacus watched his brother with the unblinking stillness of a predatory animal. The scar between Togodumnus's eyes flared red the way it always did when he was angry or uncomfortable. He had worn the scar for more than twenty years, since the day their father had encouraged them to wrestle together. Caratacus remembered the crunch as the cartilage in his nose was crushed by his brother's fist and the feel of merciless fingers round his throat. The rock had been lying just close enough for him to reach. Enough strength remained to smash it into Togodumnus's grinning, triumphant face. There had been a great deal of blood.

Their father had laughed.

'Ballan tells me your men have been busy?'

Togodumnus shrugged. 'I have many men. Am I

supposed to know what each of them does every minute of the day? They get bored. They go off. They get up to mischief. You promised them a fight, but all we do is run away whenever the enemy gets close.'

Caratacus smiled coldly. The insult was clear enough, but he chose to ignore it. 'The boy, Dafyd, ambushed the messenger I sent to the Romans.'

'You should not have saved him from the fire. He was pledged to the gods. There are other messengers. Ballan would have done the job just as well. Better.'

'It does not matter. Dafyd failed. Ballan found him lying in a stream with his guts hanging out.' Caratacus watched his brother carefully and was rewarded by a slight tic in his right cheek.

'Dafyd had the right to kill the Roman slave. If he did not have the skill, then he deserved to die,' Togodumnus said coldly. 'But I wish he had succeeded. The slave is the keeper of the beast. You have told us the beast is no threat to us. I believe you are wrong, but even if you are right and it is no weapon of war, you cannot deny it is a powerful talisman. Killing the slave would have weakened the beast. Anything that weakens the beast weakens the Romans.'

And that is why you ordered his death. Caratacus didn't say it, but he knew by the look in Togodumnus's eyes he didn't have to. 'You say you do not like running away. That is good. I have a mission for a commander who knows how to stand his ground. It will mean a fight, but I intend it to be a short, bloody fight. Then you will withdraw – not run away – withdraw in good order with your army and your honour intact. Here.' He took Togodumnus to an area of scattered sand in the centre of the hut. Inscribed in the sand was a rough map. 'You know the river, ten miles to the east? It is deep and wide, a good defensive line.' Togodumnus snorted at the word defensive, but Caratacus ignored him. 'We will not defeat the Romans here. We are not yet ready. I want you to buy me time. Delay the Romans for at least three days. Hold them on the river. You will have twenty-five thousand men; your Dobunni, Bodvoc's Regni and the Trinovantes. I will give you Adminius and the Cantiaci as a reserve. More than half our strength. Wait until the forward elements of the legions cross, and smash them. Do not get entangled. Do not look for glory. A quick victory against an inferior force, then march north to meet me.'

Togodumnus looked up at his brother. 'Where?'

Caratacus pointed to the northern edge of the map. 'Here on the Tamesa, where the sweet water meets the salt. That is where we will combine and destroy the enemy. The river will be choked with Roman dead and the bards will sing of the deeds of Togodumnus and his brother Caratacus for a thousand years.'

'Why three days? Surely it will not take three days to reach the Tamesa?'

'Because three days is what I ask and what I need. Will you give me it?'

Togodumnus grunted. 'I will give you it, but, by the wrath of Taranis, I swear this, when we reach the Tamesa my running days are over, brother.'

Caratacus smiled, and his expression was almost as wolfish as his brother's. 'All our running days are over.'

Togodumnus swaggered from the hut, shouting for his lieutenants, but Caratacus sat in silence, deep in his own thoughts. 'You sanctioned this?' he said, as if to himself.

'Sometimes my greater duty is to my people.' Nuada's disembodied voice emerged from behind a fur hanging at the rear of the roundhouse. 'Do you deny me that right?'

'I deny you the right to thwart me, priest,' Caratacus said, his voice the texture of river gravel. 'You knew my designs, knew the place the Roman had in them, yet you still acted against my will, and with my fool of a brother?'

For almost a minute the only sound in the hut was the harsh sawing of Nuada's breathing. 'I fear the great beast. I have dreamed of it each night since we learned of it, and each night its power grows greater. If killing the beast's servant diminished that power, then I would use even Togodumnus to that end.'

Caratacus gave a humourless laugh. 'There are greater powers to fear than the elephant, Nuada. The information that boy carried to his masters will help me destroy them. If he had died, Taranis would have had another messenger at the next sunrise.'

173

'Togodumnus?'

'You. Now get out.'

When the Druid was gone, Caratacus called for Ballan, and prepared himself for the long journey north. To an old love and a new hope.

She knew he was coming and had agreed to meet him. He was confident he could persuade her of the justice of his fight, but he feared the effect the shadows of their past might have on her judgement. She had always been wilful, he remembered. When she was angry, logic played no part in her calculations. Yet she was a queen, and if he could convince her that her people's cause would be advanced by joining him, surely she would act in their best interests. But she was also a woman. What could he give her, and – a shiver ran through him – what would she ask?

The way was easy and they were in Catuvellauni country for the first twenty miles, but Ballan rode as if he were in the very heart of the enemy. He had argued for more warriors, but Caratacus insisted on the minimum escort. He did not want it known that while his people were fighting in the south, their king was riding north. They had compromised on a dozen men, all, including himself, dressed in rough peasant clothing.

'You are going to get us all killed,' Ballan complained as they rode together. 'It was a mistake to let the elephant man go free. Now the Romans know where you are they will try to kill you.'

Caratacus smiled. Ballan: always watching, always thinking. 'The Romans know where I *was*. In any case, this is my land. I will know when the first Roman sets foot upon it. Take heart. No Roman sword will reach me with you at my side, Ballan.'

'It is not a Roman sword I fear, lord.'

They rode north, beyond the boundary stone of the Catuvellauni, and into the land where no man's hand ruled. Ballan's vigilance increased with each mile they travelled, for this was the haunt of thieves, bandits and incorrigibles who had been exiled from their communities, whose crimes were so terrible they would receive a welcome from no other tribe. They were desperate men, who lived on the very edge of subsistence and took from whomever they could. Even a dozen men might be prey for them. It was hilly country now, and as unwholesome as those who inhabited it: low crags with sharp scree-scarred crests and deep gullies that might have been chopped out by a giant's axe.

'Ambush country,' Ballan spat, and weighed his spear in his hand. 'Do you feel it?'

'How long have they been watching?'

'An hour, perhaps longer.'

'Will they attack?'

'I hope so.' Ballan grinned. 'My spear hasn't tasted blood for too long. It will rust away if you don't find me some Romans to kill.'

'Your spear will never rust, Ballan. I hear it is in constant use. How many is it now?'

Ballan roared with laughter, his broad frame shaking and his guffaws echoing around the hills. 'Six. Four boy brats and two useless girls. And you?'

'Only the two.'

'Medb keeps you too close to home.'

'Will she be safe?'

Ballan knew Caratacus was not talking about his wife. 'From them or from you?'

Caratacus gave him a hard look that told him he was on dangerous ground.

Ballan shrugged. 'She's not stupid enough to travel with twelve miserly warriors. She's a real queen and she'll have a real escort. This scum won't touch her.' He kicked his horse ahead, leaving Caratacus to ride onwards accompanied only by his thoughts.

Twice, they saw sign of the bandits, but something in the way the thirteen rode must have made the thieves wary, for they reached the standing stone that marked the southern boundary of Brigantia unmolested. The barren hills fell away behind them and they were in gentler, greener country, where small, fast-running streams cut across their path, identifiable from far off by the thick vegetation which fought for position and the promise of water on their banks.

'We rest here. The meeting is not until four hours after first light and we do not have much further to go.' Caratacus studied the pretty brook, its clear waters gurgling musically over sand and gravel and the shadowy forms of trout and minnows sheltering beneath the willows that drooped lazily over its banks. They found a small pebble beach by a shallow pool where they could water the ponies, and set up camp twenty paces upstream in the shadow of an old, gnarled oak. The men unfolded their blankets and laid them out in a circle, with Caratacus at the centre. Ballan formed three watches of four to stand guard. They made no fire that might alert another to their presence, but ate fire-hardened corn cakes with a few sips of honeyed ale to sustain them through the night. Caratacus fell asleep with the sound of running water in his ears. For some reason he dreamed of butterflies.

He rose with the sun, and, as Ballan readied his men for the journey, he walked downstream to the horses and unstrapped the pack from his mount's back, laying its contents carefully by the riverbank. He shrugged off his soiled riding clothes and, naked, slipped into the stream. The sun was warm on his back, but the water was cold, and he gave an involuntary gasp as it reached his groin. He scrubbed his body with clean, white sand from the river bottom. So many scars. How close he had come to death in those days of his youth when any slight had been worth a fight and any risk worth taking if it meant cattle, or gold, or women. The puckered white skin where the spear point had pierced his thigh when the guards on the Iceni village had proved more watchful than he thought; the long thin line where a Durotrige sword had opened the fleshy part of his breast. And the one he never boasted about, not even to Ballan.

The little dimple on his right buttock, to remind him of the Silurian arrow. Had she been worth it? Dark-haired and spitting like a wildcat, but with translucent skin that shone like polished marble. He tried to conjure up her face, but couldn't.

He returned to the bank and dried himself down with his blanket. The pack contained a finespun woollen tunic in a rich, dark green that was the mark of the Catuvellauni royal house, and a pair of full-length trews striped in the same green and a creamy white. When he'd dressed, he fastened a belt of heavy gold links round his waist, and from a loop on his left hip hung the ceremonial sword. The scabbard was made of bronze, but it had been polished until it glowed bright as gold. Both it and the grip were decorated with what looked like rubies, but were actually iron studs covered in scarlet enamel. He had visited the smith in his foundry on the hill at Camulodunum and had wondered at the skill and care he lavished on the sword. It had a dangerous beauty, but he would never carry it in war. The decorated hilt was too uncomfortable to hold for any length of time and the slimness that made it so pretty also made it too light to be truly a killing weapon.

Finally he picked up the torc of thick, interwoven strands of gold. It had a familiar, comfortable weight to it when he placed it round his neck. Now, he thought with a satisfaction he would have condemned in another man as false pride, I look like a king and not some travelling vagabond.

They were still six miles from the meeting place, but with time to spare, so they rode at a pace that was easy on the ponies. There was a festive air that hadn't been apparent the previous day, the escort shouting to one another and bantering. Ballan's scouts had been on constant duty shadowing the legions since the first word of the landing. They had spent long hours in the saddle, or immobile on a hilltop, always on the watch for an enemy ambush or an unwary patrol they could ambush in their turn. To be so far from danger was a blessed relief, and it showed. Not in Ballan, though. The Iceni was as alert as ever, his eyes darting from trees to hilltop, left to right, never resting.

'Lord!'

Caratacus urged his pony to where the scout waited on the crest of a ridge. Ahead of them, perhaps three miles distant, was the distinctive hill they had been told to look for. Long and low, it had the hunched shoulders and pointed snout of a sleeping boar. Its lower slopes were carpeted with trees, but the summit was bare. Caratacus thought he saw the gleam of sun on metal, but he might have imagined it. His eyes met Ballan's.

'So then,' he said solemnly.

Ballan hefted his spear, weighing it in his right hand. He nodded. 'So. I have long wished to meet this famous beauty. It is my experience that women and power do not mix well, though my sister Boudicca would spit me with a dagger if she heard me say it.

They tell me that this one will prove me wrong, but we will see.'

He kicked his pony into motion, and Caratacus followed him down the slope, his eyes never leaving the distant hill where Cartimandua, queen of the Brigantes, waited.

XVI

The rider who met Caratacus at the base of the hill carried a green branch to show his peaceful intentions, but he was dressed for war, in a shirt of close-meshed mail that had been mended many times, and a polished iron helmet with cheek pieces in a style similar to that the Roman auxiliary infantry wore. He was in early middle age, and might have been handsome, but a sword or a dagger had removed the end of his nose and the puckered red flesh gave him an unwholesome look. The wound had also affected his speech, which had a curiously nasal quality that would have been comic but for the warrior's evident dignity.

'My lady awaits you at the top of the hill. Your escort should remain here.' Ballan growled at this, but Caratacus nodded his assent. 'You will meet her by the ring of stones.'

It was obvious from the way he presented the information that he was uncomfortable with the clandestine nature of the meeting, but, Caratacus thought, he wasn't particularly comfortable with it himself. Yet there had been no other way. If her husband had known they planned to meet he would have taken steps to prevent it.

'Is your lady alone?'

The man frowned. 'No. That would not be seemly. Her sister accompanies her.'

Caratacus kept his face expressionless, but inwardly he cursed. Brigitha. Her presence was unlikely to help his cause.

He thanked the warrior and rode slowly towards the wooded hill. Cartimandua's escort had set up camp near the edge of the trees and they looked on curiously as he passed. Ballan had been right. There were fifty of them, heavily armed and well horsed. The pony picked its way up a narrow path which snaked through the wood. He was glad he hadn't worn his cloak. It was stifling and airless among the trees, and he could already feel the first prickles of sweat in his hairline. Small brown birds crept along the branches like acrobatic mice, and at one point he disturbed a deer, which bounded off through the ferns and leaf-clutter of the forest floor. It was a relief when he emerged from the trees and felt the summer breeze cool on his face. The slope was less steep here and off to his left he could just see the top of the standing stones the warrior had described. He felt a flutter of excitement in his belly and his heart beat faster. Fool, he told himself. She will have forgotten you long since, and you would do well to forget her. How long had it been? Certainly more than fifteen years. He knew he had aged; Medb made fun of the grey hairs in his moustache. At least she wouldn't see that. It had only just started to grow again since his foolish spying mission to the Roman column. Would she look at him and see the lined face of an old man? She would have changed too. He might not even recognize her. Maybe she was fat? It happened to many women after childbirth and she was surely a mother more than once. No, not fat. Not Cartimandua.

He approached the rise that led to the summit and now he could see the standing stones clearly: eight of them in a ring, with another two, or possibly three, lying in the grass. A pair of horses was tethered near the closest and he could see the figures of two women among the stones, one tall, with raven hair, the other shorter and lighter. They turned at the sound of the pony.

The breath caught in his throat.

She had always been beautiful, in a way that made every man's eyes turn to look at her when she passed. But it had been a youthful, girlish beauty and she had not fully understood the power it gave her. The woman who stared at him intently as he dismounted was probably the most beautiful he had ever seen.

'My lady.' He bowed at the waist.

'Lord Caratacus.' She acknowledged him with a slow nod of the head.

'My lady Brigitha.' He repeated the bow, knowing that Brigitha would expect nothing less than her sister.

Brigitha only stared at him. No welcome there.

What was it that made one woman beautiful and one plain? They were sisters, there was no denying it: the resemblance was there for all to see. Nose, eyes, mouth, all the same or similar. Yet in Cartimandua these things combined to create a whole that would take a man's breath away, while in Brigitha, nothing. It was as if Brigitha's flesh was cold and featureless, like a snowfield in dead of winter, while life and expression flowed from each pore of Cartimandua's skin the way heat comes from the sun, and managed to entrance, to mesmerize – and to seduce. Close up, her hair was so black it almost had a sheen of blue. It hung down her back to her hips like a waterfall, and he could tell she had spent as much time on her appearance as he had on his. The grey hairs were there, a few of them, but that was the only real evidence of the years that had passed. The slim figure was fuller and none the worse for that; the eyes were clear, the same emerald green he remembered. She wore a full-length dress of material that shimmered as she moved beneath it. The colour matched her eyes almost perfectly.

'Have you come here to talk, or just to look? Our journey was long and wearying. I hope it was not wasted.' Brigitha's voice was sharp and rough-edged. It reminded him of one of the flints the Old People had used for their arrowheads.

'I am sure my lord Caratacus suffered as much, even though he is a man, and strong, while we are mere women.' Cartimandua's voice was as sweet and soft as her sister's was bitter and hard. It sent a shiver of memory through him. 'He only seeks to confirm that we are who we are, and not some impostors come here to capture him.'

Caratacus smiled. 'If I was to be captured, lady, I could not have more agreeable jailers.'

'Come, we will walk a little. Brigitha is with me to ensure propriety is observed, but she can do so as well from here as by our side. Is that not so, sister? If you see the slightest sign of improper behaviour on the part of my lord, you have my permission to swoop like a hawk and take his eyes out with your talons.'

The tone was pleasant enough, but Brigitha's stony face made it plain she knew an order when she heard one.

Cartimandua walked towards the northern edge of the hilltop and Caratacus followed a few paces behind. When she stopped they could see ridge after ridge of high country stretching into the distance; a wind-whipped sea of green and brown and grey, frozen in time.

'It is fine country,' Caratacus said quietly.

'Beautiful, yes, but not easy country to fill bellies from. Some of my people will starve this winter unless Esus sends us a good harvest. My Druids have prayed and made sacrifices, but these are troubled times, and the gods may have business elsewhere. What do you want of me?'

The last sentence was sharp and businesslike, and most certainly not from the Cartimandua he remembered. Her father had offered her as his wife, and she had visited Camulodunum for a season. They had fallen in love, but an alliance with the Brigantes was not foremost in Cunobelin's mind. When the Dobunni king suggested Medb, Caratacus's father had seen the opportunity to secure his western border for a generation. Cartimandua was sent home. Caratacus had almost followed her, but Nuada read his thoughts and had him chained in a hut until the black rage that filled his mind faded. He had wanted to kill his father.

'The Romans will be here by the next harvest, or the one after that, and you won't have to worry about filling your people's bellies, because they will all be dead.'

'Stop them, then, with your mighty Catuvellauni warriors. They believed they were invincible, if I remember correctly?'

'I will stop them, but my warriors are not invincible, not against Romans. There are not enough of them, even with the Trinovantes, the Regni and the

186

Atrebates by their side. How many warriors can the Brigantes put in the field?'

She did not have to think before she replied. 'If I command it, perhaps fifteen thousand men, five hundred horse, two hundred chariots. It would take time. The chiefs would have to be appeased, their concerns soothed. But why should I command it? No one but the gods knows what will happen between this harvest and the next, or the next. Perhaps you overestimate the power of the Romans? In any case, what does Cartimandua of the Brigantes owe Caratacus of the Catuvellauni?'

The answer was nothing. She had given herself to him freely and pledged to be his wife, but when his father had spoken he had bowed to the old man's will and allowed her to ride out of his life. He still remembered the resentful, tear-stained face that would not look in his direction when the Brigante retinue left Camulodunum. If things had been different, if he had been the man he was now, he knew he would not have let her go, even if it meant killing Cunobelin. But then he had been young. He had shouted and lashed out, torn at the chains Nuada had bound him with, but in the end he had done nothing to get her back. In six months he had forgotten her, married Medb and made another life. Happy enough in its way, but not the life he would have had with this woman.

'With you by my side and with your warriors in my battle line we can defeat the Romans, destroy their army and send the survivors back where they came from, carrying such tales of horror as to make us safe from them for ever.'

She considered it, turned the thought over in her mind, calculating the risks and the advantages. She walked away from him again, taking the path along the contour of the summit edge. When she had gone a few yards, she looked over her shoulder at him in a way that sent a thrill through his body and set a fire in his stomach. The last time he had seen that look had been in his hut, in the week before disaster struck. Her eyes had glittered with sensuality and her bare flesh glowed like bronze in the light of the oil lamp as she offered herself to him. He shivered and fought down the wave of desire that threatened to overwhelm him.

'There is another way,' she said.

'The only other way is to make common cause with the Romans. Would you have us give up our land to the invader?'

'Not give it up. Rule it. Together we can rule Britain from north to south and east to west. Side by side we would be strong enough to force the Romans to come to terms. Offer them an alliance with a Britain that is strong and united, but no threat to their Empire.'

He was almost tempted, but knew that the Romans would never accept her bargain. They did not make bargains, they dominated. And they could only dominate the weak, not the strong. But he dared not dismiss her suggestion immediately. Better to discover exactly what was in her mind.

'How could we rule together? You have a husband. I have a wife.'

'If you put away Medb, I will deal with Venutius.' The cold way she said it, unthinking and as pitiless as a farmer slaughtering a pig, made him suddenly glad that what was, was. It made perfect sense, she was right: together they would combine the strength and power to rule Britain as a single kingdom. It was what he had dreamed of. But now the thought sickened him.

'I am sorry, lady.' He bowed so she could not see the message in his eyes. 'I have made my vows to my wife, and Caratacus of the Catuvellauni does not break a vow. It seems I must fight alone.'

'It seems so.' Her voice betrayed no emotion. Perhaps she had known it would end this way. But then why attend the meeting in the first place? 'I too am sorry,' she continued. 'I had hoped Caratacus of the Catuvellauni was above petty things, and shared my vision for a greater Britain that could take its place in counsel with the Romans. I see I was wrong, but even so there is no enmity between us. I hated you for long enough, Caratacus. I do not hate you now. When you fight, you will lose. The Romans are too strong for any army you can field. Aulus Plautius has forty thousand veterans who have never been defeated, even by the hordes of Germania. But when you have lost, know this. There will always be sanctuary for you and your family with Cartimandua of the Brigantes.' She smiled. 'You have my vow on it.'

They walked together back towards the stones, where Brigitha waited.

'Will you stay and dine with us, lord?' Cartimandua asked.

'No, lady, I must return to my people. I have a war to fight.'

When he reached the bottom of the hill, he shouted to Ballan and the scouts to get ready to move out immediately. They had erected a cowhide tent for him, and before they dismantled it he changed from the fine clothing he had worn for the meeting into the sweat-stained shirt and trews he had ridden north in. Somehow they felt cleaner.

Within twenty minutes, they formed up and moved out. He didn't look back, so he didn't see the slim figure who waved her farewell; he was too busy puzzling over the matter of how she knew so much about Plautius's strength.

'So we won't be fighting beside the Brigantes?' Ballan interrupted his thoughts.

Caratacus didn't answer, which was answer enough.

'Good. I never trusted the bastards anyway.'

The Catuvellauni war leader smiled. How fortunate he was to have this man by his side. 'And did you have the opportunity to see the wondrous Cartimandua and form an opinion of her?'

Ballan spat. 'Beautiful, but dangerous,' he said firmly. 'Almost as dangerous as my sister.'

They grinned at each other, unaware of the disaster overtaking the British cause a day's ride to the south.

XVII

Verica's skin was flushed and his eyes were lit by the fever of victory. He sat by the cooking fire surrounded by a cocoon of self-satisfaction that protected him from the glares of two people making a huge effort to let him know he was unwelcome without actually saying so. Britte stirred the cooking pot and gave Rufus a significant look that said: You're the man, why can't you get rid of him?

When they had first halted, the mood among the baggage slaves had been almost festive. The demands upon them on the march were incessant, but with the column at a standstill and safe within the ramparts of their latest temporary marching camp there was little for them to do, save a little mending and fixing of harness, sandals or clothing. Then the centurions had marched up the column calling out every third century of the Augusta and the atmosphere changed. As the soldiers marched off, in full armour and with enough food for three days, the non-combatants watched in uneasy silence; it was clear these were men heading towards a fight. When the Fourteenth Gemina, situated behind them in the column, followed in their footsteps Rufus realized this was a major engagement.

He had hailed Narcissus as he was riding by on his way from Vespasian's headquarters.

'Plautius has his battle at last, it seems,' the Greek confirmed. 'The Britons have formed a defensive line beyond a river four miles ahead. The place has been well chosen, because the banks are thickly wooded, and it is impossible to count the enemy's numbers. Our general is keen to get to grips with them, but he knows he cannot afford a setback, so he will wait until his patrols return before he moves. It may take a day or two.'

'Will we win?'

Narcissus smiled. 'Of course we will win. These are the legions and our enemies are ill-disciplined barbarians. Plautius will force the river and if the British commander is foolish enough to make a stand he will be destroyed.'

The Greek rode off and Rufus made his way back to the bullock cart trying to look more confident than he felt. He didn't share Narcissus's confidence. The memory of his ordeal at the hands of the Britons was still sharp, and he remembered only too well the

193

suicidal courage of the enemy warriors who had attacked the column in the pretty valley. Nothing was certain in war. He also understood what would happen to the baggage train if the legions were defeated. They would be hunted down and slaughtered like sheep, or end up as slaves in a British village with a life worse than any dog's. But now here was Verica roaring his triumph like a young lion fresh from its first kill and dispensing sour wine to anyone who would accept it.

'We cut them down like sheaves of corn in summer,' the Atrebate exulted. 'It was a joyous thing to behold. They stood beyond the river screaming their defiance. The clash of sword upon shield rose until it was enough to deafen you; then their champions came forward into the shallows and challenged our commander to single combat. But Plautius was unmoved. Instead, he waited and watched, studied their line and counted the hours until his scouts returned with word of their numbers. At first he believed it must be a trap, for the force opposite him was only half what he had expected to find. He called me to him and asked me to point out Caratacus, if I could divine him among that great host. I did not see him in the midst of the line, though his brother, that carrion bird Togodumnus, was there at the heart of his Dobunni. Bodvoc of the Regni stood by him, and I could identify elements of the Trinovantes by their colours. If the Catuvellauni were with them they were not visible to me. When I told him this, Plautius looked thoughtful, and turned to the legates of the Twentieth and the Fourteenth. "This is naught but a blocking force sent here to waste my time," he declared. "Take your legions forward and they will melt away in front of you. But I wish you to harry them and keep harrying them until darkness. Nothing must delay the crossing of the column."'

Verica grinned with that inane foolishness that comes with too much wine. 'You see how I was of service to our commander?'

'I see a puppy barking at a new moon,' Britte spat, but Verica pretended not to hear her. He turned to Rufus as if they were old friends who had been parted for too long.

'Then the general turned to me and said, "Prince Verica of the Atrebates and his auxiliaries will accompany the attack and identify the enemy chieftains. If there is any opportunity to take them alive, do so, and bring them to me so I may put them to the question." By now, the enemy had his forces by the water's edge. I think Togodumnus overestimated the power of the river. It was wide at this point, more than a bowshot, but it has been a dry summer and the water is shallower than normal. When the legionaries advanced line by line, it only reached to their tunics at the deepest point, enough to hamper their movement, but not to halt their advance. The warriors defending the water's edge watched them come and were overcome with battle madness. Togodumnus could not have moved them even if he had wished it.

'They charged the Romans in the shallows and it made my heart soar to see them. If courage was the currency of victory we would never have fought our way to the far bank. But the British way is not the Roman way. You saw the shield line hold in the battle of the valley? Well, it held again, and the little swords did their work, and the river ran red with the heart-blood of their finest warriors. I was supporting the right flank of the attack with my horsemen and I saw the bodies float past me on the current. Among them were men I knew by sight or by fame, great men whom Caratacus will never replace.' He shook his head and took a deep draught of wine before offering the jug around the fire. Rufus would have taken it, but the icy glint in Britte's eyes stopped him.

Verica wiped his lips. 'Fought, did I say? No. It was a massacre. First the Roman shields held, then they forced their way forward and pushed the British line back to the far bank, and then further, on to the mass of warriors on the hill behind. Some men, more sensible than brave, tried to organize a withdrawal, but they were hampered by those who wanted to fight. I saw Togodumnus urging his men into battle even when their defeat was certain.

'We were as close as our fire is to Bersheba, and I challenged him to single combat, but Togodumnus has ever been a coward who lives on past fame. He sneered at me and shouted that I was the fruit of the union between a diseased sow and a wild boar, which I took as a compliment coming, as it did, from him.

Yet my challenge had shamed him, because he sent his bodyguard to kill me. Five men.' Verica's voice was close to ecstatic and his eyes shone with the memory of it. 'Five men, warriors all, and I cut them down one by one. Flavius Sabinus, commander of the Fourteenth, saw them fall, and honoured me with his praise. "Hail, Prince Verica," he called, even as the battle raged around us. "Had you been a Roman citizen the Emperor would have awarded you a triumph, but I fear a throne must do in its stead." It was the best moment of my life.' His eyes were locked on the flames, mesmerized by the dancing tongues of orange and red and gold, and the multitude of tiny sparks spawned by the crackling branches.

'You are a hero, Verica. You should be with your friends, not with us slaves,' Rufus said quietly. 'There must be great rejoicing in the auxiliary camp.'

'Rejoicing, yes.' The Atrebate prince gave a puzzled smile and his spirit seemed to shrink within his body. When he spoke his voice had a flat, lifeless quality that matched his words. 'But not among my men. By now the general had ordered in his cavalry and they rode ahead of the legions, giving the enemy no respite. We watched as the defeated warriors were hunted down one by one, fleeing this way and that like deer caught in a stockade, but never escaping the swords. Mile after mile we rode in their wake, and mile after mile of slaughter we passed. Eventually we came to the British camp and that was where we found them.' He took another long drink.

'Them?' Rufus asked.

'The women and children. They had spared none.'

Rufus nodded. 'It is the Roman way.'

'Some of the dead were of the Atrebates. My people. I saw one woman with a small baby. She had tried to protect it with her body, but the spearman had stabbed her through so often it was difficult to tell where mother ended and babe began. It seemed . . . excessive.'

'Yet you have put your faith in Romans,' Rufus pointed out. 'You should not be surprised there is a price to pay.'

Verica shook his head to clear it. 'You are right. My restoration comes at a cost, but it is a higher cost for my people than I would have believed. Yet I must harden myself against pity in the knowledge that when I am their king they will no longer have to bow to the Catuvellauni or the Regni. I will give them everything Rome can provide: great palaces and fine temples, gold, silks, wine and oils. Every family will have a house of stone and every man will be a lord among Britons. Narcissus has promised it.'

Britte had been sitting quietly, listening, and she spat in the fire at mention of the name. 'Do not put your faith in the Greek. Where Narcissus goes, the carrion birds are not far behind.' Rufus stared at her. In all the time he had known her, he had never heard Britte put together a dozen words. Her dark eyes glittered and met his, and he realized that, though he was seldom aware of it, she was always there, listening

198

and watching, and that she probably knew Narcissus better than he did himself.

Verica looked up, his eyes red with exhaustion. 'I am not a fool, whatever you think. I do not trust Narcissus entirely.' He paused and pulled a dagger from his belt, the blade glittering in the light from the flames. 'If he betrays me I will kill him.'

XVIII

Claudius concentrated on his left leg. He could do it. If a man could rule Rome he could stop his left leg from twitching like some demented grasshopper. He chewed his lip. Was it slowing just a little?

'Caesar?'

He looked up. It was his chamberlain. 'Yes, Callistus?'

'I think Senator Galba is seeking a reply.'

Galba? Of course. His mind had drifted during the man's interminably dull monologue.

'Perhaps Senator Galba might repeat his question, Caesar?'

'Y-y-yes, I think that m-might be wise. C-continue, dear Galba. I was m-mesmerized b-by your eloquence.' Pompous fool.

It was the not knowing that made it worse. He

looked out over the receiving room; thirty avaricious, expectant faces, each one seeking some sort of advantage. Contracts for the great aqueduct system he had announced. A monopoly on the supply of grain from the east that would make a man rich overnight. Petitions for the advancement of their unworthy relatives. Until he received word from Narcissus he was as blind as any of these fawning parasites.

When the audience was completed he limped through the palace corridors and out into the sanctuary of the Palatine gardens. This was where he came to think, in the quiet shade of the plane trees, myrtles and cypresses, under the stern gaze of men whose fame was long forgotten, but whose images would live for ever in the marble statues that lined the paths. But not today. He hurried through the gardens and nodded to the doorkeeper who controlled access to the library. As he walked through the bronze-clad double doors into the cool of the interior he felt a guilty rush of pleasure. The atmosphere of this place always made him feel less anxious; he was soothed by the unmistakable scent of old leather and slow decay. From floor to ceiling the walls were lined with thousands of niches, each containing a tight-wrapped scroll in its leather case. Every book in the world, works in a hundred languages including some long dead, and, he guessed, barely a tenth of them opened, never mind read.

The librarian approached, pathetically grateful for his visit. Claudius named the book he had come to study, then took his seat at a desk beneath one of the vast windows that allowed the sunlight to slant into the building and gave the reader light to work until late in the afternoon. When the scrolls were placed before him, he unwrapped the first with studious care and pinned it flat.

Gaius Julius Caesar's *History of the Gallic Wars*, Book V.

Lucius Domitius and Appius Claudius being consuls . . . An hour later, he sat lost in his thoughts, reliving what he had just read. It was the story of Caesar's invasion of Britain ninety years before. A tale of desperate battles against savage barbarian tribes, of legions lured into cunningly devised ambushes, of epic heroism and glorious sacrifice. The history didn't say it, but it was clear that Divine Julius had badly underestimated his enemy and that their hit-and-run tactics had rattled the legions quite badly. Overwhelming force had tipped the balance, of course, as overwhelming force always would. But still . . .

Caesar, naturally, pronounced it a victory. The truth was that it was the story of a failure. He had left within weeks, burdened by a few middle-ranking hostages, treasures which were quickly spent and promises that were never kept.

Claudius shivered, despite the warmth of the afternoon, and searched again for the passage that had disturbed him more than the actual tales of war. *Most of the inland inhabitants do not sow corn, but live on milk and flesh, and are clad with skins. All the Britons, indeed, dye themselves with woad, which occasions a bluish colour, and thereby have a more terrible appearance in fight. They wear their hair long, and have every part of their body shaved except their head and upper lip.* At this very moment Plautius could be at the mercy of these terrible, blue-skinned barbarians, and where would that leave Narcissus's vainglorious plans? Where would it leave him? His mind made a circuit of the boundaries of the Empire: across the Rhine the same tribes who had destroyed Varus lying in wait, with a sense of growing pressure beyond; Africa, quiescent for the moment but never subdued; and to the east the Dacians stirring in their mountains and their forests. Each a threat that must be faced in time. Compared to them, Britain was an irrelevance. Yet only Britain could provide him with what he needed so desperately. And it was not gold, or pearls, or slaves.

A loud sniff disturbed his contemplation, and he looked up to find a small blond boy in a short linen tunic staring at him. Agrippina's son, Lucius, who, for reasons no one understood, must be called Nero. He glared back, wondering who had allowed the child access to the library. Of course! The palace staff went in terror of his mother, who insisted he have the run of the place. Should he smile? He didn't particularly like children, not even his own. In general, they tended to be dirty and to die of the most unlikely diseases at the most awkward times. Still, he supposed he should try. He bared his teeth, but the boy's expression didn't change beyond a flicker of unease. For the briefest moment, there was something about his pale, almost colourless eyes that stirred a memory in Claudius – a sort of barren emptiness, as if the person behind those eyes were incapable of emotion. Then it was gone. He realized it was the same imperious stare he received from the statues in the gardens. He'd only seen its like once before in a living, breathing human being. Caligula. Surely it couldn't be? But there *had* been rumours about Gaius and his sisters. Tales of noisy night-time visits that were, perhaps, not – quite – brotherly. But no, he was doing the boy and his mother a disservice. Any child of a sire as habitually drunken and casually vicious as Domitius Ahenobarbus would have to learn to hide his true feelings, even by the age of six – or was it five? Some men dispense death casually, almost unthinkingly. Caligula had been one. But his had been a terror born of self-preservation. Nero's father had enjoyed cruelty for cruelty's sake. Inflicting pain on friend and foe alike simply because he could. The boy had been very young when Ahenobarbus met his deserved end, but such a beginning would cast its own shadow. The long silence continued until he felt an urgent need to break it. But what does one say to a five-year-old boy with a stare as vacant as an empty cistern and – he shuddered in disgust – an appetite for the fruit of his own nostrils? Eventually he could take no more.

'Come, child,' he said as gently as he was able. 'Sit here beside me and I will read to you. It is a story of war and glory and victory.' He shuffled along the bench, and, to his surprise, the boy rounded the desk and scrambled up beside him, close enough for Claudius to feel the soft plumpness of his body and the warmth of his presence. With the unexpected human contact, he felt something change. He realized that for the first time in many months he didn't feel lonely. In a firm voice, he began to read: 'They, advancing to the river with their cavalry and chariots from the higher ground, began to annoy our men and give battle . . .'

Caratacus stood on the hill overlooking the broad river and watched the last of the survivors straggle across the narrow bridge of rough planks. So few. He closed his eyes and tried to still the killing rage that seethed and boiled inside him. He must stay in control. He had sent Ballan south as soon as he received news of the defeat. The Iceni had still to return, but the scale of the setback was written clearly in the demeanour of beaten men streaming past him.

'How many did he lose?'

'Five thousand, dead or scattered. Mostly dead.' Bodvoc's voice was emotionless. Outwardly, he had returned from the battle of two days earlier the same man, but Caratacus detected a subtle change in the king of the Regni. Defeat had taken its toll even on

205

him. Now he must defend a second river and his brash confidence had a brittle quality to it, as if it would take only one more blow to shatter it completely. 'The Trinovantes and the Dobunni bore the brunt of the assault. Togodumnus believed the Romans would be stopped or at least slowed by the river, but they weren't. I told him we should get out while we still had time – follow your instructions. He stood in his chariot howling them on, as if his presence alone could defeat them.' He shrugged. 'But of course it couldn't.'

'Adminius and his Cantiaci?'

Bodvoc stroked his moustache and looked at him a certain way. 'Were they with us?'

'Your Regni?'

'Ran with the rest. Me with them.'

Caratacus would have put his arm round his old rival's shoulder, but he knew it would shame Bodvoc. Instead, he said firmly: 'Good. It means this time when you fight, you fight by my side. Sometimes it takes more courage to run than to stand and die. That's a lesson most men learn if they stay alive.'

'Not Togodumnus.'

'No. Not Togodumnus. Should I kill him?'

Bodvoc looked up sharply. Surprised. In another man, yes, but Caratacus? 'Your own brother?'

'Why not? He is a fool. No, he is worse: a dangerous fool. Twice he's failed me, and at a cost I cannot afford. When I fight here I need to be able to trust my commanders. We can beat the Romans once and for all, but only if every man knows his place in the line and holds it until he wins or dies.'

Bodvoc thought it over. At one time he would cheerfully have killed Togodumnus himself for his monumental folly, but now he was feeling old. 'Put him and his Dobunni where they can't do any harm.' He changed the subject. 'Will the Brigantes fight alongside us?'

Caratacus shook his head. She would stay in the north, and her warriors, the warriors he needed so badly if he were to win, would stay with her.

The sound of shouting drew their attention back to the bridge. A column of chariots rattled across the wooden planking, forcing tired men to step to the side, and hurling the unwary into the river. Togodumnus was in the front chariot, urging his driver to greater speed and screaming abuse at anyone who didn't move out of the way quickly enough.

Bodvoc smiled humourlessly. 'Do I hear a dog barking? I will leave you to discuss your battle plan with your brother.' He walked off to where a guard held his pony as Togodumnus raced up the shallow slope in the chariot, swerving to a halt and leaping athletically from the fragile wood and leather structure in front of Caratacus.

'I bring news, brother,' he shouted, loud enough for anyone within thirty paces to hear. 'The Romans are checked. They now know what it is to face the warriors of the Dobunni. They lick their wounds and bury their dead.'

Caratacus stared at his brother. 'I asked you for three days, Lord Togodumnus, but you did not give me it,' he said quietly. 'I told you to avoid casualties, yet I hear Taranis now greets an army of our honoured dead at the doorway to the Otherworld. The only thing the Romans now know, Lord Togodumnus, is that they can slaughter your Dobunni warriors like sheep.'

Part of him hoped the insult would anger Togodumnus into challenging him. He was tired of his brother's stupidity and plotting. It would be a relief to kill him. But he knew he wouldn't, because spitting Togodumnus on the end of his sword now would leave the Dobunni leaderless, or, worse, half a dozen factions fighting for the dead king's throne. He couldn't afford that. 'How many Romans did you kill?'

Togodumnus shrugged. 'I didn't stay to count them. Hundreds. Thousands. The river swept many away.'

'And your own dead?'

Togodumnus looked away.

'Five thousand?'

'Fewer.'

'How many fewer?'

'Fewer.'

'And the supplies I gave you and asked you to protect? The women and the children who followed you?'

'They would only have slowed us down.'

'Coward,' Caratacus hissed in his brother's face. And now he didn't care if he provoked Togodumnus into a fight, would take pleasure in butchering him where he stood, because he could see the twisted bodies of the innocent lying among the sacks and the slaughtered animals, and the killing rage was back. 'Coward,' he repeated.

Togodumnus took a step away, his face white and his hand shaking as he reached for his sword hilt.

'Lord?' Caratacus heard the shout through the red cloud that filled his mind, but he ignored it. He wanted blood. He wanted Togodumnus dead and all the nameless warriors and helpless infants who had fallen because of his stupidity avenged.

'Lord?' He swept the sword – his battle sword, not the ceremonial toy he had worn to meet Cartimandua – from its scabbard and exulted at the sound of its metallic song. A hand grasped his shoulder, and he would have shrugged it off, but it was Bodvoc's hand, and no man could break Bodvoc's grip if the Regni king did not choose to allow it.

'Caratacus, look.'

His vision cleared. He followed Bodvoc's pointing finger past where Togodumnus was staring away to his right, beyond the mass of warriors who had gathered behind the low grass-clad hill overlooking the river.

And he knew he would not have to kill his brother.

Because Scarach had come.

*

'Welcome, lord king.'

Scarach nodded his acknowledgement. He had been given the place of honour beside Caratacus, and took it as his due. A slave handed him a silver flagon and he studied its contents curiously. 'Beer? Do we have no wine?'

Caratacus gestured to the slave, who returned a moment later with another flagon. Scarach put it to his lips and took a deep swallow. 'That's better. I like Roman wine. I'd like most things about the Romans if only they'd stay where they belong.'

'Then let us send them back there.'

Scarach raised his cup in a salute. 'To victory.' He was a stout man, bordering on fat, but still powerful, and he was accompanied everywhere by a bearded giant whose suspicious gaze swept the assembled gathering. 'My boy Keryg. Don't mind him. He's a sullen bastard, but terribly handy with a sword or a spear, or even with his bare hands. I use him as my executioner. Very effective. Might even be a match for you, Bodvoc. Or have you given up fighting for shagging?'

Bodvoc laughed dutifully, and Caratacus gave him a grateful glance. It was time to get down to business.

'He looks a mighty warrior. His father's son. How many like him do you lead?'

'Ten thousand.' The figure brought a murmur of appreciation. 'Ten thousand Durotriges, plus another five thousand Dumnonii, who are better off getting killed by the Romans than staying behind and

210

plaguing my borders. Most will be here by tonight, the rest tomorrow.'

Fifteen thousand warriors, Caratacus calculated; fifteen thousand to add to the thirty-five thousand already gathered along the river. Fifteen thousand extra mouths to feed, but they would cope with that. They would have to. It was a mighty host. Together they would outnumber Plautius's whole army, perhaps outnumber the best Roman legionary troops by two to one. He would beat them, but the battle must be fought on his ground and his terms.

He looked up and saw Scarach staring at him in a significant way, and he realized he had missed something.

'I said does our bargain still hold?' the Durotrige war chief repeated. 'The Dumnonii will only fight for pay.'

'They will have their gold.'

'And the rest?'

'Our bargain holds.'

'What bargain is this?' Togodumnus was on his feet. 'Was the council consulted?'

'This is a bargain between myself and Lord Scarach.' Caratacus looked to Scarach for support, but the Durotrige saw an opportunity for mischief that was not to be missed.

'But surely Lord Togodumnus is a vital component of it?' he said innocently.

Caratacus could feel every eye on him, and realized he had no choice. 'I have pledged to provide a force

211

of warriors to fight for Lord Scarach against the Irish sea folk who raid his coasts – once we have defeated the Romans.'

Scarach nodded his head in acknowledgement of the favour, but everyone in the room knew there was more to come.

'I have further agreed to build and equip a fleet of ships to carry those warriors and a force provided by Lord Scarach to sweep the Irish coast, to wipe out the pirate bands and to take slaves.' Scarach had driven a hard bargain. It would strip Caratacus's treasury bare to find enough gold to build the ships. The only consolation was that once the Romans had gone he would annexe Adminius's kingdom of the Cantiaci to help pay for the expedition.

'How many men?' Togodumnus demanded. 'Whose men?'

'Why, yours, Lord Togodumnus.' Scarach smiled. 'Five thousand of them. Are not the Dobunni the finest warriors in Britain?'

Togodumnus gave a strangled snarl and would have spoken again, but Bodvoc got to his feet. 'Enough of this,' he growled. 'When do we fight?'

'The Romans will be here in three days,' Caratacus told him. 'They will not attack immediately. I estimate another three days at most. Then we fight.'

XIX

'We should attack now, when they do not expect us.'

Plautius stared. There was something in Vespasian's tone that was not quite respectful, particularly in front of junior commanders. Still, there was nothing to be done about it. The legate might be a boor, but he had friends at Claudius's court and in the senate and must be humoured. The annoying thing was that from a purely military standpoint he was correct. Caratacus must be off balance after the slaughter five days ago. Whatever force he had been able to gather since would be demoralized and disorganized. He believed himself to be safe behind the river, and therefore would be off guard. He underestimated the legions, and commanders who underestimated the legions were defeated before they even fought. Nevertheless, Plautius stood his ground.

'We will rest and resupply, deploy the legions for attack . . . and wait.'

They had set up the invasion commander's pavilion on rising ground south of the river. It was a fine day, and the front and side cloth walls were raised, allowing Plautius, his legionary commanders, their aides and the Emperor's representative Narcissus an unbroken view of the far bank. Sunlight glittered on the swirling, shadowed waters, and occasionally a substantial fish would leap, causing a splash near the centre. The river was wide here, possibly as much as three hundred paces, and, if the sluggish flow was anything to go by, also deep. But there had been a bridge – the top few inches of the blackened piles stuck out from the surface like so many broken teeth – and where the British had built a bridge the Romans could build a better one. Of course, the British bridge had not been built under attack. The crossing would be opposed. They would lose men, but that was what men were for.

Plautius studied the far bank. The point he overlooked was on a gentle bend in the river, but it was clear the river itself was not always gentle. Regular flooding had cut away the bank, leaving a sharp edge and a steep climb of perhaps four feet. There was no beach that he could see, although there might be one at low water. He guessed that the river bottom was not uniform. The bridge was evidence of that. His engineers had identified that it stood on a gravel ridge which cut diagonally across from just below where they sat to a point slightly further upstream on the north side. Beyond the steep bank, a lush green meadow stretched away to a long, low hill – a whaleback – where his enemy stood and watched him in his turn.

It was a good position, one he might have chosen himself. The British warriors were arrayed along the crest of the low hill, most of them on foot, but the line was broken at intervals by the taller figure of a horseman or a chieftain standing in his chariot. He knew there would be more chariots, but it didn't concern him. They were an annoyance, that was all. When a man had fought a chariot-borne warrior once, he had the measure of him. The horsemen, too, had only nuisance value. Cavalry tactics were alien to the barbarians. They used their horses to carry them into battle and away from it. Transport for the chiefs and the nobles, nothing more.

Plautius cocked his head to one side as he thought he heard a howl and he wondered if they had dogs. Realized they almost certainly would have. The British war dog had a fearsome reputation. Huge, powerful beasts with razor teeth and sharpened claws. A charging man might not break the line, but if a dozen snarling hounds started tearing at the legionaries' unprotected legs it might be a different story. He would give it thought.

From time to time an individual or a small group of warriors would come to the water's edge and scream what must have been insults, but they were much too far away to make out the words. He knew he was seeing only a fraction of the British force, and only what Caratacus wanted him to see, but it did not concern him. When the time came, there could be no doubt about the final outcome. The augurs had done their work, the sacred chickens had been consulted and the corn had danced in the most positive omen of all.

Vespasian, however, wasn't finished.

'If we wait we give the barbarians the opportunity to strengthen their defences, reinforce their army and recover from the beating we gave them. Tactically, there is no purpose to be served in waiting.'

'Sometimes there are other imperatives than the tactical imperative,' Narcissus said indulgently, but if he expected his words to mollify the Second's commander he was mistaken.

'What would you know of tactics, spy? I see no triumphal regalia on your chest.'

'I would ever bow to your tactical knowledge, General, but I recognize a reality when I see one, and the reality is that the army must conserve its strength for the coming battle. There can be no mistakes.'

Vespasian scowled. 'Do you allow this informer to dictate our movements?' he demanded.

Plautius's face turned almost as scarlet as his cloak. 'You overstep your position, Legate. You command the Second. I command the invasion force by the authority of Emperor Claudius, whom you also serve unless you have changed your allegiance in recent days.'

Vespasian growled at the insult, but he was interrupted by his younger sibling, Sabinus, commander of the Fourteenth, who was as polished as his brother was coarse-grained.

'I think that what the legate of the Second is attempting to convey, and I might add, respectfully, with the full support of his fellow legionary commanders, is that he is . . . perhaps the best word is *puzzled* by our dispositions. You estimate a halt of a week to ten days, yet he sees nothing to be gained and much to be lost by such a delay. Naturally, we accept the authority of our commander, Aulus Plautius, but we feel that a more . . . detailed . . . explanation of his dispositions might be in order.'

Plautius glared at him. It didn't matter how thoroughly it was cloaked in diplomatic language, Sabinus was challenging the authority he claimed to accept so readily. Yet Plautius was commander enough to know he had been outmanoeuvred by the Flavians. He looked to Narcissus for confirmation.

'Perhaps we might continue our discussions on a more private basis,' the Greek agreed.

'Junior commanders are dismissed,' Plautius barked.

When they were alone with the four legates, Narcissus signalled to an orderly for wine. The six men sat in silence until it arrived, a delay which allowed the tensions in the room to abate, as Claudius's freedman had intended it should.

'Other imperatives.' Narcissus dropped the words into the silence.

'If the blood of a single legionary of the Second is spilled unnecessarily as a result of your "other imperatives", spy, I shall give his comrades the pleasure of watching you die slowly on a cross.' Vespasian's words were threatening, but his voice was more controlled now. 'What other imperative can there be but the destruction of the barbarian forces and the bringing of civilization to this benighted land?'

'The imperial imperative,' Narcissus said simply.

The four legates turned from Narcissus to Plautius, who sat back in his padded chair, thinking deeply. He looked up to find them watching him.

'I have dispatched a message to the Emperor Claudius in Rome calling for reinforcements. The message states that, defying all nature, the British tribes have united against us and have forced us to a halt. It further states that other British forces are active in our rear and threaten our lines of supply. It is my belief that the Emperor will act upon this communication and send another legion to our aid.'

For a moment there was a puzzled calm, before the full impact of his words came home to the four officers. They all started to speak at once.

'But . . . none of this is true,' spluttered the legate of the Ninth, an elderly politician forced on campaign by his wife's ambition to be the spouse of a consul.

'We have the barbarians at our mercy,' Sabinus pointed out. 'Our supply chain may be stretched, but I have heard nothing of any attacks.'

The legate of the Twentieth shook his head. 'No, this cannot be. We require no aid. Victory is certain.'

'There is more to this than is at first apparent.' Vespasian stared at Narcissus. 'It will take weeks for another legion to reach Britain from Rome, if a legion is available in Italy. More likely the Eighth will need to march from Dacia. By the time this unnecessary reinforcement arrives we won't have to attack the Britons, they will have died of old age.'

'The Eighth legion will join us in ten days,' Plautius said steadily.

'Pah! A legion cannot fly. It would take five of those days to reach us from the coast and that at a forced march.' Vespasian's voice was thick with disbelief. 'I mean no disrespect to you, Commander, but what you say is impossible.'

'You mean you think I have gone mad.' Plautius smiled his eagle's smile. 'Yet what I say is true. The Eighth will land at Rutupiae on the Kalends of July and we will not attack until after that auspicious day.'

'But how?' Vespasian shook his head in confusion. 'I do not understand.'

'Because I sent the message requesting reinforcements several weeks ago.'

'But that was . . .'

'A few days after we landed on the soil of Britain,' Plautius confirmed. 'As soon as I could be reasonably certain of our progress and success.'

'This is madness.'

'Not madness, my dear Legate.' Plautius nodded

towards Narcissus who stood by the doorway, his face expressionless. 'Politics.'

'We will attack Caratacus on the day the Army of Plautius becomes the Army of Claudius,' the Greek said quietly.

'The Emperor . . . ?'

'That is correct, gentlemen. The Emperor will assume command of the army in ten days. You have ten days to prepare your forces. Ten days to ensure your Emperor the triumph he needs to be proclaimed *Imperator* and to enshrine his and your places in history.'

Now they all saw it. Victory. A triumph. *Imperator*. Conspiracy was what won an Emperor his throne, but these . . . these were the currency that allowed him to keep it.

They were interrupted by a commotion at the doorway, where a rotund, richly dressed Celt swept in as if the pavilion belonged to him, with two large bodyguards at his back. The small man stared contemptuously around the room until his eyes fell upon Narcissus.

The Greek smiled a welcome. 'May I introduce Adminius, king of the Cantiaci, and half-brother of the British leader Caratacus. He has a multitude of reasons to hate his brother and I believe he has news which may be of interest to you.'

XX

Four days after the meeting by the river, Claudius lay beneath a bright awning on the wide deck of his galley and tried to ignore the interminable creaking of planks and ropes. It was well past the fourth hour after dawn, but all he could see was grey. Grey sky, grey mist, grey sea. All the same dull, uniform grey. How he yearned for the familiar multi-hued contrasts of the *Mare Nostrum*; the deep blue and the aquamarine of the waters and the stark, glistening white of the sands. The journey had been long and tedious, but the captain assured him they would soon reach the shores of Britain. He felt a faint thrill of apprehension. What awaited him there? It had all seemed so simple when Narcissus had explained it, but weeks of interminable boredom had given him ample opportunity to explore every avenue of failure. There were so many, and each of them seemed inevitably to lead to his death. He tried to suppress the habitual tingle of panic. Whatever the next few days brought, he must retain that spirit of absolute confidence with which he had set out for the Senate that day five weeks ago; the day when he had truly become an Emperor.

He remembered each detail as if it were cast in stone. Messalina had been visiting her artistic friends, but his niece Agrippina had been there with the boy, Nero, when the messenger arrived. Sweet Agrippina was so attentive these days, always with some new tonic that calmed his nerves or helped him sleep. There were two messages. The first, from Plautius, bore its dread news of obstruction, failure and potential defeat. Callistus presented it with grave ceremony; the chamberlain already knew its contents, which would soon reach the ears of the palace servants and from there, inevitably, the streets, where rumour of disaster would spread like flame within a summer-dry thicket. The second was from Narcissus and was in a simple coded cipher which had been developed for just such confidential correspondence. This told the true situation, which filled Claudius's heart with hope.

'Callistus, prepare my chair and call an emergency session of the Senate.'

He had kept his face suitably grim as he made the short journey from the Palatine to the forum. As his bearers reached the foot of the Clivus Palatinus he could see that a crowd had already gathered among the marble columns and the gleaming temples along the Via Sacra. The steps of the Domus Publica and the frontage of the House of the Vestals nearby were packed with staring, wide-eyed faces. Of course the mob would be aware of some impending crisis, but he ignored every shouted call for information. Instead, he admired the perfect proportions of the temple of Divine Julius and paid a silent tribute at the little shrine to Venus Cloacina. Then he was there, in that hallowed place. The Senate House.

Why was it only here that he truly felt like an Emperor; when he was faced by his rivals, his enemies and his detractors? Look at them, dewy-eyed and solemn, yet every one of them exulting in his discomfort. Each ready to take what advantage they could from his dilemma. Why, Galba was even snivelling like a child, no doubt lamenting the greatest military disaster since Varus lost his legions among the swamps of the Teutoberg forest. Well, let him snivel. It was difficult to keep from feeling smug. No. The mask must not slip. This was his time. Remember. The performance.

He looked out over the rows of tiered benches and felt the power rising in him, his brain taking on the icy sharpness of the surgeon's scalpel. He kept his face immobile, and as the seconds stretched into minutes the fat backsides filled with aristocratic blood began to fidget on the worn white marble. Let them wait. The gods had given him a gift to offset the disabilities and the humiliations they had heaped upon him at the moment of his birth, but they had hidden it well. Only Augustus, that most prescient of Emperors, had recognized it. Had seen that, while Claudius dribbled and stuttered like the most ill-starred lunatic when confronted on equal terms by anything born of mortal woman, he was still capable of charming, seducing and convincing when he spoke to an audience. What had the old man written to his grandmother? Oh yes. The pompous, growling voice filled his head as if he were mimicking it. 'Confound me, dear Livia, if I am not surprised that your grand-son could please me with his declaiming. How in the world anyone who is so unclear in his conversation can speak with such clarity and propriety when he declaims is more than I can see.'

He felt a smile threatening at the memory, but was just able to suppress it. Now. Now was the time. He got to his feet, hitching the toga over his shoulder. His eyes ranged over the benches once more, acknowledging the powerful and the influential, ignoring the others. 'Senators of Rome.' He projected his voice so that it seemed to rattle from the marble columns of the house, and those in the front ranks of the crowd beyond the ropes outside the building could hear each word and pass it on to those behind. 'Senators of Rome, I have called you here on a matter of the gravest importance. The honour – no, the very future of the Empire lies in the balance.'

A murmur of dismay ran through the white-clad

ranks on the benches. He raised his hand for quiet.

'General Aulus Plautius, whom all here know, and I tasked with the long overdue annexation of the peoples of Britain, reports a setback. The British tribes, which he had supposed defeated, have united under the command of a new and resourceful leader, Caratacus, king of the Catuvellauni. This Caratacus now gathers a mighty host to his standard, a host which threatens the very existence of General Plautius's army. Four Roman legions – four, I say – are now held with the point of Caratacus's spear at their throat, beyond reach of their supplies, without reserves, with no hope of succour, unless,' he paused to let his words and their message be absorbed, 'unless we, the conscience and the conviction of the Empire, give them hope.'

He stopped again and allowed his head to drop slightly. His voice seemed quieter, but somehow still reached every ear he intended it to reach.

'I blame myself for placing Rome's bravest and most honoured in such deadly peril. General Plautius asked for more troops – indeed, he outlined this very situation – but I – and you – denied them to him.' He shook his head as if he couldn't believe his own foolishness, and with that one act included every man in the Senate House in his guilt. 'Too expensive, we said. We need them in the east, we said.' His voice rose in volume again, its power growing with each word. 'What price do we put now on Roman blood, what price on Roman honour? Is there any price we would not pay, any gift we would not give, to turn defeat into victory?'

'No!' 'None!' 'Anything!' The words were repeated along the benches, taken up by one senator after another, and he knew he had them. Had them all.

'Then I propose we send the Eighth legion to the aid of our beleaguered commander. I have already taken the liberty of alerting their legate at his base in Dacia, and they have begun a forced march through the Alpine passes.'

There was a murmur of assent, but one senator ventured his concern. 'Will a single legion be proof against an enemy who have the measure of four already?'

Claudius allowed himself a grave smile. Thank you, Lucius Vitellius, for playing your part. You will have your reward.

'Not just a single legion, Vitellius. The expedition will be accompanied by a force consisting of the Praetorian Guard and auxiliary cavalry, which is equal to a second legion.'

He waited until the full impact of his words was rewarded by a murmur of surprise. The Praetorian Guard was the élite of the Roman army, headquartered in Rome and the personal bodyguard of the Emperor. He never went anywhere without them, or they without him.

'Yes, senators of Rome, I, an old man, will personally lead the relief force.' He let his eyes range across the tiered benches. 'But who will join me? You? You?

Or you? Will you come to General Plautius's aid and redeem the glory of Rome?'

What could they do, when the senator seated next to them was clamouring to be included? To gainsay him would be to admit cowardice or lack of patriotism. So one by one his enemies stood and clamoured with the rest. And, one by one, he swept them up.

'Yes, you brave Marcus Vinicius. I accept your gracious offer. Valerius Asiaticus, you live up to your noble name. Lucius Sulpicius Galba, I am humbled by your sacrifice and will willingly serve beside you. Gallus, old friend, and now comrade.'

One after the other he netted them, the cunning and the ambitious, the plotters and the backstabbers, until every danger of consular or senatorial rank was safely in his basket. When it was done he studied his haul like a hunter weighing his bag at the end of a long day. Asiaticus and Vinicius had both married into the imperial family, and been involved in the plot to kill Caligula. But for the accident of Claudius's discovery by the Praetorian Guard, Vinicius could have been sitting here in his stead, for he had been nominated by the plotters to replace the Emperor. Nobody had more reason for hate than he. Gallus was a fool, but he could not be left behind when he wore his contempt for the Emperor like a badge of honour and waved his ambition like a flag. Sulpicius Galba was more dangerous still, since he was the most able of them all, and kept his ambition hidden behind his patrician scowl. Yet he talked ceaselessly of what was *needed* to make Rome great again, and all knew that he believed what was *needed* was Lucius Sulpicius Galba.

It could not have gone better, and when he had them eating from his hand like caged lovebirds, he convinced them to appoint his most trusted ally, Lucius Vitellius, to govern in his stead during the campaign.

Yet, when it was over, elation had been replaced by a strange melancholy. Would there ever be another day like this? Would he ever reach these heights again? He knew he had only won a brief respite from the pressures ranged against him. To truly cement his position he needed a victory and a triumph.

So he had returned to the Palatine – to arm himself for war.

XXI

Why don't they come?

'Why don't they attack?'

Caratacus kept his eyes on the far bank where the Romans waited, the tents of their geometrically precise encampments stretching as far as the horizon. It was the eighth day he had watched them. The sky above the camps was made hazy by the smoke from a thousand cooking fires. On the flatland beyond the river he could see squadrons of cavalry wheeling and manoeuvring as they'd done every evening for the past week. The Roman engineers had begun building three separate bridges within hours of their arrival. They were sited four hundred paces apart, which Plautius obviously believed was far enough to stretch the British forces but close enough for each bridgehead to support the other in case of need. But the work lacked urgency and each slim artery seemed to progress only a few feet a day, inching out as if the Romans were nervous of reaching the British bank. At this rate it could be weeks.

'I don't know, Bodvoc. Perhaps they are frightened of us.'

The Regni war chief didn't smile. 'We have supplies for only another few days.'

'So do the Romans.' It was true. His spies had reported a dwindling stream of wagons reaching the four great legionary encampments. But the Roman commander, Plautius, had cut his men's rations by a quarter to eke out his food. Caratacus knew that if he did the same his army would melt away around him. He could almost feel the ripening harvest calling to the farmers among his vast force. There had already been desertions among the Dumnonii; it seemed greed for gold could not outweigh the reality of Rome's legions massed on the other side of the river.

'Scarach grumbles. He says if the Romans do not attack us, we should attack them.'

'Scarach was born to grumble. He knows we cannot cross the river, but he howls like a wolf to impress the rest of the pack. They will come, and when they come we will defeat them.'

The utter conviction in his voice surprised him and seemed to convince Bodvoc, for the big man just nodded, and strode off the hilltop towards the circle of rough huts where the Regni had set up camp. Caratacus could see the bright flame of a funeral pyre outside the ring of huts. A change in the wind brought him the familiar reek of cooking fires and carelessly ejected shit. They had been fortunate so far; the disease that always followed an army on campaign had not found them yet. The few men who had died were already sick. If the Romans did not come soon it would be different.

He closed his eyes and his hand strayed to the brooch at his shoulder. Come now. Taranis, use your power to make them come. He inspected the men working below him, screened from the Romans by the uneven mound of sand-covered flood debris that lined the bank for miles up- and downstream. He knew he could not have chosen a better position. It was perfect.

From the point where Plautius had set up his garish pavilion it appeared the terrain on the north side of the river was a flat meadow which stretched for perhaps two hundred paces before sloping gently upwards to form the grassy hill. The Roman commander would calculate that he would lose men, maybe hundreds of men, making the crossing. But once they were on the British bank and formed up he would be certain that no matter how hard the British fought, the outcome was inevitable. What he did not know, and what Caratacus sacrificed to the gods each night to ensure he did not find out, was that the 'meadow' and its approaches had been turned into a killing ground.

The harmless-looking bank where the legionaries

would disperse when they crossed was full of deep pits, dug each night by reluctant warriors who thought wielding a shovel was slaves' work, but many of whom would live because the Roman line would be fractured before it had fully formed. When they emerged from the river in their cohorts, the Romans would march straight into an ambush from mixed squads of slingers and spearmen hidden in the hollows. Those who survived, and Caratacus acknowledged there would still be many, would be held back by their officers until they could form the disciplined lines which made them impossible to defeat. But the delay would give the British ambushers time to flee back to their comrades ready to cause more carnage. That was when the legions would realize they had walked into a trap. But by then it would be too late.

The meadow which looked so inviting from the safety of Plautius's pavilion a mile away was in reality a featureless bog. In itself it would have made a formidable obstacle for heavily armoured men, but Caratacus's fertile mind had added its own deadly refinements. He had ordered his men to carve thousands of wooden stakes sharpened to a point at each end. When they were ready, the stakes were jammed into the soft mud of the bog, with three feet above ground angled towards the advancing legionaries at groin height. When the stakes were fixed to his satisfaction, the British war leader ordered the small stream which ran through the centre of the bog to be dammed a few feet from where it met the river. Now the bog was a shallow lagoon which stretched for two miles along the British front and was laced with invisible gifts from the gods which would kill and maim. He could imagine the tight, orderly lines struggling through the placid waters, tripping and stumbling, then the first man going down with a scream, writhing against the unseen horror that had punctured his lower belly. Then the next, and the next, until the water turned red.

By the time they reached the temporary safety of dry soil, they would be exhausted and demoralized. That was when he would launch his first attack. It would be his élite: the champions of the Catuvellauni and the Trinovantes, the Regni and the Atrebates, the Durotriges and the Iceni – Britain's mightiest warriors. They would smash the Roman line as it struggled to free itself from the grasping mud of the bog. The weight of the assault would force the Romans back into the ranks behind them, creating a tight-packed logjam into which the spearmen and slingers would cast their deadly rain of missiles. As his men screamed and died and drowned, Plautius would throw in reinforcements, but they would only add to the chaos, more cattle to the slaughter. That was what Caratacus counted upon; what he had planned for since the night his conversations with the slave Rufus had divulged Plautius's fatal weakness. The Roman commander was under so much pressure to win a quick victory he would accept battle wherever he found it. Even on British terms. Togodumnus, in his stupidity and his arrogance, had unintentionally helped lay the trap. The easy victory on the first river could only have made Plautius more certain of his overwhelming superiority. Caratacus had led him onwards to this place, the doom of his army, in the certain knowledge that Plautius would follow as a dog follows a bitch in heat.

He waited on the hilltop until the sun was almost down, enjoying the aloneness of it and listening to the different sounds of the two camps; the Roman was silent apart from the occasional shouted order or strident trumpet call, while from behind him came the raucous clamour of men arguing and women shrieking. When would it start? Ah, there it was, the roar of massed voices singing some repetitive marching song. It happened every evening at this time and would last until just before daylight. Was this some Roman superstition – a rite to be performed on the eve of battle – or was Plautius attempting to keep the British warriors from their beds in the hope they would fight less well? Either way it would not affect the outcome of the battle.

But first the Romans had to come to him.

'Why are they singing?'

'Soldiers like to sing. They have few enough pleasures.'

Narcissus had taken an almost fatherly interest in Rufus since he had returned to the column. He had insisted the young slave enjoy the most nourishing foods from General Plautius's personal supply: fillets of fish and breasts of fowl, great slabs of suckling pig and slices of succulent, fat-heavy beef. Rufus was pleased enough to accept the Greek's unexpected generosity, but sometimes he couldn't rid himself of an image of a calf being fattened up for slaughter.

'They seem to be singing the same song over and over again.'

'Yes. I believe it's entitled "The March of Marius". Some of the verses are quite obscene, but it has a rhythm that keeps going round in my head. I much prefer it to that other dirge, what is it? Oh yes. "The War Anthem of Mars" – it hardly stirs the blood, does it?'

They stood in silence for a while, listening to the pulsating chant, which always seemed to come from their right, downstream. When Narcissus spoke again his voice took on a commanding edge and his words sent a shiver through the young slave. 'It is time to fulfil your oath. Tomorrow after dusk I will send a messenger for you and your elephant. You will accompany them where they direct you, and when you reach your destination you will follow your orders to the letter. Is that clear?'

Rufus nodded. 'Is it time, then?'

The Greek pursed his lips. It was something he had considered, but one element of the puzzle still remained to be put in place before the contents of Bersheba's wagon could be revealed. 'No, but you, I

235

think, would be wise to wear the uniform of the Guard. And Rufus?' Rufus stared at him. 'Say nothing of this matter to anyone. Your life may depend upon it . . .'

Rufus returned to the baggage train, his mind ablaze with visions of battles and wounds and terrible ends. But men survived battles. He had fought before, when he had killed Dafyd, and at Cupido's side when they had saved Caligula from the assassins, and again, on that awful day in the passageway from the theatre when the world had changed for ever. He thought of Cupido, the calm stillness of the man and the reassurance in his pewter-grey eyes, and knew that the gladiator would keep him safe, or, at the very least, save a place beside him in the feasting halls of his ancestors.

He didn't expect to sleep that night, but when he woke at dawn his head was clear and his mind sharp. Neither was matched by the day, which was a sulphurous, brooding trial of airless heat crushed beneath a blood-red ceiling of low cloud. Soldiers called days like these ominous, and with good reason; a sky the colour of new offal seemed to be filled with omens for a legionary on the eve of battle. It was the kind of day Rufus had learned promised rain, and plenty of it, but the rain never came and the heat never abated. Instead, the air crackled with an almost physical tension. Men who had never exchanged a sour word cursed each other as they worked.

Centurions lashed out with the thick vine sticks of their office at the slightest provocation. And there was no lack of provocation.

It was clear by now that the Second's preparations for the river crossing were close to culmination. The camp was abuzz with activity. Carpenters worked ceaselessly to ensure the great wooden catapults and the *ballistae* that could punch a heavy four-foot arrow a quarter of a mile through the air were in good order and ready for action. Armourers sharpened swords by the dozen and met last-minute promises to mend the weak points in legionary plate armour or auxiliary chain mail that might cost a man his life. Vespasian stalked the camp with his aides like a lion marking its territory, reassuring, checking, and repeating his orders again and again to his junior commanders. There was only one word on every man's lips. Tomorrow.

XXII

On the far side of the river Caratacus was back at his station on the low hill at the first hint of daylight. There was something different about the Roman camps, a new intensity of purpose that wasn't particularly visible, but was there all the same. The cavalry went through the same routines, but their formations were more compact; tight and efficient. The riders carrying dispatches and orders between the four camps seemed more numerous, while beyond, in the great supply compounds, it was as if he could sense the increased activity of thousands of soldiers and slaves, even if he couldn't see it with his eyes. Nuada joined him at noon and together they considered the dread sky and brooding atmosphere. He hadn't forgotten the Druid's part in Togodumnus's folly and Ballan had returned from patrol three days previously hinting there might be more he didn't know. But on this of all days he needed Nuada's support.

'I want you to make a sacrifice to discover the meaning of this strange weather,' he ordered.

Nuada sniffed the air. 'I don't need to sacrifice anything to understand the weather. A child could read the signs. It means rain tomorrow, or perhaps the day after. The clouds are heavy with moisture, the sun heats them and the gods stir the mixture. The clouds will give birth to a storm in their own good time. In any case, we have no prisoners. Your brother couldn't achieve even that.'

'Not prisoners. A goat.'

The Druid spluttered. 'A goat! What good is a goat? A goat won't win you the support of the gods. We should line the riverbank with Wicker Men, fill their bellies with slaves and send their souls to Taranis. That will bring you the gods' favour and put terror in the heart of your enemies.'

Caratacus smiled grimly. 'If the gods do not favour us now, Nuada, then they have deserted us for ever, and you and your kind have failed this land of Britain. There are many mere children in our army and I have seen the fear in their eyes when they look at that sky. You will sacrifice a goat and the portents will be favourable, and perhaps their bellies will be filled with courage instead of beer.'

'And what if the omens are not favourable?'

'If the omens are bad, I will fulfil my promise to sacrifice a Druid to ensure the gods' favour.'

239

'Then I will choose the goat with the utmost care.'

'That would be wise.'

'Tomorrow?'

'Yes,' Caratacus said quietly. 'Tomorrow.'

If nothing else told him with certainty they would come tomorrow, the bridges did. Since dawn each of the three crossings had been an ants' nest of activity, with Roman engineers scurrying back and forth along their length carrying the building materials which had now brought them close to halfway. This was the first time he had witnessed the true power of Roman ingenuity. A British bridge was a fragile, expendable affair of thin planks, supported by the closest available timber, jointed and held together by rope. It could – no, it was expected to – be swept away by the next flood. Romans built to last. They used small, tethered wooden boats which they must have carried in their long baggage trains to create the initial framework. When they were anchored in place, the legionaries swarmed over and among the pontoons, slipping in and out of the water like otters as they sited large baulks of timber cut days, perhaps even weeks, before for the bridge piles. These were then driven into the river bed by an ingenious weighted device like nothing he had ever seen. Even before the piles were properly set, engineers and carpenters were working among them, placing and testing the planks of each section. The result was a structure as sturdy as any he knew. Yet it was not the bridge that impressed him most, or was responsible for the chill that ate into him even on this thunder-hot summer's afternoon. No, it was the way the men worked together, each knowing his place and his task, never obstructing or colliding. There were no screamed orders or wicked slaps of whips on idle backs. It was almost inhuman, this clinical control. For the first time he felt, low in his gut, the wolf-gnawing ache of doubt. Could his crude stratagems succeed against a people capable of all this?

Nuada was staring at him and he knew what he was thinking was written on his face. He forced a confident smile. 'Don't you have a goat to sacrifice?'

When he was alone, he went over the plan again in his mind.

The hill was the key. Here, in the centre, where the massed ranks of Plautius's army would strike, the most fearsome warriors of the Catuvellauni, the Trinovantes and the Iceni, reinforced by Scarach's Durotriges, would wait; the rock upon which the legions would break themselves.

On the far left, ready to fall on the Roman right flank, would stand the Atrebates of Epedos and Bodvoc's battle-eager Regni. He had spent hours with the Regni king reinforcing the need for patience. Wait. Wait. Only when he was certain the Romans were exhausted and their line stretched thin as a butterfly's wing along the river's edge should he strike, but when he did strike it must be with the speed of a lightning bolt and the force of a hammer blow. There would be no second chance. When the warriors in the

241

centre had sucked the power from the legions it was Bodvoc and Epedos who must destroy them. Utterly.

Togodumnus, naturally, had demanded this honour, but Caratacus knew his brother, and after the rout on the first river the kings and the chiefs of the army of Britain were no longer impressed with his bluster. He would hold the British right with his Dobunni and a coalition of the lesser tribes, convinced after hours of persuasion that it was the place of greatest danger. Here the ground was broken and wooded, less favourable for the attackers, but where Togodumnus would wait, ready to fall upon a routed enemy already defeated by the crushing flank attack.

Caratacus rubbed his forehead where it throbbed and bubbled as if his thoughts and his schemes were trying to escape from his head. There was so much to consider. So much at stake. Was there anything he had missed? He went over it again, was satisfied he had done all he could – apart from one nagging doubt.

'Ballan.'

The squat Iceni horseman jogged up from where he had been waiting with his scouts on the rear slope of the hill. 'Lord?'

'About ten miles upstream, close to a place where the river passes below a ridge of yellow rock, there is a ford where a horseman might cross. Ride there and sweep for any signs of Roman cavalry. I think we would know by now if any major force had passed that way and got behind us, but I want to be certain.'

Ballan grinned. 'I know that place. I sent Uda and his troop at first light. If he sees anything suspicious he will dispatch a courier and you will hear within the hour.'

Caratacus laughed. 'So, an Iceni horse thief knows my mind before I know it myself. I am glad you are not with the Romans. And to the east? Do you perceive any threat from that direction?'

Ballan's leathery forehead creased in a deep frown of concentration.

'No ford there that I know of. A man might cross by boat when the tide and the current are right, but not an army. We've been patrolling the bank for a week and seen nothing suspicious. But something concerns you?'

'Ships. The Romans came to this island on ships. Is it possible they could land a force far downstream in the flatlands that edge the estuary?'

Ballan considered for a moment before replying, running the soggy, creek-channelled landscape through his mind. 'Possible. But not likely. Nothing but mudflats down that way. A transport ship would have to beach a mile from the shore and a man in full armour would take a day to reach proper dry land, if he ever reached it at all. A commander would have to be a fool to attempt that way.'

Caratacus pursed his lips in thought. 'Foolish, yes, but possible, you say?'

Ballan shrugged. He'd said his piece; let Caratacus do with it what he willed.

Finally the king decided. 'Take a few men there and find the highest point. The country is flat as one of Medb's corn-cakes and from any sort of height you should be able to see many miles of coast. Do not stay long. Either they are there or they are not. Probably not. But best to know for certain. A fool's errand, I know, Ballan, but I *must* be certain.'

The Iceni nodded. 'I will return before daylight, to stand by your side.'

Caratacus smiled. He had expected nothing less, but he couldn't resist teasing the earnest tribesman. 'Do you never rest, Ballan?'

Ballan gave him a look that fathers reserve for a naughty child. 'I will get all the rest I need in the Otherworld.'

Alone again, the British war chief turned back to stare at the slick, black surface of the river. The closest of the three bridges – the one in the centre – was almost within a spear's throw of the near bank. A group of Scarach's young warriors had gathered close to the water's edge and were noisily competing to see who would reach the Roman engineers first. Their spears were dropping yards short of the nearest pontoon, but if the bridge progressed at the present rate it could only be minutes before the builders were in danger. He knew he should stop them – those weapons would be needed tomorrow – but he remembered the way the blood boiled and fizzed through his body on the eve of his first battle. Let them have their sport.

As he watched, a small group of lightly armoured men jogged towards the point of the centre bridge. He opened his mouth to shout a warning, but he knew he was too far away and that any runner he sent would never reach the Durotriges in time. The Romans halted and knelt on the boards just behind the foremost engineers. Caratacus sighed. He knew what was coming. One of the young Britons ran up to the bank and launched a spear towards the hated enemy. It was a mighty throw, the best of the day, and splashed into the water just short of the bridge, but where the boy would normally have slid to a halt in the sand and watched the flight of his weapon, instead he pirouetted in a parody of a dance and flopped bonelessly to the ground. Leave him, Caratacus thought, leave him and run. But the lad's comrades gathered around his body. The next perfectly flighted arrow took a second warrior in the throat, and was instantly followed by another, which lodged itself in the thigh muscle of a third and left him limping as he scurried away, leaving his two dead friends bleeding by the water's edge.

There was no victory shout from the men on the bridge. The archers trotted back to the bank in a disciplined column, followed by the engineers. They had done enough for the day, but Caratacus knew they would be back at work at sundown and the bridge would reach the shallows at dawn. He breathed deeply, sucking in the thick, warm air, and tried to dispel the melancholy that enveloped him like a blanket. He stared at the still bodies lying amongst the brush between the flooded water meadow and the river. What was it Ballan had said? 'I will get all the rest I need in the Otherworld.' How many more would be resting in the Otherworld, and how many of them would have gone to their deaths cursing his folly . . . tomorrow?

XXIII

The rain slanted from the darkness and twinkled as it was caught in the flickering light from a hundred torches.

Rufus had still been awake when the messenger from Narcissus tapped him on the shoulder, taking care not to disturb Gaius, who slept dreamlessly at his side. He felt a pang of regret that he had no token he could leave, no message of reassurance in case he didn't return. But the Greek's orders had been clear. There was one thing he could do, though. He bent his head low over the russet curls and gently kissed the little boy's forehead, producing a faint whimper that made his breath catch in his chest. He wished more than anything that he could stay; this was where he belonged, not out there in the dark unknown, his fate in the hands of men he hadn't even met. But he could not let Narcissus down. He took Bersheba by the harness and led the elephant carefully through the baggage carts into the open. He had hidden the Praetorian uniform in the base of the wagon beside Narcissus's great secret. Now he donned the black linen tunic and the sculpted armoured breastplate with its wolf symbol. On his head he placed the heavy metal helmet with its wide cheek pieces. When he had fastened his sword-belt, he slid the short, razor-edged *gladius* from its scabbard with a hiss that made the hair rise on the back of his neck. It was comfortably heavy in his hand and he couldn't resist two or three practice cuts before he returned it to its sheath.

He expected the messenger to lead them towards the river where Plautius's four legions must already be forming up in preparation for the dawn crossing. Instead, the man turned in the opposite direction, away from the three bridges which would carry the Roman army into the centre of the British battle line.

Rufus struggled to hide his confusion, but he knew better than to ask questions. He was in Narcissus's world now; a world where the unexpected must be taken for granted and where nothing was ever quite as it appeared. It was full dark, but his escort was well versed in his business, for he never deviated from the path as they marched across the rough country south of the river. Only twice did he hesitate, and both times it was to stop and listen.

'Did you hear anything?'

Rufus shrugged. 'An owl. A rustle in a hedgerow. Just night sounds. Why?'

'It's nothing. A little nervous maybe. There's word of British scouts this side of the river. Wouldn't want you getting your throat cut.'

They continued for ten minutes before they topped a low rise and Rufus stopped so abruptly Bersheba almost walked over him. The grassy bowl below his feet stretched for perhaps four hundred paces in each direction and it was overflowing with the shadowy figures of men. Legionaries. The extent of the enormous mass of soldiers was defined by pinpricks of light from the torches which identified the pathfinders who would lead them through the night. It was a full legion, he realized. No, it was more than a legion. There must be five or six thousand men.

The messenger touched him on the shoulder and they made their way carefully down the rain-slick slope towards a group of mounted men waiting on the right. Vespasian's aides looked as if they would prefer to be hooded against the relentless drizzle, but if their commander noticed the conditions he didn't acknowledge them. The legate wore the gilt armour breastplate that signified his general's rank and had his cloak thrown back from his shoulders so all could identify it. His face was a frown of concentration, but his expression softened when he saw Bersheba.

'So, our secret weapon. I hope you are right, Master Narcissus.'

Rufus blinked and turned to find the Greek

249

standing behind him, with Verica, his eyes bright with excitement, by his side. The young Atrebate studied the black and silver of Rufus's Praetorian uniform with interest and nodded his approval.

'Oh, I don't believe either the Emperor's elephant or his handler will let you down, General. They have been of great service in the past – and will be again in the future,' Narcissus replied.

Vespasian gave a thin, tight-lipped smile. 'If they survive. And who but the gods can say if any of us will survive this night?' The Roman general shouted a name that Rufus couldn't quite identify, and an officer marched briskly out of the darkness. 'This is Justinius Frontinus, prefect commanding our Batavian auxiliaries, and tonight he commands the Emperor's elephant. What say you, Frontinus? Will the beast do?'

Frontinus, an earnest young man with prematurely ash-grey hair, looked Bersheba up and down, giving Rufus an opportunity to gather his thoughts. Will she do for what? He had expected to be part of a battle – had prepared for it – but what madness had Narcissus trapped them in this time?

'Oh, I think it will do, sir. If it is as strong as it looks.'

'Well, elephant keeper?' Vespasian demanded. 'Is the beast as strong as it looks?'

'Stronger.' Rufus tried to think of some feat of Bersheba's that would make his point more forcefully, but the legate had heard enough.

'Then she will do indeed. I had hoped to have her beside me in my battle line, but she has other duties tonight.' An orderly spoke quietly in his ear and he nodded. 'It is time. Do your duty, young man, and your Emperor will reward you; fail him and your only reward will be death. But I do not think you or the elephant will fail him. If you survive, visit me tomorrow and I will give you my own reward, insignificant though it is. Perhaps when we next meet we will have made history.'

In the darkness around him, Rufus felt the mass of troops begin to move off and Vespasian and his retinue turned their horses to keep pace with them. They were heading east. Downstream, away from where Caratacus's army waited. He expected the order to follow, but Frontinus stood and watched them go. Narcissus strode off, calling for his horse.

'So, tonight you will be given the opportunity to prove yourself in battle, you and your elephant,' Verica said. Whenever he'd spoken to Rufus in the past it had always been in the patronizing tones of a social and physical superior, but here, standing in the soft rain with the muffled sound of gently clinking armour all around them, there was a new respect in his voice. 'Do not fear. It is not so terrible. Keep your guard up and always stay on the move. I have watched you; you are strong and you fight well. I think you will survive this night. I have fought a dozen battles, but I will never forget the first. It is what makes a man a man.'

Rufus smiled in the darkness. Verica could never keep his natural arrogance at bay for long, even when he was making an obvious effort. He decided it wouldn't be out of place to do a little boasting of his own.

'I have fought before. In Rome, my friend and I saved our Emperor from assassins.' He saw Verica's head come up in surprise. 'It was during the procession for the Divine Drusilla, the Emperor's sister. Cupido was an officer of the guard and Bersheba pulled the goddess's golden statue. We saved Gaius Caligula from men sent to kill him.' And later I killed him myself. He didn't say it, but he couldn't suppress the memory of that blood-soaked duel in the passageway.

'You saved an Emperor, yet you are still a slave?' Verica's voice betrayed his doubt. 'If you had done the same for me I would have freed you and given you gifts of great worth. Where is this friend now? He must have been a mighty warrior to be part of the Emperor's guard.'

'He is dead, killed by the man he protected.'

Verica grunted, as if Cupido's death somehow made him less interesting. On another day, Rufus might have reacted to the slight, but tonight they were two comrades on the eve of a battle. Tomorrow, both of them might be dead. Apart from Narcissus, Verica was the closest thing he had to a friend, and tonight he needed the companionship of such a one. There was a shout from the shadows and Verica

252

turned to go. Rufus felt a momentary pang of regret. 'Prince Verica?' The Atrebate hesitated. 'I will pray to Mars to bring you through the battle safe, give you victory over your enemies and return your kingdom to you.'

There was a flash of white in the darkness and Rufus imagined Verica grinning. The shouted reply came amid the jingle of harness as he struggled to mount his horse. 'I thank you, Rufus. Stay safe, and when we meet again tomorrow you will be a hero, and I will be a king.'

XXIV

A touch on his right arm made Rufus turn and he found the auxiliary officer, Frontinus, by his side. 'Is it possible your beast can move quietly in the dark?' he asked. 'We must close on the enemy without being discovered. They may have spies on this side of the river. Silence will be essential to our success.'

Rufus thought for a moment. 'That depends on what kind of country we are crossing. In heavy forest I wouldn't give much for our chances of going unde-tected, but over open ground, and if I lead her rather than ride her, Bersheba can make less noise than an ant.'

The Batavian looked doubtful, but he nodded. 'Very well, then. I will make space for you in the centre of the column, between the third and the fourth cohorts. I will guide you there.'

'What are our duties to be?' Rufus asked the question that had been tormenting him for most of the day. 'No one has given me any instructions.'

The prefect shook his head. 'The army never changes. General Vespasian, in his wisdom, has decided that our little force will be the left wing of the attack. It is a great honour, but one I fear we may not live to appreciate. Now, follow me, and make sure that thing doesn't crush any of my men. I've few enough to do the job as it is. I will join you later if I can.'

The Batavians were ranked six abreast in their centuries and the line stretched away into the night. Facing west – upriver – away from the bulk of the Second Augusta. As Bersheba passed along the column, Rufus heard the murmurs of surprise and awe. Many of these men would have heard of the Emperor's elephant, but few would have set eyes on her. Now she was here, joining them on whatever perilous mission they had embarked upon. Some of them would be encouraged by the massive grey presence among them; others would fear her, for that was always the way with Bersheba. Rufus saw that a few of the younger Batavians sported full beards and wore their hair long, in defiance of fashion and military practice, and these he noted also wore neck rings, made not of precious metals but of rough-smithed iron. Frontinus explained the puzzle while they walked. 'They are the' – he used a word of

255

unashamed coarseness that approximated to virgin – 'of our tribe, who have yet to kill a warrior in battle. Only when they dip their spears in another man's blood will they cut their hair and cast away their childhood along with the torc they wear, which will be presented to Donar, the chief of our gods.' As they passed each century of mail-clad soldiers, the prefect had a word for an individual officer or a soldier. Had Macrinus received the equipment he'd requested? How were Taurinus's feet, had the blisters healed? Eventually they came to a gap in the ranks and Frontinus halted. 'This is your position. Hold station on the unit in front. Do not lose them. I don't want half my force to go missing on the way to the river. When we get where we need to be I'll send word for you.' With that, he marched off.

Rufus stood close to Bersheba, whispering reassuringly to her. Though his heart was racing, she was at her most placid. Night-time escapades like this were alien territory for both of them, but there was something in her nature that allowed her to accept, even to enjoy, the unusual. He slipped her one of the sweet apples he always carried and she gave a soft grunt of thanks as she crunched it. While they waited for the order to march, a man from the century ahead approached cautiously, carrying a length of rope. 'My commander bids you take hold of this. The other end is tied to a man in the last section. It can be confusing in the dark, and this will ensure you stay in contact.'

Rufus thanked him. It meant one fewer problem to rattle round his head. The night was pitch dark and the rain dampened any noise; there was a fair chance he would have lost touch with the ranks ahead of him. The auxiliary centurion's foresight proved he was in good hands. There was no command, but a short tug on the rope told him they were on the move. Walking silently through the darkness, he kept Bersheba at a steady pace, maintaining station on the shadowy silhouettes and the occasional glint of light on an armoured helmet in front. He tried to concentrate only on the moving backs, but his mind was inevitably drawn to the imponderable question of what lay ahead. They were part of the attack, yet their route was taking them *away* from the main body of the enemy. Frontinus had said they were making for the river, but what would happen when they got there? Could there be a ford the Britons had left unguarded? It seemed unlikely. Had the engineers constructed a fourth bridge? Less likely still, for the enemy would certainly be aware of it and their welcome on the far side would be a shower of spears. Nothing made sense. Eventually he gave up his pointless brooding and forced himself to focus on the ground beneath his feet and the men to his front.

Frontinus was as good as his word. Rufus had no way of measuring how long they had marched, but at one point he found the auxiliary commander keeping pace beside him. Rufus asked the question that had been gnawing at him. 'You say we are to close on the enemy? How is that possible when the barrier of a mighty river separates us? Do you have a sorcerer who will lift us over its waters undetected?'

'Not a sorcerer.' Frontinus laughed. 'River rats.'

'River rats?'

'That's right. River rats and an elephant.'

Rufus must still have looked mystified.

The auxiliary commander explained: 'It is what my men call themselves – river rats from the wetlands between the two great rivers of Germania. Water rules our life from the day we are born. When we take our first breath our father sacrifices to the water gods. One of the great trials of manhood among the Batavi is to swim the Rhenus, a river twice as wide as this rather pitiful thing we approach, and when we die our bodies are consigned to its waters. The rivers provide us with everything: fish and wildfowl for food, driftwood to build our huts, the beaver and otter pelts that clothe us. The only thing they cannot give is gold, and that is why we fight for the Romans. Every family of my tribe supplies a son of military age to serve, and when these men return home they come with bounty and plunder that gives them the pick of the women, and the Roman citizenship which guarantees an honoured place in our society and the patronage of Rome. We are attached to the Fourteenth Gemina, but for this operation General Vespasian has asked for our specialist skills.'

Frontinus's face mirrored his pride in his men. Rufus realized that, for all his fine manners, he was a barbarian chieftain at heart. The men he commanded were the same warriors he would have led as part of his tribe, if the Empire had not enticed them into its service. There was no need to ask what the specialist skills were that Vespasian believed so important.

'If your men are so good, why do you need me – and Bersheba?'

Frontinus turned to study Bersheba, who swung out her trunk to take his scent. Some men would have flinched in the face of that mighty implement, five feet of solid muscle that could smash a man to the ground, or lift him from it, but the Batavian commander smiled and allowed her to run her sensitive nostrils over his arm. 'How deep a river could she cross?'

Rufus frowned. 'That would depend. Eight feet if the current was not too strong.'

'And if your life depended upon it?'

Rufus felt a thrill of alarm. 'Ten,' he said.

'Eight will be enough. If the rain doesn't get any heavier and if we ever find the crossing point.'

'But what will she have to do? She is not a war elephant. She can't fight the Britons for you.'

'She won't have to.' Frontinus laughed again. 'My river rats can cross the Tamesa even with their weapons and equipment.' He saw the disbelief on Rufus's face. No man could swim a broad river in full armour, not even if he had webbed feet. 'Oh, there are ways, have no fear of that. But to achieve what General Vespasian asks of us we must land as a unit, and that is where Bersheba can help.'

By the time they reached the riverbank, there was activity all around them. The men closest to Rufus were working in small groups, each certain of his duty even in the sullen darkness.

Frontinus explained. 'We constructed the rafts yesterday, and they were carried by the lead group, but the goatskins have to be inflated, tested and properly secured. Then the weapons, clothing and armour are covered by oilskin cloth and loaded. Everything goes on the rafts, everything but the men. They do what they do best. They swim. But tonight they won't swim on their own. They'll be towed by Bersheba. Even in a gentle current the rafts would drift downstream, and this current is far from gentle. By the time they reached the far bank my men would be scattered for miles and they'd walk straight out of the river on to the enemy spears. They would have no time to unpack their weapons. It would be a massacre. Worse, it would be a pointless massacre. We are soldiers, and happy enough to die, but none of us wants to be sacrificed in a useless cause. If Bersheba can tow six rafts and four times as many men, six crossings will secure us a bridgehead. We'll put twenty ropes across and use them to relay the rest of the unit. We can have two thousand on the far side long before daylight.'

'And then?'

'And then we do the other thing we do best. We fight.'

While the preparations were going on around him, Rufus took the opportunity to study the river. What he saw knocked all the bravado from him. He estimated they were three miles above the place where Plautius's main force faced Caratacus. The river was narrower here, but this was no gentle stream. It was a formidable barrier a good two hundred paces across, probably more. The surface was dark and dangerous, full of swirls and eddies that were a sure sign of broken ground on the river bed. That was the key. What was the bottom like where they planned to cross? If it was gravel, hard-packed and solid, he was confident Bersheba could do what he had boasted she could. She had forded deep rivers before, enjoyed nothing better than to frolic in the clean water. But what if the bottom were mud, or, worse, composed of large rocks with gaps between them like mantraps? She would lose her footing, might even break a leg. He reached up to stroke the yellowing lion's tooth charm and sent up a silent prayer to Fortuna.

When he returned to Bersheba, Frontinus was already at her side. At the Batavian's instructions he led the elephant through the small groups of soldiers making a final check of their rafts by the river, where the grassy sward shelved steeply into the water. Rufus had a momentary vision of Bersheba stumbling and throwing him into the depths. The fact that he had never learned to swim properly suddenly became very important.

Frontinus appeared beside him. 'Six, you understand? You are certain she can tow them? Once you are out there it will be too late to turn back.'

Rufus nodded. These men were more important than his fears. 'Six, and twenty-four men.'

'Then truly she is the Emperor's elephant. May the river gods protect you!'

Then Frontinus was gone, replaced by naked Batavian infantrymen who tied the cords of their rafts to Bersheba's harness with practised fingers. The closest, Taurinus, the centurion whose feet had so concerned his commander, explained what would happen next. 'Just take it slowly. We'll carry the rafts down to the river at your pace. Once we're in the water there'll be a little confusion at first, there always is, but we'll soon get it sorted out. Don't worry about us. Just concentrate on getting this beast to the far side and we'll be right behind you. When we reach the bank we'll untie the rafts.' The tall, heavily muscled soldier patted him on the shoulder. 'Strength! Never thought I'd say that to a fucking Praetorian.' He laughed and disappeared towards his men. Rufus climbed on to Bersheba's knee and up her great slab of a flank.

When he was ready, Frontinus appeared beside the elephant, glancing worriedly back to where his men were completing their preparations. Eventually he was satisfied. 'Go,' he hissed.

Rufus urged Bersheba forward into the unknown.

XXV

The first lurch as she hit the slope almost pitched him straight into the river, but his hold on her harness was strong enough to keep him in his seat. Bersheba placed first one mighty pad and then the next into the water with barely a ripple, and Rufus breathed a sigh of relief. There was no steep drop off into the depths. The waters reached just above her knees.

Two more steps and they were on their way, the surface quickly rising until it reached her belly. Behind him, Rufus heard soft splashes and muffled gasps as the rafts and their escorts entered the river. Instantly, the cords tightened as the rafts were pulled downstream by the current. Rufus felt the elephant shift her weight to take the pressure and he heard the centurion cursing as he organized his men. He'd feared Bersheba might be disturbed by this unfamiliar

263

task, but she accepted it in her usual unflustered fashion. When she had gone a dozen feet from the bank, the darkness folded around them like a cloak. At first, Rufus lost all sense of space and time in this impenetrable black prison, but the solid warmth of Bersheba beneath him helped steady his nerves. He could see nothing ahead, but, below him, the eternal, implacable flow of the water restored his sense of direction and he urged the elephant onward.

They were well into the crossing now and his sense of unease returned as the current grew stronger. The river rose until it reached Bersheba's lower shoulders, forcing Rufus to bend his knees to keep his toes clear of the water. He grimaced as the force of the stream tugged at his sandals. They must have been a third of the way across when the elephant suddenly lurched to the right and Rufus cried out in alarm as the solid bulk beneath him took on a curious weightless quality. Bersheba had stumbled and lost her footing. He held his breath. If she didn't regain it quickly they would be swept away. With one hand he grabbed for the lion's tooth at his neck and he placed his destiny with the gods. If she had truly been out of her depth, they would have been doomed, but she had marched into a shallow depression in the river bottom, and her flailing feet quickly found the firm ground that allowed her to continue on her imperious way. Rufus bit his lip and breathed again.

With Bersheba steadied, he took the opportunity to look over his shoulder. It was clear the Batavians knew their business. The cords attaching the rafts to the elephant's harness had been cut at different lengths, so a few feet separated each floating platform from the next, ensuring they didn't become entangled. The rafts rode high in the water on their goatskin floats, keeping weapons, armour and clothing well clear of the surface. Each raft had the swimmers stationed on its downstream side, kicking upstream. In this way they stayed in a more or less direct line behind the elephant, eliminating the drag and allowing her to use all her strength to force her way forward through the relentless current. They were past halfway now and, in front of him, he could just make out the faint line that marked the far bank: a deeper dark against the old lead of the rain-saturated sky. He peered into the night, struggling to distinguish between what he was truly seeing and the optical tricks his eyes were playing on him. Where was it?

'We sent a patrol across two nights ago. It was a risk, but a risk worth taking,' Frontinus had explained before they reached the river. 'They identified a landing place where the bank has eroded and the bottom slopes up to a gravel beach. It is perfect for our purposes. Behind the landing is a stand of tall trees. That is where you will see the sign.'

The sign was a white flash cut into the bark of one of the trees about halfway up its trunk. It had sounded entirely plausible when the auxiliary commander explained it, but now, in this stygian tomb, it was laughable. The only flashes he could see were the ones caused by his over-tired eyes. It was impossible. Eventually he stopped looking and placed his faith in Bersheba. She felt her way forward, one impassive, lumbering step at a time, instinctively finding the safest route to the bank. Slowly, the waters retreated down her flank and her speed increased. Rufus began to distinguish individual objects. Driftwood piled high where it had been deposited by some long-ago flood. The almost feminine undulations of a giant sandbank. The distinctive outline of a tight-packed stand of trees taller than anything around them. A pale flash in the surrounding gloom.

Frontinus's Batavians went into action even before Bersheba placed a foot on dry land. The rafts were dragged from the shallows on to the shore. Two men from each raft swiftly stripped off the oilskin covers and retrieved clothing, weapons and armour. Meanwhile, the two other auxiliaries ran into the nearby trees and firmly secured the long ropes the rafts had also carried.

They made the crossing six times in the next few hours. It was hard, gruelling work, but Bersheba never faltered, and, eventually, Frontinus was satisfied he had enough ropes to ferry his remaining force across without the elephant's help. On the final trip, Rufus persuaded the Batavian to forgo the pleasures of a freezing swim and be carried across on Bersheba's back. When they reached the bank, the auxiliary commander slid down the elephant's side and stood listening, gauging from the sounds around him whether all was going to plan. Eventually he was satisfied and motioned Rufus to leave Bersheba and follow him.

'Now we must wait. Time is short and we still have far to go, but I have my orders.'

The Batavians had created a wide perimeter around the landing ground, an unbroken half-circle of kneeling men staring into the dark from beneath the brims of their iron helmets. When they reached the picket line, Frontinus took his place just behind it, staring as hard as any of them. The prefect was clearly nervous and Rufus, who had thought him unflappable, decided that should make him nervous too. He fingered the hilt of his *gladius* and gained comfort from it, if not courage.

'Listen.' The urgent whisper came from a Batavian officer in the front line.

Frontinus's eyes narrowed and his face took on a look of total concentration. Rufus listened too, straining his ears for any sound that was alien to the natural rhythm of the night. Even so, he saw them before he heard them. They came out of the darkness, a line of silent shadows that turned into solid, all too human figures as they approached. A hundred tall, moustached men, clad in trews and chequered shirts, well armed and moving with a disturbing sense of purpose. One of Frontinus's men raised himself and lifted his spear to hurl it into the mass of enemy warriors.

'Hold,' Frontinus snarled. The approaching line halted within a few paces of the auxiliary troopers, and opened to allow a stocky figure to march to their front. Frontinus turned to Rufus. 'The Greek who advises General Vespasian said you would recognize him.'

Rufus stared hard at the small man and nodded. He was just as Narcissus had described him two nights before: short, stout and full of his own importance.

'Are we to scowl at each other all night, or may we go?' Adminius, king of the Cantiaci, demanded. 'Our enemies await us.'

XXVI

Caratacus stared into the darkness.

They were out there. He knew it as he knew the scent of his firstborn. A natural knowing made without effort or thought.

The three bridges were close now, almost to the point where the charging hordes who would thunder across at daylight could reach the shallows with their first leap. His best archers and spearmen had spent the last hours peppering the night with unaimed fire, rewarded occasionally by a loud splash or a shrill scream that testified to a legionary engineer who would not be alive to fight in the morning. He knew it wouldn't stop them, didn't intend it to. But they would expect it, and he was eager to give Plautius what he expected.

'Epedos, you understand what you must do?'

The war chief of the Atrebates nodded gravely. All the kings of the united tribes of southern Britain had gathered on the whaleback hill overlooking the crossing point. 'We wait until you have the enemy pinned against the river. They will be forced to deploy left and right, thinning their line. When they are at their weakest, we strike.'

Caratacus turned to Bodvoc, whose Regni warriors would man the British left flank alongside the Atrebates. 'Remember that, Bodvoc. When your blood boils in the furnace of battle and the clash of iron calls you like a bed-ready maiden, you wait. You must not act without Epedos. This is our chance to crush them. Yours is the vital blow; you must strike it with all the force you have. And when the Romans are driven in chaos and confusion across our front, you, Lord Scarach, will fall upon them with your Durotriges, our Iceni friends and my Catuvellauni and Trinovantes, and it will be as a wolf falls upon an injured doe, swift and deadly.'

Scarach's face split into a grin. 'Hear that?' He slapped his enormous son on the back. 'Like a wolf. Booty and plunder and blood. And all before breakfast.'

'And I?' Togodumnus didn't appreciate being left to last and his voice mirrored his petulance.

'You, Togodumnus, will be the knife in the heart of the Roman attack; the anvil against which we destroy them for ever.' Caratacus's brother gave no sign of appreciating his flattery. 'With Epedos and Bodvoc on their right, unbearable pressure on their centre and the river at their back, they will inevitably be forced to retire to the west. Then you kill them.' He turned to the men on the hill, looking each in the eye in turn. 'You kill them all. This is the day the Romans learn the true price of stealing our lands and enslaving our people. No slaves. No prisoners. Only souls for Taranis. The legions of Plautius must vanish into the mist as if they had never existed, so their fate is the stuff of Roman nightmares for fifty generations and more.'

'Aye.' A dozen voices sounded in unison.

Caratacus closed his eyes and allowed himself a vision of victory. He saw a river choked with Roman dead, running red with Roman blood. A Roman baggage train burning. A shining eagle trampled in the dirt. He thought of his wife Medb and the boy Tasciovanus. They would be proud. Then, with a pang of guilt, he remembered the day on the hill. And Cartimandua. Would she leave her mountain fastness to seek his forgiveness and an alliance, or wait until he inevitably made his way north to impose his over-lordship on her Brigantes?

'Yet these are Romans.' His thoughts were interrupted by the quiet, life-weary voice of Antedios of the Iceni. 'We have seen how the Romans can fight. They are both flexible and disciplined. What if . . . and I defer to your wisdom in this, Lord Caratacus . . . what if this Plautius does not see fit to stray meekly into your trap? What if he has a trap of his own?'

Caratacus felt the liquid ice in his guts as the question he had not dared ask himself was put into words, but when he replied his own voice was hard and unyielding. 'Then, Antedios, we fight the Roman on his terms . . . and we win or we die.'

Five miles downstream Ballan rode westward along the riverbank to join his lord. He had been right, it had been a fool's errand, but he didn't grudge Caratacus his certainty. It was that kind of attention to detail that made the Catuvellauni a leader worth following. They had reached the high ground where the estuary met the sea just before last light. It wasn't a hill, exactly – just a gentle elevation in the flat landscape – but there were signs that people had lived in this inhospitable, wind-scoured place; the rotting fallen timbers of a building and blackened stones that had once been part of a hearth were just visible among the tufted grass. From this platform they were able to see far along the coast to north and south, over the bog and marshland inhabited only by ducks, herons and frogs, and the mudflats that were just visible as the tide turned. Ballan saw nothing to fear. No war galleys or troop transports, not even the timbers of an ancient merchant ship that had fallen foul of this treacherous, ever-shifting coastline. When he was certain, sure enough even for Caratacus, he and his eight men turned their horses west. They could have made better time cutting inland, but the Iceni scout elected to follow the twisting river. If Caratacus believed there was even the slightest chance of a small enemy force crossing this far down he might as well check. They would still be back with the king by daylight.

Four hours later he was regretting his decision. In the darkness and the rain that now drifted down to soak their clothing he could barely see beyond his horse's ears. The river was blanketed by swirling mist that men's eyes turned into sprites and ghostly figures come to relieve a warrior of his soul. The ground beneath their feet was as treacherous as the shoals of the estuary, full of sink holes and soft spots, buried branches with spikes as sharp as any spear and gullies that could swallow a man and his horse.

Behind him, his men rode with their heads down, praying that Ballan would see sense and end their misery. He could feel their resentment and he grinned. He hadn't proved to Caratacus that an Iceni was worthy of the position of chief scout by being sensible. He had proved it by doing the impossible. Again, and again and again. He had spent more time in enemy territory in the last month than he had by his own fire. When word of the Roman invasion was first brought by the refugees from the coast, whom had Caratacus dispatched to confirm it? Ballan. And when his lord had decided to see for himself, who had brought him by the secret ways and placed him so close he could almost smell his enemy? No, they would stick with their fool's errand. Let his men curse him.

He wasn't sure at first; how could a man be sure of anything on a night like this? They had just reached a point where the action of the river had taken a massive circular bite out of the soft material of the bank. It was nothing unusual, but it meant another half-hour detour and an extra element of care. If the river could undermine one piece of dirt it could undermine another, and a horseman had to be wary of ground that might fall away beneath him and pitch him straight into the water. Still, the cloud blanket seemed to be thinner, and there was even a glimmer of shadowy moon showing somewhere up there. At least they would have the illusion of light to ease their way. The rain continued to fall gently and the river mist was thick as his wife's oatmeal porridge, but there was a hint of breeze that made it whirl and eddy in an ethereal imitation of the water it covered. He sighed and was about to turn and follow his men when he saw it.

It wasn't a shape, nothing as substantial as that. Just a section of mist that was more . . . solid wasn't the word. Perhaps there wasn't one? He told himself it was only another eddy in the fog, but it awoke something in him. He felt a shiver run through his body, as if a dead man had just run cold fingers down his spine, and he stared harder, trying to understand what the mist was telling him. For a few more moments it was still just mist, and he thought he was imagining what he had or hadn't seen; had or hadn't sensed. Then the wind shifted again, and the vapour curtain was twitched aside, and he was more frightened than he had ever been in his life.

Romans. And they were walking on water.

XXVII

Claudius had never liked tents. True, this was more of a silken palace, with its six separate rooms, wall hangings of golden cloth and a raised floor covered with soft rugs – even a small shrine where he could pray to his ancestors for the success of this enterprise – but it was still a tent. He had been brought up in real palaces. Monuments of stone and marble that gave a man a feeling of security and superiority. A tent could be blown away by a puff of wind, and no one, not even an Emperor, could do anything about it.

Still, he was better housed than the *comitatus*, the gaggle of consuls and senators who accompanied him and who had grumbled all the way from Rome; a thousand miles of whining and complaint. Most of them had served in the army at one time or another, but you would never have believed it. The food was 'bad', the accommodation 'uncomfortable', the latrine facilities 'unacceptable'. When he had pointed out that they ate a hundred times better than the legionaries packed into the stinking transport ships bobbing a mile upwind, they had sniffed and replied that they were representatives of the Empire, and not mere plebeians who had been brought up to expect nothing more than slops and discomfort.

The fleet had landed on a wide beach on the southeast coast of the island and they had made their leisurely way here, a day's march south of the main army encamped at the river. He had been nervous at first, there was no denying it. But his confidence had grown with every mile they advanced north and west through a landscape cleared of any threat. There had been no need to hurry; Narcissus had arranged everything. The legions of Plautius's force would do their duty and – though they did not know it yet – their Emperor would arrive in the hour of their triumph, dispense the honours their valour had won them, and lead them onwards to the final conquest of Britain.

Nothing he had seen on the march had changed his attitude to the place he had decided should be Rome's greatest conquest. It was a miserable country, with none of the grandeur even of Gaul, which was hardly memorable itself. Green, yes, verdant even, but poor. He had seen nothing but poverty. The people lived in mud hovels and worshipped gods who drank blood.

Well, he would change that. He would give these people civilization whether they wanted it or not.

A small desk had been set up for him and his secretary had placed on its rosewood surface the papers he couldn't escape even on campaign. It was after midnight, but the Empire wouldn't run itself. Vitellius would keep those thieves and vagabonds in the senate as honest as they would ever be, but the important decisions would be made here. He signed the order which finally authorized a start on the harbour at Ostia. Picked up another from the pile. Hesitated. One scroll had been placed discreetly to one side. He knew what it was. Knew who had sent it. Didn't want to open it, but knew he must. He reached for it and noticed his hand was shaking. The stiff parchment between his fingers felt somehow unclean. He knew it was his imagination, but the thought persisted as he unrolled it and pinned it to the desk. The trembling increased. It was worse than he had imagined. How could she think this would go undetected? Even if his own spies hadn't been watching her, someone would have informed him. Agrippina had warned him of what was happening, but oh, Messalina, not in public, and not with him.

'General Plautius is here, Caesar.'

He straightened and drove all thoughts of Valeria Messalina's infidelity from his mind, unpinned the scroll and turned it face down on the desk. He would deal with it later. Plautius marched briskly into the tent with two of his aides. The invasion commander was burned brown by the sun, and the weathering of his skin emphasized the lines in his face and made him look more like a startled eagle than ever. His expression was cold, but his eyes held a message that made Claudius's heart quicken.

'Welcome, General.' He waved a hand towards a pair of couches set by the wall of the tent. 'You must be tired. Bring the general some wine.'

They sat in silence for several moments, each man taking the measure of the other. They were related, distantly, and Plautius had quietly supported Claudius through the years of trial under Caligula. In the interim he had excelled in his governorship of troublesome Pannonia. His reward was command of the invasion of Britain and an honoured place in history.

'Are the barbarians defeated?' Claudius already knew the answer, but some questions had to be asked.

Plautius shook his head. 'Not yet, Caesar. But I can assure you victory will not be long delayed.'

'Yet you are here, on the eve of battle, a battle which could be decisive – the outcome of which could be . . . fatal.' To both of us. He didn't say it. Didn't need to. 'Are you so confident?'

Plautius nodded, not arrogant – he was too astute for that – but assured. 'My forces are disposed. My orders are given. My men are in good hands. And my enemy's doom is certain. So, yes, I am confident. By the time you reach the river the battle will be won and, if the gods will it, I will present you with this Caratacus's head.'

'And it will be a great victory?'

'A victory worthy of the Army of Claudius.'

'And after?'

Plautius stared. He was giving this man the triumph which would place him beside Julius Caesar in the ranks of Roman heroes and still he wanted more? Yes, he thought, of course he wanted more. The more battles won, the more the glory, and the more glory, the more secure his position. And every Emperor craved security above all things.

'Afterwards, you will lead us to more victories and your valour will rank above any Roman's since Romulus made Rome the greatest city the world has ever known.'

'Then a toast.' Claudius raised his golden goblet. 'To victory.'

'To victory.'

Victory was far from Rufus's mind. The only thing that concerned him, as he steered Bersheba through the darkness towards the encamped enemy, was survival. Each of Frontinus's centuries was guided across the broken country north of the river by one of Adminius's bands of Cantiaci warriors. The prefect was understandably wary of his new British allies, but the column made steady progress through the night and they halted two hours before dawn in a forest a mile from the crossing point. Frontinus called

Rufus forward to a small clearing where his officers gathered for a conference at which Adminius did most of the talking. The Batavians created a tent wall around the clearing to mask the torches that lit the forest floor where the Cantiaci king used his sword to sketch out the enemy positions among the leaves.

'Caratacus is here, in the centre.' He circled a low mound close to the line of the river. 'His forces are stretched to the east and west of his position, from the Atrebates and the Regni here at the farthest point downstream, to the Dobunni farthest upstream, here, less than two miles from us. I have selected a defensive position for you at this point,' he jabbed with the sword, 'where a line of cliffs runs down towards the river. There is a gap about three hundred paces wide. I was told this was the ground you would need.'

Frontinus nodded. He knew that if Adminius had chosen the wrong position they would all be dead before morning. 'It will do.'

'The cliffs can be climbed, but only with difficulty. Any attempt to flank you will take more time than Caratacus can afford.'

'And the enemy?' the Batavian demanded. 'He would be foolish not to patrol his flank, and nothing I have heard about this Caratacus tells me he is a fool.'

Adminius's eyes shone in the torchlight. 'Not Caratacus. His brother Togodumnus, who is as lazy as he is arrogant. He sulks in his hut because Scarach of the Durotriges stands in the place of honour at

Caratacus's right hand, while the Dobunni skulk like dogs waiting to be fed scraps from their master.' He laughed. 'He believes the only honours to be won tomorrow will be in the battle of the three bridges and that is where his attention is drawn. He cares nothing for flanks, only glory.'

'Then it will be the death of him,' Frontinus declared.

Adminius bared his teeth. 'Just so.'

The Batavian commander gave his orders in a firm, deliberate voice. A thousand men would be dispatched to the enemy camp, there to cause havoc among his cavalry lines and his supplies. 'Hit hard,' he urged. 'Hamstring the horses and kill everything you meet. Burn what you can, but don't get involved in a pitched battle. Hunt like wolves, in packs, but like a wolf be a shadow in the night, appearing, then vanishing, to appear again where they least expect it. Make them believe they have been attacked by a full legion, and when they gather forces to fight you, withdraw and return here, where we will have formed line.' He pointed to the short stroke Adminius had scored on the ground, the line between the cliffs and the river. 'They will be drawn after you, eager for vengeance, but instead of vengeance they will meet their deaths.' He turned to Adminius. 'How many of these Dobunni do you estimate will face us?'

The Cantiaci chief shrugged, as if such a calculation was beneath him, but one of his warriors spoke quietly in his ear. 'Perhaps fifteen thousand.'

Frontinus grinned at his officers and they smiled back. 'So, fifteen thousand against two thousand. Enough, even for my Batavians. Go now, and return before dawn. The watchword for tonight is Claudius and the reply is Victory.'

'Claudius and Victory,' the auxiliary commanders chorused in their thick German accents, and the words sent a shiver down Rufus's spine.

XXVIII

Four miles downstream from where the Batavians were forming their line and a mile beyond the left flank of Caratacus's position, Ballan's heart thundered so hard he wondered it didn't burst from his ribs. He was looking at an army of ghosts.

'Esus save us,' he whispered. His eyes told him he was seeing what he was seeing, but the impossibility of it overwhelmed his mind and the thin fabric of his sanity threatened to tear apart inside his head. Every instinct told him to run. To get away from this haunted place to somewhere, anywhere, he would be safe. Most men would have fled – the frightened shouts and the sound of horses charging through the riverside scrub told him his scouts already had – but he was Ballan. Ballan of a hundred battles. Ballan of a dozen secret missions. And some power within that

Ballan forced him to face his fears and stay. He closed his eyes and shook his head, but when he opened them again the only thing that had changed was that the ghost-soldiers were closer to the north bank. He could see now that the spirit-general leading them through the swirling vortexes of the mist wore a plumed helmet and was mounted upon a magnificent white horse. A cloak of scarlet covered his burnished armour. The pale horse pranced and high-stepped as if it was on parade, and, as the mist cleared for a fragmentary second, Ballan could see it was splashing through water that only just reached its fetlocks, water that could only be a few inches in depth, but he knew – *knew* – was a dozen feet deep at the very least. Behind the phantom general came his phantom legion, only their helmeted heads and the points of their throwing spears showing above the mist. Close-ranked, disciplined sections eighty men strong, each separated by a few feet and kept in position by a centurion. Slowly Ballan's brain came to terms with what he was witnessing. Surely it was only the setting that filled him with dread? Everything else was familiar, almost comfortingly so. He had watched the Romans for weeks now and the only thing different about these men was that they were doing the impossible. If anything, the ranks were a little tighter. They were marching so close together they were almost getting in each other's way.

His fear evaporated, the way the mist on the water would evaporate with the first rays of the morning sun, and that same mist drifted slightly once more, allowing him to see the little poles rising out of the water. The poles that showed the Roman legion where to march. The poles that marked the underwater bridge they had constructed beneath the very noses of Caratacus's army. The singing – that was it! Each night the voices of a thousand men had masked the sound of construction. How had they managed to build a bridge below the water? He didn't know, but if anyone could do it, the Romans could. He shuddered as he realized the full implications of what he was seeing. This was a full legion, perhaps five thousand strong. Once they completed the crossing they would wheel and take Caratacus's army in the flank. He concentrated, trying to remember who had the left flank of the British force. Togodumnus was on the right, furthest upriver; Caratacus in the centre with his Catuvellauni and Trinovantes, the Iceni and Scarach's Durotriges. That meant it would be Epedos and the Atrebates, and Bodvoc and his Regni who faced the flank attack. Could they hold the fighting power of a full legion? Yes, if they had time to prepare for the attack. But not if they were caught by surprise. He hauled on his pony's reins and dug his heels into her flanks. He had seen enough. He galloped through the sand-blown scrub in the wake of his fleeing men. Caratacus must know.

It was thirty minutes before he was able to round up the rest of the scouts and gather them shamefaced on their blown horses. He didn't blame them for running. There were some things it was sensible to run from. He had seen exactly what they had and he'd been close to running himself. But there were also some things that had to be said.

'You think you ran from ghosts?' he sneered. 'You didn't. You ran from a few Romans – the same Romans you've been laughing at for the last four weeks because they couldn't find their cock under a blanket. Who's laughing now?' He flayed them one by one until he saw the expressions on their faces turn from shame and defeat to hate. All right, it wasn't the Romans they hated, but it would do. 'Those Romans you ran from are the doom of your army, understand that? The death of those sluts you call wives and the worm-ridden brats you call children. They'll spit your babies on their spears and laugh while they're doing it. But that doesn't matter. No, what matters is that if Caratacus doesn't know about them they'll defeat him. He'll die cursing my name, but that doesn't matter either. What matters is that Caratacus is the hope of Britain. Without Caratacus we'll all be slaves or we'll be dead. And that's why we're going to get through to him or die trying.' The heads came up then, and the hatred was replaced by pride and he loved them for it. 'Every minute we've sat here on these spavined wrecks, the Romans have been marching to cut us off from Caratacus. But if we ride as though Taranis is behind us and use every trick we know one of us might just make it. If one man gets through he will restore the honour of us all.' He saw that the ponies were almost fully recovered, and his words became brisk. 'We head north and then west. Once we're sure we're clear of their patrols we'll split into pairs. All Caratacus needs to know is that there's a Roman legion on his left flank. Understand? His left flank.' Eight heads nodded in unison. 'Ride!'

How long did he have? Two hours, maybe less, for the Romans to get into position to attack. Riding hard and taking a direct route it would take at least an hour to reach the British camp where Caratacus waited for the enemy, never suspecting that his carefully baited trap was about to turn into an ambush. But there was no question of taking the direct route. They would have to ride in a wide circle away from the river, and they would have to take risks.

But Ballan didn't have two hours, not even one. It was well done, he had to give them that; just what he should have expected of them. They came from a fold between two flat-topped hills. A thunder of hooves masked, until the last second, by the thunder of his own. A death scream he recognized with a sundered heart, followed in quick succession by a second, louder still, as lances wielded by troops who knew how to use them twisted and bit into the spines of the last two men of his little column.

'Turn and fight,' he yelled, not knowing how many of them there were. It didn't matter: the little British ponies could never outrun Roman stock. He and his scouts had survived this far by stealth. Now they would have to survive by their skill as warriors. But as soon as he hauled his pony round to face the enemy he knew no amount of skill would save them. There were twenty attackers, probably more. It was difficult to distinguish friend from foe as the mêlée surged and whirled around him, shouts and cries and the clash of iron echoing in the semi-darkness. A horse flashed past close on his left side and he recognized in the faint moonlight the livery of the Gaulish auxiliaries who had annihilated the foolish British attack on the Roman column.

Something twitched at the corner of his eye and he turned his pony instinctively to meet the cavalryman who had singled him out. He was coming at the charge, crouched down in the wooden saddle the Romans used. Everything about the way he rode said he was certain of an easy victory. Blond curls spilled out from beneath the sideplates of a pot-shaped helmet and Ballan could see the glint of eyes beneath the curved brim. His own gaze never deviated from the lance point. The weapon was held low and loose in the rider's right fist, but Ballan knew that when the iron tip swept up to rip his throat or blind him the grip would tighten and the arm tense to take the shock of the blow. He counted the seconds in his head, matched time to the strides of the galloping cavalry horse and calculated the closing speed of his pony. Now! The little mare danced right, taking them down the German's left flank, and he felt the wind as the killing blow swept over his left shoulder, the strike made awkward by the split-second change of course. As they passed, he attempted to bring his own spear across to rake the exposed flesh of the Roman's thigh or his mount's haunches, but the horse was gone in an instant and he was in the open again on the verge of the vicious little battle.

He circled, man and pony breathing hard. His scouts were hard-pressed. Another two were down, at least, and more wounded. He knew to return to the fight was death. But he still had his spear, and the long sword at his waist, and what was death to Ballan of the Iceni? A passing shock, a grunt of pain? Then the Otherworld. He laughed, a laugh of the pure joy of battle, and prepared to kick the pony forward.

'Ballan!' The shrill cry came from Cerda, the youngest of his scouts. A spear or a sword had scored the boy's forehead and his face was a mask of blood. He was using his pony's manoeuvrability to dodge a big trooper who was trying to finish the job. Well, there were worse ways to die than aiding a friend. He started to turn the pony. Cerda saw the movement and understood that his leader was about to ride to help him. 'No!' he called and his words came clear over the sound of the fighting. 'Our honour, lord. One man can restore our honour. Ride. We will hold them. We will buy you time. Ride, to Caratacus.'

Mentally, Ballan shook his head. No. He would not do it. He would not abandon these men he had ridden with and fought beside for so long. But, in the real world, he knew Cerda was right. Caratacus must be told. He whirled the pony and galloped towards the shelter of a nearby forest. Before the trees closed in around him he turned and looked back at the little drama being played out in the silver shadow-light of a broken moon. One of the big Roman horses smashed into the flank of Cerda's pony, pitching the boy to the ground. A spear shaft quivered as the point flashed down into the helpless body on the bloody meadow grass.

Of course, they hunted him. Hunted him and found him. The cavalrymen flushed the wood as if they were beaters flighting a covey of partridge, and this time the Gaulish troopers had been joined by the strange, green-clad archers he had noted guarding the flanks of the Roman legionary columns. He had gone less than a quarter of a mile when the arrow thudded into his back just below the left shoulder. It struck with enough force to knock the breath from him and he knew he was sore hit, perhaps even mortally. He never understood how he stayed in the saddle, but somehow he did, just long enough to force his pony through a deep thicket that let him roll from its back as the animal galloped on. He hit the ground with his right shoulder and his momentum carried him through the leaf-mould for a few feet. Heart pounding, he lay motionless for less than a second before an unthinking instinct for survival made him scramble for the concealment of the dry watercourse that split the thicket. The shaft of the arrow was still protruding from his back and he closed his eyes and reached for it, fearful of what he would find – then froze. A horse's hooves padded by inches from his head. The low branches that concealed the rider also concealed him from his enemy. He allowed his hand to creep towards the dagger at his belt. If the horseman stopped, he would take him, whatever the risk. He held his breath and tensed, ready to make the leap, but the seconds passed and the beast continued placidly on its way.

He allowed himself to breathe, a function that caused a streak of raw pain to split his back and chest. Tentatively he reached backwards for the arrow once more. If it was buried deep, he would have to leave it. If the wound was superficial he would haul it clear. The sweat stung his eyes and he felt a wave of nausea. He knew that if he pulled the arrow from his skin and it was buried deeper than he realized there was a chance he'd bleed to death. But it was a gamble he had to take. He gripped the shaft as firmly as he was able with his hand twisted awkwardly up his back and his body pushed forward to make the arrow more accessible. One, two . . . three. He almost fainted with relief. The arrowhead had been fired from relatively short range with enough force to pierce the tough, half-inch-thick leather of his outer tunic, but it had barely penetrated the mail shirt he had looted from a dead Roman auxiliary. Only the point had reached his skin and the wound was barely a scratch. The pain came from his ribs, where the missile had struck with the power of a charging bullock. He winced as another bolt of pain tore his chest. One rib was broken, maybe even two, but he would live with that. If he lived at all.

XXIX

A few miles upriver, Rufus stood beside Bersheba
close behind the centre of the Batavian force.
Frontinus had inspected the defensive line all the way
from the river to the place where the red cliffs rose,
giving quiet words of encouragement to his men and
directions to the two centurions and the clerk who
accompanied him. When he returned, Rufus could
see the frown of concentration on his face as his mind
went over every challenge the day would bring
and how he would meet it. Frontinus knew there
would be disaster as well as triumph, and chaos
amidst the carnage, for that was the way of battles.
But there would be a moment – there was always
a moment – when the unexpected, or perhaps a
combination of unexpecteds, would bring the crisis
that would win or lose the fight. Nothing he did,

no amount of preparation or thought, would prevent its happening and it was the way he, Frontinus, reacted that would swing the balance one way or the other. That was why he had placed Rufus where he was.

He explained: 'No matter how many pretty speeches I make, how brave I sound, or how much my men respect me, the only certainty is that at some point we will be outnumbered, perhaps by as many as ten to one. I must use every weapon, every stratagem at my disposal to offset that fact, and no matter what you or your friend Narcissus say, the elephant is a potential weapon. The barbarians fear her. Adminius confirmed it, and even if he had not, the reaction of his warriors would have convinced me. So I want you here, at my side, in the place of greatest danger. She may make no difference, probably will not, but I can't take the chance of losing any advantage she might give us when the lives of my soldiers may depend upon it.'

The wall of shields ahead of them was not yet an unbroken line. It was breached by four distinct gaps through which the survivors of the raid on Togodumnus's horse lines would retreat when they fled before the barbarian host Frontinus thought – hoped – would follow them. Only when the last man was within the ranks would the gaps close. Adminius had demanded that his warriors be allowed to accompany the Batavian raid and take their revenge upon those who had humiliated them and ravaged their lands, but Frontinus refused. When Adminius talked of vengeance the prefect heard plunder, and in any case he did not need one more complicating factor in an already complicated plan. Instead, he suggested the Cantiaci king take his men to the top of the cliffs and protect the Batavian flank. The rain finally stopped, and the night was pleasantly mild after the suffocating heat of the day, but still Rufus found himself shivering. He tried to disguise it, for it was evidence of the fear that made his belly feel on fire and his bladder as if it might burst.

Frontinus appeared at his side. 'Do not think you are the only man here who is afraid, Rufus. Look at them.' He gestured to the wall of chain-clad backs in front of them. 'Experience of war does not make it any less frightening. There are men here who have fought a dozen battles and shown dauntless bravery in each one. But a man's reservoir of courage is not bottomless, and when the enemy is screaming in their faces their first instinct will be to flee – just as yours will. But they will stand, because they are soldiers and because their fear of the enemy is less than the shame of letting down the man next to them. When the time comes, Rufus, I will stand next to you and you will not run.'

That was when the soldiers came.

They saw the flames first, downstream and set back from the river. Quite small and then growing, feeding off the thatch and wattle of whatever house or storage hut the Batavian raiding party had set afire, until they reached up into the night sky like so many fingers clawing for support. One, then two, five, a dozen and finally too many to count.

They were too far away to hear the screams of the crippled ponies, hamstrung by the pitiless blades of the auxiliaries so they could be of no further use to their masters. But Rufus knew it was happening, because he had heard Frontinus order it. He imagined the carnage and panic as the sinister shadows slipped furtively among the tethered beasts, hacking this way and that, leaping to escape the lashing hooves as the stricken animals thrashed and shuddered and choked to death on their tethers. The British would hear it, though, and would have seen the flames of the burning huts. By now they would already be in their battle positions along the river, waiting for the Romans to come. But the Romans had tricked them, and they would rush to take revenge. How many had Adminius estimated? Fifteen thousand? Against two thousand. Rufus slipped his short sword from its scabbard and tested the blade.

The flawless black of the night sky had faded to sullen pewter by the time the raiders returned. They came in small groups, and at the run, but there was no panic. Every man knew his allotted place in the line and made unswervingly for the gap closest to his position. Frontinus had forbidden any looting, but Rufus noticed that a few of the Batavians at least were carrying prizes and cheerfully displaying them to their comrades. A small leather bag containing some nameless treasure. A Samian-ware drinking bowl that must have been imported from Gaul. The severed head of a small girl dangling by her blonde hair. The flow of soldiers slowed from a rush to a trickle and finally the space Frontinus had cleared between the defenders and the riverside scrub was unnervingly empty. Two thousand men held their breath and waited.

It was just light enough to see now; a ghostly, shadow light that made the impending tragedy all the more intimate. The Batavians must have been among those furthest into the British positions when Taurinus was wounded. The centurion was a big man, made heavier by the mail shirt he wore, and he was still semi-conscious, although he had taken a spear thrust in his upper leg that had crippled him. Two of his comrades carried him, stumbling over the rough ground beneath his weight. A third came behind, his face and his sword towards the enemy, and he was screaming at them to hurry. At first it was a shadow among the trees and bushes, a solid dark line against a lighter background a few dozen paces beyond the Batavians. Then the shadow took form and solidified into running men who stuttered to a silent, disbelieving halt when they saw the Roman ranks before them. As Rufus watched, the line thickened and became a wall, with the sense of an immense mass pushing behind it, urging the reluctant vanguard forward. Three hundred paces separated the pursuing British warriors from the Roman line. Taurinus and his rescuers were a third of the way across the cleared ground when the Britons noticed them. With a savage cry, a group of around thirty warriors broke clear and sprinted towards the little quartet. Rufus saw what was happening; understood the inevitable outcome.

The auxiliary acting as rearguard screamed a warning and ran for his life past the trio he had been protecting. At first, the two men carrying the injured centurian were so exhausted by the physical effort that they didn't recognize the danger. Then Rufus saw them stop and look at each other. They knew what they were doing, understood what their decision meant to Taurinus. The very fact that they had risked their lives to stay with him was testament to the comradeship they felt. Yet there was a greater imperative: survival. They dropped their burden and ran. As he flopped to the ground, their friend was bewildered by the sudden change in his circumstances. He had been part of a unit – part of something more than a unit: a brotherhood. When the spear pierced his leg he had known, without doubt, that his comrades would bring him home. Now he was faint from lack of blood, disorientated by the shock of his wound and dumped among the filth and the sand. He opened his eyes and saw three retreating backs, closed them again. Where was he? Why had they left him? He reached out, tried to use his arms to force himself to his feet, but the strength he had always accepted as his right had deserted him. He lay back, trying to understand, but the waves of pain and exhaustion tossed him like some piece of ocean flotsam. Once more, he attempted to gather his thoughts; opened his eyes to see the roseate light of the dawn rising glorious above the trees. He had seen many such dawns. Dawns in far Germania, dawns in the sharp icy air of the Pannonian mountains; in the heat and dust of Spain. So many dawns. His mind picked him up and he ran among the woodlands of his youth, felt the sun on his back and lay down, waiting. She came then, as he always knew she would come. He couldn't remember her name, but she was the one everyone wanted, and now she was his. A shadow covered the sun and he waited to feel the softness of her body upon his. He smiled.

Rufus saw the soldiers drop the wounded man. Knew it was the only thing they could do. Hated them for it. The pack which had broken free from the British force soon realized they would never catch the three able-bodied auxiliaries. They slowed, and very deliberately approached the crumpled form abandoned in the dirt. He watched the swords rise and fall, rise and fall again, faster and more frenzied, wisps of moisture clouding the air around the blades. Above the compact mass of British warriors first one object was raised, then another. He tried not to think what they were, but his eyes wouldn't lie. An arm. Part of a leg. A head still encased in its helmet. A howl – more than a howl – a sound more animal than human rose from the British ranks, and Rufus realized they were not fighting an army; not fighting individuals. They were fighting a beast that craved Roman blood.

XXX

How Narcissus wished Verica would shut up. The more time he spent with these barbarian Britons the more he realized they liked nothing more than the sound of their own voices. The Atrebate prince was babbling about the deeds he would perform in the next few hours, the honour he would win and the kingdom that would at last be his. Claudius's freedman had long since stopped listening, so that Verica's voice had become a background drone, as meaningless as the steady clop of their horses' hooves or the dull clunk of armour carefully packed with cloth or grass to deaden the unmistakable sound that would alert an enemy a hundred paces away.

They were stationed behind Vespasian's headquarters in the centre of the column formed by the Second Augusta. Even though he had been aware of its construction, Narcissus had been hugely impressed by the submerged bridge the engineers had built under the cover of darkness and the sound of legionary marching songs. The plan was Plautius's, but Vespasian had implemented it and it was he who had added the cunning embellishment of the Batavian diversion, which would draw the attention of Caratacus and his warriors to the west in the crucial moments while the legion was converging on his un-suspecting eastern flank. Thus far Mars, the god of war, had smiled upon them. Manoeuvring five thou-sand infantry and an *ala* of cavalry across the miles of rough ground between the crossing point and the enemy would have been demanding enough in day-light; in darkness it should have been a general's worst nightmare. But Vespasian placed his trust in his chief of engineers and the man had not been found wanting. A score of pathfinders blazed a trail ahead of the column, tying white cloths to trees on each side of the route in imitation of the way the ingenious little poles had identified the position of the bridge beneath the dark waters of the river.

Only one incident had threatened the perfection of the operation. A cavalry patrol had ambushed a British scouting party close to the bridgehead, killing all but one of the riders. Vespasian had frowned when he heard of the man's escape even though the scout had been wounded and unhorsed. He dispatched another dozen cavalry troopers he couldn't spare to scour the woods with orders not to return without the Briton's head.

'What?' Something Verica had said had penetrated Narcissus's reflections.

'Epedos,' the young Atrebate repeated. 'I said that after I kill Epedos I will have his body flayed and hang his preserved skin on the wall of my palace at Calleva so that all men shall know the fate of a traitor.'

Narcissus smiled at the sublime arrogance of youth. What guarantee was there that the boy would survive the battle in which they would undoubtedly be enmeshed in a few hours' time? Verica was brave – it was one of his most appealing traits, along with his honesty – but brave to the point of foolhardiness. Where the fighting was hottest and the danger greatest, that was where Verica would be when the sun came up. The laurels he claimed to have won at the first river crossing were no idle boast. Sabinus had been genuinely impressed by the young man's courage. But that was in a rout. Today would be another matter. While the lines – British and Roman – held, and order prevailed, a soldier knew where he was and whom he could trust. But when one side or the other broke and friend and foe surged and fought and bled together, it was different. That was when no amount of skill could save the bravest warrior from an arrow in the back, the spear that came out of nowhere or the sword thrust that was meant for another man, but took your throat out by mistake. Still, it didn't do to dwell on such things. He decided a little flattery was in order.

'I am sure men will sing of your deeds for a hundred years, Lord Verica,' he said smoothly. 'Emperor Claudius has been informed of your valour and commends it. When your kingdom is restored he has let it be known that no other hand but his will be allowed to place the crown upon your noble head.'

Verica's chin came up and Narcissus knew he was imagining the weight of the gold upon his brow. 'And when shall I be crowned?' the young Briton asked, his voice taking on a new authority.

Narcissus thought for a few seconds. 'First we must defeat this Caratacus. Once that has been achieved, Caesar is determined to take the king's capital at Camulodunum, where he will declare Britain a province with the full protection of Rome.' And where he will begin the process of recouping his investment, he thought but did not say. Verica didn't need to know quite yet the price he was going to have to pay for the return of his kingdom. They rode along in blessed silence for a few minutes, following the indistinct shapes of the riders ahead. It had been almost two hours since they had crossed the river and Narcissus calculated the Roman column must be close to its destination.

'I wonder how Rufus and his elephant fare?'

The Greek stared at Verica in surprise. It was most unlike the Briton to give a thought for anyone but himself. Had he become close to the slave? That could be awkward – or useful.

'Do not concern yourself. Rufus is a seasoned campaigner and a member of the Emperor's Praetorian

Guard. In any case, the Batavians will look after him. Frontinus is a good commander. The best.' Narcissus shifted painfully in the saddle. When he got back to Rome, he vowed, he would never sit on a horse again, not for all the treasures in the temple of Mars Ultor. The ground beneath them was rising now and the low scrub was replaced by the twisted shapes of a few scattered trees.

'Halt. Halt. Halt.' The hissed commands ran down the column, and they reined their horses to a stop. The headquarters group in front of them moved out of the line and the clerks and aides began to lay out the panoply of command. 'Officers to the centre.'

There followed a shuffle of jogging figures as the commanders of the legion's cohorts converged on Vespasian. Narcissus watched them form a little group around the legate. It took less than a minute to pass on his orders. Moments later the Greek sensed a mass movement all around as the legionaries deployed into battle formation. He cast his mind back to the map on the wall of Plautius's gilded pavilion. It meant the tribes of the British left flank were on the far side of the hill; an extended line stretching a mile up the riverbank to the point where Caratacus would have positioned himself in the centre of his army opposite the three bridges that were the bait in the Roman trap. Beyond the Catuvellauni leader, another mile of warriors waited in the darkness for Plautius's attack, and beyond them were Frontinus and his Batavians.

Caratacus would undoubtedly have ordered flank guards to patrol beyond the limit of his formations, but the vanguard of the Second Augusta had encountered none. Narcissus allowed himself a small smile of satisfaction. Vespasian had been unsure that his stratagem would succeed, but the pieces were falling into place just as he had predicted.

Verica raised a hand. 'I must join my men. We fight alongside the Gauls today. If . . .'

Narcissus smiled and patted him on the shoulder in a way that was almost fatherly. 'No ifs. We will meet again tonight and you will be a king once more.'

Verica nodded solemnly and rode off into the darkness. The Greek watched him until he disappeared before giving a deep sigh. Shaking his head, he dismounted and led his horse towards Vespasian's command post, where an aide took the animal's reins and ushered him forward.

'So, spy, it seems your trickery has not failed us.'

It was still too dark to make out the general's features, but Narcissus could imagine the brutish face with its etched lines and permanent frown, the gimlet eyes boring into him. He knew Vespasian didn't like him, but was neither daunted nor offended by it. He had Claudius's protection, and, besides, even straightforward, upright and honourable soldiers like the general were sometimes required to dirty their hands in the foul waters of the clandestine world. It might be distasteful, but it saved lives.

'I never doubted it, General.' Not quite true, but it

struck the right note somewhere between arrogance and outright disrespect. He could almost feel the legate's hackles rise. There was a long silence and the sound of shuffling feet as the headquarters staff waited for the inevitable reaction to this insubordination. Instead, Narcissus was surprised when a solid figure detached itself from the group and took him by the arm.

'Come.' Vespasian led the way upwards through the trees towards the barren crest of the hill. When they were just short of it, the Roman general surprised him once more by removing his helmet, dropping to the ground and crawling forward on his stomach. Vespasian must have sensed his reaction, because he turned and when he whispered there was a smile in his voice. 'An old soldier, but a soldier still, Master Narcissus. I would not be the first general to lose a battle because he was so anxious to see his enemy he allowed himself to be silhouetted against the skyline. On your knees, man.'

Narcissus obeyed and a few seconds later they lay on the hilltop, peering into the darkness. At first it was just that, a black curtain that cloaked everything, but very slowly his eyes adjusted and he was able to pick out the line where solid land met the night sky, a few almost invisible stars hanging motionless in the murk above, and, to his left, a very faint strip of dull silver that he realized must be the river. Somewhere out there in the darkness, if the gods had been kind and the British patrols were asleep, the Batavians would be ready to strike. But where were they?

Narcissus hardly dared breathe as the minutes passed with infuriating slowness.

'There!' A sharp-eyed young aide saw it first, just a tiny pinprick of light that quickly flared into something bigger, then another, and another. It was the signal Vespasian had been waiting for. He wriggled backwards down the slope until he was certain he wouldn't be seen, then stood up as the others followed suit. Replacing his helmet with exaggerated ceremony, he turned to the senior tribune.

'Order the men forward. And remember, every man beyond this ridge is an enemy of Rome and will be treated accordingly.'

Narcissus stood at the general's shoulder as the long lines of Roman soldiers moved past them and disappeared over the brow of the hill. There was no urgency in the movement, only discipline and precision; the same discipline and precision that had carried these men and their forebears to the ends of the earth and defeated every foe; the discipline and precision that had won Rome the greatest Empire the world had ever seen.

He felt a hand on his shoulder and Vespasian's strong voice in his ear.

'You have shown you can scheme, spy. Now we will see if you can fight.'

XXXI

'Lord?' Caratacus heard the concern in his shield-
bearer's voice and suppressed a small stirring of
irritation.

'What is it?' He didn't turn his head. He had been
concentrating on the river, attempting to interpret the
sounds from the bridges and gauge the extent of the
Roman progress. It was a bad moment to disturb him
and he knew his voice was brusque.

'Lord,' the lad was pleading. 'Look. To the west.'

Now he turned, and when he followed the pointing
finger he was frozen by a momentary shiver of panic.
At least a dozen huts, probably more, were blazing in
the Dobunni encampment. It was impossible. There
must have been some kind of accident. He shook his
head. Don't be a fool. This is no accident. Antedios
was right, and he had underestimated the enemy. He

willed himself to be calm. Fear was contagious. The chiefs around him must believe this was something he had prepared for.

'Send a runner to Togodumnus,' he ordered, deliberately keeping his voice steady. 'Tell him I must know what is happening. Every detail of it.'

A messenger trotted off into the darkness, but he had only been gone for a few minutes when one of Togodumnus's Dobunni warriors appeared, gasping for breath.

'My . . . my . . .'

'Wait,' Caratacus admonished him gently. 'The knowledge you carry is only of use if I can understand what you are saying. Recover your wind and be calm.'

The warrior nodded and stood sucking in air for a few moments. When he was ready, he straightened and looked the king in the eye. 'My lord Togodumnus bids you to send reinforcements immediately. The Dobunni have been attacked by a force two legions strong.' A murmur of dismay ran around the men surrounding him and Caratacus realized he should have received the message in private. But it was too late now. He raised a hand for silence and told the messenger to continue.

'We are hard-pressed, but holding them. My lord is of the opinion that with the Iceni and the Durotriges under his command he will be able to crush the Romans and slaughter them to the last man.'

Caratacus felt Scarach stiffen at his side and put out a hand to calm him. Whatever he decided there was little chance the Durotrige war leader would agree to serve under Togodumnus. 'And what does your lord believe we should use to fight the Romans here, where the main attack will come, when he has taken half my forces?'

The man chewed his lip. What he was about to say was not the sort of thing messengers wanted to tell kings, particularly not kings with Caratacus's reputation. 'My . . . my lord Togodumnus is of the opinion that the Dobunni are facing the main attack. He says . . . believes . . . you have allowed yourself to be tricked by the Romans and urges you to join him against them and leave a small force here to hold the diversionary attack from the bridges.'

Scarach growled, but Caratacus ignored him. He walked forward to the edge of the hill and stared into the darkness. What was happening out there? He waited, feeling the pressure from the men behind him who wanted an instant decision, but knowing he must not react to it. Every instinct told him the main attack would come across the bridges. It was the Roman way. An assault in overwhelming strength that would grind the enemy into dust. Togodumnus must be wrong. It was impossible for the Romans to have crossed the river upstream with so many men. There wasn't a ford for ten miles and Ballan's riders had searched the whole length of the bank. For a moment his thoughts turned to the Iceni scout. Surely he should have returned by now. No. No time for that. He made his decision.

'Tell your lord he must hold the Romans in place. Tell him I do not wish him to attack them, but to find a defensive position where he can protect my flank and hold it. Nuada?' He called the Druid across. 'You will accompany this man to the king of the Dobunni, see for yourself the strength of the enemy and his dispositions so that I may assess the threat, and return immediately you are certain of the position.' He nodded in dismissal. Nuada didn't like it, but what could he do? He needed to know what was happening, not what Togodumnus's overactive imagination was telling him. He could see the messenger was reluctant to go and he didn't blame him. Togodumnus was unlikely to take the reply well. He turned back to the assembled chiefs of the Catuvellauni, the Iceni, the Trinovantes and the Durotriges.

'The main attack will come here, and when it comes we will choke the river with Roman corpses. The gods will it.' The final four words echoed in his head and in the same instant his heart soared when he heard a clap of thunder as the gods reaffirmed their will. It took a second before he realized the sound was not thunder. It was the clash of wood and leather and metal as two mighty walls of shields met with a force that shook the earth. And it came from downstream.

It was impossible. How had they crossed the river in the east? It didn't matter. All that mattered was that they were there. His army was caught between three Roman forces, any one of which might be strong enough to destroy him. The fine trap he had manufactured would become the graveyard of his warriors. His first instinct was to gather the bulk of his forces to meet the most obvious threat, from downstream, but he dashed the thought from his head. There was a greater danger, and it would come from across the river where he still sensed the bulk of the legionary force waited. His mind, which had been on the very brink of panic, cleared, and in extremity, he decided, there was an opportunity. Plautius had split his command. If – and it was an enormous if – he was given time to defeat the main thrust from the south, across the river, he could then attack each of the diversionary forces in turn. He undoubtedly still outnumbered his enemy and the deadly obstacles still lay submerged under the placid waters of the lagoon. It would be costly, bloody work and there would be many thousands of weeping widows by nightfall, but it was still possible to shatter the Romans, here, on the Tamesa.

But first he must buy himself time. Epedos and Bodvoc would have been surprised by the assault from downstream, but the very fact they were able to organize a defence line to meet the attack meant someone had reacted swiftly enough to ensure a crisis hadn't turned into a disaster. Still, they would be hard-pressed.

'Antedios? Take your Iceni and support the Atrebates and the Regni.' He was giving up his precious reserves, but it had to be done. He was conscious of a greater pressure from that direction than from upriver, where he felt certain Togodumnus had overestimated the threat. 'If it is your judgement that the Romans have been stopped you may return here to your positions, but I must have time to meet and destroy the main attack across the river. This is still the greatest danger. Do you understand?'

The Iceni king nodded. He was unused to being given orders like some beardless boy before his first battle, but he was aware of the gravity of the situation and had pledged his support for Caratacus. The sky was clearing now, heralding a sharp, crisp morning that reminded a man he must look to the crops that would see him through the winter. He had fought in more battles than he could remember, but his bones were creaking with age and his body was beginning to fail him. Would this be his last? With ponderous dignity he was helped on to the back of his pony, and he gave a final salute as he rode off at the head of his tribe.

At last, Caratacus could turn his attention to the river. It was light enough to see the far bank now, but the morning mist still blanketed any activity there or on the river itself. The only evidence was the sound of the bridge builders at work, and the frantic hammering and splashing told him they were close to completing their task. Every warrior on the hill listened intently. The hammering stopped and there was a momentary silence that was quickly replaced by a noise that sent a shiver through the defenders. A sharp, rhythmic rattling as thousands of feet shod in hobnailed sandals marched in step over the three wooden crossings.

The sun broke clear above the eastern horizon and the mist burned off the river as if it had never existed.

Caratacus felt his warriors tense all around him; a mass tightening of muscles, thousands of fists firming their grip on sword or spear, the shuffling of feet as warriors readied themselves to fall upon the enemy. The enemy. He saw them arrayed below him and he found himself breathing hard as if he had just tackled some strenuous physical task. His heart beat faster and his mind raced. Calm, he told himself. Stay calm. Of all men here, you and only you have the will to prevail.

They frightened him. Of course they frightened him; he would be a fool if they didn't. He had seen them from afar with Ballan as well as when he had disguised himself as a cavalry trooper to infiltrate the baggage train. But this was the first time he had witnessed them in full battle order. When he was a child, he had once found a giant insect, a long sinuous thing with a body made up of many parts and countless legs on either flank. It didn't walk so much as ripple across the ground. The legions reminded him of it. The men, and the sections, and the centuries and the cohorts, were the body parts, each a separate entity, but creating a single unit which moved as one. Their armour glinted in the sun as they marched, just as the armoured carapace of the insect had gleamed as it flowed from place to place between the stones. The monstrous thing had been a bright, sulphurous orange, but the predominant colour in the monster that was a Roman legion was red. The cloaks and the vestments of the officers were a uniform scarlet, but the tunics of the rank-and-file troops varied according to their length of service and the conditions they had served in. Some were sun-bleached to a pale pink, others so dark they could almost be called brown, and in between was every colour of that spectrum.

A rush of air heralded the arrival of the first of the catapult-launched missiles he knew would flay the British line all day. But they must be ignored. If the gods wanted him, they only had to take him.

Plautius had ranged a single legion as if they were on parade at the far end of each bridge, and that convinced Caratacus he had been right to leave Togodumnus to cope alone. Three legions to his front, another on his left flank where Antedios should by now have reinforced the battle line of the Atrebates and the Regni. That meant Togodumnus must be facing a relatively small force of auxiliaries. It was the vanguard of each legion who now thundered across the bridges. Caratacus knew these would be crack troops. The heavy infantry. He watched them advance, short, squat men heavily burdened by their weapons and armour, but running as easily as if they were naked. They were close, perhaps twenty paces from the end of the bridges, when they began to fall. An officer, a centurion, at the very point of the centre column, spun and dropped from the bridge to disappear soundlessly and instantly into the swirling waters of the river. Another fell, jerking convulsively, and the British leader watched in admiration as the legionary deliberately rolled over the side – to certain death – so as not to impede his comrades. What mark of men these were, he thought; an enemy worthy of any king.

He turned his attention to the near bank where the slingers, spearmen and archers he had placed sweated to kill as many of the charging men as they could before they were overwhelmed. They had orders not to get into a fight, but to retire to the battle line along cunningly sited paths to a position at the base of the hill where they could kill and kill again. Not all would escape. A few would stay to cover the retreat of the others. The Romans were not the only people who knew the meaning of sacrifice.

The first legionaries leapt from the end of the bridges into the shallows and the Britons on the bank launched their final few missiles as the enemy floundered knee deep in the water. But as one fell he was replaced by two more and two more still, and at last the red-clad figures reached the shore. They spread out, forming a perimeter, just short of the swamp he had turned into a death-laced lagoon. He believed he detected confusion among them, and his heart soared. Let them come. Let their pathetic diversions smash themselves against the rocks of his champions. He had them now.

A shout from behind distracted him. He turned to see Scarach, white-faced, listening to a bear-like man who knelt before him. Ballan, but a Ballan worn thin by whatever horrors he had experienced in the last few hours. The Iceni scout's clothing was torn and mud-stained and his face was so swollen as to be almost unrecognizable.

Ballan saw him, and raised himself to his feet, reeling with exhaustion. 'Lord,' he croaked from a throat serrated by thirst. 'You must reinforce Lord Bodvoc.'

Caratacus stared at him. He trusted Ballan more than any other man he had ever met, but the scout's mind must have been unhinged by his ordeal. 'I have already sent your Iceni compatriots to support Lord Bodvoc and Lord Epedos. Surely twenty thousand men can hold a single legion?'

He turned away. He had no time to spare for conversation with fools, even if the fool was Ballan.

'Not twenty thousand,' the Iceni whispered, and Caratacus froze. 'No more than ten. King Epedos and the Atrebates vanished in the night. Antedios, my king, is dead. Bodvoc fights alone.'

XXXII

Rufus was puzzled. He was still alive. They were all still alive.

The British force on the far side of the western battle-ground dwarfed the thin line of auxiliaries. One all-out charge was surely all it should have taken to sweep the Batavians aside, yet they had made only three half-hearted attacks before withdrawing to the far side of the clearing. Occasionally, one of their champions would emerge to shout insults and a challenge at one of the Roman officers, but the auxiliaries only jeered at their antics. The high tide of the barbarian attack was visible in the scattering of crumpled bodies just in front of Frontinus's shield wall, the harvest of Batavian throwing spears, but they were only a tiny fraction of the losses the Britons could have afforded to ensure a quick victory.

'Why don't they come?' he asked Frontinus.

The Batavian shrugged, unmoved as he had been when the British attacks had splintered on the Roman spears. 'Perhaps they are afraid of Bersheba?'

'That would be like Bersheba being afraid of a rabbit.'

Frontinus grinned. 'Then I think they lack a leader. By now they will know they are attacked on three sides.' He had informed Rufus of Plautius's battle plan once he was certain the Second's crossing would be complete. 'They will be nervous. If two forces have crossed the river by stealth, why not three? Even now an army could be cutting off their retreat and ensuring their annihilation. They are brave, but their women and children are in the camps yonder, and even a brave man will look to his family when all hope of victory is gone.'

His words made Rufus think of Gaius, back with the Roman baggage train. Was he wondering where his father had gone, or was he too young to understand? Whatever the answer he wished he was with his son now.

'Commander!' The warning shout came from one of the auxiliaries in the front rank. Frontinus marched over to him and looked to the far side of the field, where a horseman in a silvery grey robe rode at the side of a British chariot, the first they'd seen that day. The man standing beside the chariot driver wore the glittering symbols of his rank, heavy golden torcs which ringed his neck and arms. His green cloak was pushed back from his shoulders, but otherwise he was naked to the waist, and even from three hundred paces Rufus could see he was powerfully built.

'There is your leader,' Frontinus shouted back to him.

Nuada had finally tracked Togodumnus down to his hut in the centre of the Dobunni encampment. It had been evident as soon as the Druid set eyes on the tiny Roman force that Caratacus's brother had exaggerated the danger, and equally evident that Caratacus would not have ordered Togodumnus merely to hold his line if he'd known the paucity of the Roman forces. The sub-chiefs of the Dobunni were unable to meet his eyes when he demanded to know where Togodumnus was, but he'd soon discovered the king had retired, sulking, to his hut when he'd heard of his brother's refusal to support him. He could have used subtler methods to stir him from his torpor – Togodumnus was a king, after all – but Nuada was a Druid, and a Druid of little patience. It hadn't been difficult. A man who has been brought up in the shadow of priests will be for ever susceptible to their magic. The knowledge that his private parts would turn black and fall from his body if he remained where he was soon restored Togodumnus's courage, if not his spirit.

But now that he was back with his army, it seemed he was having another change of heart. Nuada reined in his pony in the centre of the Dobunni line and Togodumnus told his charioteer to halt. He stared towards the Batavian shield wall.

'Caratacus ordered me to hold the Romans, not to attack them. Am I to disobey his orders?'

Nuada smiled through gritted teeth. Worm, he thought, it will be the first time you have obeyed them, and the last. But when he spoke it was with the silken voice of reason. 'Your brother was unaware of the true circumstances, Lord Togodumnus. The two legions which attacked you have evidently retreated across the river in fear of your vengeance, and left this paltry force of mercenaries as a sacrifice to appease your wrath.' He waved a disdainful hand at the Roman line, which looked pathetically thin and weak when compared to the Dobunni host facing them. 'Lord Caratacus would squash them like a flea, and he would expect a mighty champion like his brother to do the same.'

Togodumnus stared across the gap towards the Romans. The defeat at the first river line – despite his protestations to the contrary, he was forced to admit it had been a defeat – had left him nervous of the power of the legions. Yes, there were comparatively few of the lightly armed auxiliaries, but he had seen them fight and had learned to fear them. There had been reports of movement in the trees along the clifftops to the Roman left that he didn't like. He turned to Nuada, who had dismounted from his pony. 'I understand your concern, Nuada, and I share it, but in all honour I cannot disobey my brother's orders without a counter-order or . . .' he gave a smile that made the Druid's hackles rise like a brindle hound's, 'a sign from the gods.'

Nuada stared at him for a moment, not hiding his contempt. He looked to the skies, hoping a convenient cloud would cover the sun, but the heavens were a dome of perfect blue. Not even a solitary hawk to claim as a messenger.

'I—' He had just opened his mouth to reason with the fool, when a gigantic, impossibly loud roar shook the trees and shattered the silence. He felt his heart swell and said a swift prayer of thanks. As he turned in triumph towards the Roman lines he had a glimpse of Togodumnus's face, ivory white. Why had he not noticed it earlier? Of course, it was almost perfectly camouflaged against the grey stone at the base of the cliffs.

He raised his bear claw and pointed it towards Bersheba, the Emperor's elephant.

'There!' he roared, so all could hear it, even those at the furthest wings of the Dobunni attack. 'There is your sign. Kill the beast and the gods will wash these accursed invaders from our land and hurl them into the sea. Kill the beast and free this land of Britain. Kill the beast and ensure a hundred years of peace.' More quietly, but in a tone even more commanding, he said, 'There, Lord Togodumnus, is your honour and your fame. Kill the beast and none will dare say the name of Caratacus in your hearing again.'

Togodumnus stared back at him, his eyes bright with . . . what? Fear? No, the opposite. The Dobunni king's thin lips drew back from his teeth in a feral snarl and he tapped his charioteer on the right shoulder.

'Attack!' His scream rent the air and was taken up by hundreds, thousands, all along the line. The Dobunni multitude broke into a run as one man and fell on the Batavian line like a pack of howling wolves.

The day was still young when that first terrible assault came; by the time it had been repeated more times than he could count Rufus felt like an old man. He wasn't alone. Frontinus had the lined face of an ancient to match the premature grey of his hair and a haunted look that was shared by all the survivors of his dwindling, parch-mouthed band of heroes. A line that had started the day four men deep was worn down to a single thin strand. The dead and the wounded had been hauled clear and lay together with nothing to distinguish one from the other but the occasional shudder or moan. Those injured still able to walk wandered among them handing out the last of the dwindling water supply to the ones most likely to survive, but no one else raised a hand to aid them. They were saving what was left of their strength to meet the next charge.

Rufus had watched the Britons come from his place beside Bersheba, his guts a twisted ball of fear and his feet telling him to run. At first only the elephant's calming presence had given him the courage to stand, but as wave upon wave of attackers surged and broke against the Batavian shields his fear was replaced by despair – and with despair came a different kind of courage. The courage of the damned.

Three times he had stepped forward to take his place in the line as men went down. He had picked up a discarded spear and forced himself between two of the Batavians in the second rank and jabbed the point between a pair of auxiliary helmets in front of him at moustached, sweat-slicked barbarian faces that came and went, screamed and snarled, bled and died. As he fought for his life he had discovered a curious calm born of close proximity to the men beside and in front of him. Mail-clad shoulders pushed against his on either side; from behind, a shield forced him forward so that he was in physical contact with the auxiliary in front and adding his strength to the frontline defender's own. He had no shield to protect him, but when one of the long barbarian spears threatened, the man at his side would nudge his own shield forward to take the blow. Comradeship, was that it? No, what he was feeling was more than comradeship. It was brotherhood. His battle was limited to that narrow corridor of half a dozen friends and the enemy who faced them from between the two polished iron helmets that limited his vision. His nostrils were filled with the acrid smell of fear, and he knew that it was his own. But there was also sweat, the bitter metallic stink from the sparks that flew when two iron blades met in a certain way, and above it all the now familiar scent of butchered carcass and torn bowels. He wondered how any man in the line was able to hear an order, if orders came at all. The soldier's aural world was one of grunts and unintelligible growls that rasped from dry, dust-filled throats; of fear-filled challenges in an unfamiliar language, and shrieks of mortal agony sung out against a background rhythm of shield against shield, sword against shield, and sword against flesh and muscle and bone. Of man against man.

Three times Frontinus had sent him back. 'Your place is beside the elephant, soldier,' the Batavian snarled on the third occasion. 'Your time will come, but disobey my order again and it will be my sword that kills you and not a British spear.'

So he had retired to his position and witnessed the martyrdom of the Batavian cohorts. Men didn't die from a single wound. The mail that covered their torsos and the protective helmets they wore meant it was difficult for the Britons to inflict a mortal blow from beyond the shield. Instead they stood beside their comrades until they had taken a dozen cuts and dropped to the ground from exhaustion or loss of blood, then crawled clear to die without complaint among the bodies of friends who had already fallen. For every Batavian casualty the Britons suffered tenfold. With each successive charge, the mound of dead and dying in front of the Roman line grew higher and hampered the surviving attackers' progress. It was only Nuada's exhortations and faith in their gods that kept them coming forward. Togodumnus used his warriors like a giant club, battering again and again against the thin metal sheet that was the Batavian defence, and he raged and screamed his frustration as his men died in vain and the sheet bent and buckled, but did not tear. But there came a point as the sun reached its mid-point when not even the gods or Togodumnus's rage could make the British champions charge again. They must rest.

A breathless hush fell over the battlefield, and where there had only been the endless clash of iron against iron and the agonized screams of men suffering and dying, Rufus could hear the sound of birdsong. It seemed inappropriate, unfair. While they had been trapped in this gore-slick enclave of carnage, life continued around and above them unnoticed. It made him want to weep. One of the auxiliaries came to his side and offered him a drink of precious water from an almost empty goatskin. He reached for it, but dropped his hand and gave the man a tired smile.

'No,' he croaked. 'I'm not thirsty.' The truth was that his tongue was cloven to the roof of his mouth as if it were set there in mortar. But he would not drink when better men were thirstier still. He waved towards the line of exhausted defenders.

Frontinus staggered up to them. The Batavian commander had lost his helmet and his face was coated with dust, making him look as if he were already long dead. 'It is over, I think,' he confessed. 'If they have the spirit for just one more charge, I believe we are done.' His voice was cracked and broken, but thick with pride. 'Only Vespasian can save us, and I fear his troubles are as great as our own or he would be here by now. Take to your elephant's back. If time is to be our saviour, then it may be that you can buy us a little more of it before . . .' His voice tailed off and he nodded before limping back to be with his surviving auxiliaries.

As Rufus watched him go he absently rubbed Bersheba's forehead where she liked to be scratched, and the elephant grunted in appreciation. Her trunk reached out and she sniffed his tunic, searching for the scent of the little pink apples she loved, but he had none to give her. 'I am sorry, Bersheba, sorry for everything. I should never have brought you to this barbarian land and this dreadful place. You deserved better.' He looked into her intelligent brown eyes and saw that, despite everything, she still trusted him. He bent to untie the ropes that held her. 'When this is over you will never again want for an apple or sleep without a roof over your head,' he promised, giving her the command to kneel. 'But first, we have one last battle to fight.' In a single movement he leapt on to her back and manoeuvred her behind the centre of the Batavian position.

On the far side of the clearing Nuada urged the exhausted Dobunni warriors to a last effort. He had watched in frustration and fury as Togodumnus launched his forces in one futile bull-headed charge after another, allowing the Romans to harvest his men the way a scythe harvests a field of corn. Now he drew Togodumnus to one side. Caratacus's brother had the look of a man caught in a nightmare. His eyes flickered as if he were seeking an avenue of escape, but they never rested in one place long enough for him to identify it. If he didn't win this battle, he knew he was finished. If his brother didn't kill him, the Dobunni survivors would.

'You have one opportunity,' Nuada hissed, gripping the king by his cloak where a large golden brooch held it closed at his neck. 'Do you understand me? One opportunity. Your warriors will follow you, but only if you lead them. This is what you must do.'

XXXIII

Caratacus's brain felt as if it were about to explode. How could one man cope with so many different problems? How could a single mind deal with the myriad divergent dilemmas created by an army on the brink of defeat? Had he underestimated the threat to his right flank, from where Nuada had failed to return with word of Togodumnus's position? He had been betrayed by Epedos, that was clear, but who else was about to betray him? He had been certain the left flank could be held – now he was certain Bodvoc would be overwhelmed unless he was given aid. He tried to feel the ebb and flow of the battle around him, but there was only chaos. His people were dying and he was helpless.

'Lord?' Ballan's voice pierced his despair. 'Lord, you must act. There is still time.'

331

He blinked and his mind cleared. He saw Ballan staring at him. Saw the trust in the Iceni's eyes. Beyond him, Scarach stood with his enormous son, waiting. There was still a chance. One chance.

'Lord Scarach, take your Durotriges, the Trinovantes and the lesser tribes. Join with Bodvoc and smash the forces facing him. One attack. Every man you can gather on the way.' Scarach stared at him. He had been waiting all day for a fight and at last he was going to get one. And what a fight. But he understood the implications of Caratacus's order.

'That will leave you with—'

'I know. It is the only way.'

The Durotrige hesitated; did his honour require a refusal? He saw the certainty in Caratacus's eyes and knew it did not. He nodded and turned away, shouting his orders, but Caratacus had one final instruction. 'Scarach, you must control your forces. Don't let them off the leash. When it is done bring them back here. I promise I will leave you more Romans to kill.'

Scarach laughed. 'Don't worry. I'll keep my dogs to heel. We'll rip a few Roman faces off and slaughter so many of the bastards they won't stop running until they reach the ocean. I'll leave Bodvoc to clean up like the housewife he is and then come back and show you how it's done.'

With a last salute the king of the Durotriges ran from the hill and Caratacus again turned his attention to the legionaries pouring from the three narrow bridges. There were hundreds now, already linking the three bridgeheads into a single entity. Soon there would be thousands. His strategy had failed. There was no question of sucking Plautius into a trap, for the trap was already sprung. He must stop the three legions where they were and buy time for Scarach to defeat the force on his left.

He waved his war chiefs forward. It was now or never.

'Catuvellauni!' he roared. 'Attack. Kill them! Kill them all!'

The vast warrior host had been waiting in the lee of the hill since long before sunrise, tormented by and taking casualties from the catapult missiles landing in their midst. Caratacus had dispersed them as widely as he dared, but rocks the size of a bull's head bounced and skipped and ricocheted over the hard ground, turning men to red ruin in an instant, removing arms and legs and heads. But the British warriors knew nothing of their king's despair. They had not fought, so they did not consider defeat. They knew the Romans were on the other side of the slope with their backs to the river. The invaders. The enemy. The Catuvellauni were blood-crazed and battle-ready and they charged with all the unstoppable power of a mountain avalanche.

With a surge of pride, Caratacus watched them as they breasted the hilltop in one screaming mass and accelerated down the slope with their fearsome champions in the lead, leaping ahead, tall and powerful and showing their contempt for the enemy by their nakedness. He felt his heart lurch when they reached the bottom of the shallow slope and slowed in a gigantic splash of disturbed water, all their momentum lost in an instant. He had known it would happen. How could he not? The water-filled bog which had been such a key part of his strategy was now the bane of his own people. It was they who were forced to struggle through the glutinous, feet-deep mud to reach the enemy. Moving towards the river, they didn't have to fear the underwater obstacles he had placed to delay the Romans still further, but the slow-moving mass trapped in the swamp was a target even a blind legionary couldn't miss.

His eye was drawn to a warrior in the forefront of the British assault. The man was a giant and Caratacus recognized him as Arven, champion of one of the clans who made up the Catuvellauni. Even from a hundred paces away on the hilltop he could see the man's muscles bulge as he forced his way through the thigh-deep water. He looked magnificent. Immortal. Mighty Arven was screaming defiance at the Romans forming up by the river when his abdomen sprouted six feet of wood and metal. He stopped abruptly, before folding, almost gently, into the bog to be trampled deep into the mud by those following. He was the first of many. Caratacus saw water stained with blood indeed, but it was not the blood of his enemies.

He wanted to turn away, but he forced himself to watch the suffering of the Catuvellauni. This was his responsibility, no one else's. His plan, that now depended on ten thousand of Britain's finest warriors throwing themselves to their deaths against the spears and the swords of three Roman legions. Could he have done anything else? Did he expect anything else? The answer to both questions was no. How he wished it were otherwise. When he had sent the Durotriges to aid Bodvoc, he had known the only way to slow the main attack would be with the flesh and bone of his own people. He felt a twitch in his cheek, just below his left eye, and gritted his teeth. He would not weep.

Something had changed, he realized. When the fighting began he had been surrounded by his aides and his under-chiefs and those who wished to supplant them in the hierarchy of the tribe; each more eager than the one before to give him advice or offer unlikely support. Now he found himself alone in the centre of a ring of men who looked at him with either fear or compassion, as if he were suffering from some contagious disease. Even his personal bodyguard kept a respectful distance.

He knew what it was. They could scent defeat. He came to a decision.

'Ballan.' The squat Iceni scuttled to his side. 'You have eaten and rested?'

Ballan nodded. Caratacus knew it was a lie, but exhaustion and hunger were minor privations on this

335

day of days. He dropped his voice. 'I wish you to return to the encampment and gather the women and the children, the sick and the old, and furnish them with enough supplies to reach Scarach's fortress at Mai-den.' Ballan's eyes widened and he opened his mouth, but Caratacus silenced him with a shake of the head. 'Your scouts will provide an escort. The day may yet be won, or it may be lost. If we are victorious I will send a rider after you. If not . . .' He didn't have to complete the sentence. If not . . . it would not matter, because he would be dead.

Ballan knew better than to argue. He left without another word and Caratacus turned his attention once more to the bridges, fearful of what he would see. But an unfamiliar feeling caught his chest as his eyes roved over the battle below. Hope. The three landing areas between the river and the swamp were so crammed with legionaries they barely had room to swing their spear arms. All along the Roman line a huge press of British warriors was hacking and cutting in a bid to breach the wall of shields that protected the bridgeheads. The flow of Plautius's men over each bridge had slowed to a crawl and the far ends were crowded with units waiting their turn to cross. It was working. The sacrifice of the Catuvellauni was not in vain.

By now Bodvoc and Scarach would have destroyed the threat to the army's left. Soon he would recall the Durotriges and together they and the Catuvellauni would throw the Romans back into the river. He began to make his plans for the attack that would finish the Romans once and for all.

A wail of dismay broke his train of thought. As calmly as he could manage he walked to the rear of the hill, where he could look down upon the British encampments. He would have expected chaos where Ballan was organizing the army's followers for the journey to Mai-den, but this was different. Hundreds – no – *thousands* of men were streaming from the east through the huts and the horse lines, singly and in small groups, occasionally in larger, more disciplined units. He recognized the insignia of the Durotriges, the Regni and the Iceni among them. He knew what he was seeing. A retreating army. A defeated army.

He ordered up the leader of his bodyguard. 'Bring me someone who can tell me what has happened. I must know. Go now, and return quickly.' Was that urgency in his voice, or panic? He shook his head wearily. It didn't matter. He returned to the river side of the low hill and looked down to where the Catuvellauni were still fighting and dying. Still managing to pin the Romans in place against the river as he'd asked them to do. Should he withdraw them? Could he withdraw them?

'Lord?' The guard held a shaking figure by the arm, a young boy not yet out of his teens. The youth had lost his sword and shield, but was unwounded. It was very obvious he thought he was going to be killed. Caratacus gave a sign and the boy was released and fell to his knees, where he began to babble incomprehensibly. Caratacus laid a gentle hand on his shoulder. 'Enough. Take a deep breath and tell me what happened. What of King Scarach and King Bodvoc?'

The boy went quiet and his chest rose and fell as he did as he was ordered. When he had recovered sufficiently he looked up, his eyes still clouded with fear. 'King Bodvoc was holding the Romans when we reached him, lord, though he had lost many warriors and we were only just in time. Scarach of the Durotriges led us, and ordered an immediate attack, because the Romans were as hard-pressed as the Regni who faced them.'

'Your tribe?'

'The Parisii, lord,' the boy said, his voice shaking with pride. 'We were in the forefront of the fighting. Three times we charged, and three times they held. But their line buckled and was close to breaking. One more charge, Lord Scarach said, and he was right. One more charge and we would have sent them fleeing from the field and such slaughter we would have done, but . . .' His voice faded and his head dropped. Caratacus lifted his chin and looked into his eyes.

'I need to hear it all, lad. All.'

'When we were massing for the final attack a great force of cavalry and infantry smashed into our flank. Where they came from none knew, for it seemed every Roman was needed to hold what they had. But they came, and with such power they cut us almost in two, and as they came the general commanding the legion to our front ordered them to attack. They should not have had the strength.' The boy's voice was bewildered, as if he had been cheated in a game of touch rather than being part of a routed army.

'Yet they did,' Caratacus said gently. 'And you ran.' He could see it in his head. The Roman general had chosen his moment with the utmost precision. He had husbanded his forces as Bodvoc and Scarach flayed his front line, had probably been tempted to reinforce his men as they suffered and died, but had never given in to that temptation. That was a measure of the general he was. And at the moment the British believed he was beaten he had launched a flanking movement that had torn his attackers in two and, in the same instant, thrown everything he had into an all-out assault that had spread panic and dismay among the undisciplined warriors facing him.

And they ran.

It was over.

He didn't need to withdraw his Catuvellauni. Word of defeat, or the scent of it, had already reached them and they were conducting a fighting retreat back up the hill with the Romans growing bolder and more numerous on the north bank with every passing second. He reached for his sword and felt it, heavy and comfortable, in his hand. Not the toy ceremonial sword – some Roman would no doubt find that when the huts were looted and take it as a trophy – but his killing sword; the sword he had been itching to wield all day. But it was a commander's duty to command, not fight. And a commander's duty to die with his men when the dying needed to be done. Strange that, with everything lost, he felt clean and free for the first time today. Or perhaps not so strange.

He walked through the running men down the slope towards the Romans.

XXXIV

As Caratacus succumbed to the despair of defeat, a mile to his west the sullen mass of Britons confronting Frontinus had been motionless for so long that he dared to hope they had given up. It was Rufus who shouted a warning that told him what he had always known. They were coming again. The Batavian commander drew his sword, reminding himself to mend the new nicks that marred its razor edge, then remembering he probably wouldn't have to. He took a deep breath.

'Prepare to receive the enemy.'

His calm voice was echoed along the line by the few surviving officers. Three hundred shields were raised as one and three hundred swords came free of their scabbards in a ragged parody of the nerve-tingling song the two thousand had created earlier.

Rufus saw the British advance from high on Bersheba's back. It was obvious they were weary, and some were reluctant, the fire in their blood extinguished by the carnage they'd witnessed, allowing themselves to drift behind the main force of attackers. But there were still thousands of them and they knew how close they were to winning.

Frontinus had used the lull to send out foragers to collect what they could from the heaped British dead, and now the most able-bodied of the wounded were frantically straightening the metal points of throwing spears and handing them forward to their comrades in the line. The Britons were just beyond the mound of their fallen when the shape of the attack changed. A group of forty warriors, champions all, sprinted ahead of the main force and formed an unconscious imitation of the Roman wedges that had destroyed the last cohesion of the ambushers in the battle of the valley. Frontinus screamed a warning, but his men had no time to react. The arrowhead of charging warriors hit the pitifully thin Roman line like a battering ram and Rufus saw the exhausted Batavian defenders smashed aside, opening a gap that was an invitation to the thousands of warriors following behind.

'Rufus!' He heard Frontinus's shout, but he didn't need it. He was already urging Bersheba forward past the Batavian officer into the gap. He could feel the fear and the anger in the elephant and she flared her ears and raised her trunk and gave an almighty roar of fury that split the skies. The first Britons saw her

342

come and recoiled in terror before the enormous grey monster that was the stuff of their worst nightmares. But behind them came Nuada and Togodumnus, and neither was daunted by the elephant's power.

'Kill the beast,' Togodumnus screamed as he sped forward with a long spear in one hand and a sword in the other.

'Kill the beast.' Nuada echoed the cry, and by some trickery or piece of magic a flaming torch appeared in his hand. He thrust the brand into Bersheba's face and now it was the elephant who recoiled, squealing as she lifted her head to expose the loose skin of her throat to the point of Togodumnus's spear. The movement threw Rufus off balance and he felt himself being pitched over Bersheba's shoulder, but even as he fell he still had the presence of mind to draw the short sword at his belt. Every fibre of Togodumnus's being was centred on the elephant and he barely noticed the sprawling bundle that landed off to his side. With a cry of triumph, the Dobunni king dropped his sword and raised the spear in both hands to thrust the lethal, leaf-shaped point with all his strength into the soft flesh of Bersheba's neck.

To Togodumnus, it was the merest glint at the corner of his vision, but Nuada saw it come and he cried a warning that was a heartbeat too late. Rufus had launched his *gladius* overhand with the timing of an athlete and the sure eye of a warrior. It was one of the crude arena tricks Cupido had taught him, but it saved Bersheba's life. The needle-tipped iron took

Caratacus's brother in the left side of the chest, piercing flesh and bone and heart muscle. Togodumnus felt the breath knocked from his lungs in the same moment he screamed his victory cry. He was surprised when he found himself staring up at a pure blue sky; more surprised still when his mouth filled with liquid and he began to drown in his own blood. He cawed once, like a hungry crow, before he slipped into the eternal darkness of the Otherworld.

Rufus gripped the hilt of the sword in both hands and it came clear from Togodumnus's lifeless flesh with an obscene sucking sound. Their king was dead and the warriors of the Dobunni were stunned by the loss, but Bersheba was still the only thing holding the gap in the Roman line and Nuada the Druid screamed at them to avenge their leader. He advanced towards the elephant across the dead and dying of both sides, with the sinister bear claw held out before him as he chanted the incantations that would bring his god to his aid.

Rufus didn't know whether it was the power of the words or the sight of the man who had been within a second of sending him to a fiery death, but he felt himself suddenly gripped by a numbing paralysis. Bersheba shifted uneasily beside him. For a moment there was nothing on the battlefield but the three of them. No Dobunni warriors. No Batavian defenders. No heroes or cowards. No dead. No living. Just man, and beast, and the Druid. Nuada looked him square in the face and smiled as he saw his enemy quail.

344

The Druid's amber eyes, which reminded so many men of a stooping falcon, glittered with hatred, but, in a moment of revelation, Rufus looked into them and saw not a hawk but the memory of a saviour. He heard the earth-shaking roar of a male lion in his head and his hand automatically sought the worn charm at his neck. In that instant his strength returned and Nuada's spell was broken. The high priest felt the moment too and frowned in puzzlement.

'You have no hold over me, Druid,' Rufus cried in a voice distorted with contempt. 'Go back to the black pit you came from and take your dogs with you.'

In the same instant there was a blood-chilling howl from the left and a new army fell from the tree-cloaked heights there. Adminius and the Cantiaci had come to the battle. The traitor king had watched as the drama was fought out below him. More than once he had been tempted to leave the Romans to their doom, but always something had made him stay. Now he sensed victory and loot the way a soaring buzzard senses the stink of a rotting carcass.

The Dobunni saw them come and ran. With a final venomous curse at Rufus, Nuada ran with them.

Two miles downstream Caratacus waited at the foot of the low hill above the river and watched the disciplined lines of legionaries wading towards him through the flooded lagoon he had created. There was nothing to slow them but mud and the floating

345

corpses of dead Catuvellauni warriors. The traps he had set had all been trampled by his own advance. The army that should have been waiting to slaughter them was gone, scattered like autumn leaves in a sudden gale. Only his small rearguard stood between the legions and the retreating British tribes. Here they would stand, and here they would fall, and he would fall with them. He had failed, and he knew that in failing he had condemned his country and its people to Roman domination and all that meant. Death, for some, certainly. Slavery for more. What wealth they had would be taken to fill Roman coffers and what honour they retained would be trampled beneath Roman feet. But not his honour. His honour would die here with him and he would feast with his fallen warriors – like brave Arven – in the halls of the Otherworld.

He felt a firm hand grip his shoulder, and shrugged it off.

'Leave me,' he snarled, half turning and surprised to see Ballan, and behind him the men of the royal bodyguard. 'You had your orders. Your place is protecting the women and children.'

'No, lord, my place is with you, and your place is with your people.' The Iceni's voice was hard-edged with urgency. 'Don't you understand, lord? You are Britain's hope. Without you they are nothing. With you, they will fight.' Caratacus shook his head. No, they wouldn't fight. They were defeated and demoralized. Their fighting days were done. Ballan persisted.

'Yes. They will fight because you are there to lead them.' He pointed to the crest of the hill behind them. 'Twenty thousand warriors and more are waiting for your call. Yes, they are beaten and, yes, they will need time to recover their strength and their courage, but they will fight. Throw your life away in some pointless gesture and you are betraying them and every one who fell today. Those men died for you. Live for them.'

The Iceni's words were echoed by the captain of the rearguard. 'He is right. Go, lord. Do not let our sacrifice be in vain.'

Caratacus bowed his head. He didn't have the strength to suffer this again. Wouldn't. But neither did he have the strength to resist the hands that pulled him away from the advancing Romans and back up the whaleback hill towards the encampments. He stopped just once, and forced himself to look down over the battlefield that should have been Plautius's bane, but instead had become his own and that of his people. The long lines of armour-clad legionaries were halfway across the shallow lagoon now, advancing with dogged, purposeful steps towards the rearguard. Behind them, the flooded plain was dotted with British dead, while, at the river's edge, the three Roman bridgeheads were linked by a pale rampart of Catuvellauni flesh. Beyond that, the Tamesa flowed on, unmoved and unhindered, except by the narrow bridges that dissected its broad waters and still carried the last

347

elements of the three legions across to the north bank. 'Lord!' He heard the concern in Ballan's voice, knew he was endangering them all, but knew also there was one last thing he must do. His eye was drawn to the brightly coloured cloth pavilion where he knew Plautius had watched the battle. He tried to stretch his mind across the gap, to seek out what he did not want to know, but what he must endure. For if his warriors had suffered the spears of his enemy, surely he could suffer his enemy's scorn? Yet, as he stood there on that field of blood, he realized that the man who directed this terrible killing machine had already forgotten the name of Caratacus of the Catuvellauni. And that was worse than any insult.

He allowed himself to be led in a dream through the chaos of defeat. Among the huts of the encampment a hundred small battles were being fought between the retreating Britons and the victorious legionaries of the Second Augusta. A hundred small tragedies played out.

Not every legionary had pursued the fleeing tribesmen, and it was clear that if they had stood and fought, the remnants of the Regni, the Durotriges and the Iceni could have comfortably kept the Romans at bay to cover the retreat of their women and children. But defeat drives logic from a man's head and those who had lived through the carnage of the day's fighting had only one thought: survive. An auxiliary cavalryman who should have stayed with his unit speared a fleeing British chief in the spine with a roar of triumph, but a second later he was hauled from the saddle by a dozen of his victim's tribesmen and butchered among the obscene filth of a latrine area. Moments later, muffled screams attracted Ballan's attention to a scattered clump of rowan trees beside their path between two encampments. He knew he didn't have time to investigate, but an image of his woman and the bastard children he affected to despise convinced him he must. Two Romans were holding down a Catuvellauni maid of about fourteen, while a third humped and bucked between her legs. Without a word, he cut the rapist's throat and Caratacus's royal bodyguard chopped the accomplices to pieces as they screamed for a mercy they knew would never be forthcoming. One of the guards took the girl by the arm, but she slipped from his grasp and ran, screaming, into the chaos and the confusion. Men on both sides who showed no inclination to fight simply ignored each other. Two Romans entered one hut looking for plunder, while five paces away a British family gathered what they could for the long retreat. One of the Romans threw a British child a loaf of bread and the boy's father nodded his thanks as they departed. A few paces ahead, Ballan found his way blocked by twenty surviving champions of Bodvoc's Regni involved in a savage little battle against a similar number of legionaries from the élite first cohort of the Second Augusta, whom they had faced in the morning. The two sides stopped hacking at each other long enough to allow

Caratacus and his bodyguard to pass before resuming their personal war.

They had almost reached the horse lines when Caratacus halted. 'Wait here,' he told Ballan, and walked over to the group who had caught his attention.

Scarach of the Durotriges was a warrior feared in battle and a ruler who would bend the knee before no man. But he was a father too. Now he knelt at the centre of his royal guard, head down over the still body of his giant son. As Caratacus drew closer he could see the king's shoulders shuddering, shaken by grief that was torn from him in great heart-bursting sobs. He almost turned away. No man should see a friend like this. But just as Ballan had shown him his duty, Caratacus required Scarach to do his.

Two of the warriors lifted their spears to stop him, but a third ordered them to allow him to pass and he stood over the weeping Durotrige. The boy's face – what was his name? Keryg? Yes, Keryg – was marble white, but otherwise unmarked, and he might have been sleeping. He was bare to the waist and Caratacus could see no wounds on his torso. It was a few seconds before he realized what had killed Scarach's son. There was a small nick just below his right ear where an arrow had sliced through his flesh. It wasn't a deep wound, but deep enough. It had cut through the big artery in Keryg's neck. Caratacus had seen such wounds before. A man just bled, and bled,

350

and bled, until he could bleed no more. He touched Scarach on the shoulder. 'Lord Scarach?'

The king turned to look up at him, his eyes wet and red-rimmed, and Caratacus could see that the front of his tunic was black with the dried blood that also covered his arms to the elbow. He imagined the awful minutes as Scarach had fought to save his firstborn, the terrible, certain knowledge that it was all in vain, and the final moment when the light faded in the boy's eyes. He made his voice hard, knowing that sympathy was the last thing this broken man needed. 'Your son is dead, but others live. You have a duty to them.'

At first, Scarach stared at him, unseeing, but gradually recognition dawned. 'It is finished,' he said bleakly. 'Do not talk to me of duty. My only duty is to give my son an honoured resting place.'

Caratacus shook his head. 'It is not finished, and you dishonour your son's memory with every minute you waste here.' He felt the guards shift uneasily at the insult. What a fool he would be if he ended the day wriggling on the point of an ally's spear. 'We will gather our forces and make for your fortress at Maiden. There we will wait until we have regained what strength we have and are able to strike back at the Romans.'

He saw a flicker of life flare in Scarach at the mention of his legendary hill fort, which he had vowed no enemy would ever overcome.

'It will take time until we are fit again for a battle,

351

but from Mai-den we will be able to strike out. We cannot yet destroy the invaders, but we can hurt them and make them pay for what they have taken from us today.' He deliberately moved his gaze from Scarach's eyes to the corpse of his son. 'You will honour Keryg more by avenging him than by burying him. Come.' He held out his hand. Scarach hesitated and Caratacus thought his appeal had failed, but eventually the king's bloodstained fingers reached out for his and he pulled him to his feet. 'Ballan! A horse for King Scarach. We ride for Mai-den.'

XXXV

Dusk was falling when Rufus noticed Narcissus and Verica picking their way on small British ponies through the Dobunni dead. He had spent the time since the battle ended helping the pitifully few Batavian medical orderlies patch up those wounded who would survive. The mortally injured were dispatched with a well-placed sword thrust that ended their pain, but there were hundreds more suffering from lesser wounds which would heal if they didn't mortify.

He swayed on his feet. He felt terribly tired. It wasn't just physical exhaustion, but something deeper and more fundamental, as if a huge rock weighed him down. At times he would stir from a kind of waking sleep to find his mind was as dead as any of the lacerated bodies around him. At others, his brain was filled with images he didn't realize he'd seen and memories of things he didn't know, or want to know, he had experienced. The only thing he knew for certain was that the last thing he wanted to do was meet Narcissus.

'Still alive, Rufus,' the Greek hailed him cheerfully, waving a languid hand towards the mounds of British bodies. 'I'm terribly impressed. You will be almost as famous as King Verica here.'

'King?'

Verica's face took on a look he had decided was what other men called modesty, but which Rufus had last seen on a cat that had just feasted on its master's caged songbirds. 'The enemy is defeated, Caratacus is missing and Togodumnus dead . . . He is dead, isn't he?' Rufus wearily pointed to a heavily built corpse in a green cloak that had lost its head since the last time he'd looked at it. 'Good. The way is open for me to return to my rightful place at the head of my people. When Emperor Claudius arrives tomorrow . . .'

'Claudius?'

Narcissus nodded. 'That is one of the things I am here to tell you, Rufus. When you have rested, the Emperor will have work for his elephant. He is even now marching here with the Eighth legion to complete the conquest of Britain.'

Rufus shook his head. It didn't seem possible. Claudius here? The man was old and frail. He could barely walk from one end of the Palatine gardens to the other; how could he command an army?

But . . . 'You knew!' Everything fell into place. Claudius had always been coming. Why else would he have made his ceremonial elephant part of the invasion force? 'This is your doing. All of it. We're not part of the invasion of Britain, we're just pieces in one of your games.'

Now it was Narcissus's turn to try to look modest, but Rufus noticed he didn't deny the accusation. 'I merely attempt to pre-empt my master's wishes. If he requires a new toga, I will see that it is provided. If he decides to expand the Empire . . .' He shrugged. It was all one to Narcissus. He stroked his long nose. 'I have one more job for you before the day is done.'

A few minutes later Rufus was saddling a borrowed pony.

Before they left, Frontinus approached him. 'I will ensure Bersheba is kept safe. But I believe you should reconsider accompanying this man. You have served well today, and served enough. Be sure Vespasian will know of your valour.'

Rufus shook his head wearily and tried to explain. 'I don't have any choice, Frontinus. Narcissus is right: Verica and I are the only people who can identify Caratacus. Whether he is dead or alive could make a difference to what Plautius . . . what the Emperor decides to do next. It could save lives, and I've seen enough lives spent today.'

On the way to the bridgehead they passed the newly constructed marching camp of the Twentieth legion. Not even a battle could spare a legionary from

355

the back-breaking effort of building a secure base for the night, but Rufus noticed there were many fewer men working on it than there would normally be; a testament to the casualties the Britons had inflicted.

As they travelled, Rufus and Verica swapped stories about the events of the previous twenty-four hours. It was apparent that Narcissus had already heard the Atrebate's tale a dozen times, but he was interested in Rufus's stand alongside the Batavians.

'Frontinus and his men are to be honoured for the river crossing, and you may include yourself in their renown. You did well, Rufus, you and Bersheba, and be sure the Emperor will know of your actions. The Batavians would have been relieved sooner if our crossing had gone to plan, but the Britons surprised us. They always seem to surprise us.'

He told how, even though they had been unnerved by Vespasian's appearance on their flank, a combination of Regni and Iceni warriors had reacted with a speed and suicidal courage that had set the Roman forces back on their heels.

'They died where they stood and they won their leaders enough time to bring up reinforcements who should have been pinned in place by Plautius's attack. The bridge crossing was poorly executed and not pushed with the kind of drive the Emperor would have expected. But Vespasian did not panic. He hoarded his resources until the very moment they were required. It was also King Verica's moment.' He nodded acknowledgement to the Atrebate.

Rufus thought there was something odd in the way Narcissus kept repeating 'King' Verica, but the recipient of the title didn't appear to mind and he interrupted hurriedly, keen to offer his own version of events. It was as if he were composing a song that would be sung in his hall at Calleva. 'Three times they came, and three times we held them. The massed ranks of the Regni, the Iceni and the Durotriges; a solid wall of warriors half a mile wide and a hundred paces deep, and every one a champion.' Narcissus shot the Atrebate a sideways glance. He had seen the bodies of twelve-year-old boys among the dead. Brave fools, perhaps. Heroes even. But not champions. By the time the excitable Verica was done there would probably be fifty thousand of them. Still, the boy must be allowed his hour of glory. 'That was when the tribune Gnaius Hosidius Geta approached me. "Prince Verica," he said. "Your valour is hailed throughout the army of Claudius. Accompany me on a mission of the utmost peril." So I attached my riders to the cavalry who screened the flanking march of the fourth and fifth cohorts. By now the enemy had stopped to draw breath before the final assault which would annihilate Vespasian and the Second. They were arrayed before us, all unawares, like a covey of partridges before a hungry fox, and like a fox we fell upon them.'

Narcissus interrupted. 'The idiot should be dead.'

'Who? Verica?'

'No, Geta. A sensible commander would have

made a demonstration and retired. Instead, he sent his men against an enemy who outnumbered them ten to one. Verica saved him when he persuaded the prefect commanding the auxiliary cavalry to charge with the infantry. And Vespasian, of course. He took full advantage of Geta's suicidal folly and attacked the Britons just when they thought he was finished. They'd taken heavy casualties themselves and that charge broke them.'

'They ran like chickens, and we slaughtered them.' Verica drew his sword and slashed the air around him. 'And now I am a king again.'

'They were your people,' Rufus pointed out quietly. 'Not your tribe, but your people.'

The young Atrebate shrugged. 'I told you once before, there was always going to be a price to pay. I will ensure it was worth paying.'

By the time they reached the foot of the low hill above the river where the rearguard of the Catuvellauni had made their last stand it was full dark, and shadowy figures moved among the fallen warriors.

'Where there is carrion, you will always find vultures,' Narcissus complained. He hailed a decurion who was passing with a section of men from the Twentieth. 'Clear this looter scum away and bring me torches. Quickly now. We are on imperial business.'

When the decurion had completed his task Narcissus led the way among the anonymous dead. 'Don't fear, they are all harmless. The Twentieth made sure of them hours ago, and if any survived the looters will have seen to them.'

The flickering torches cast an unearthly light across the battlefield, illuminating slack-jawed faces deformed by the manner of their owners' passing and reflecting dull eyes that would never see again. Rufus was struck by the commonwealth of death. A few hours earlier these men had been divided by riches and status and strength, but now they were all equal. There were no chiefs giving orders, or nobility to pass them on. No bards to sing of valour, or Druids to commit their deeds to memory. These were shadows of men, and he did not fear them, for today he had also walked in the shadows and he felt only a brotherhood with them.

Of one thing he was quickly certain: they would never find Caratacus's body here. More of the dead faces were hidden by darkness than not and Narcissus hurried among them, giving the occasional corpse a cursory glance and often not even bothering to turn over those of obvious rank. Rufus thought it extremely unlike the Greek, who was normally fastidious to the point of obsession, but he left it to Verica to complain.

'How can I identify him when you don't give me the chance to look at them?' the young Briton demanded. 'Wait, here's one who's the right build.'

Narcissus ignored him and kept moving until he reached the rear slope of the hill, where he stood with his torch raised. 'This is where the survivors withdrew. If he isn't on the hill, he will be down here.'

Rufus exchanged a puzzled glance with Verica. Was it any more likely the British leader had died among the trampled bushes and spindly rowans than with the main body of his men? Narcissus edged his way carefully down the darkened slope and Verica made a face as he and Rufus followed.

Down here, the bodies were less numerous and Narcissus's interest in the individuals suddenly revived. Now he was at his most painstaking, turning the likeliest corpses over and putting his torch close to their blank-eyed faces. They passed close by the rowan coppice where, although Rufus could not know it, Ballan had earlier rescued the raped girl. Surprisingly, one of the two Roman legionaries who had been butchered by Caratacus's bodyguard still lived, though a sword had taken a slice from his skull, along with an ear and part of his right shoulder. To ensure he would never rape again, one of the guards had thoughtfully removed his manhood and at the same time ripped open his belly, tearing a terrible ragged gash that left his bowels exposed. He knew none of this. All he knew was pain. Thrice he had regained consciousness during that interminable day of agony and thirst. Thrice he had prayed he was dead and in the halls of his gods. Thrice he was disappointed. Now he lay, more dead than alive, only vaguely aware of his surroundings. But he was sure he could hear voices, and the suffocating blanket of his torment was pierced by a single reality. Voices

meant people. People meant a merciful end to his suffering. He tried to cry out, but his tongue filled his
mouth like a gag. He wanted to weep, but even that
privilege was denied him. He dozed for a while, if
such a living death could be called dozing, and when
next he woke the voices had been replaced by another
sound. A gentle snuffling and a rustling of leaves. It
came closer and he felt something touch his face;
whiskers and a cold nose. He was transported back
to his childhood and the faintly reassuring memory of
some animal, perhaps a pet dog, licking his face. The
snuffling went away and he sensed the animal
inspecting his lower body. Now his puzzlement
turned to concern.

Without warning, the dog fox and his vixen began
a vicious, snarling skirmish for possession of the
dying soldier's entrails, ripping the long strings of
offal clear of his belly cavity. From somewhere deep
inside, he found the strength to scream.

Rufus half turned at the sound, instinctively reaching for his sword. He was about five or six paces
behind Verica, who cheerfully ignored the agonized
cry and walked on, reciting his plans for rebuilding
his capital. The young Atrebate's path took him a
yard closer to the stand of rowans and Rufus noticed
a flicker of movement in the corner of his eye. It was
almost pretty, a spark arcing from a winter fire; a
singing half-circle of torchlight reflected on polished
metal. Verica's blond hair twitched and his head spun
six inches upwards from his shoulders and dropped

with a sharp thud at Rufus's feet. For a long moment the boy's body stood upright as if it wasn't sure it was actually dead; then a dark fountain of heartblood erupted from the severed neck and it toppled forward on to its chest with an audible thump.

Rufus's sword was still midway out of its scabbard, but he allowed it to stay exactly where it was. 'Do not make a move or a sound. Your life depends upon it.' Narcissus's voice was very quiet and very persuasive, but not as persuasive as the dagger point that pricked at Rufus's throat. Very carefully, he allowed the sword to slide back home.

Two Britons stepped from the shadows into the torchlight. The first of them, a hulking dark-haired brute with eyes set too close together and a face fixed in a permanent sneer, wiped his bloody sword clean on the cloak of the decapitated torso, and stooped to pick up Verica's head by the long blond hair he had been so proud of. He inspected the dead prince's face, which wore a look of surprised indignation as if he were annoyed that his speech had been interrupted. When the warrior was satisfied he had the correct victim he delivered the head to the second man, who was tall and slim and wore his nobility like a badge of honour. He had sharp, almost fox-like features and a severe expression that might or might not have been his natural demeanour. The intricately worked gold torc at his throat would have kept a family of equestrians for a year.

Narcissus withdrew the knife from Rufus's neck.

'May I introduce Epedos, now undisputed and unchallenged king of the Atrebates?' The noble nodded gravely at the sound of his name. 'And this, lest I miss my guess, is Gavan, his bodyguard, or perhaps his executioner.' The brute's sneer turned into an evil gap-toothed grin. Narcissus added something in the sing-song language of the Britons, and Epedos replied in the same tongue.

'King Epedos and his people have lately become allies of the Emperor and friends of Rome. He tells me he has decided to take a Roman name, Tiberius Claudius Cogidubnus, in honour of his meeting with the Emperor.' Narcissus smiled. 'He is certain of great rewards for his remarkable diplomatic gifts and his even more finely honed sense of timing.'

Epedos/Cogidubnus stared at Rufus. When he spoke again, the melodic rhythms of his native tongue took on a harder edge and Gavan's grin grew broader.

'The king believes we should kill you,' Narcissus explained, before replying with a similarly jagged-edged burst of incomprehensible syllables. Rufus tensed and allowed his fingers to drop towards the hilt of his sword, which drew a barking laugh from the bodyguard. Narcissus laid a hand on Rufus's arm. 'I have said no.'

With a last suspicious look, the warrior and the king of the Atrebates withdrew into the cover of the trees, still carrying Verica's severed head. Rufus allowed his shoulders to slump. 'Why?'

'Why did I bring you here? It's quite simple. Verica

was becoming suspicious. He would never have accompanied me into a darkened battleground alone. He only agreed when I told him you would be with us. He thought you were his friend, you see.'

Rufus resisted the urge to vomit. 'No. I meant why did he have to die? Epedos was not the only . . . friend of Rome.' He heard the Greek's feet shuffling among the fallen leaves and turned round. Was Narcissus feeling guilty? No, he was kicking piles of leaves together to camouflage Verica's headless corpse.

'There was always a price for our commitment to Verica, he understood that. He told you himself he was prepared to sacrifice anything for what he wanted. The truth is that Verica had become an embarrassment. Rome needs strong allies. He would never have been able to hold his kingdom against men like Epedos and Adminius. Better a dead hero than a live problem – and what is another body on a battlefield? In any case, King Cogidubnus insisted.'

Rufus took a deep breath. Just for a moment Verica's laughter filled his ears, the arrogant, smiling face taunted him, and he felt a compelling need to kill Narcissus. It didn't last, as he knew it wouldn't. He would fight for his life – give his life even – for his son. But he was no executioner. Somehow that knowledge made him feel cleaner. He turned, and he could see in Narcissus's face that he knew.

The Greek waved a languid hand and two more dark figures separated themselves from the shelter of the rowans. Each held a short bow with a notched arrow at the ready and Rufus recognized one of them as Hanno, the Syrian archer who had saved him from Dafyd. The little man grinned, showing white teeth against the brown of his skin.

'I never like to take chances,' Narcissus said enigmatically. 'We have work to do, you and I – and the Emperor's elephant. Tomorrow we will honour the living and the dead. The following day we will fight another battle.'

He turned away, and the two Syrians trotted close behind, leaving Rufus alone with Verica's body. He said a silent prayer to whichever gods would listen, to carry the Briton's spirit to the Otherworld. When he was done, he walked into the night with his mind in shadow and his heart filled with dread. He was to fight another battle. Bersheba's battle.

XXXVI

'The enemy are destroyed?'

'They are, Caesar.' Narcissus noticed a bloom in Claudius's cheeks that had never been apparent in Rome. Campaigning – and victory – obviously agreed with him. Even his habitual stutter had gone. The Emperor sat upright in a cushioned chair in the private quarters of his tented palace.

'And this Caratacus? Dead?'

'It can only be a matter of time, Caesar. He flees as a hare before the hounds, but General Vespasian and the Second are close on his scent. You will have his head within the week.'

Claudius nodded as if it were his right. It had not been a joyful reunion, but meetings between the two men had never been joyful. Businesslike, yes. That was what characterized their relationship, even before he had given Narcissus his freedom. In the dangerous years with Caligula, and before, Claudius had depended on Narcissus's wiles to keep him alive and the Greek had been so successful that he had placed his master on the throne of the world's greatest Empire. Now the Emperor needed him even more – to keep him there. He had always admired Narcissus's enormous intellect – even when it was accompanied by an enormous conceit – but he had never been comfortable with it. What was going on behind those hypnotic, azure eyes? What schemes was that fertile mind concocting that he wasn't aware of? Yet, if he needed Narcissus, did the Greek not need him too? Imperial patronage could be a profitable commodity and none had used it with more aptitude. Narcissus had grown so rich that he now depended on Claudius's protection to keep his enemies at a safe distance and to retain the fortune that had been won at the cost of so much effort. Claudius swept the thought from his head. He was being ungrateful. Narcissus had given him his victory. The barbarians were routed and their army slaughtered. The bodies strewn across the riverside battlefield were already beginning to rot beneath the summer sun. The stink of decaying flesh had been thick in the air when he crossed the centre bridge at the head of the Eighth legion, and they had set up camp well upwind to the north of where the wreckage of the barbarian roundhouses still smouldered.

Victory. It should have been enough. But for

Narcissus there was never enough. On this occasion, however, he was right. The Emperor allowed his expression to soften. 'You have made the arrangements for the next phase of the campaign?'

The bald Greek smiled. 'The venue is chosen. The stage is set. All that is required is that the players know their parts.' He knew the statement was evidence of conceit, arrogance even, but it was he, and no one else, who had directed this piece of theatre, and none other could have achieved it. Claudius caught his mood.

'Then let the play begin.'

It was time. 'The Emperor will require his elephant at dawn,' Narcissus announced. 'You know what to do. This is your day, Rufus, yours and Bersheba's. Garb her in her armour of gold. It is time these barbarians witnessed the Emperor's elephant in her true splendour.'

Its presence in the bottom of the cart hidden beneath Bersheba's hay had gnawed at Rufus every hour of every day since they had left Rome. It was an enormous responsibility, a vast treasure in any man's currency; an Emperor's ransom. Of course it should have been guarded. That was the first question he had put to Narcissus when the Greek had supervised the carpenters who cut the hidden compartment in the base of the cart. But the imperial aide had already made his decision. 'Once its presence was known it would take a full legion to guard a prize of this magnitude, and our legions have more pressing duties. It would also send out a certain signal – one which I have good reason for not wanting to send.'

Rufus completed his preparations as the first smear of dawn dusted the horizon and consigned the fading stars to oblivion amidst a dense blanket of misty blue. Narcissus had at last allocated an honour guard of Praetorians, and their help proved invaluable. First Rufus had fitted the great headdress with the perforated eye coverings that gave Bersheba the look of a bug-eyed Babylonian monster. A lethal golden sting in the shape of a two-foot spike jutted from her forehead. Even her foot-long tusks were tipped with gold. The great mantle, which would have covered the floor of a small house, would have been too heavy to move without help. Not as heavy as pure gold, it had to be admitted, but heavy enough. The elephant armour had been manufactured from silver and each piece then plated with a thin layer of gold, but the effect was the same. Under Britte's eagle eye the vast metal blanket and the intricately carved wooden howdah that would seat the Emperor were hoisted on to Bersheba's back and buckled firmly into place.

When he had pulled the final strap tight and polished the last immaculate leaf of burnished gold, Rufus stepped back and examined her. With a perfection of timing that only the gods could have decreed, the sun cut through the shredding curtain of the morning mist and caught each scale of that immense golden carapace, reflecting its glory a thousand fold. She looked majestic. Terrifying.

As they marched to their position in the line a buzz of excitement ran through the legionary ranks at the sight of the armoured giant their Emperor had brought to fight alongside them. Here was the glory of Rome. Here in this fearsome gold-encrusted killer of men was combined the raw power and the prosperity of a civilization the barbarians could never match in a thousand lifetimes. The veterans among them knew her for what she was, an ungovernable, unreliable ally in the heat of the fight, but even they looked upon Bersheba and saw victory.

A sharp blast from the long funnel-shaped trumpets carried by the *cornicens* of the leading legion was taken up by others along the column. It was followed immediately by barked orders from tribunes to centurions and from centurions to decurions, and finally they were moving. To war.

Three hours later, the horns signalled the halt, and the legions began to disperse into their battle formations. For Rufus it was like being at the centre of someone else's dream. The cohorts and centuries ahead and around him flowed in tight columns to left and right, the muted thunder of thousands of marching feet pounding the dry earth and the metal of their equipment clashing to the same hypnotic rhythm. In the distance, he saw sunlight glinting on polished metal as troops of auxiliary cavalry scoured clumps of trees and bushes for the inevitable scouts and ambush parties of the enemy. The precise, choreographed movements brought back a half-forgotten memory of the machine that had crushed the grain so long ago in Cerialis's bakery. Mechanical and relentless; not quite human.

As suddenly as it began, the noise was replaced by a silence as shocking in its way as any unexpected fanfare. Rufus knew he could see only a fraction of the field of battle – that assigned to the Eighth – which he assumed was on the far right of the army. The legion's ten cohorts were in a staggered formation, with six cohorts in the first line followed by two further lines of two cohorts each. The individual cohorts were tight-packed formations of six centuries, nominally four hundred and eighty men, but sickness and administrative absences would have whittled them down to less than four hundred. Only the first cohort, the long-serving élite of the legion, had more: eight full-strength centuries.

Every man knew his place and his job, in attack or in defence. Hundreds of hours of muscle-tearing training and hundreds more amid the tumult and madness of battle had made them what they were. In tight formation, if they stood squarely behind the shoulder-high protection of those brilliantly painted shields, no enemy of equal force could move them. Well aimed – and it was always so – the first cast of javelins from the front-rank cohorts could kill or disable a thousand attackers and it would be followed

371

by a second in the time it took a man to draw back his throwing arm. Only against overwhelming numbers were they vulnerable, when the enemy could overlap their flanks and surround them. But even in that dire situation, when another army would panic and be destroyed, the legions had an answer. The testudo. In a well-practised manoeuvre they would lock shields over and around the century like the shell of a gigantic tortoise and cut themselves clear with the razor-edged, needle-pointed gladius each man carried.

The Eighth, alone among the Army of Claudius, had not yet fought a battle on British soil. They had heard the stories of their enemy's exploits – of tattooed giants who took a dozen wounds and still fought like madmen – but if they knew fear, they did not show it. Even from his position hundreds of yards away Rufus could feel their stillness. They stood, row upon red-tunicked row behind their tribunes, trumpeters and standard-bearers, waiting grimly for the order that would send them forward against the barbarians.

But when the order came, it was for Rufus, and it was Narcissus who brought it.

'Time to stop dreaming and start working.' The Greek was on foot and had been watching him as he watched the legions. 'Follow me and I will lead you to the Emperor, but be sure Bersheba takes care where she treads. I do not want to be the first casualty of this fight.'

They threaded their way through the baggage carts and the auxiliary units held in reserve, and Narcissus explained the situation facing the Roman army. 'The barbarian chiefs have taken up a strong position on the far side of that shallow valley yonder, with the wood at their backs and boggy ground to their left and right. That is clever, Rufus, because it means it is impossible for the general to use his cavalry to attack them from the flanks, where they are most vulnerable. There will be no Tamesa tricks today.'

He stopped, arms flapping as he almost backed into a hulking, stony-faced auxiliary officer, and mumbled an apology before continuing.

'Emperor Claudius will gamble all on a direct, frontal attack with the heavy infantry of his legions. First, he will use the power of our artillery to strike fear into the enemy, then he will send in his most secret weapon, his mighty elephant and her fearless—' Narcissus ducked his head to avoid a roundhouse swing of Bersheba's trunk. 'I know, great Bersheba. I should not joke at a time like this, but I am nervous, as you should be, for this is your hour. No, then. Not his mighty elephant and her fearless handler. Once the barbarians have felt the power of our *ballistae* the legions will advance. It will not be easy; the enemy have the slope. The soft going on either side will funnel our soldiers on to the ground held by the greatest of their champions. It will be bloody work, but the Emperor's priests have sacrificed a fine white bull to Jupiter and it is their view that we will prevail.

He is keeping the auxiliaries in reserve, for this is to be Rome's day. They will only join the attack if the legions are hard-pressed or cover the retreat if – Mars aid us – the barbarian warriors and their gods prove the stronger.'

By now they were approaching the mound where the Emperor's tented palace had been raised. To its left, Rufus was puzzled to see what appeared to be a reviewing platform. He asked Narcissus what it was.

'That,' the Greek sniffed, 'is reserved for those who wish to enjoy the spectacle but care not to smell the blood or hear the cries of the wounded. No doubt Senator Galba will have reserved a position in the front row, with his fellow giants of the Senate, Asiaticus and Gallus, at his shoulder. Watch them scuttle off like hermit crabs on an open beach at the first sign of danger. Yet they are already heroes. The Emperor has decreed that every man among them should be awarded the triumphal regalia, for if they are rewarded, must not he be rewarded tenfold?' Rufus detected a note of resentment. It seemed one faithful servant who had been risking his neck for his Emperor had not yet received *his* reward. He hoped Verica was looking down on them. He would appreciate the irony.

Claudius and his aides waited in front of the tent, surrounded by a double guard of Praetorians. At first, Rufus found it difficult to believe this was the same man he had known for four years. The drooling, hunched cripple was gone, replaced by a grim-faced, straight-backed figure who looked every inch a soldier, from the simple legionary's sandals on his feet to the scarlet-plumed general's helmet that fitted him like a crown. But this was no ordinary soldier. Beneath the purple cloak that fell from his shoulders he wore a sculpted breastplate of gleaming gold that set him above every other man on the field. The display had a message for all who looked upon it: Rome is here this day, and I am Rome.

Narcissus moved unobtrusively away, and Rufus, sweating not only because of the heat inside his heavy tunic and armour, manoeuvred Bersheba carefully towards the steps set up to help the Emperor mount the elephant. Claudius climbed gingerly into the howdah on Bersheba's back and Rufus glanced back at the man seated three feet behind him. The Emperor stared into his eyes from beneath the brim of his polished helmet and nodded to indicate he was ready to move. He was struggling to suppress a smile.

Rufus would never forget that slow, deliberate advance towards the front of the Roman battle line. To a man they cheered their Emperor; forty thousand throats opening in unison to hail as *Imperator* the ruler who had come to fight and, if necessary, die with them. A few years earlier he had been a figure of contempt; now, as he sat straight and proud in his golden armour upon Bersheba's broad back, he came as close as he would ever do to fulfilling his destiny – to becoming a god.

They had been reluctant to fight for him. Some had

come close to mutinying against him. But he had bribed them with gold and with the promise of land, and he had sent them to victory. They knew their enemy now. Knew they had the beating of these barbarians and the Druid priests who sacrificed Roman prisoners to their greedy alien deities. And now he was here, on the soil of Britain, to see them win and to share their glory. They shouted themselves hoarse.

'Claudius!'

A few feet behind Rufus in the swaying howdah, Claudius felt the power grow in him. It was like the day in the senate, but multiplied a hundred – no, a thousandfold. *Imperator*. He had never thought to hear the word coupled with his name. But there could be no doubt. Wave after wave of cheers washed over and around him, caressed him like the warm waters of a temperate sea and lifted him until it was as if he were floating far above everyone and everything around him. He wanted to laugh, but kept his face grim. The sternest part of the task was still to come. Would he have the courage to face the enemy and prevail? They were close to the front line now, among the foremost cohorts who would lead the attack, and he could see Plautius frown as he studied the barbarians a quarter of a mile away.

They were spread along the crest of the slope on the far side of the shallow valley that separated the two armies. A vast warrior host that formed a solid wall of defiance. An uncountable swarm of screaming, bare-chested warriors, each more desperate than the next to bathe his spear in Roman blood. To the front were their kings, their arm and neck rings of twisted gold glinting in the sunlight, and beside them the naked champions who would lead their charge. They were too far away to identify individuals, but Rufus could imagine them: huge men, made even taller by long hair formed into bleached spikes by lime wash. The legions who had fought them in the river battles believed they were drugged, so great was their strength and endurance.

He brought Bersheba as close to Plautius as he dared. The invasion commander stood with his scarlet cloak flapping gently in the slight breeze, surrounded by his aides and messengers, the glittering eagles of the legions held aloft by the *aquilifers*, each identified by the animal-skin headdress that distinguished him from his comrades.

Plautius didn't say a word. He looked up at the Emperor and their eyes locked. Claudius raised his right hand before dropping it in a sharp, chopping motion. All along the line came the distinctive solid 'thunk' as the *ballistae* hurled their instruments of death towards the barbarian horde across the valley. The big machines, with their catapult-driven bows, fired artillery bolts as long as a man's arm at a velocity that made them all but invisible to the eye. They called the five-foot arrows 'shield splitters' and now those fearsome missiles were being soaked up by the mass of living flesh in front of the trees five hundred paces distant. Volley after volley arced its way into their ranks and Rufus couldn't believe any man could endure the terror of waiting for the next strike. But the barbarians did not flinch. It was as if the heavy bolts were plunging into a bottomless swamp. Rufus saw the frown on Plautius's face deepen as he realized his heavy weapons were failing him. He turned to his closest aide and murmured an order which the man passed on to the cornicen behind him. The harsh, spiralling tones of the attack call echoed across the field, raising hairs on the neck of everyone who heard them.

It was time for the legions.

And Bersheba.

'Forward.' The order came from within two feet of him, but Rufus couldn't believe what he was hearing. He turned to stare at Claudius, hoping he'd misheard. But the Emperor waved a bejewelled hand impatiently towards the enemy. 'I said forward. But not too quickly. We don't want to reach the barbarians before the troops.'

Automatically, Rufus gave Bersheba the signal to advance, but his brain was turning somersaults and his stomach seemed to be somewhere close to his knees. This wasn't meant to happen! You'll be in the centre of the line, Narcissus had said, safe among the headquarters troops. Bersheba would be a figurehead, nothing more. Now the figurehead was past the Roman artillery and ambling slowly behind the long, neat ranks of the assault force. The attack proceeded at a steady, deliberate pace made fearsome as much by its ordinariness as by its discipline. Unlike the savages who waited for them, these soldiers were not driven by hatred or revenge. They were professionals doing a job of work. They knew some of them would die, but, like killing, that was part of the job. The screams of defiance from the barbarians gained in volume as the attackers' remorseless march brought them within bowshot of the archers ranged in front of the main British force.

A single flight of arrows darkened the sky and dropped towards the leading ranks, who hunched their shoulders like men caught in a shower of summer hail. Not a man faltered and Rufus wondered at the good fortune that had brought the soldiers through such a missile storm. Claudius saw the arrows fall and prayed to Mars to see him end this day safely. He had heard the phrase 'death or glory' often enough and had always sneered at the ridiculous sentiment it expressed. But now he was experiencing the reality and he felt nothing but exhilaration. It was madness, but a divine madness. He was *brave*. How he wished old Augustus were here to see him. Narcissus had been right. Eternal glory awaited the Emperor who personally led his troops to a victory. They could never take this away from him. He felt a lightning bolt streak across his left temple and thought for a moment he had been struck by an arrow. But there was no pain and no blood. The only difference between now and what had gone before was that *he* was different. He looked out upon the world from the swaying back of the elephant and experienced a clarity that was . . . yes . . . that was god-like. That set him apart from other men. He had always known the blood of gods ran in his veins, but had never thought to feel their power. His blood did not flow; it fizzed like the foaming torrent at the foot of a mighty waterfall. His heart didn't beat, it thundered. And when he filled his lungs to breathe it was with the force of an ocean tempest. He laughed with the insanity of it. He was in a battle. This was what Divine Julius had felt; what had made Augustus great. It changed everything, for ever. Never again would he have to hide the true Claudius behind a mask. Never again would he have to play a part. He was no longer Claudius the actor. He was Claudius – the war god.

'Onwards. Onwards to glory. Onwards to immortality. For Rome.' The words erupted from his throat in a clarion call. The soldiers closest to Bersheba turned in disbelief. Not one of them had looked back since the opening of the attack. They had known their Emperor had come to witness the battle, but they had never expected him to share their danger. The closest of them pleaded with him to go back, not to risk his life, which was more precious than their own. But Claudius waved their pleas away. Something stirred in him, some long-forgotten memory of his brother Germanicus, father of Caligula, and the soldier's soldier he had always sought to emulate as a young man. What would Germanicus have said? Yes!

'Where the legions of Rome venture, their Emperor may venture too,' he shouted, and his voice was carried far along the battle line on a fortunate gust of wind. 'Did you really believe I would march with you only to shirk my duty when there is barbarian blood to spill and barbarian lands to conquer? I will rest when you rest and slake my thirst from your water skins when you slake yours. We will fight together and we will win or we will die together. Your enemy awaits you, there!' He stood up in the shaking, precarious howdah and by some miracle kept his feet for long enough to point an imperious outstretched arm towards the waiting British warriors.

For a moment there was silence . . . then the cheering began.

Claudius. *Imperator*. Victory.

The whole Roman line swept forward in an entirely un-Roman fashion, driven not by discipline but by the same madness that infected their Emperor. They were gods, every one, and this was their day.

The barbarians turned and ran.

XXXVII

The Army of Claudius fought three battles in the next five days, and won three great victories.

On each of those days the Emperor would awake with a divine knowledge of the intentions and whereabouts of the enemy and lead the legionary columns unerringly to the place of battle. No matter how disadvantageous the position, he would order an immediate attack and, taking to the back of the Emperor's elephant, join his troops for the assault.

'Plautius and the others are astonished at the transformation in our Caesar,' Narcissus said as he sat with Rufus in his tent the night after the third victory. 'They attempt to dissuade him from placing his life in danger, but it is as if the word *Imperator* has convinced him of his immortality. The men talk of him as a god.' He laughed. 'Gallus and his friends speak of witchcraft. You have been closer to him than anyone these last few days. What do you think?'

Rufus thought for a few moments. 'I think he *believes* he is a god, and he has changed. If good fortune is the mark of a god, then he carries the mark. The men love him, because he is sparing with their lives. They already talk of these as bloodless battles, but that is foolish. How can it be a battle if it is bloodless? Yet there have been very few casualties. When Bersheba carried the Emperor on that first day I had the impression that the enemy were being slaughtered by the *ballistae*. But when they ran away there were only a dozen dead. Did you notice that most of the bolts fell short? The first flight of arrows they loosed against us should have killed or injured a hundred men. I saw three. Strange, don't you think?'

Narcissus read the look Rufus gave him. Perhaps he had underestimated the boy? There was a decision to take here, but for once he was reluctant to take it. He didn't like many people – had none he would call a friend – but he had come to like the keeper of the Emperor's elephant more than most. They shared secrets that went back to Caligula's assassination, and further. And he always seemed to find a use for him. Besides, the young man enjoyed Claudius's confidence, and who else would look after the Emperor's elephant?

'Cogidubnus.'

The word filled the space between them and it grew

until Rufus felt as if it were forcing him out of the leather-walled tent.

'Cogidubnus leads the Britons we face. The *same* Britons we have faced in each of the three battles. Verica was the price of his co-operation. Now do you understand?'

Rufus shook his head. What the Greek was saying sounded like insanity.

Narcissus nodded. Very well, further explanation was deserved. 'I have studied war, and the more I read the more I understood how much chance plays a part in it. Even the most carefully planned campaign contains an element of risk. When Emperor Claudius donned the purple he brought many qualities to that office, qualities which even I had not recognized in our many years together. It was apparent to those who worked closely with him that he could be a very great Emperor indeed. Yet it was equally apparent it would take a great deal of good fortune if he were to be allowed to give Rome the leadership it deserved after Caligula. His detractors in the Senate outnumbered his supporters, and those detractors saw none of his strengths but all of his weaknesses. We became aware of some of the plots and were able to circumvent them. But it was clear that it was only a matter of time before one of them succeeded.'

He took a long draught of well-watered wine before continuing. 'To survive, Claudius needed the unequivocal support of the army. The only thing the army respects is strength. The most obvious way to show strength is to lead them to victory. Which brings us back to war – and chance. Throughout my studies one name stood out again and again, but I didn't see its true potential until I stumbled upon Verica's letter.'

'Britain?'

'Yes, Britain. The same Britain which Divine Julius invaded, but never conquered. The Britain which promised so much, but delivered so little. The Britain where the friends of Rome – like Verica – were ridiculed, driven out or murdered. Verica told of a Britain more divided than in Julius's time. Not only were the tribes in constant conflict, but certain of the leaders were secretly pro-Roman. Adminius, of the Cantiaci, had traded with his Celtic brethren in Gaul and had travelled there, as far south as Lugdunum. He had witnessed the might of Rome, but more important he had seen the *prosperity* that peace with Rome could bring. He had tasted Roman wine, bathed in Roman spas. Now he wanted more: the public buildings, the games and the sumptuous villas that the kings of Gaul enjoyed as their right.'

So Narcissus had dispatched Verica back to his native land and the fragile mortar that bound the Celtic tribes first cracked, then crumbled away.

'He returned with secret documents that pledged the true allegiance of the coastal tribes to Rome. The Cantiaci, the Atrebates and the Belgae would make a show when it was required of them – they could not entirely dismiss the wrath of Caratacus and

385

Togodumnus – but they would not fight. Verica also brought news of those who would provide the key to Britain: the Druids.'

Rufus flinched. 'I have been closer to Druids than I ever wish to be again. I have no love for them, but I do not think they would be easy to corrupt.'

Narcissus made a gentle tutting sound. 'Corruption is such an ugly word. I do not corrupt. I impress. I seduce. I convince. I persuade. I may occasionally purchase and I sometimes even suborn, but I never corrupt. The reason? Those who are corrupted once will undoubtedly be corrupted again, and who is to know who will be the corrupter? But to return to the point: the Druids. They are the cement that binds the peoples of this island. As a group, they are revered – it is still a great honour for a young man of good family to be taken in and trained by them in their dark ways – but Verica's chatterings unwittingly revealed their weakness to me. They believed themselves to be above kings and princes. They were arrogant. They were overbearing. They were disliked, even hated, by those who were jealous of their power. And now I had the names of the jealous and the names of the slighted. With names I was able to unearth further weaknesses and so I was able to separate the priests from the kings, and destroy their influence among those who mattered.

'It was never my intention that Verica should die.' He stared hard into the flames of the torch outside the tent and just for a moment Rufus believed him. 'If he had proved capable of ruling, or even capable of discretion, he might have lived. But I had to be certain of victory, and Epedos was my guarantee. Only he had the will to oppose Caratacus. Only he had the strength to persuade his warriors to withdraw from the battle line at the crucial moment. Only he had the power to use the gifts I gave him to build a new army, an army that would posture, but not fight. Verica was the price he asked, so Verica had to die.'

He gave a sad, almost boyish smile that reminded Rufus of the one Cupido had used to disguise the reality of his life in the arena.

'It all went to plan until the first battle after the Tamesa. Claudius was meant to awe the Britons by the magnificence of his presence on mighty Bersheba, the Emperor's elephant, safe within our own lines. Instead, he convinced himself he was a warrior. When I heard him order you forward I came close to fainting away and I swear by Jupiter that Plautius almost had a seizure. It would only have taken a single arrow to destroy everything. All my fine plans brought to nothing by the divine madness of the man they were devised to serve.'

'So the invasion is just one giant deceit?' Rufus's voice betrayed his indignation. 'Thousands of lives placed at risk – my life and Gaius's, and Bersheba's – so you could have the satisfaction of engineering a victory and a triumph for a man who deserves neither.'

'Not deceit, diplomacy. Thousands of lives, perhaps

hundreds of thousands, placed at risk not for one man, but for the security of the Empire; for the security of a million lives and more. Would you rather Vinicius sat in place of Claudius on the Palatine, or that Gallus or Galba wore the purple of Caesar? I would not have done it if I didn't believe the Emperor was capable of something those others were not. Of combining prosperity and peace. Of making Rome truly great again instead of the giant beast decaying from its very heart that we both know it is.'

Rufus could barely believe what he was hearing. 'You call this peace – a land filled with ghosts? If you truly believe so, you are as blind as poor Verica. It is barely a week since we walked among countless dead men who fell defending what was theirs. But at least they died for something that was worth fighting for. Can you say that of the legionaries of the Second Augusta, or the Batavian river rats?'

Narcissus's eyes narrowed. 'Do not talk to me of sacrifice. I have dedicated my life to Rome.' Rufus snorted in disbelief and the Greek gave him a dangerous look. 'Those men died for Rome, just as I would die for her. Just,' his voice went cold, 'as you would die for her, elephant man, the moment I decided the time was right. Never forget that I hold your life in my hand, not once, but twice, and the lives of Aemilia in Rome and your children too.'

Rufus had felt the anger rising in him, the way a flame grows in a well-kindled fire, and with the threat to his family a red curtain blurred his vision. His hand swooped on the sword at his belt and drew it clear of its scabbard. 'Then take it if you can, Greek,' he said, his breath rasping in his chest. 'But before I die I will ensure you will never be a danger to anyone again.'

Narcissus came to his feet, his face pale with fury, and for a second Rufus thought he would reach for the sword hanging from the tent pole at his side. His grip tightened on the *gladius*.

'Guard!'

Rufus didn't bother to turn. He tensed to launch himself at Narcissus before the man could reach him.

'Guard? My friend requires more wine. Bring another jug of the Falernian.'

The tent flap fell back and Narcissus let out a long sigh and closed his eyes. 'I apologize for the threat to your family. I allowed anger to cloud my reason.' He shook his head. 'It has never happened to me before. There is so much at stake and I am so very tired. I am no soldier, Rufus. I want nothing more than to return to Rome and to serve my Emperor. Sit . . . please.'

Rufus hesitated for a second. He knew how dangerous Narcissus could be. But there was something about the Greek he hadn't noticed earlier. He looked worn, worn threadbare as the old cloak a rich man passes down to his slave. He sheathed the sword and took his place again on the rickety camp stool.

'Believe me, Rufus, that Emperor must be Claudius,' Narcissus continued. 'You saw what happened in the days after Caligula's death. The Empire

389

was on the very cusp of a civil war that could have destroyed her. Without Claudius there might be no Rome. Earlier you accused me of engineering a triumph and a victory for a man who deserved neither. Think back. When you and he joined the attack on the Britons was he not brave? He did not have to march with his legions, he chose to. Can you, who faced the enemy beside him, say there was no danger? All it needed was a single bow, bent double with the strength of fear, to fire its arrow a few yards further than intended and Rome would have been left without an Emperor. Men died in that battle, Rufus. They died unintentionally, but that does not make them any less dead. Tell me now that Claudius does not deserve his triumph.'

Rufus remembered the moment the sky was turned black by arrows and the thrill he had felt when the Emperor had stood high on Bersheba's back and urged his legionaries on to victory, to immortality. Engineered or not, there were no guarantees on a battlefield. He shook his head wearily. 'No, I cannot deny it.'

Narcissus stroked his nose, the way he did when he had some unpleasant information to impart. 'The Emperor has one final task for Bersheba. At Camulodunum.'

XXXVIII

The tip of Bersheba's trunk swept over Rufus's body in swift, desperate little circles, stopping here or there to pluck at some interesting part of his clothing that might contain what she sought. Eventually, she gave up her search with a tiny groan of frustration and fixed him with a dewy, walnut-brown eye that filled him with guilt.

It had been days since he'd run out of the sweet, moist-fleshed apples and he had been so busy doing Narcissus's bidding that he had never been able to find time to seek out a new supply. What made it worse was that she had never deserved them more. The Emperor's elephant was cheered wherever she went in the Army of Claudius. The bravest would touch her wrinkled skin for luck as she passed, and when they went into battle they knew that with

Bersheba at their sides they had Fortuna's favour.

The legions had trudged eastwards from the site of the Emperor's last victory, until they were a day's march from the final piece in the complicated jigsaw that would give Claudius his place in history: the fortress named for Camulos, the British war god. Camulodunum had been the capital of the Trinovantes until Cunobelin of the Catuvellauni had claimed it for his own. Now it was the capital of Cunobelin's son, Caratacus, but he was far away in the west, with Vespasian's Second legion on his heels and a ragtag army of fugitives at his back. Every day spawned a rumour that the British king had been taken and there was word of a great siege at a place called Mai-den.

Rufus smiled to himself. He had more important things to concern him than the fate of kings or the fall of mighty fortresses. Where would a slave find a reliable source of sweet apples in a land stripped bare by the quartermasters of four legions? He reached into the bullock cart, now free of Bersheba's golden armour, which had taken its rightful place among Claudius's imperial treasures, and found the cloth bag that normally contained the elephant's favourite treat. He picked it up. Strange. It was unexpectedly heavy. He grinned. Maybe he had missed an apple after all.

But, when he fumbled inside, what he found in his hand was more valuable than any fruit. It was a brooch and, judging by its weight, a brooch of pure gold. It was round – slightly less than the diameter of his clenched fist – and the workmanship was as fine as he had ever seen. In the centre was the partially complete emblem of a charging boar, with a fiery red stone for its eye. The stone flashed and glittered in the sunlight as he turned the brooch to study it. On the outer circumference of the metalwork were what he assumed to be words, but in a script that was inde-cipherable to him: short vertical and horizontal strokes in columns and groups, occasionally joined as if some wading bird with wide-spread toes had walked across them. It was beautiful, and undoubt-edly worth a fortune. He felt a thrill run through him. Suddenly freedom wasn't the slow death he had feared. With the money he could get for this in Rome he could set himself up in business – even rent a small house. He knew a goldsmith out by the Appian Gate who wouldn't cheat him too much. But where had it come from? He cast his mind over the past few days. His first thought was that the brooch might be a reward from the Emperor, or more likely Narcissus, for his services over the past weeks. But the reward he had already been promised was his freedom, and Gaius's. And it would be unlike the Greek to have slipped such a great prize amongst his belongings with so little ceremony. The Narcissus he knew would have made an occasion of its presentation, and ensured that Rufus was bound all the closer to him. So, not Narcissus. Who then?

A vague memory stirred, like the reflection of a

cloud drifting across a faraway lake; a scene played out behind a veil of exhaustion at the end of a death-weary day of awful carnage and limitless fear. He saw a corpse covered by a green cloak and another man crouching over it, then rising, triumph written over a face that had aged ten years in an afternoon, ivory teeth shining in a dusty mask. Frontinus. In his hand he held the heavy golden torc of a British chieftain. A wonderful object made up of five thick woven strands of gold. At each end of the torc was a ram's head the size of a small plum, and between them a golden chain that had secured it round the dead man's neck.

'This will buy me a fine wife and a fine position in Rome when my service is done. I will be able to represent my people there and perhaps even influence the Senate on their behalf. See how heavy it is. But wait.' The Batavian prefect gave a little half-shrug, half-smile, that made him look very young. 'You killed this man, who is Togodumnus, brother of Caratacus. The reward must be yours. Here.'

Frontinus had held out the torc, but Rufus could see he was offering it out of politeness. He couldn't take it. 'No. If anyone deserves a reward it is you, who held the line with your courage and your presence. Keep it and use it well.'

Frontinus's face had broken into a wide grin. 'Then at least you must have something. This,' he held up one of the smaller arm rings Togodumnus had worn, 'or this . . .' But Rufus had already waved a weary hand and turned away. All he truly wanted was rest.

Now he looked down at the brooch in his hand. It was the one Togodumnus had worn at his throat. Frontinus must have waited until he was distracted and placed it in the bag. And there was something else about it, something familiar . . .

'That is a pretty trinket.'

Rufus hurriedly replaced the brooch in the cloth bag and looked up to find Narcissus studying him. 'It's nothing. Just a piece of rubbish I picked up on the field.'

The Greek's smile didn't waver. But Rufus was certain he didn't believe the lie. Narcissus was a man who knew the value of everything down to the last sesterce. Claudius's aide shrugged. 'Perhaps, but I suspect it will be most helpful once you have your freedom.'

That word again, that twisted his heart with both terror and hope.

'You will have your freedom, Rufus, and soon. I have spoken to the Emperor. Once we have captured Camulodunum, you will take the Emperor's name, Tiberius, and you will be a freedman, just as I am, with a freedman's rights and a freedman's liberties.'

Rufus sucked in his breath. Words like 'rights' and 'liberties' were not ones a slave heard often, unless it was someone else's rights and someone else's liberties. He struggled to place the words into a context that meant something in his regimented, sharply defined world. And failed. It would come, but first there was a reality to face. 'Is Camulodunum truly as mighty as they say?'

Narcissus's fathomless blue eyes met his for a moment. 'No place is strong enough to hold against a Roman legion. But I think you will find that Camulodunum is like no other fortress.'

It was unique in Britain, and perhaps the whole world. A hundred years before, or more, a beleaguered Trinovante king had demanded of his closest counsellors how he could protect his people and their cattle in a land with so few natural advantages. The Trinovantes were many, but their warriors were few. Their neighbours, the Catuvellauni, were strong and took what they wanted. It was the way of Britain. If the king could not stop them, he would be a king no more. The advisers deliberated and discussed, they wandered the land and looked, and looked again, but all they could see was woods, and rivers and bottomless swamps. Men could take refuge in the woods or escape down the rivers to the sea, but the king already knew that. The advisers were ready to give up. But one of them, not a warrior, but a thinker, looked at the landscape in a different way and found an answer.

The walls of Camulodunum.

It took the whole tribe – men, women and children – an entire season to build. A wide ditch backed by an earthen bank five times the height of a man was constructed across the western approach to the settlement. It was three miles long and linked the river which formed the southern boundary of the site with an area of impenetrable marshland, and, when the marsh ended in firm ground, carried on to intersect with the line of a second river in the north. When it was complete, nature and man had combined to create an unbroken barrier that separated the Trinovantes from their enemies to the west and the south. In the coming years they would add others, stronger still. When danger threatened, the tribe streamed in from the surrounding countryside to seek sanctuary behind walls that would be lined with warriors prepared to die to hold them.

This was what faced the Romans.

At noon the following day Plautius had his army drawn up just beyond bowshot of a single gateway in the long grassy mound that split the land straight as a sword blade as far as the eye could see. The legions were in battle formation, with the cavalry on the flanks holding their nervous mounts in check and the auxiliary units in reserve to the rear. Rufus took pride of place in the centre, astride Bersheba, her ceremonial armour gleaming and the howdah on her back ready for the Emperor.

The ranks stirred as a single tall figure rose from behind the rampart to stand at its peak, to be joined by others, until dozens, then hundreds and finally thousands, lined the crest. A faint rattle ran through the legionary lines as the soldiers automatically tightened their grip on their weapons and their muscles bunched in anticipation of what was to come. But there was something unnatural about these enemies.

Where was the screaming and posturing of the earlier battles? Where was the menacing clatter of spear on shield? Instead, they stood in silence, staring down at the legions in frank curiosity.

Finally, the great gate opened, and the legionaries tensed anew as a single chariot drawn by two chestnut-brown native horses hurtled from within the walls. It careered in a tight circle, the bare-chested driver parading his skills as the finely muscled warrior who was his passenger stood casually erect beside him. The golden torc round the warrior's neck showed his high rank and his long blond moustache flowed in the breeze as he studiously ignored the enemy who waited only yards away. The charioteer skidded to a halt in the broad meadow midway between the legions and the wall – and waited. Within seconds the first chariot was followed by a second, then another, and another, until twenty of the two-wheeled vehicles formed a guard of honour leading towards the gate.

Behind him, Rufus heard Narcissus say quietly: 'Great Caesar, I give you Camulodunum.'

XXXIX

The preparations for the surrender of Britain began immediately, but it would take time to bring together the men – and the woman – who would give Claudius the total victory he had bought at so high a price. Narcissus could rightly have taken his place in the Emperor's retinue with a dozen aides at his beck and call, but the Greek set up his tent among the staff of the Twentieth legion, where the comings and goings of his British messengers invited less comment. There were other reasons for his choice of quarters.

'I would be safer dining with Caratacus himself than the political peacocks who have followed my master here,' he complained when Rufus visited him that night. 'With him, at least, I would know where the knife had come from and I could drink my wine without wondering if it had been flavoured with hemlock.'

The legions had created a great tented camp close to one of Camulodunum's enormous ramparts and the engineers of the Twentieth were busy preparing the ground for the permanent fortress they were to build on a rise a mile to the east above the river's bend. In many ways the British capital was a disappointment to the men who had fought so hard to reach it. They thanked their soldiers' gods that the Emperor had at least spared them the last battle, but they had expected a mighty fortress, or a city worthy of a king and therefore worthy of their efforts, where they could reap the traditional soldiers' rewards of women and wine. But all they found was a piece of the island much like any other. A gently rumpled blanket of greens and browns that faded away into the shimmering, hazy blue of the middle distance, the skyline above pierced by the smoke of an occasional cooking fire. The only settlement worthy of the name was on the hill beside the bend in the river where the barbarian craftsmen had their homes and workshops. Otherwise the landscape was populated by small, scattered groups of roundhouses, each accommodating a few families who lived side by side with their cattle, hogs and sheep amid well-maintained fields protected by hedges and banks and connected by paths and droveways.

Only Narcissus seemed satisfied. 'A capital is not just a place where kings and princes dispense their rule,' he explained. 'It is a symbol; a symbol of power. Claudius now has that symbol in his grasp. He came

400

here to conquer Britain. As far as Rome is concerned, Camulodunum *is* Britain. If he has this, he needs nothing else. Oh, he will get the rest in time: gold from the west, whatever the northern wilderness has to provide; even Caratacus. But that is the future. Camulodunum and the surrender of ten of this country's rulers will guarantee his immortality.'

They began to straggle in over the next day. Adminius was the first to arrive, heralded by the raucous blare of a British war horn, full of his own importance and eager to ensure his service against the Dobunni was not forgotten. The principles for the gathering had been set by Narcissus, with each delegation limited to fifty in number, including advisers, priests and warriors. Rufus noticed without surprise that the king of the Cantiaci had dispensed with religious or political counsel and that the band which followed his chariot along the colour-splashed avenue of legionary standards and banners to the camp consisted entirely of his tribe's champions, their shields freshly painted and their weapons polished silver bright.

Cogidubnus made them wait. He lingered for a day before he made his entrance, as relaxed with his new Roman name as he was with the promises he had already prised from Narcissus: the guarantee of his kingship and the subsidies and trading rights that would make him the richest man in the new province. His bodyguard numbered less than thirty, and, as Rufus watched them ride in, he saw with a shock that Verica's murderer, Gavan, was at their head. The black-browed warrior grinned and raised a fist in mock salute as he rode past, but his compatriots were as alert as cats and their eyes never strayed far from the royal contingents who had preceded them. Including Adminius, these now numbered eight. Bodvoc was there, but the strength that had made him so formidable had been gnawed away by the parasitic doubt that breeds deep in the heart of the defeated. Rufus saw Cogidubnus staring with the hungry eyes of a winter-starved wolf and wondered how long it would be before the Regni found a new ruler.

Only one other war band drew Rufus's attention. They trotted in an hour before Cogidubnus, every man well horsed on one of the little British ponies and with sword and spear at the ready. Something about the way they sat their ponies placed a single word in his head. *Iceni*. These were Ballan's people. Their queen was stationed half a length behind her much older husband, who must be King Prasutagus, heir to dead Antedios. Rufus studied her as she rode past. She wasn't beautiful; even if the fierce expression she wore ever softened, her features were too strong to be described as pretty. A heavy brow and a nose that might have been Roman. But striking? Yes. Her tangled mane of russet hair and the queenly way she held herself caught the eye the way a more beautiful woman never could.

Nine kings and one queen. But not the queen Narcissus had expected or wished for.

As the sun rose towards its noonday peak the Greek visited each of the British compounds in turn to present the Emperor's compliments and pass on his instructions for the following day. Everything had been prepared. The Twentieth had constructed hut circles in the Celtic style so that the vanquished should at least have familiar surroundings as they came to terms with their new status. They had felt the power of the legions; now they would discover the benevolence of their new ruler before they were introduced to the realities he imposed. Cogidubnus would have his Roman citizenship and his subsidies, but he would still be subject to Roman taxes. Prasutagus would be free to trade the horses for which his tribe was justly famed, but his far-spread lands would be shackled by Roman roads and his every movement studied by Roman watchtowers. The minor tribes would pick the crumbs like little brown sparrows from the Emperor's table, but they too would have a price to pay. To each of the kings, Narcissus presented a suitable gift from his Emperor – a matched set of drinking cups fashioned from gold and fixed with precious stones; a king's ransom – and each courteously accepted it in his own way. But for two.

The first surprised him. Prasutagus of the Iceni seemed an amenable man and a pragmatist who was aware of the new reality. But when he saw the first glint of gold as the goblets were unpackaged the king frowned and the hand he reached out was quickly withdrawn as the leather curtain that split the hut behind him was pulled back. Narcissus glanced up to find two unsettling green eyes staring at him from beneath a tangled crown of red hair.

'We will take your gold, Roman, but do not think you can buy us with it,' Boudicca of the Iceni announced dismissively. When he left the hut the Greek realized he had learned something. He thought he had seen it in every form, but now he knew the true meaning of hatred.

The second was Adminius. The Atrebate chief's face lit up when he recognized the quality of Claudius's offering, but, with an effort that was blatantly obvious to an experienced dissembler like Narcissus, he quickly replaced it with a look of pained disappointment. 'I had expected more for my services than a few pots and pans,' the Briton sniffed. 'Surely the man who killed Togodumnus should have Togodumnus's lands and Togodumnus's possessions. It is our way. Our tradition.'

During the time he had spent with Verica, Narcissus had absorbed every piece of information he could glean about British ways and traditions, and he knew with certainty they were not Adminius's way. He also knew that Adminius hadn't killed Togodumnus. But the Briton was a king, and kings must be humoured. 'I apologize for the poor quality of the Emperor's gift,' he said in a voice heavy with irony that was wasted on the Cantiaci. 'Perhaps we can find some other thing among his treasures to replace it?'

Adminius saw the glittering trophies before him fading to be replaced by some obscure, unwanted relic. 'No, no. That will not be necessary. I am happy to accept the Emperor's bounty, but . . .' Narcissus pursed his lips. With men like Adminius there was always a but. 'When Togodumnus died . . . when I killed him . . . he wore a token of our father's favour. It is of no great significance, but I value it for my family's sake. In the heat of battle and with my enemies around me I had not the time to recover it from him, but now . . .' He shrugged. 'I had thought to claim it as my reward.'

Narcissus almost laughed. The words 'of no great significance' dripped from Adminius's lips honeyed with sincerity, but he had never heard a more naked lie. What could Cunobelin have given Togodumnus that ambitious Adminius coveted enough to risk pleading for its return? And what value would another place on it?

'Tell me more about this . . . token?'

The Greek remained a further twenty minutes with Adminius, and, when he left the Cantiaci king, altered his planned route to visit the compound of the Atrebates, where any spy – and Narcissus was not the only spy among the legions – would have noted that he spent almost twice as long as he did with any of the other British rulers. When he completed his tour he returned to his tent. And waited.

He'd hoped that Cartimandua would arrive with her retinue as they had agreed, but his dealings with the queen of the Brigantes had taught him that nothing was straightforward as long as there was an advantage to be gained from it. In a way she reminded him of himself, and that gave him a respect for her that didn't extend to her fellow barbarians. So when the rider was brought to his tent bearing greetings from his queen, he welcomed him with the courtesy he would extend to an imperial envoy. The messenger was a grizzled warrior with a nose horribly split by an old sword cut. Narcissus had met the man before – indeed had trusted his life to him on the long ride north to the meeting that had driven the wedge between Cartimandua and Caratacus – so was happy to dispense with the guards who normally attended such meetings.

'Please, sit.' He smiled. 'I had expected your lady, Queen Cartimandua, but I see she has been delayed. Not some ailment, I pray? If so, I will see that she is attended by the Emperor's physician himself.' The messenger shook his head and Narcissus smiled again. The offer had been a double-edged sword. Cartimandua's illness would have to be grave indeed before he entrusted her to Scribonius Largus.

The envoy cleared his throat and repeated the message he had obviously learned by rote. 'Should the queen of a free people take her place alongside a rabble of the defeated and the cowed? The Atrebates and the Regni, the Cantiaci and the Iceni may have bent the knee before Roman swords, but not the Brigantes, who are a proud nation and happy to

406

contest that pride with any. If we are to be a bulwark between the wild savages of the north and the west and the civilizing influence you bring' – there was an edge to the words 'civilizing influence' that made them an insult, but Narcissus chose not to notice – 'then we should be recognized as an ally and given an ally's place – and an ally's rewards.' So there it was. He had misjudged her. The guarantees of military aid and the promises of an annual tribute he had given were not enough. She was like all the rest of these people: greedy, avaricious and duplicitous. But the envoy was not finished. 'If the lady Cartimandua is to come here to accept the Roman peace, she must have something to set her apart, something of great value, from the Emperor's own hands.'

Narcissus closed his eyes; he was wearying of this island and these barbarians, but he felt a flare of relief. This, at least, could be straightforward. Cogidubnus had been remarkably forthcoming when he had discovered Adminius's interest in the 'insignificant token', particularly when Narcissus hinted that he would be happy to return it to the Cantiaci ruler. Something of great value? Why not, if it would bind her to the Roman cause? Was it even possible that Cartimandua had heard of the brooch; was aware of its potential?

'Your lady will have her gift, and it will set her apart from all men on this island, you have my promise.'

'From the Emperor's own hands?'

407

'From the Emperor's own hands,' Narcissus confirmed. 'A thing of great worth and great beauty that was precious to the rebel Caratacus.'

Mention of the Catuvellauni king's name made the envoy's eyes widen and the Greek realized he might have underestimated the value of this thing that every Briton wanted to own.

When Cartimandua's messenger had left, he settled down to work on the final details of the following day's ceremony. He had only been writing for a few minutes when he heard a warning challenge from outside the tent. The flap opened to allow a burly figure to enter. He looked up. So his informant had been correct. How many surprises could a single day hold?

XL

They were gone. At first Rufus was puzzled, but puzzlement was quickly replaced by concern, and then by outright fear. He looked out over the sea of tents, hoping to catch a glimpse of Gaius's red hair, but saw nothing he recognized. He called out, praying they were close, but his only reward was blank stares from the other slaves. 'Has anyone seen my son?' he asked. 'Has anyone seen Gaius? Or Britte, the German woman?'

Eventually he found an ox driver with the information he needed. 'The big lass? She went off with the boy out thataway.' He pointed towards a distant wood about a mile beyond the fortress wall. 'Maybe she's got a boyfriend?' He sniggered, making Rufus want to smash his teeth into his throat.

He set off at a trot towards the distant shadow of

the forest. There was no sign of the pair between the fort and the trees. Gaius he could lose among the tall grass, but not Britte, who would have stood out like a harvester's cart in a hayfield. Why would they leave the safety of the encampment? Britte knew the dangers well enough. This was a conquered land but there were many in it whose spirits remained unbroken. The indignities they had suffered were more than enough to prompt them to seek easy revenge from a Roman slave girl or a Roman child. The thought made him increase his speed.

He was halfway to the trees when the sharp sound of hoofbeats on the hard-packed earth made him turn. A faint prickle on the back of his neck told him he wouldn't like what he found. He was right. Five of them, Britons dressed in rough shirts and trews; hard men with warrior-scarred knuckles and blank, compassion-free expressions. All but one. Gavan was in the centre, wearing the same sneering grin he'd worn when he'd just sliced Verica's head from his shoulders. Hand never leaving the hilt of his sword, Cogidubnus's executioner slid from his pony and walked forward until Rufus was close enough to smell the rank odour of his unwashed body. He stared into Gavan's eyes and there was no mistaking the menace there. His mind swiftly went through his options. Running wasn't one of them. The ponies would cut him off before he got a dozen yards. He was unarmed. No, he was *almost* unarmed. He reached for the little blade he used to trim Bersheba's feet. Gavan laughed and drew his sword. For a long moment, they stared at each other. Then, with the speed of a lightning strike, Gavan feinted left, making Rufus jump back, which brought another guffaw of laughter from the big man. Rufus watched him, reading his face for the sign that would betray his next move. He was content for the Briton to play all day if he wanted. At least he wasn't killing him.

The oldest of the horsed warriors shouted something to the man on the ground. Advice on the etiquette of execution? A polite suggestion to hurry the murder along so they could go back to their women and their beer? Whatever it was it had its effect. Gavan hefted the sword in both hands and spat out a string of words in the British tongue. Rufus tightened his grip on the knife. He recognized a single word in the long sequence: *Togodumnus*. At the same time Gavan reached up and touched the simple brooch that held his cloak at the neck. The brooch! Rufus cursed; the golden brooch he'd thought he'd hidden so well. Cogidubnus had learned of it and now Cogidubnus wanted it. Had he taken Gaius and Britte as hostages for its return?

'Gaius?' Gavan's expression didn't change. 'Woman?' Rufus used the British word which was in common use among the legionaries. He saw understanding in the Briton's eyes, followed by a bitter laugh. *Now* he thought he'd been insulted. Gavan reached up to the brooch once more. It was clear his patience was wearing thin. Rufus changed his grip on the knife, weighing it for an overhand throw. The calculations ran through his head. He couldn't let Cogidubnus's champion get close enough to swing that long blade. Even if the knife throw didn't kill Gavan instantly it would slow him down. They'd catch him in seconds, he knew that, and the long swords would do their work. But he had to try. For Gaius. He tensed for the throw.

A fluted 'phhhhutt' like the hiss of an angry swan stopped his arm in mid-cast and in the same instant the earth at Gavan's feet sprouted an emerald-flighted arrow, immediately followed by a second. Rufus recognized the arrows, and almost laughed aloud, feeling the battle-heat grow in him, the way it had when he had killed Dafyd in the rock-strewn gully. Gavan looked from the green-feathered shaft to Rufus's face, then very slowly turned his head to his left, where two men sat their horses with an unnerving stillness. The first was a slightly built soldier in the green tunic and pot helmet of the mounted archers who served the Romans. He held a short, curved bow with a third green-flighted arrow notched to its iron-taut string and pointed in the general direction of Gavan's broad gut. Rufus waited, knowing that to move or speak would break the spell cast by the two arrows. The Atrebate rider who had spoken earlier barked a command, and Gavan's head came round like that of a hunting dog hitting a scent. Clearly it was very well to ambush a Roman slave, but to attack three armed men, with no guarantee of success, was not part of their mission. The Briton stared at Rufus and his fingers twitched on the sword hilt. The order was repeated, this time with more authority. Gavan spat before turning abruptly and vaulting on to his pony. With a final glare at Rufus he rode off towards where the British huts shimmered in the ground haze.

For the first time Rufus looked towards his two saviours. Hanno, of course, grinning like a maniac through the thicket of his black beard. The other man sat his horse as solidly as one of the great mountains Rufus had known as a boy: squat, almost square, and glaring out from beneath heavy brows. A bear of a man, armed with a long spear and an iron sword. Ballan. But it could not be. Ballan should be with Caratacus and his defeated army in the west. What was he doing in the middle of a Roman camp where the ten tribes of southern Britain waited to give up their freedom to an Empire he despised and feared?

'It seems that trouble follows you, Roman,' the Iceni said when he'd dismounted. Rufus hurriedly explained about Britte and Gaius but Ballan insisted they make sure that Gavan was gone for good. While Hanno looked after the ponies he explained his timely reappearance.

'I was never oath-sworn to Caratacus. After we were defeated . . . when the Romans drove us like cattle' – Rufus could hear the shame in the Briton's voice, but there was pride there too – 'we fled west. Fled, but never broke, for if we had broken the

413

Romans would have slaughtered us. But the west is not my land and the Catuvellauni are not my people, and when we had gone but a few miles Caratacus summoned me before him. "Ballan of the Iceni," he said, "your obligation to me, if obligation there ever was, has been fulfilled ten times over. Go to your people and aid them through this time of trial that is upon us. They will need strong hands and strong minds and men who can wield sword and spear." Thus he thanked me and regretted that he could not reward me, but I told him that to serve him was reward enough. You understand that, Roman? You understand what it is to serve a lord like Caratacus? I took twenty heads and yours would have been twenty-one if Nuada had not required it for the sacrifice when you were saved from the belly of Taranis.'

He told how he had travelled east, avoiding the Roman cavalry patrols, until he had joined a band of Parisii noblemen who gave him news of a great gathering of tribes at Camulodunum.

'You could have been recognized,' Rufus pointed out. 'You risked death or slavery by coming here.'

Ballan grinned. 'I am a noble of the Iceni and the Iceni are now bound to Rome. Did not my sister receive gifts and a blessing from your Emperor, though she cursed the one and will deny the other?'

'Your sister?' Rufus noticed for the first time that Ballan had forsaken his leather tunic and chain armour for the clothes of a Celtic lord, and an honoured one if the gold at his neck was anything to go by.

'You saw her today, when my people rode into the Roman camp. The red-haired girl.'

Rufus remembered the proud, flame-haired figure who had ridden behind Prasutagus. 'The Iceni queen? Your sister is a queen?'

Ballan laughed. 'And what a queen. Prasutagus may make accommodation with the Romans, but only if Boudicca sees advantage for her people. The king did not want me here – he fears anything that makes his wife more powerful – but she had her way, and here I am.'

There was still one thing that puzzled Rufus. 'But how did you discover me, a single slave among this multitude?'

'I am Ballan,' the Iceni boasted. 'Would a man who stalked the legions for a hundred days be troubled finding an elephant in a flock of sheep?' He shook his head and gave a little smile, as if he was embarrassed, an expression that looked out of place on that war-worn face. 'Narcissus,' he said. 'Narcissus told me where you would be. Somehow he had word of my arrival and he sent for me. He questioned me about Caratacus.' Ballan shrugged. 'Perhaps I gave him the impression I would be his man. This Narcissus spoke of a thing that was of interest to him; an insignificant thing he had given a slave in error. I was to prove my new loyalty by returning it to him.' He met Rufus's eyes. 'Narcissus would ensure the slave would leave his tent empty by using Hanno to order the slave's woman and child on some errand.'

Rufus shook his head at his own folly. Gaius and Britte were safe. 'So you searched my tent, but you did not find what you sought, which is why you followed me here?'

Ballan grunted what might have been a laugh or a dismissal. 'If I had known the way of it, I would have given a different answer. This smells of palace plots and I want nothing more to do with it, though I am interested to know what he would have had me steal. A brooch, he said, but a man like Narcissus could buy a hundred brooches, or send a dozen legionaries to fetch this one from you. And now I find you with an Atrebate sword at your throat. What is it like, this insignificant thing that has so many men seeking it out?'

Rufus stared at him. Just how much did he trust the Iceni? It was a question that only had one answer. The few hours he had spent in Ballan's company had created a bond between them that went beyond time shared and made the gulf between their two cultures irrelevant. It was a bond of true friendship and he had experienced it only once before. Ballan was as different from Cupido as any man could be, but he had the gladiator's heart and unfailing honesty. He had trusted Cupido with his life; how could he do less with Ballan? 'The brooch Narcissus seeks is the brooch Togodumnus of the Dobunni wore at his throat. A brooch of gold, wrought with the figure of a charging boar. It is a beautiful thing, and of cunning construction, but I fear it is cursed, for it seems death follows it.'

Ballan's dark eyes blazed. 'And you are right to fear it, but not for any curse. Did we not speak once of a charm that Caratacus held dear?'

Rufus remembered the exchange at the mouth of the gully where he had killed Dafyd. An image of the brooch Caratacus had unpinned when he had given him his cloak filled his head. 'Then this is the same brooch? But—'

'Not the same,' Ballan said triumphantly. 'The twin. Cunobelin, who ruled here, had them from his father, and his father before him, even back to Cassivellaunus. Cunning construction, you said? Yes, and for a reason. Caratacus wore the one and Togodumnus the other, for they were the signs of their kingship, but there was more. The brooches are two halves of the same whole, and brought together, with a Druid saying the proper words, it's said they will allow a man to divine his enemy's thoughts. Thus did Cunobelin bind his two sons – only acting together could they unlock the true power of the talisman.'

Rufus snorted. 'Much good it did them at the battle of the river. The one is dead and the other flown.'

Ballan shrugged. 'Such things are in the gift of the gods. Perhaps Togodumnus did not prove worthy of their gift.'

Rufus shook his head. Enough! He would find

Britte and recover the brooch from her. He would give it to Narcissus and be well rid of it. 'Where did Hanno send Britte and Gaius on their errand?'

The little Syrian, who had been sitting apart, shook his head, and Ballan looked puzzled. 'Did I not say? When we reached your tent it was empty. They were already gone.'

XLI

Rufus was up and running before Ballan could get to his feet. The Briton called him back with a shout, but the young Roman shook his head. 'I don't have time to explain. My son is in danger.'

Ballan didn't hesitate. 'Then take this.' The Iceni unsheathed his sword and threw it towards Rufus. 'We will follow as we can.'

Rufus caught the sword in his right hand and turned for the trees. When he reached them he found there was no path, and he had to hack his way through thick undergrowth on the forest edge. The sweat was soon coursing down his back but when he was beneath the broad-leafed canopy it chilled on his body and he felt as if he had been doused with a bucket of icy river water. As he moved forward the entangling brush quickly thinned to a carpet of fern and stinging nettle, and the gaps between the trees became greater. At times it seemed he was walking among the Corinthian columns of some darkened temple, and not in a silent wilderness where danger threatened with every step. He walked slowly, careful not to tread on fallen branches or hidden twigs that would betray his presence. And as he walked, he listened for any sound that would provide a clue to the whereabouts of Gaius, or Britte – or his unknown enemy. The forest floor was mottled with delicate patterns of sunlight that had somehow pierced the dense canopy above, and insects and dust-mites danced in the rays. On another day it would have been pleasing, but he was conscious of a feeling of dread. The silence of the forest was the silence of the dead.

After another hundred paces he realized he was approaching a clearing. It wasn't so much a sound as a disturbance in the air that alerted him; some change in atmosphere that made him stop and crouch down in the shadow of a giant hornbeam. He understood the feeling was a warning from the gods, but which gods ruled in this strange and frightening place? Roman gods had dominated his life: mighty Jupiter, great Mars, fearless Diana. But in his childhood there had been other gods. He knew the world was divided into three, just as there were three deadly gods and three benevolent gods. The earthly world, where humans lived and suffered. The divine world where the gods looked down upon the earthbound and imposed their will upon them. But there was also the shadow world, inhabited by those trapped between. Perhaps he had already entered the shadow world. He waited for the physical manifestation of the warning to become clear.

A rasping cough that might have been a bear, but wasn't, gave him his answer. He peered into the gloom ahead. Silhouetted against the dim light was a broad-shouldered figure with the lime-spiked hair of a British warrior. Rufus's fist tightened on the unfamiliar grip of the long sword and he stood, slowly, took a single, deep breath and readied himself for the attack.

A call from beyond the silhouetted figure stopped him just in time, and he watched in relief as the man silently disappeared from view towards whoever had spoken. That was when the singing began; a song that sent a shiver down Rufus's spine. The last time he had heard the sonorous, mournful notes he had been trapped in the belly of the Wicker Man and he knew full well their portent. Then, the words had been bellowed from a dozen throats; now, a single, piercing voice split the air among the trees. Nuada!

He slipped to the ground and bellied through the leaves towards the spot where the warrior had vanished. What he saw made the blood freeze in his veins.

The sacred grove was as broad as a legionary parade ground and half as long, with a low man-made mound at its centre and two huge oaks standing like gateposts at its eastern edge. Britte was roped to a wooden stake fixed to the west of the mound, held upright by the bonds which cut into her body, her screams silenced by a leather gag. To her left stood Nuada; a different Nuada, worn skeletally thin by the privations he had endured since the defeat by the Batavian river rats. The Druid's grey hair hung in filthy matted strands and his robe was rent in so many places that it seemed more gap than cloth. He appeared as if he barely had the strength to stand, but he still had his hate and it burned bright in the amber falcon's eyes that seemed too large for the skull they inhabited, and in his voice, which soared ever higher as he reached the climax of the gift song.

The Druid reached out and Britte attempted to jerk her head away as the fearsome bear claw stroked the long strands of her dark hair. To the right of the stake stood a warrior with the shoulders of a bull and the emotionless expression of an executioner. Nuada's eyes rolled back in his head and he raised both arms towards the sun that was now high above them. At the same time, the warrior almost gently moved Britte's hair to one side, placed a noose of thin cord over her head and tightened it round her throat until it stood out against her flesh like an obscene necklace. He then produced a short piece of wood and fitted it carefully through a loop in the cord at the base of her neck. He looked towards Nuada and the Druid nodded. Rufus saw Britte's face contort as the warrior made the first turn of the stick and she felt the noose bite into her throat.

He was so transfixed by the terrible drama being played out before him that he barely noticed the two heavy-set figures enter the clearing from his right. They were naked to the waist and between them they held a squirming naked bundle. Rufus almost cried out when he recognized his son. Gaius snarled and bit behind the cloth they had used to gag him, and his russet-mopped head shook left and right as he tried to fight them with every step they took. Rufus's heart filled with a father's pride that was instantly replaced by a father's terror. The first warrior moved slightly aside as he killed Britte by inches, allowing Rufus his first sight of the second stake. It was lower – perhaps four feet high – and narrower; the bark was a deep, rich brown, but the fresh heartwood at the tip showed clean and white where it had been carefully sharpened to a needle point.

A shock ran through Rufus as he recognized it and the thought of what was about to happen pushed him beyond the edge of reason. With a cry he threw himself into the sunlight towards the two men. They turned in surprise at this violation of the sacred grove and their free hands went for their swords, but a shouted order from Nuada stopped them. Instead, the warrior on Gaius's left pulled the little boy's head back to expose his throat and at the same time drew a bone-handled knife from his belt and placed it very deliberately against the taut, white skin. A nerve twitched in Gaius's throat and he froze as he felt the razor edge of the blade against his flesh. The warrior laughed as Rufus stumbled to a halt, knowing that one more step would kill his son. His mind raced as he sought a way out of the trap Nuada had set. But there was none. It didn't matter what he did. One way or another Gaius would die. In any case, his body had made the decision for him. Fear had turned him to stone.

He watched Britte die.

She fought them, as only Britte could fight them. She threw her head back, attempting to smash it into the face of her executioner. Her teeth bit at the gag that silenced her. But it was never going to be enough. The shadowed grey eyes bulged as she fought for air; her flesh turned first marble white, then a dull blue. She was dead long before the last turn of the stick broke her neck with an audible crack and her head flopped nervelessly on to her chest.

Now the Druid's attention turned to Gaius. Rufus looked on helplessly as his son was carried towards that obscene spike. He cried out the boy's name as he fought the paralysis that had seized him as surely as if Nuada had cast some Druid's spell. He pleaded to die in Gaius's stead. Even wished he had burned in the bowels of the Wicker Man so he would not be forced to see what no man should see. And as he watched, Nuada looked on in his turn, with a thin, pitiless smile. The two warriors were feet from the stake when they raised Gaius up to place him precisely on the jagged wooden point.

Rufus was puzzled by a soft thud, like a heavy footfall on a silk-carpeted floor. At first he wasn't certain what he was seeing. But the initial sound was followed by a second, clearer than the first, and the warrior on Gaius's left side gave a sharp cry and clawed desperately at his back, half turning so Rufus had a clear view of the twin green-flighted arrows buried deep in his spine. The second warrior's face was a mask of disbelief. Snarling, he dropped Gaius to the ground and clawed for the sword at his belt. But he was too late. Much too late. Even as the two arrows were speeding towards their victim, a bulky shadow had detached itself from the woods and moved with astonishing speed across the grove. Ballan. Rufus saw the long spear slice into the warrior's throat, the blade tearing skin and muscle and cartilage and showering a fountain of blood from the ruined neck that bled the man dry in less time than it takes to tell it.

A father's instinct screamed at Rufus to rescue Gaius as he wriggled like a hog-tied piglet amongst the blood of his two sometime impalers. 'No!' Ballan pointed to where Nuada was racing for the trees. Rufus nodded acknowledgement and sprinted after the Druid. The warrior who had killed Britte moved to cut him off, but Rufus ignored him, his eyes never leaving Nuada's back. A second later his faith was rewarded by a clash of arms and a shrill cry as the last of the grove's guardians died on the point of Ballan's spear.

By the time Rufus reached the forest edge the Druid had disappeared into the gloom. The young Roman kept the long British sword raised and at the ready. Old man he might be, but Rufus had no illusions how dangerous Nuada could be. He touched the charm at his throat and moved carefully into the trees. The trunks were close-ranked here, and the branches above him formed a continuous roof that starved the forest floor of light. As he cautiously advanced, he could hear the shuffle of his feet through the leaf-mould and the nervous sound of his own breathing. The trees and the rotting leaves gave off a distinctive but not unpleasant scent, and the whole atmosphere below the leaf canopy was somehow mesmeric. The word rang inside his head like a warning bell. He stopped. Listened. Was the feeling some Druid magic of Nuada's? He shook his head to clear it and set off again, his eyes searching left and right, up and down, for any hint of danger.

A single sunbeam saved his life.

In the corner of his eye he saw it glint on one of the claws on Nuada's bear paw as it was swung with lethal savagery at his head. The blow came from behind and Rufus only had a heartbeat to react; no time to bring the sword round, but he had to try. He ducked and swung in one movement. In the same instant his head exploded in a lightning rush of pain and he instinctively threw himself to the left, away from the attack. He lost the long sword as he fell and cursed himself for the carelessness that was about to cost him his life. Half blinded by blood, he fought his way to his feet, fingers scrabbling for the knife at his hip. His mind told him he wasn't dying: the bear paw had only caught him a glancing blow – there was still hope. Suddenly a blurred figure filled what remained of his vision and he threw up his right arm to block the blow he knew was coming. He heard the unnerving crack at the same time as he felt the throat-filling agony as one of the bones in his forearm was shattered by the force of Nuada's strike. Lost in a fireball of pain, he fell backwards, and the Druid was on him like a hunting leopard. Rufus could smell the carrion-reek of his breath and the stink of his body. He blinked away blood and was only just in time to wrap the fingers of his left hand round the Briton's wrist as the bear claw descended towards his face in a killing blow. Nuada snarled a curse and his own left hand groped for Rufus's throat, where his fingers closed like an iron ring as the young slave choked and struggled for life. He knew he had only seconds left and he ignored the pain in his right arm as he tried to dislodge the Druid, but his hand only flapped uselessly and the effort almost made him faint. He was dying.

But as he fought for consciouness, the weight on his chest vanished and he could no longer feel Nuada's fingers at his neck. Which meant he was dead or . . . ? He opened his eyes and saw the Druid sprawled a dozen feet to his left, where he appeared to have been thrown by some giant hand. Towering over Rufus, a great, grey mass that gave a gentle snort of affection blotted out what little sun the branches allowed through, and he felt warm dampness on his cheek. Bersheba? It was impossible. The questions flooded his spinning head, but he knew he wouldn't find any answers today. It was enough that she was here. Enough to know that she had saved his life. He struggled to his feet, his useless arm hanging at his side, and her liquid brown eye caught his, full of compassion and, perhaps, reproach. And why not? After all, he had abandoned her again.

He heard a scuttle behind him, and turned to see Nuada disappearing into the trees. He stared into the murk. How many more innocents had he condemned by leaving the Druid alive? He shook his head and tried to work out the way back to the sacred grove. At the same time Bersheba brushed past him and ambled off, following the path Nuada had taken.

'Bersheba!' He put all the authority he could command into the order, but she ignored him entirely, leaving him swaying on his feet. He was still there when Ballan and Hanno found him minutes later.

'You should be more careful when you walk in the woods, Roman,' the squat Iceni said, eyeing Rufus's battered scalp. Before Rufus could reply, a tiny figure darted from behind the Briton and rushed towards him. Forgetting his injured arm, he stooped to pick up his son and winced as the pain hit him like a hammer blow. Ballan stepped forward to retrieve Gaius, but Rufus shook his head, and shifted so he could hold his son in the crook of his left arm. For a moment, he revelled in the warmth of the little boy's body and the gentle beat of his heart; the soft breath that caressed his cheek and the damp tears that mingled with his own. His body shook as he remembered what might have been. Gaius was engulfed in a blood-stained shirt retrieved from one of the dead guardians. Rufus studied his son, searching for some outward sign of his ordeal, but in the same instant the little boy lifted his face and his blue eyes shone in a smile of such untouched innocence that he knew there was no lasting damage.

He turned to Ballan. 'Britte?'

The Briton shook his head. 'We would need a wagon. I—'

The Iceni was interrupted by an inhuman shriek that made Hanno fall to his knees with his hands held over his head. The cry was followed by a thundering of giant feet and a roar that almost shook the leaves from the trees. Ballan muttered a silent prayer and raised his spear to meet whatever terrible end the gods had decreed for him.

Did she remember Nuada from the day the Batavian shield wall broke? Was the scent of Britte's dying somehow transmitted through the forest to her? Only the gods would ever know, but it was the Druid who paid the price. First Nuada scuttled into view at a speed Rufus wouldn't have believed possible. He was followed moments later by a grey-brown shadow that dwarfed the man it pursued. Bersheba hunted the Druid through the forest as unerringly as a stoat chasing a rabbit. Nuada was exhausted, but he was agile and he dodged energetically, using one tree then another as a shield as he fled for his life. But if the Briton was nimble, Bersheba was nimbler still. She ghosted amongst the great oaks and the slender elders as easily as if she were in an open field, never quite narrowing the gap between herself and her quarry, but always giving the impression she had the ability. Time and again Nuada must have believed he had escaped, only to find Bersheba at his heels like some god-sent nemesis.

In other circumstances Rufus would have felt pity, but the memory of Britte's death was too fresh in his mind and he only wanted it to be over. He covered Gaius's eyes. As if she had read his thoughts, Bersheba increased her speed and Nuada, feeling her presence, panicked. His foot caught a hidden tree root and a despairing cry escaped his lips as he went down among the leaves and nettles. In an instant the elephant towered over him, her trunk held high, trumpeting her victory roar.

Nuada cried for mercy, but there was no mercy in the forest of the sacred grove.

With one swift movement, Bersheba lowered her head and hooked her left tusk below Nuada's ribs. The Druid's howls of agony split the forest as he squirmed like a worm on a bone hook and that terrible ivory spear bit ever deeper into his vitals. It was a mortal wound, but still Bersheba's revenge was not complete. With a flick of her neck she tossed Nuada's body high into the air. When he landed, she was on him in an instant, grinding his body into the forest floor with one great knee so Rufus could hear the Druid's ribs snap like so many dried twigs. Still she wasn't satisfied. Rufus had seen her do many things in their years together, but he had never seen her dance. She danced over the Druid for more than a minute, until his body was little more than a red pulp beneath her enormous pads.

When it was over, she stood by the body for a few more moments as if she were considering the morality of what she had done, and once she was satisfied she ambled through the trees to where Rufus stood, no longer a terrible, unstoppable weapon, but gentle Bersheba once more.

Rufus handed Gaius to Ballan and walked to Nuada's shattered body. He looked down at the bloody smear on the ground and gingerly reached for what had once been the Druid's cloak. It was there, as he knew it would be, and, amazingly, undamaged. He unpinned it and walked back to where the Briton held his son.

'Here.' He handed Ballan the brooch of Cunobelin, which so many sought and so many had died for. 'Take it and do what you will with it. But do not keep it long, Ballan.' He stared at the place where Nuada had died. 'If it can kill a Druid, then no man is safe from its spell.'

He took Gaius's hand in his, and, with Bersheba following, set off in the direction of the camp. Ballan watched them go, then looked down thoughtfully at the treasure in his palm.

XLII

Claudius stared out across the wide expanse of grassland Nacissus had chosen for the surrender of Britain. Was it worth it? He had invested the wealth of an empire to be here this day, had risked the lives of fifty thousand soldiers; his own life. Was it worth it? Yes. Definitely, yes.

He breathed the heady air, felt the power grow in him, and turned to survey the might of Rome. They formed three sides of an enormous square that seemed to stretch for miles across the flat plain. Four legions and their attached auxiliary units were on parade – the Eighth, Ninth, Fourteenth and Twentieth – an army forty thousand strong, even without the Second Augusta and the bulk of the cavalry, who had marched west after the fleeing Caratacus. The fourth side of the square consisted of the Emperor's reviewing stand with three cohorts of his Praetorian Guard forming a wing on each flank of the huge structure of purple and gold.

To the front right of the stand, in which Claudius and the politicians who had accompanied him took their ease, Rufus stood beside Bersheba, resplendent once more in the golden armour. He was aware of the spectacle around him, but his mind was still numbed by what had happened in the forest, his head filled with the obscene vision of Britte's last moments. Poor Britte, who had asked nothing but a full belly and a warm bed. He would miss her. A fanfare rang out and he realized the presentations that would precede the surrender were about to begin. He was close enough to the Emperor to see the pride on Frontinus's face as he marched up on behalf of the depleted ranks of the *Cohors Prima Batavorum* to receive the unit citation from Claudius's own hand, and the sadness in his eyes as he remembered the absent comrades who had truly earned it.

'None deserves it more.' Rufus flinched as Narcissus spoke the words from a few feet behind him. 'You should be with them, you and Bersheba. The feat of the river rats and the Emperor's elephant is still the talk of the army. They're saying the Batavians swam the Tamesa in their full armour like a shoal of leaping fish.'

'Verica should be out there too.' Rufus didn't particularly mean to say it, but when the words came out of his mouth he didn't wish them back. 'He earned his place among the heroes. Even you wouldn't deny that?'

Narcissus gave a hurt sigh. 'Verica did his duty, Rufus . . . as we all did. Verica is the past while Gnaius Hosidius Geta, the horse-faced tribune you see before you, is the future. Geta will receive the honours poor Verica earned and more, but in life he has not done half the service for the Emperor that Verica has in death.' They watched Geta march up to Claudius to receive his prize and Rufus was puzzled when the Roman's face went pale. 'Overwhelmed by the Emperor's generosity, and well he might be,' Narcissus explained. 'The first occasion in our history someone not of consular rank has been awarded the triumphal regalia. They tell me Vespasian is quite put out.'

Rufus tensed and Narcissus moved to one side; the last of the honours had been dispensed and the Emperor was approaching. Rufus touched Bersheba's flank and the elephant bent her knee so he was able to vault smoothly on to her back just in front of the gold-embossed howdah with its bearded image of Mars, of whom Claudius was now the earthly embodiment. A set of wooden stairs was hurriedly brought forward and the Emperor carefully took his seat two feet behind Rufus.

'Take her forward – close enough for them to smell her,' he ordered.

Ten kings, Narcissus had promised, and from a grass-clad mound in the centre of the wide plain ten kings and two queens had watched in wonder as all the terrible power and the awesome glory of Rome marched past. Forty thousand men moving as one behind the eagles of their legions. Forty thousand spear points glittering in the morning sunlight. Forty thousand reasons to obey.

Now the rulers of Britain shifted uneasily as Rufus manoeuvred Bersheba's huge bulk towards them, bringing her to a halt a few feet from the kneeling line so each was forced to stare upwards at their new Emperor as he sat atop a living mountain of gold that blinded them with its lustre. One by one they rose to pledge their loyalty to Rome.

Cogidubnus was first, head held high and secure in the knowledge that his people would prosper. Adminius, who had watched his rival with undisguised hatred, followed to reap the rewards of his perfidy. Of the others, Rufus recognized Prasutagus of the Iceni, and Bodvoc, the Regni king, who had the glazed eye and unsteady feet of a drunkard. One king did not look like a king at all; a small, wiry figure in shabby clothing whose eyes darted nervously and who looked as if he believed Bersheba was about to devour him.

And finally the delicacy that made the rest of the banquet seem like ashes on the tongue. Rufus felt the Emperor shift in his seat as Cartimandua, queen of the Brigantes, walked barefoot across the sward until she could almost touch Bersheba with her outstretched hand. She wore a shimmering gown of translucent blue that hinted at transparency but didn't quite achieve it.

'Down.' Rufus was surprised by the command; this had not been part of the order of ceremony. But an Emperor's order was an Emperor's order. He touched Bersheba's shoulder and she went to her knees, allowing Narcissus to help Claudius from the howdah.

He gestured to Cartimandua to approach. She really was strikingly beautiful. In a way she reminded Claudius of Messalina, only darker – and more dangerous. 'Welcome, lady. Your fame and your devotion to your people have reached our ears.' Narcissus handed him a long, cloth-covered bundle. 'A gift, Queen Cartimandua, from your Emperor's own hands, in recognition of past loyalty – and future service.'

Cartimandua bowed her head and accepted the parcel, but her eyes were puzzled. She slowly unwound the cloth wrapping and the Emperor was rewarded by a gasp of what might have been either admiration or outrage. The gift was a sword; a beautiful ceremonial sword in a bronze scabbard that had been polished until it glowed bright as gold. Scabbard and grip were decorated with what looked like rubies, but she knew were not. She recognized the sword. She had last seen it on Caratacus's hip and though she did not know it, it had been found among his possessions in the aftermath of the battle. Perhaps the gift would do after all. She smiled her thanks and turned smoothly to return to the line of rulers, making certain all could see the worth of the Emperor's gift. As she went, her eyes fell on the flame-haired figure who had stood emotionless by her husband's side throughout the humiliation of the parade and the oath-taking. Boudicca of the Iceni gave a little half-smile that could have been mistaken for pity, and pushed the green cloak that matched her eyes back from her shoulders. For a moment, Cartimandua was dazzled by a blaze of light. When her vision cleared she recognized the golden brooch at Boudicca's throat; the brooch in the shape of a boar with a ruby for its eye.

Narcissus saw her stiffen, and understood the reason for it. How . . . ?

'Two formidable ladies. I am glad I have neither for my wife.' The Greek nodded dutifully at Claudius's comment, though no one knew more than he that the Emperor would have been better served by either than the wife he had. 'Ten rulers of Britain I believe you promised me,' Claudius continued. 'Though I think I counted eleven. Who was the little man, the one who smelled of the sea and was dressed like a street urchin?'

'Why, Caesar, that was the most important king of all.'

Claudius stared at him. Narcissus was allowed licence beyond other courtiers, but not so much as to mock his Emperor.

'King Donnal rules the Orcades,' the Greek explained.

'The Orcades?'

'Islands, I am assured, at the edge of the known world. He must have been at sea for weeks. Apparently his island was once visited by Roman ships which brought gifts. He considers himself a client of the Empire.'

'And why should the king of a few fishermen trouble the Emperor of Rome?'

'Because, Caesar,' Narcissus said with the utmost patience, 'King Donnal's submission extends your dominion to the very ends of this land and beyond.'

The realization dawned on Claudius slowly. Now he could go home.

XLIII

'I am sorry for your loss.'

Rufus raised his head sharply and stared hard into Narcissus's eyes. They were sitting in the Greek's tent, which had been moved back among those set aside for Claudius's closest aides.

'Your son is well?'

'He is well, but no thanks to you.'

Narcissus winced. He was forced to acknowledge that, this once, he had been wrong. He'd thought to spare them both a painful confrontation over Togodumnus's brooch. If Ballan had retrieved it, Rufus would never have known. What was one more lost treasure in a camp full of thieves?

'I should have realized Cogidubnus would seek the brooch out and that he would calculate you were the source of my knowledge. Owning it would have given him a hold over the Catuvellauni and the Trinovantes, perhaps the Dobunni too, and King Cogidubnus is an ambitious man. He has petitioned Claudius to create a new title – King of all the Britons, no less. Of the Druid's movements I knew nothing. That was a lapse on my part, for which, I repeat, I am sorry.'

Rufus had a vision of Nuada's predator's eyes and shivered. Narcissus had recognized the power of the brooch's symbolism, but he had scoffed at its so-called magic. Rufus was not so sure. He wondered at its potential in the hands of a woman like Boudicca. Perhaps it would have been safer with Caratacus. He said none of this. It didn't matter any more. They were going home. Narcissus had just completed packing his effects when Rufus had arrived.

'You have been a good soldier, Rufus. The Emperor wishes you to keep your Praetorian uniform, and creates you an honorary member of the Guard.' The Greek reached inside the folds of his tunic and held out a small bronze plaque. 'He also wants you to have this. He fulfils his promise.'

For a moment Rufus felt light-headed, and when he reached out his hand it was trembling. It was his manumission. He was free. 'I . . .'

Narcissus held up a hand. 'There is a condition.'

'I . . .'

'You must never return to Rome.'

It was as if the words were jumbled or spoken in a foreign language, the message was so improbable.

'But why? I have never let him down. I belong with him. He—' He stopped abruptly. 'Who will look after Bersheba?'

Narcissus laid his hands on Rufus's shoulders and forced him to look into his eyes. 'That is the Emperor's final gift to you and your son. Bersheba will remain here, in Britain, with you. You are free to come and go as you please in this land, but the legate has orders that you are to be kept on the ration strength as a soldier of the Twentieth. Bersheba too will retain her status, on condition that if she can be of use to the legion, you will provide her. You must understand, Rufus, that this is for the best. You have seen and heard too much for the Emperor to be comfortable in your presence.'

Rufus opened his mouth to protest, but the truth of what he was being told suddenly became clear. The Emperor's gift wasn't only freedom, it was life itself. How much easier to rid himself of this nuisance on the voyage back to Rome, with a knife in the back and a weighted sack into the depths? Who would miss a slave and his son?

Narcissus continued, his tone almost kindly. 'You have two great assets. The first is your self. You are intelligent and hard-working and many a man has made his fortune on those qualities alone. Never underestimate your worth. The other is large and grey and cleverer than both of us put together. Use her well, and kindly, and you and Gaius need never go hungry.' He smiled and turned to go, then hesitated as if he had changed his mind. 'I almost forgot. Here is my gift.'

He held out two small leather bags. Rufus took them. They were heavy and he realized that they were familiar. Even Narcissus's gifts were not what they seemed. The last time he had held the bags was when his friend Cornelius Aurius Fronto had shown them to him in Rome, promising him their contents would buy his freedom. Narcissus had claimed they were lost for ever.

On another day he would have been angry, but not this day.

He reached up to touch the lion's tooth charm at his throat. It was time.

Claudius stared out over the stern of the galley from beneath the awning erected for him in the centre of the deck. The grey-green contours of the land stretched as far as he could see on either side of the same river that ran past the partially constructed fortress a dozen miles upstream at Camulodunum. Aulus Plautius had chosen the settlement as the site for a permanent base from which he would conquer the rest of the island, but Claudius had his own plans for the place. One day, the gods willing, it would be a city of stone – a monument to his victories.

The invasion of Britain had been a triumph of war and it would win him his own triumph when he returned to Rome. His messengers had already carried news of their Emperor's glory to the capital. His rivals, Gallus, Galba, Asiaticus and the rest, had seethed and grumbled when they discovered word of the victory would reach home months before they would. They still had doubts, of course; Narcissus's subterfuge had been too enormous, too blatant, to go entirely undetected. They would gossip and sneer at him among their own kind, but too late to do him any damage.

He shivered. The truth was that he was glad to be free of this island, with its damp and its fogs, its alien gods and its dangerous barbarian inhabitants. Each night he dreamed of the day he had led his legions into battle on the Emperor's elephant and in the mornings he woke up sweating in fear. How could he have been such a fool? How could he have allowed his enthusiasm and his emotions to carry him on a surge of super-heated blood into the very heart of danger? He didn't want to be brave. He wanted to be alive.

And he was alive – alive and returning home. To Rome. But here too was a contradiction. For in Rome Valeria Messalina awaited, and, no doubt, further tales of Valeria Messalina's wrongdoings. There was a reckoning to be had there, but it was a reckoning he did not wish to face. He had already decided he would delay it until after his triumph. Let her enjoy her day in the sun when he was carried from the Campus Martius at the head of his soldiers, and on the Capitol where he would sacrifice to Jupiter in thanks for his victories. He let his imagination take him there. The cheering crowds and the chariot with its matched white horses, the great temple looming above him on its squat hill, the laurel crown above his head and the slave whispering again and again in his ear, '*Memento mori* – Remember thou art mortal.'

Something flared on a hill inland and to the north of the river mouth. A fire of some sort. A party of woodworkers or some wicked barbarian rite? It didn't matter. His time in Britain was past and he intended never to return. The soldiers and the bureaucrats could have it now. He had been on the island for all of sixteen days.

The little group on the hill stood mesmerized by the flames clawing their way into the bruised purple of the evening sky from Britte's funeral pyre. Rufus tried not to see the cloth-wrapped bundle in the centre turn black and disintegrate as the west wind whipped the flames through the carefully stacked cords of pitch-soaked timber. A Gaulish trooper of her tribe had performed the rites as best he could, but for Rufus it was enough that she should know he was here, and had attempted to fulfil her wishes. When it was done, he would gather the ashes and, if the wind was still fair, let it carry what they contained of Britte to the land of her birth. Some instinct told him that she – or what she had been – was already gone.

A small hand gripped his, and he looked down to see Gaius staring into the fire with troubled eyes. They waited until the sky above and the far-off sea below were dusted with gold by the light of a harvest moon. When the last timbers of the pyre crashed down, sending a flurry of sparks into the heavens, Rufus finally turned away and led his son back down the hill. To a new life, in a conquered land, among a conquered people.

Epilogue

Summer AD 51

Caratacus looked down upon the battlefield from his refuge among the rocks and watched his family being led away through the heaped bodies that had once been the combined might of the Silures, the Ordovices and the Catuvellauni. Eight long years he had resisted the Romans. Eight years of pain and death, of heroism and epic endurance. Eight years of mistrust and betrayal. Now the last battle was fought, the last of his strength gone. Three warriors, all that survived of his personal guard, rode with him, and, but for them, he would have been down there among Britain's bravest and its best, his life gone, but his honour intact. He sighed and closed his eyes. He was so tired, tired unto death. It was over . . . unless?

Two days later four ragged figures rode on horses more dead than alive through the gates of the Brigante capital at Isurium. Curious onlookers lined the dirt avenue between the huts to follow their progress but made no move either to welcome or to impede them. Caratacus saw that their coming had been expected. A small group of richly dressed figures waited in the centre of the main gathering place.

He reined his pony to a halt and slid painfully from its back, almost staggering as his feet touched the hard-packed earth. A hand reached out to steady him, but he shrugged it away. He no longer had a kingdom, but he still had his dignity. Alone, he approached the Brigante court, feeling filthy and unkempt, oblivious of the noble figure he cut. Among the small group he recognized her husband, Venutius, and Brigitha, but he only had eyes for the slender, dark-haired figure in the green gown who stepped from their ranks to meet him.

He stopped three paces in front of her and dropped to his knees, in the same movement drawing his sword from its scabbard. He heard gasps of alarm and the sound of other swords singing free. Felt the moment she shook her head and her bodyguards relaxed. He bowed his head and held out both hands palm upwards with the slim blade of the sword balanced upon them. It was his battle sword, scarred and grooved; the last token of his honour.

'Caratacus of the Catuvellauni begs aid and succour

from Queen Cartimandua of the Brigantes. This is his gift to her and the pledge of his allegiance.'

The words fell into the silence, and it seemed an age before she replied. 'Cartimandua of the Brigantes also has a gift for Caratacus of the Catuvellauni.'

He felt the sword being lifted from his hands to be replaced by the weight of the heavy iron shackles her bodyguards secured over each wrist. He closed his eyes for a moment. Why, when he should feel betrayed, did he only experience a sense of blessed relief?

He raised his head to accept her scorn, but her face was blank. She bent forward and nimble fingers worked where his cloak was pinned at his shoulder. When she straightened she held the brooch that had secured it. He saw her eyes shine as she recognized the boar symbol and the ruby stone. If he'd known she coveted it so much he would gladly have given it to her.

He had expected death, would almost have welcomed it; instead he was confined in the royal household, shackled, but kindly treated, though they kept him apart. At the end of the third week she appeared at the doorway of the room where he was being held. She looked extraordinarily beautiful and he wondered if she had made an extra effort on this day of all days.

'You are to be reunited with your family,' she said, but the tremble in her voice did not match the sentiment of her words. He understood why when she stepped aside and another, larger figure filled the doorway. Caratacus closed his eyes, but not before he recognized the blood-red tunic and the shining plate armour, the unwarlike little sword that had done so much to destroy his hopes.

They docked two months later in stifling heat at a busy port where small multi-coloured boats scuttled like water beetles among the larger ships, unloading cargoes that smelled and looked like nothing he had ever encountered. Once ashore, they dressed him in fine clothes in the British style, exchanged his iron fetters for gold and placed a torc of the same precious metal at his neck. He almost laughed. Did a man have to be well dressed to die in Rome?

He knew he should be fearful; did not all men fear death, even kings? And to die in an alien land so far from home . . . But there was a comfort, if the Romans kept their word, in that he would soon be reunited with Medb. And then there was curiosity. He had always been a curious man, eager to discover and understand what others thought mundane and uninteresting. By the end, he had understood the Romans. True, he had not been able to defeat them, but he had made them pay dearly for their forays and raids into the mountain fastness he had made his own. Yet skirmishes and ambushes were not battles and it was battles that won wars. The minds of her commanders had been clear to him, but he had never been able to defeat Rome's soldiers. Now he was curious about Rome. He remembered his conversation, so long ago, with the keeper of the great beast that had accompanied the invasion force. Even then he had felt a flutter of excitement at the descriptions of buildings as tall as mountains, palaces of pure gold and homes fit for gods. Now, in the twilight hour of his life, he would see the reality of it.

They sent fifty men to guard him; fifty of the Emperor's élite, in unfamiliar dark tunics and breastplates embossed with silver. All this for a single vanquished enemy who was no more a threat than the women who lined the route hoping for a glimpse of the barbarian in the imperial carriage. And they had given him a travelling companion. Was this part of the insult to a defeated enemy, to be awarded a jailer who had barely begun to shave? The soldier seemed absurdly young for the legionary officer's uniform he wore; fresh-faced and pink-cheeked, and staring with a frank curiosity that might have been annoying but for the intelligent humour in the pale eyes.

'I am interested to know what lies ahead.'

The young man blinked, surprised that his exotic prisoner had command of Latin. He looked thoughtful for a moment, the eyes moving from Caratacus's face to his chains. No harm in answering a question from the condemned man.

'Gnaeus Julius Labienus, tribune, at your service,' he said politely. 'There is to be a parade, from the Campus Martius to the Emperor's palace upon the Palatine Hill.'

The word Palatine stirred another memory of the long-ago conversation. A hill. One of how many? Six, or was it seven? 'And I am to be part of this parade?'

'You are to be the object of it. Its purpose. A thousand captured warriors will be your vanguard, and the trophies taken from you – the gold and the silver, the arms and the standards – will be piled high so all can see the wealth the Emperor has won for Rome.' Caratacus suppressed a wry smile. He was a king, and kings understood the need to justify wars, but he wondered where this enormous treasure had come from. Arms he had lost in plenty – crude swords made in forest clearings and spear points forged in mountain caves – but the only gold he owned was at his neck and he knew nothing of standards save the eagles he had sought to wrest from the legions. Labienus continued. 'There will be a fine turnout. Your fame precedes you. The fame of a mighty warrior who never surrendered and won the respect of our commanders and of our Emperor.'

'And at the end?'

The young Roman studied the man opposite him on the padded bench seat of the carriage and felt an unexpected pang of regret. Perhaps in his mid-forties, the tale of his capture and the long ordeal of his captivity were etched deep in the lines of his face, but his eyes told a different story. The man might have been defeated, but the spirit and the will still burned strong. Tall and severe, greying hair to his shoulders and his moustaches drooping below his chin,

Caratacus wore his chains like a badge of honour. Labienus felt an involuntary shiver as he imagined meeting the Briton in battle. Everything about him could be encapsulated in a single word. Pride.

'At the end your fame will be greater than at any time before.'

Caratacus nodded. 'May we draw back the curtains? I have travelled far to see this Rome.'

At first, it was a ghost city that danced in the shimmering midday heat. Nothing had prepared him for the scale of it. Mountains he had seen, and great forests, but these were creations of the gods. His imagination could barely accept that men had made this vast escarpment of stone that stretched from one horizon to the other and shone in the sunlight as if it were encrusted with gemstones. Soon they came to the first buildings lining the roadway: pillared and pitch-roofed constructions of golden stone with marble statues staring down from their summits. Each was different in its own way, in either design or scale. Some were small, smaller even than the round-houses of his homeland, but others were vast, more temple than home. One thing puzzled him. 'I see no entrances. Do you Romans spirit yourselves in and out of your houses?'

Labienus smiled. 'Oh, these are not houses. They are graves: the tombs of our forefathers. The greater the man, the greater the memorial.'

They soon reached an area where the true houses rose like cliffs tight on either side of the carriage, and what little space was left between was filled with clamouring crowds so that their progress slowed to a walk. The apartment blocks were so high they shut out the sunlight and Caratacus's mood darkened with the deepening shadow. For a moment he felt the helplessness and rage of a bear trapped in a pit, and he had to restrain the urge to launch himself across the carriage at young Labienus. One twist of the chains and the tribune's neck would have snapped like a chicken's. But the impulse was gone as quickly as it had come and the carriage emerged once again into the sunlight. They crossed a broad river, a sluggish, unwholesome stream that gave off the stench of raw ordure and rotting meat, and the carriage came to a halt. Labienus turned to him. 'We have arrived.'

When he emerged from the carriage he found himself at the centre of a vast open space encircled by buildings and dominated by the curve of a structure so huge he could see only a small part of it. In front of the buildings an enormous crowd of Romans had gathered and now they stirred as they caught the first glimpse of the rebel commander who had fought the legions to a standstill. He closed his ears to their insults and concentrated on his surroundings. To his front, stretching away towards a wide gap in the wall of stone, a broad column of cowed figures stood motionless, save for a dozen or so at the rear who straightened as they recognized him. As he stared at them, a chained arm was raised in salute and a single

454

word echoed from the marble and the granite and the brick.

'Caratacus!'

He saw heads rise at the shout, and a murmur ran through the column of slaves as the name was repeated again and again and again, ever louder, until the word turned the space into a great cauldron of sound that made his hair stand on end and his skin prickle with sheer joy.

'Caratacus!'

A weaker man would have wept, but he was not yet that man. Not even when Labienus appeared at his side leading a slight, dark-haired figure by her chains and he held his Medb in his arms again for what might be the final time. Not when they took her away from him and linked his golden chains to the rear of a gilded chariot drawn by two milk-white mares. Not even when the chariot jerked into movement and he was drawn like a common criminal between rows of jeering faces along a broad avenue lined with more members of the Emperor's dark-tunicked guard. It was a few minutes before he realized with disbelief that the crowd wasn't jeering; that the words they shouted were not insults but *encouragement*. He held his head high and looked to neither right nor left, able to stride out steadily behind the chariot as it advanced at walking pace. What strange people these Romans were, bringing him to this place, where the only gardens were gardens of stone, and the only forest where a man might hunt was a forest of marble pillars, not to debase him, but to *hail* him as if he were their own Emperor. A mountain appeared before him, a mountain topped by an enormous multi-pillared, marbled edifice he felt certain must be Claudius's palace, but the procession skirted it and passed through thronging narrow streets to a second long avenue, dominated, to the right, by a second mountain. His feet stumbled on cobbled paving and he was surrounded by extravagant structures that outshone everything that had gone before, but he only had eyes for the mountain – because it wasn't a mountain at all. Could men truly have made this? At first glance, it was a single structure, walls and columns, great arched windows, soaring frontages that made his head spin, and statues wrought of gold and silver that might come to life at any moment, they were so human in form. As his mind grappled with its complexity it turned into not a single building but many, placed one on top of the other or locked in close embrace, so that the one appeared to be supporting the next. For the first time he came close to losing his composure. How could he have believed he could defeat a people capable of creating this?

The column of prisoners disappeared over a low rise at the end of the avenue, Medb with it, but the chariot came to a halt at the foot of a roadway leading towards the great palaces that towered above. Caratacus allowed himself a bitter smile. He had quite forgotten why he was here. Soon. With the gods' will it would be quick. If not? He was

Caratacus of the Catuvellauni; let them do what they would. A phalanx of Praetorians closed in around him and an officer took his chains and led him upwards. To the Emperor.

Claudius sat on a golden throne beneath a broad canopy on the balcony overlooking the forum. The palace, like the throne, had once been Caligula's and it had taken years to uncover all its secrets. Even now, he was certain, old bones waited to be discovered in their unlikely resting places. His heart was still fluttering with excitement from the moments earlier when he had watched the tall, noble figure being paraded below him. Every available vantage point in the forum was packed with faces looking upward for the moment when conqueror met conquered. When Emperor met king. The moment when his conquest of Britain was finally complete after all the long years.

'You say he speaks Latin well?'

'So I believe, Caesar,' Narcissus confirmed. He felt Agrippina's eyes boring into him. Would the woman never let him be? He had been right. Claudius should never have married her. She came with too much baggage, including her brat of a son. And spite. He remembered looking down upon Valeria Messalina's twitching body; the beautiful face swollen to ugliness by the poison she had been forced to take. He wished the face had been Agrippina's. The thought made him smile. He saw her eyes widen and he realized Caratacus must have been brought in. She had always

457

had an eye for a man. He turned and confirmed what he had been told. The British king was taller by a head than the Praetorians who surrounded him. Somehow, he managed to convey the impression that the guard was his to command and the balcony his to dispose of as he willed.

Caratacus in his turn studied the figure on the golden throne; small and sickly pale but with bright, intelligent eyes, almost lost in his white toga with the broad purple stripe. A laurel wreath of gold rested on his thinning hair. So this was his nemesis; the man who had sent the legions to his country with their blood and their iron and their fire. The man who had enslaved half the tribes of Britain and corrupted the rest. And, yes, he acknowledged, the man who had defeated him and was about to kill him. He allowed his gaze to rove over the others in the little group. A tall, bald man with dark eyes and an inscrutable expression. A plump woman who studied him hungrily, and a boy, who must be her son, with the coldest eyes he had ever seen.

'You may kneel and seek my forgiveness.'

Caratacus understood the imperial command, but he stared back as if the words had never been spoken. The Druids had told the story of Vercingetorix, the Gaul, who had knelt before a Caesar and whose reward was the strangling rope. They could strangle him if they wished, but he would not kneel. He heard the song of a dozen iron swords being drawn and he waited, stone-faced, for his fate.

Claudius stared at him, realization dawning as he studied the stern, unyielding figure in the golden chains. This giant of a man, this warrior, this *king*, was a reflection of *his* glory. No. More than that. He magnified it a thousand times. He had intended a public execution; an example to all that the only reward for any man who stood against Rome was a painful death. But it could not be. Caratacus of Britain would live, he decided – a wolf in a gilded cage. But first the formalities must be followed.

'Caratacus, enemy of Rome, you have forfeited your life a hundred times by your actions. You are guilty of sedition and rebellion, and, by association, of common murder, rape and the torture of innocents. By your actions you brought war, death, famine and sorrow to your people.' The words rang out, sharp and clear, and Caratacus knew they were aimed, not at him, but at the crowd below. This was the justification for his execution, though he could deny or defend every word of it. Claudius continued: 'Yet you fought hard and you fought well and, though your cause was unworthy, you fought with honour and valour and won the respect even of your foes. At the end, mighty Rome brought you low, and now you are brought before me, defeated, but not subdued; for you are a king, and a king prefers death before dishonour. Death is your right and is your due. As is your right of reply.' The Emperor gestured graciously towards the balcony edge.

Caratacus recognized the moment he was meant to

plead for his life, but there was no honour in pleading and he was certain no purpose would be achieved by it. He would not make some self-serving address that these Romans could use to tarnish his memory. But there was one thing. He turned and looked out beyond the gawping multitude among the marble-columned temples below and over the endless sea of terracotta that sheltered the countless thousands of his enemies.

'Why, when you have all this, did you need our poor huts?' he asked.

The Latin was slow and unnatural, but the voice was strong and the words were understood. Claudius's face froze. Narcissus blinked. The tang of fresh grass on a diamond-bright British morning filled his nostrils. He saw again the sea of dead, snarling faces on the day of the ambush. An Emperor, who was a god, on a great golden beast. He wondered what had become of the young man and his elephant.

Acknowledgements

Thanks to my editor, Simon Thorogood, and the team at Transworld, and to Stan, my agent at Jenny Brown. Graham Webster's excellent books *The Roman Invasion of Britain* and *Rome against Caratacus* provided the foundations for Claudius's Britain, but shouldn't be blamed for any assumptions I've made or liberties I've taken in the search for a better novel. I'd also like to say a special thanks to Blairdrummond Safari Park for allowing me to meet Toto, who gave me a true insight into the character Bersheba, the Emperor's elephant.

Caligula

By Douglas Jackson

Can a slave decide the fate of an Emperor?

RUFUS, A YOUNG slave, grows up far from the corruption of the imperial court. He is a trainer of animals for the gladiatorial arena. But when Caligula wants a keeper for the emperor's elephant, Rufus is bought from his master and taken to the palace.

Life at court is dictated by Caligula's ever shifting moods. He is as generous as he is cruel – a megalomaniac who declares himself a living god and simultaneously lives in constant fear of the plots against his life. His paranoia is not misplaced however: intrigue permeates his court, and Rufus will find himself unwittingly placed at the centre of a conspiracy to assassinate the Emperor.

'Jackson brings a visceral realism to Rome in the days
of the mad Caligula'
DAILY MAIL

'Light and dark in equal measure, colourful,
thoughtful and bracing'
MANDA SCOTT, bestselling author of the BOUDICA SERIES

'A gripping Roman thriller'
SCOTLAND ON SUNDAY

9780552156943